No One but Paul Erdman Could Have Written *THE LAST DAYS OF AMERICA!*

As he did in *The Crash of '79* and *The Silver Bears*, Erdman reaches into his vast knowledge of international finance to create one plausible event after another, weaving fact and fiction into a tightly meshed novel that wraps you up totally!

Books by Paul Erdman

The Billion Dollar Sure Thing
The Crash of '79
The Last Days of America
The Silver Bears

Published by POCKET BOOKS

THE LAST DAYS OF AMERICA

PAUL E. ERDMAN

PUBLISHED BY POCKET BOOKS NEW YORK

This novel is a work of fiction. Names, characters, places and incidents are either the product of the author's imagination or are used fictitiously. Any resemblance to actual events or locales or persons, living or dead, is entirely coincidental.

POCKET BOOKS, a Simon & Schuster division of
GULF & WESTERN CORPORATION
1230 Avenue of the Americas, New York, N.Y. 10020

Copyright © 1981 by Paul Erdman

Published by arrangement with Simon and Schuster
Library of Congress Catalog Card Number: 81-5287

ISBN: 0-671-44717-3

First Pocket Books printing July, 1982

10 9 8 7 6 5 4 3 2 1

POCKET and colophon are trademarks of Simon & Schuster.

Printed in the U.S.A.

PART ONE

1

BEING AN AMERICAN in the 1980s was not always easy—as you remember. When the decade began, most of us were convinced that we had no place to go but up. After all, we had gotten by Vietnam and Richard Nixon and Iran and Jimmy Carter. What else could go wrong?

Ha!

Not that anything catastrophic had happened, thank God. It was just that we all still had to eat and live somewhere and move around now and then. But who could still afford to do any of these things in style any more? Very few—with gas at $3.85 a gallon for unleaded premium, with a 1985 model Cadillac costing $42,000, with that house in Woodside that we bought for $400,000 in 1982 now going for well over a million according to our neighbors who kept track of such things, and with steak now at $16 a pound at Safeway.

Still, when we Americans compared our situation with that of most of the rest of the world, we really had nothing to complain about. I don't mean this in terms of dishwashers and swimming pools per capita; I mean it in terms of our freedom, our right, to work and live and play in any *place* we chose and in any *way* we desired. Hardly anybody else on earth could do that in 1985.

In Eastern Europe the Soviets had decided, already back in '83, to abandon all pretense of civility. In Poland, in Czechoslovakia, and even in Hungary, you did what the Russians told you to do or you disappeared. In Brazil, and since 1984 also in Mexico, if the ruling junta did not like the way you parted your hair, especially if you parted it to the left, ditto. Even in Italy, that wonderful, wonderful country, they had had to finally choose between utter chaos and the Black Shirts. Naturally, they chose the latter.

And everywhere they hated us Americans. Because they envied us. So when Thanksgiving rolled around in 1985, you could not have enticed Nancy and me to spend it abroad for anything. We decided to do what we always did during Thanksgiving week—make our annual sojourn at the Mauna Kea Beach Hotel on the Big Island of Hawaii in the good old U.S. of A. And that was where we were in the late evening of November 18 when it all began. Little did any of us know then how tenuous it all was. That not even America would be able to withstand the . . . but that comes later.

On that particular evening I had finished dinner and, instead of going up to the room with Nancy, had decided to walk down to the sea and watch the manta rays go through their nightly performance. That was when the manager sent a bellman with the word that Herb Patterson had just called from the mainland and wanted urgently to speak to me.

Before I get into what he wanted—and it had to do with Germans—let me explain about Herb Patterson, and then about the manta rays.

Herb was chairman of the board of Missile Development Corporation of Sunnyvale, California, and I was the company's president: in other words, he was my boss. Patterson's

8

character was such that he would actually call up the manager of a posh hotel like the Mauna Kea Beach and ask him to act as his messenger boy, as he did that evening. Patterson's power was such that the manager—Bob Butterfield was his name, and I think he is still there in case you ever need help in arranging accommodations on short notice—would actually acquiesce.

Now about the manta rays. Back in the early 1960s, Laurance Rockefeller decided to put up a hotel on the Big Island on the Kohala coast, which has all those beds of black lava, a few beaches, and little else. It is remote and quiet, and that is why I liked to go there. Anyway, when the hotel was essentially complete, to add a few finishing touches, the landscapers decided to install a couple of really powerful spotlights on the rocks below the main dining room, to illuminate the sea. Apparently the light attracted the plankton, and the plankton attracted the manta rays. Since then, almost every evening, sometimes as many as half a dozen of these huge monsters from the deep cavort right in front of everybody's eyes, starting around ten o'clock—which is just about the time Herbie Patterson called me that evening.

You may suspect that I've overdone this little anecdote to indicate some symbolic linkage between stingrays and Herb Patterson, and if you do, you are right. But that would be getting way ahead of the story.

First, that phone call. I decided to take it up in the suite, where my wife was already in bed, reading.

"How are your pals doing tonight?" she asked when I walked in. She found my fascination with the sea monsters a bit out of character. She knew that I was more attracted to the recycled air of boardrooms and banking offices than the nocturnal waters of the Pacific.

"Herb Patterson wants me to call him back," I said. "Didn't he call here?"

"Somebody wanted you person-to-person. I said you were out."

9

"Thanks." Sometimes they can drive you nuts.

I picked up the phone. The fact that Hawaii is on the same direct-dialing system as Newark and Cleveland tends to take away a bit of the romance of the Islands, but when you come right down to it, by the mid-1980s there was very little left of it anyway.

"Herb, it's Frank," I said.

"Good of you to call back, Frank. Look, we've got some trouble in Europe. Maybe big trouble. Can you come back tomorrow? Let's meet in the city." By that Patterson meant the city of San Francisco and not the town of Sunnyvale, down on the Peninsula, where we had our corporate offices.

We decided on the Pacific Union Club. That was where the elite of Northern California lunched, and occasionally dined. Patterson and I were definitely of that elite. And intended to stay that way for a while.

"Would seven be all right, Frank?" Patterson wanted to know.

"Sure," I answered.

"Okay, see you tomorrow. Best to Nancy."

Nancy was, of course, taking all this in, and pretending not to. I had met her in the late 1950s. She was from Virginia and I from California. We got to know each other in Switzerland, where we were both Americans doing graduate work at the University of Basel. Her field was philosophy, with a smattering of theology on the side. Her principal professors were Carl Jaspers and Karl Barth. My field was economics and finance. We both graduated in the fall of 1962 with our doctorates. I received a *summa cum laude*, she a *magna cum laude*. We got married three days later and have managed to stay that way ever since. Thank God, as later events proved.

On the United flight back the next day she never said one word about Herb Patterson, Missile Development Corporation, Germans, or the cruise missile. She later told me that during the entire trip she was on the verge of telling me to simply resign. Immediately, without giving any reason to anybody. But obviously she didn't.

After landing at San Francisco International we took separate cabs—she with the baggage to our home in Woodside. I to my meeting with Patterson at the Pacific Union Club.

2

Franz Josef Strauss, the Chancellor of West Germany, described by some as "a fat Hitler with brains," summoned his Minister of Foreign Affairs, Graf Otto von Amsburg, to an unscheduled meeting shortly before lunch on that same Monday, November 18, 1985. Upon returning to his office, von Amsburg made a slight change in his plans: the following day he, not his deputy, would attend the NATO forward-planning meeting in Brussels. This change in schedule would ultimately have extraordinarily profound implications for all of us. In fact, without referring specifically to this particular action, Henry Kissinger later described the process that was thus set in motion as "affecting the very future of mankind."

It hardly seemed so at the time. On the agenda in Brussels the following day were two rather serious matters, but hardly new ones, and hardly any that seemed to have apocalyptic overtones. The first was a motion to confirm that NATO would deploy 572 American ground-launched cruise missiles

(GLCMs) without further delay, and that the governments of Britain, Italy, West Germany, Belgium, and the Netherlands would agree, irrevocably, to allow such missiles—all to be armed with nuclear warheads—to be deployed on their territory. The second motion referred to the type of missile system to be deployed by NATO. Three competing systems were still in the running: that being built by Boeing in Seattle, the one developed in St. Louis by General Dynamics, and the weapons system being offered to America's allies by Missile Development Corporation (MDC) of Sunnyvale, California.

The outcome of both votes was assumed to be a foregone conclusion in NATO circles. It was now known that the Dutch and Belgian governments were reluctantly prepared to finally come around and stop their eternal stalling on the cruise-missile deployment issue. After all, with the Russians now firmly entrenched in Yugoslavia, did they really have any choice? Equally certain seemed the selection of Missile Development Corporation as the prime contractor for the NATO GLCM. It was common knowledge that Boeing's cruise missiles kept crashing all over the state of Washington, burning down more than a few trees in the process, while General Dynamics' prototypes simply kept getting lost: some over the Pacific, a few over the Caribbean, and one over Mexico.

Before the meeting actually got under way, Graf Otto von Amsburg was seen in the corridors of the NATO headquarters building chatting briefly first with the Minister of Defense of Belgium and then with the commander-in-chief of the Dutch armed forces, an Air Force general. What was discussed seemed to have caused a bit of a flurry, since both the Dutch and Belgian delegations immediately went into what was quite obviously an unscheduled caucus. The result was that the general meeting started a half-hour late.

The first vote went as predicted, and it was unanimous.

The second did not; in fact, the second matter on the agenda did not even come to a vote. This was because Graf Otto von Amsburg moved that the decision regarding the selection of the particular weapons system to be deployed be postponed for two weeks, until Monday, December 2, 1985. He gave no reason as to why he was making this request. His motion was immediately seconded by the leaders of the Belgian and Dutch delegations. It was then adopted, also unanimously. One of the generals in the American delegation was seen making quite a fuss among his colleagues prior to the vote, but in the end the United States went along with everybody else in acceding to the German/Belgian/Dutch request.

Otto von Amsburg was back in Bonn by noon that same day. The Brussels–Bonn flight time is only thirty-five minutes. He then made four phone calls, all to destinations inside West Germany. The purpose of these calls was to arrange for a meeting that he was scheduling, tentatively, for two weeks and one day later, to be held at the Gasthaus zum Sternen, a little country inn about eleven kilometers north of Bonn on the old road to Cologne. The scheduling was tentative because it was too early to tell which way the Americans would jump. Three of the four men he spoke to said that they would be there. Dr. Reinhardt Kreps, Generaldirektor of the Deutsche Bank, was not in—he was in New York—so von Amsburg simply hung up the phone rather than talk any further with the secretary. He would catch him later.

Then Graf von Amsburg called the Chancellor. When he had finished his report, Strauss said to the German aristocrat who was serving Germany as Foreign Minister in the tradition of Bismarck: "Ausgezeichnet. Die Amis merken nichts. Die Scheisskerle werden täglich einfältiger. Lass uns hoffen, dass wir sie jetzt endlich los werden. Mach nur weiter so, Otto."

This translates more or less as follows: "Excellent. The Americans notice nothing. Those shitheads are getting more

15

simpleminded every day. Let's hope we are now finally going to be rid of them. Proceed, Otto."

Franz Josef Strauss may have brains, but he certainly does not have class. But he was right. We shitheads did *not* notice anything; at least, this particular American shithead did not.

3

IF YOU HAVE BEEN to the Fairmont Hotel in San Francisco, you may have wondered what that huge stone mansion was on the square across the street. Well, that's the P.U. Club. For some reason, I remembered quite a few of the faces around the main dining room that evening: Steve Bechtel, Jr., who controls the largest privately owned corporation in the world, was there, sitting with Keller, I forget his first name, head of Standard Oil of California. Then there was Prentice Cobb Hale, the department-store tycoon, who a decade earlier had absorbed Neiman-Marcus as if it were some Texas hot dog stand; he was there with the senior Senator from Illinois. There were a couple of Swiggs, the family that owns the hotel across the street, and also a couple of Haases—they've got Levi Strauss. I am telling you this so that you can get an idea of who belonged there, who could belong. It was not enough that you ran a big company or a big bank or a big whatever. You also had to *own* a reasonable percentage of it. That, my friends, is what really separates the men from the boys in the United States, and the Pacific Union Club was one of the last places willing to recognize that fact and to hell with the public. To hell also with women, by the way. Not allowed. Which was rather natural, since there was not a woman within hundreds, probably thousands of miles of downtown San Francisco who ran and owned anything of any importance.

How did Herb Patterson and I rank among the big boys in the room that day? I guess Herb Patterson would have been right up there with Steve Bechtel or Prentis Cobb Hale, in that he owned a very substantial part of the business of which he was chairman. Me: well, like everybody else brought in from the outside to be president of a company, I had my stock options and not a hell of a lot more. But that hardly kept me out of the Pacific Union Club. When Herb Patterson sponsored somebody there, he was automatically approved.

But enough of that stuff. I was already seated at the table with a double gin with a twist in front of me when Patterson walked in the evening of that nineteenth day of November. Herb ordered a double vodka with three olives.

"All right, Herb, what is it?" I asked.

"Our general. He called me last night from a phone booth at NATO headquarters in Brussels just after he got out of that meeting there."

"Probably as safe as any procedure," I said.

"I guess so. Now let me tell you what he said. Something went wrong with the vote. Not only did they not approve our system, but he tells me that the Germans, the Belgians, and the Dutch are now all leaning toward Boeing or General Dynamics. It's unbelievable."

"What do we do?" I asked.

"You want me to put it nicely or straight?" asked Patterson.

"Straight."

"Okay, look, Frank, we are back where we were a few

18

times in the past. I think somebody has gotten to the defense ministers or the generals or I don't know who over there. You know full well and they know full well and everybody knows full well that our cruise missile and especially our guidance system is a hundred percent better in every respect than their versions. You know that, the Pentagon knows that, and until yesterday the majority of NATO's members agreed. I am repeating myself, but bear with me, Frank. The swing votes in NATO on this issue are Germany, Belgium, and the Netherlands, as you also know. We had them in our pocket. Now . . . ?"

"Wait a minute, Herb. This is not the 1970's, you know. I simply don't believe that anybody is trying to pull stuff like that any more. Now: what or whom *did* they vote for?"

"They voted to go ahead with the procurement and the deployment. But they postponed for two more weeks the decision on which weapons system they want to buy."

"So we've got one more chance," I said.

"Yeah, one more. But if it goes against us next time . . ."

Well, as I recall there was a bit of a lull then. The waiter came and we both ordered steaks and a nice bottle of wine. The P.U. has a good cellar. It also has fast and efficient service. The result was that within thirty minutes we had no further excuse to postpone the matter at hand.

"All right," I said. "How do we make sure that it doesn't go against us next time?"

"I think," said Patterson, "that we are going to have to reactivate Herr Dr. Zimmerli in Switzerland. And Aeroconsult in Liechtenstein."

Now, I could say right here that I threw up my hands in horror and tried desperately to convince Herb Patterson that there were such things as morality, ethics, codes of conduct, and all that sort of thing. I could also say that I told Patterson that at least as far as I was concerned, principles were more important than the survival of a corporation like MDC as an independent company, or even the survival of Herb

Patterson as its chairman, or finally the survival of Frank W. Rogers as its president.

But . . . I am afraid that would not exactly accurately describe what ensued. For what I *did* say was this: "Are you going to handle it yourself, Herb, or do you want me to do it?"

"You don't know Zimmerli, do you?"

"Not personally, no. But I know, at least vaguely, about—"

"I know you know, Frank. I think you came on board about three years after we put that whole thing over there in the Deep Freeze."

"Well, let's see, I joined in 1982—in the fall."

"Right; then it was about three and a half years after we deactivated Aeroconsult."

"Does, ah, anybody else, by any chance, know about the old arrangements there?" I asked.

"Sam Jackson knew about it. He's dead."

Sam Jackson was my predecessor as president of Missile Development Corporation. He died in 1983 of natural causes . . . I think.

"You know," I said, "it's a pity that we have to go this route."

Patterson answered in a low, cold voice: "We don't have any choice. You think that I just intend to stand by and let Boeing and General Dynamics siphon billions of dollars of business from us?"

"Herb, that's not—"

"Their missiles are no damn good! With their speed and that goddamn TERCOM guidance system they're using, the Russians will be able to shoot down the sons-of-bitches just as fast as they're fired. Is that what you want, Frank?"

"But how do you know that somebody was bought over there?"

"Because I've been in this business my whole life. Something fishy as hell has been happening over there. But Frank, now listen to me, if you want out, right now, just say so, and

20

I'll understand. When I brought you into Missile Development Corporation, frankly, I did not think it would come to this."

"Look, Herb, I didn't spend eighteen years working for Citibank and Chase Manhattan around the world without knowing probably a lot more about what we're doing here than you can even dream of. So let's cut the horseshit and get down to procedures, and I repeat my question: Do you want to handle it or you want me to handle it?"

"If I were younger, Frank . . ." Patterson's voice kind of tapered off.

"All right, where do I start?" With our general?"

"God, no!" exclaimed Patterson. "Start with Zimmerli in Basel. He'll know where the hanky-panky is going on if anybody does. You know, I've seen some bent lawyers in my time, but Herr Doktor Zimmerli takes the cake in any country and in any language as far as I'm concerned."

"I think," I said, "that I am going to have to know a few more details about, you know, how much is stashed where, and how I can break it loose without making any unnecessary waves."

"Everything you need is in a dossier. It's in a safe in Zimmerli's office. It's been gathering dust there for quite a while. But it will tell you everything you need to know. Needless to say, Frank, I don't think you should let that dossier get too far away from you. I would also like to suggest that I don't think there is really any necessity for you to get into any of this with Nancy. You know what I mean?"

"Sure, Herb."

"Better come down to the plant with a suitcase ready to go tomorrow," Patterson continued. "If Nancy asks, just tell her you're going to London or something."

When I told Nancy about going to London, she didn't even bother to look at me. When I asked her about it later on, she said she figured I was a big boy and knew precisely what I was doing.

Well, I was a big boy. And right here I'd like to just stand back a minute and discuss in plain terms what Patterson and I were waltzing around about at the P.U. Club that evening. In a word, we were embarking upon a program of bribery.

Now, I think that for many years there has been a total misunderstanding, at least in America, about just what exactly goes on in this world under the general heading of "bribery." I mean, there have been some truly pathetic instances of what I term the penny-ante variety, the most sickening being the so-called Abscam affair. Here we had obscure congressmen from obscure districts accepting 50,000 bucks from an FBI agent of Lebanese origin disguised as a Saudi Arabian businessman after a gambling license in New Jersey. That, my friends, is not the sort of thing that Patterson and I were embarking upon.

Nor were we about to get involved in one of those usual operations involving the so-called multinational corporations —you know, the sort of thing that ex-Senator Frank Church used to investigate. Again, so what if IT&T was bribing customs inspectors in Chile? And what if Textron—remember Mr. Miller who used to be Secretary of the Treasury? well, *his* company—so what if they were greasing the wheels a bit with some colonels in Iran to get them to buy three lousy Bell helicopters? The whole thing was small potatoes and boring.

Now let me tell you what bribery is really all about in the latter part of our twentieth century. It is not penny-ante stings, and it does not involve greasing palms in some Latin American customs shed, and it is not that something that came up very often in one of Senator Church's investigations. If anything, in this area as well as in most others, Church's biggest fault was his lack of imagination. He is a small man who obviously thought small. He missed all but a few of the really big ones. Now, I am not going to talk about some of the things that my former competition at McDonnell Douglas, or Lockheed, or Boeing were doing in the world of the 1970s and early 1980s. But what I would like to do is just make things clear about the attitude that I had when I went into this whole thing in the latter part of 1985 by citing two examples of what I believe are historical parallels.

First, the story of General Douglas MacArthur and the President of the Philippines. It's a short story. The Philippines' President, Manuel Quezon, was trapped on Corregidor at the end of 1941. Understandably, he wanted out before the Japanese got to him. MacArthur, for whatever reason, refused to help him. On January 3, 1942, President Quezon issued an executive order that $500,000 be transferred from the account of the Philippine treasury in New York City to MacArthur's personal account. On February 19, 1942, MacArthur received confirmation that the funds had arrived in his account at—where else?—Chase Manhattan Bank. On February 20, Quezon left Corregidor in an American submarine. To this day the Philippine Republic is a good friend of the United States, and MacArthur proved to us all that, in the words of that old song, "Old soldiers never die, they just fade away . . . rich."

Example number two: Henry Luce. Yes, the sainted Henry Luce who cofounded *Time* magazine and ran it for decades. If you page back through the *Time* magazines of the 1960s and '70s you will find that one of that publication's big heroes, along with such great men as Chiang Kai-shek, was the Shah-an-Shah of Iran. Why? Perhaps it had something to do with the fact that agents of the Shah disbursed from account No. 214895.20 of the Union Bank of Switzerland in Geneva $1 million to the account of Mr. Henry Luce in 1962.

How do I know this? Well, as I told Patterson that evening in San Francisco, when you've worked for Chase Manhattan around the world, you've learned and done a lot of things. MacArthur used to bank with us, and the Union Bank of Switzerland in Geneva was just down the street from our office there, and we used to swap war stories sometimes, provided the parties involved were long deceased.

The point of all this is to show that there is a type of bribery on a very high level which really produces results. It can actually change the path of history for the better. Are the so-called perpetrators of such payoffs such evil men? I doubt it. Just think—if someone had blown the whistle on General MacArthur in 1942, what could have happened? We might still be bogged down on Guadalcanal. Right? Or take Mr. Luce and his friend the Shah of Iran. Sure, the Shah ended up where I guess he had to end up, but at least he kept the Russians at bay in Southwest Asia for twenty-five years. Without the support of Luce and his friends in high places in Washington how long would he have lasted? To be sure, when he went, Iran went. And partly because it went, Missile Development Corporation and the Germans and the Russians somehow found themselves on a type of collision course in 1985. And we were on that course because, perhaps, somebody in a very high place had once again been bought.

I think Herb Patterson's mind was full of similar thoughts that evening of November 19, 1985. Because he said, just as we were parting on California Street after that dinner, each about to head in his own direction: "Keep something in mind, Frank, because I suspect you are going to be mulling this over before you go to sleep tonight. In 1962 Lockheed Corporation made the deal of the century by selling West Germany three hundred and fifty F-104 Starfighters when a man called Franz Josef Strauss was Minister of Defense of West Germany. After Germany bought, both Belgium and the Netherlands also went Lockheed. The F-104 was such a lousy aircraft that eventually more than half the planes crashed. But that's not the point. My point is: Strauss is now Chancellor of Germany, after spending almost twenty-three years in limbo. It seems to me peculiar that just a few months after his reappearance on the European scene this new 'procurement problem' has suddenly cropped up."

He paused.

Then: "Strauss' chief aide is Graf Otto von Amsburg.

Strauss appointed him Foreign Minister, as you know, but the relationship goes much deeper than that. I think Zimmerli knows von Amsburg's family."

He paused again.

"Everybody over there is going to be very, very cagy on this sort of thing. I know, since I've been through it before. What I suggest is that you keep these names in the back of your mind, but let Zimmerli go through all the various motions he feels necessary before you really get to deal with the principals. If that sounds a little vague, it's because we are fishing in very murky waters. See you tomorrow, Frank."

The next morning I left home at seven fifteen and as usual took Sandhill Road past the linear accelerator and Stanford Medical Center, through Palo Alto to 101 and onto the freeway leading south to Sunnyvale.

Now, Sunnyvale, California, is not a place that exactly strikes one as being ominously capable of global reach. Until, that is, one is confronted with the massive facilities of Missile Development Corporation. Like Boeing up in Seattle or Lockheed down in Burbank, it has its own huge private airfield, situated between Highway 101 and San Francisco Bay. Impressive as the airfield is on its own, even more awesome are those huge hangars behind the landing facilities where the MDC ballistic missiles are—or at least, were—assembled. Occasionally those huge doors were left open to tease the imaginations of those never-to-be astronauts working their way south on the freeway to an appointment in San Jose—not at 5,000 mph in a MDC missile, but at 55 mph in a Ford LTD.

That morning instead of going directly to my office I decided to stop off at Plant 5 to see how things were going. Plant 5 is where the final assembly operation of the MDC cruise-missile prototypes was taking place. When I stepped into the huge building I could not, as usual, fail to stop in admiration of what our American technology had once again wrought.

There were eight of them "laid out" that morning. Our cruise missile was just under fourteen feet long, colored a glistening steel blue and resembling very closely an elongated version of those Navy torpedoes we are all so used to from World War II submarine movies. But as any observer that day would immediately have concluded, these modern weapons were infinitely more complex. Each of the eight prototypes was hooked up to hundreds of wires, which led in turn to dozens of mobile racks of highly sophisticated electronic instrumentation surrounding them.

In Plant 5 there was no hammering, no shouting; there were no huge cranes, no hissing, no whining. The place in no way resembled the usual scene at aircraft or aerospace plants. If anything, our Plant 5 more closely resembled a research laboratory than an industrial factory. Even the dress of the "workers" was somewhat similar. Dozens of technicians wore white coveralls; many others were dressed in tweedy jackets, Brooks Brothers shirts, and conservative ties. Not a blue collar in the lot. And if one continued to analyze the scene, another aspect soon became apparent: the average age of the people was not much over thirty. The median education of the men in that building was somewhere between a master's and a doctorate, and not from places like North Dakota State, either: Stanford, Cal, and Cal Tech were most heavily represented; then MIT and Georgia Tech. The majority of them had specialized in the field of electronic engineering—the older ones going back to the days of first Frederick Terman and then Joe Pettit at Stanford: in other words, the best in the business.

We paid our people minor fortunes. For which they had produced two major miracles, the keys to our cruise missile: first, the unique electronic guidance system which our corporation had developed over ten years, and second, an amazing new jet engine which incorporated an electronic fuel system a decade ahead of the current state of the art. These miracles involved an R&D expenditure of over one point five billion dollars—that's $1,500,000,000—by our company. They meant that our company now possessed a cruise missile with a truly astounding capability, astounding in two chief respects: the 572 missiles which NATO intended to deploy, if all were launched within a ten-minute time frame, and assuming that just under 50 percent were intercepted, would kill about one hundred twenty-five million Russians—that's 125,000,000. That is amazing, isn't it? In fact, so amazing that the financial fortunes of Missile Development Corporation were insured to the end of the century.

At least, we had thought so.

"Mr. Rogers," came a voice beside me. "Mr. Patterson's secretary was on the phone, and asked me to tell you that Mr. Patterson is expecting you in his office. Now."

It was somebody from the chief engineer's office. He seemed embarrassed. He didn't seem to realize that even presidents of companies can be ordered around too. By chairmen of boards.

When I appeared outside the boss's office a few minutes later, Chairman Patterson's secretary waved me right in.

"Morning, Frank. I think we're ready to move. We've booked you on that Lufthansa direct flight to Frankfurt which connects with the Swissair feeder to Basel. You will be met. You did bring a suitcase?"

"Yes."

"I hope you don't mind all the hurry. But there is no question in my mind at all that we must move fast, before the Germans' new position—or apparent new position—jells. After you've established your program in Basel, give me a call. You know where."

Patterson had managed to deliver his instructions without once referring by name to either Dr. Zimmerli or Aeroconsult.

"I hardly need remind you how important this is, Frank,"

continued Patterson, now rising to his feet. "If you succeed in this, I think there can be little doubt left that you will succeed me behind this desk."

I just nodded. Patterson was sometimes just a bit too transparent.

"How far are you willing to go on this, Herb?" I asked.

"As far as the situation in Basel might indicate, Frank."

Ridiculous that two grown men running a major American corporation had to talk in riddles like this in their own office building, for God's sake. But one never knew.

We shook hands, and I left for the airport.

4

DR. ZIMMERLI WAS WAITING about thirty yards the other side of the gate through which you pass onto Swiss territory after clearing customs at the Basel airport. The runways, the tarmac, and most of the terminal are in France. It is a peculiar airport, just as Basel is a peculiar city.

Zimmerli was a tall, thin man; "gaunt" would perhaps best describe his body. The head was narrow; the eyes almost black, and piercing. The first time I saw the man I was reminded of pictures I had seen of old John D. Rockefeller. Not that Zimmerli was that old. My guess was somewhere between fifty-five and sixty.

"*Sie sind Herr Doktor Rogers*" were his initial words. His voice was flat. And there was no smile. Nothing.

"*Herr Doktor Zimmerli?*" I asked.

He gave a curt nod.

"Will it be English or German?" he then asked, still standing without a move, and without blinking.

"English for now, if you don't mind."

29

He shrugged. "As far as I am concerned, it could also be French or Italian or Russian or Spanish or—"

"Yes," I interrupted. "Where is the car?"

He motioned to a man standing about ten feet behind him.

"Your driver," he said as the man approached. His name is Hans-Peter. He is absolutely reliable. Mr. Patterson always used him when he used to come here. Mr. Patterson always used a Mercedes 600. Black. So that is what we have outside. If you prefer something else, I—"

"That's fine," I said, again interrupting. "Let's go."

The weather was about as inhospitable as it comes. Gray sky, light drizzle, temperature probably just a couple of points above freezing. When one lives in California for too long, one forgets about the misery in which most people live at least half the year. And I should hardly have forgotten. For Basel, its weather, the general air of depression that pervades the Rhine valley in which it is situated were quite familiar to me. After all, I had gone to university there for three years, had met my wife there, had, indeed, astounded the local intellectuals by receiving my doctorate with the predicate of *summa cum laude*, an honor reserved for a couple of graduates at best each year, but seldom for foreigners, and never for Americans. They did not forget such things in Basel.

"Doesn't change much, does it?" asked Zimmerli, as we started to pass through the Spalenquartier.

"No. But you people seem to like it this way. How long has your family been here?"

"Came from France at the end of the sixteenth century. Huguenots, you know. When was it you graduated here, Rogers?"

"Nineteen sixty-two."

"With a *summa*, wasn't it?" he continued, proving my point.

"Yes. And you?"

"Oh, much earlier, of course. Nineteen fifty-one, to be exact."

"No, I meant the predicate."

"I forget. *Magna*, I think."

What bullshit! That was one thing nobody forgot. Academically, I was one up on Zimmerli. He obviously did not want to dwell on that unfortunate fact too long.

"Your wife stayed home, I presume. Nancy is her name, I believe," he continued.

"You knew her?" I asked, more than slightly surprised.

"No. But some friends did. Children?" Zimmerli asked.

"No. When was Mr. Patterson here last?"

"Patterson? Oh, that was quite a few years back. When we put the operation here more or less on ice."

"I presume you know why I am here?"

"Yes. To defrost it."

"Well, I would not exactly say that. I would hope that we should be able to solve our problem through the use of normal channels."

"Really" was Zimmerli's dry response.

"Is Graf von Amsburg aware that I'm here?"

"*Who?*" And the word was spoken sharply.

"Graf Otto von Amsburg."

"No. Why should he be?"

"Mr. Patterson thought that perhaps he might be helpful in this matter."

"He did, did he? I wonder why."

"He said that you knew his family."

"That I do. Well, let me put it this way. Perhaps we shall come to Graf Otto von Amsburg. But all in due time."

"And what, in your judgment, Herr Doktor, is due time?"

"First we must talk here in Basel. Tomorrow. And then, probably, we must visit a friend in Brussels. And then, perhaps after that, we shall see a friend or two in Germany."

"Tomorrow? But I was thinking we would definitely start

this afternoon. In any case, I think we should first go to your office and pick up that dossier. I want to go through it if we can't meet today."

"That will not be possible."

"What exactly does *that* mean?"

"Exactly what I said. No one sees that dossier until I am given explicit instructions from Mr. Herbert Patterson."

"I think I should make something quite clear, and right now, Dr. Zimmerli," I said, and now I was, to put it mildly, quite bloody mad.

"Please do."

"Mr. Patterson, and thus the company, have given me an absolute *carte blanche* in this matter. In other words, all decisions will be made by me and will be final."

"But of course," replied Zimmerli. "I am and will remain, my dear friend, your humble and obedient servant." He paused. "After I am told to be so by Mr. Herbert Patterson."

We were at the Hotel Euler on the Centralbahnplatz.

"Hans-Peter," said Zimmerli to the drive, "take Mr. Rogers' bags in."

And to me: "I think I will stay in here out of the rain. I am sure you need a rest. Be at my office at seven-thirty sharp tomorrow morning. Then we shall start."

And I was dismissed. Not the most auspicious of beginnings.

The hotel personnel could not have been more solicitous. I had a martini at the bar. Then a most delicious lunch in the restaurant. And decided to take a nap. Come tomorrow, I would take charge of Herr Doktor Zimmerli once and for all.

5

SABINE VON LATHEN CALLED ME in my room about four hours later. I remember because I had decided not to nap past five o'clock, in the hope that I would be able to get a full night's sleep later on and get over the jet-lag problem in one easy go. My phone had rung only seconds after I turned off the alarm.

"Is that you, Frank?" asked the voice. It was a low voice, what one probably would describe as being on the "throaty" side.

I was absolutely stunned to hear it. I had never expected to talk to Sabine von Lathen again. By mutual agreement.

"Frank?" This time softly.

"Yes. Sabine." I tried to make it flat. Cut-and-dried. Curt. Uninterested. Bored.

"Can we see each other?" she then asked.

"I don't—"

"I'm in the lobby."

"Well, I—"

"I'll come up. Just for a minute."

She was there in less than a minute. She was probably more breathtaking than I remembered her. And over the last three years I had remembered her quite a bit. She was a woman of magnificent build, of patrician face, of long, flowing hair. And she dressed, always, as if she had just stepped onto the Faubourg St.-Honoré after having been kissed lightly on the cheek by Yves Saint Laurent.

She was, frankly, the most desirable woman I had ever met in my life.

We shook hands. And my hand—in fact, my whole arm—was actually trembling.

"Dammit, Sabine," I said.

"I know. We both promised. But I simply could not keep it."

"I also promised Nancy," I added.

"I know. I don't want you to break that promise."

"How did you know I was here? I just got to Switzerland a few hours ago, for God's sake."

"I'm with the Staatsanwaltschaft. Actually, I am an assistant prosecuting attorney. I am also still single."

"Congratulations. On both counts. But what has either got to do with me?"

"You are on the police surveillance list at the airports in this country. You go through Immigration control and they let the police know immediately."

"Why?"

"I don't know. All I do know is that I was walking down the corridor of the courthouse after lunch today and the local head of the Fremdenpolizei, who is a very smart number, told me that you had just arrived in town. He referred to you as my 'Ami boyfriend.'"

"How could I possibly be on their list? I haven't even been in Switzerland for three years."

"No. Three years and four months. You left on September 16, 1982. Remember?"

I remembered. It was exactly two weeks before I had joined Missile Development Corporation as that company's number two man. The month of total transition: from international banker to president of an aerospace company; also from married man with the most terrific mistress in the world to married man, period.

It was not as if Sabine had given me any "fish or cut bait" ultimatum. "I'm perfectly happy this way," she had told me, countless times.

It was Nancy who had given the ultimatum. And I swear to God, I had never even suspected she knew. In fact she had never, not once, ever mentioned Sabine's name. And we'd been having that affair for three years. And during the entire three years not one peep out of Nancy.

We'd been living in London, where my bank was. And Sabine had been associated with a law firm in Zurich that handled some of our Swiss business. Sometimes that required our getting together—as banker and lawyer—in Paris, or New York, and one time it was Istanbul. We'd financed a tobacco export operation there that traded through Switzerland. There was how our Swiss lawyers got involved.

Sabine had met me at the Istanbul Hilton with the documents providing a Swiss-bank guarantee for our loan to the Turks. That evening we'd decided to spend the night together. We'd closed the deal the following morning. But we'd stayed in Istanbul for four more days and never left the grounds of the Hilton once. That was in September of 1979. That was the year Salt II was signed in Vienna. Brezhnev and Carter. Both long gone. Hell of a way to remember the beginning of the best romance I have ever lived. Or even imagined.

"Why the prosecuting attorney's office? And why Basel?"

"I'm *from* here. You know that. And I wanted to do something different. Afterward. It was not difficult. My father arranged it."

Her father was president of Hoffmann–La Roche, the

world's largest pharmaceutical company, which was situated in Basel and which had given a hungry world such marvelous solutions to its problems as Valium and Librium. Her family had been among the founders of that company in the late nineteenth century. They were rumored to be collectively worth about a half-billion Swiss francs as a result. When the von Lathens wanted something in Basel, they got it.

"What do you do there?" I asked.

"Fraud squad is about as close as I can get in English. Officially: Wirtschaftsdelikte."

"And I'm on your list, huh?"

"Now, Frank. You are not on our list or anything like it. I just, by chance, was told that you are on some list or other of the Fremdenpolizei. And you know that they have lists that hardly end."

She was, of course, right. The Fremdenpolizei is a Swiss police organization which comes as close to the Gestapo as you can find in Western Europe. In Eastern Europe they are, of course, the rule, not the exception. These police are there to supervise the activities, all the activities, of foreigners. If any foreigners break the rules, they are either deported or imprisoned. Deportation requires no judicial action. Prison sentences are handed out in a perfunctory fashion. Now, this does not mean that the Swiss themselves are subject to such a police state. Not at all. Their civil liberties are almost as avidly protected as those of the British or even Americans. The Fremdenpolizei are there to protect the law-abiding white Christian Swiss from foreign elements, such as Italians and Turks, just as the Gestapo was there to protect the law-abiding white Christian Germans from such foreign elements as the Jews or Gypsies in the 1930s and '40s.

The Swiss, in many ways, have the same Germanic traditions as their neighbors to the north—with the exception that they have retained them uninterrupted throughout the entire twentieth century, since they were never forced to abandon them because of having lost a war. The Swiss never lose wars. Because they never fight them. They are neutral. Even where Nazis, Jews, Gypsies, and Americans are concerned. As I was to find out.

"Could you find out why I'm on the list?"

"Probably."

"Now?"

She walked past me. We'd been standing between my bed and the door the whole time. She picked up the phone and dialed.

"*Fremdenpolizei? Geben Sie mir bitte Herr Doktor Wettstein*," she asked. Then a pause.

Then: "*Herr Doktor Wettstein? Sabine von Lathen hier. Bitte können Sie mir mitteilen, warum sich mein Freund, Herr Doktor Frank Rogers aus Amerika, auf der Fahndungsliste des Flughafens befindet?*"

She listened for no more than thirty seconds, said, "*Vielen Dank*," and hung up.

"So?" I asked.

"It's not the Swiss who put you on the list."

"Who, then?"

"The Germans. The West German Federal Police in Wiesbaden. With instructions not to hold. Just to inform them immediately of any arrival or departure."

"Which you did."

"Frank, *I* did not inform *them*. I am informing *you*. It is our Fremdenpolizei who do those things."

"But if the order had been to 'hold,' you *would* have been involved."

"Of course."

"Do you just do what the Germans want you to do all the time?"

"Of course not. Only when explicit agreements are involved."

"What kind of agreements?"

"Those involving reciprocity."

"You mean through Interpol?"

37

"No. Interpol has nothing to do with it. It's bilateral. In this instance, a Swiss–German understanding that goes back years. Interpol would not allow itself to be involved."

"Why not?"

"Interpol will not have anything to do with political cases."

"Political?" Now my voice began to rise. "What in hell is political about me?"

"Frank, I will try to find out. All I do know is that when we get requests like this directly from Germany—or France, for that matter—on a bilateral basis, there is usually some political element involved. Like terrorism."

A long silence followed.

"Sabine," I finally said. "I'm sorry. This is ridiculous. You were only trying to help, I guess. I don't know what got into me."

"I understand, Frank. I guess I'd better leave."

"No, for God's sake. Look, let's go downstairs and have a drink. If you don't mind being with somebody that's on your wanted list, that is."

"I really think I should probably just leave."

"Come on, Sabine. Just kidding, right?"

After which I went over and kissed her. Following which she slowly kissed me. And . . .

"I'd better put on a tie," I said, interrupting a process that was heading straight back to where we had left off three years and four months before, with disastrous emotional results.

The Euler bar is small, resembles an English bar more than a Continental one, and is boring. We had one drink, then mobilized Hans-Peter and the Mercedes and headed across the Rhine to the Red Ox Grill, which also had a bar that looked like an English bar, but was not boring. After two more drinks there we went into the grill and sat down to dinner consisting of two well-aged *entrecôtes* covered with *sauce Café de Paris, pommes frites,* and *salade.*

"Glad to be back?" she asked as we killed off the rest of the

Pommard '69 which, in dollars, was setting me back the equivalent of a small cruise missile.

"I hate to admit it, but the answer is yes. The goddamn food here is absolutely unbeatable."

"And the people?"

"Definitely beatable. With a few exceptions. One in particular."

"May I assume that—"

"You may."

And her hand came across the table to touch mine, and it felt just the way it had felt three years and four months before.

Then she asked, "Frank, what exactly are you doing here?"

"Why?"

"Maybe I can help."

"I came here to see Dr. Amadeus Zimmerli."

And her lips came together in a silent whistle.

"I think you have a word in America for him."

"Yeah?"

"Heavy."

"In which way?"

"Very powerful friends."

"Do you people have an interest in him?"

"We people?"

"The prosecuting attorney's office, dear Sabine. Let's not go into the Dumb Swiss act."

"We have no interest in Dr. Amadeus Zimmerli. That I can state categorically. My boss and Zimmerli are very big friends, if you know what I mean. Therefore Herr Doktor Amadeus Zimmerli's name never comes up."

"Should it?"

"Perhaps. We have laws here, you know, concerning arms exports. They are forbidden into areas of potential military conflict."

"I thought those laws applied only to weapons manufactured in Switzerland proper."

"That's a matter of opinion."

"And your boss's opinion is that as long as—"

"I think we'd better get off this subject, Frank."

"How come you seem to know so much about Zimmerli?"

"He is also a friend of my father's."

"Small world."

"Frank, Switzerland is a lot smaller world than I think even you imagine. Just one suggestion. Be very careful with Zimmerli. And don't think that you can possibly beat him on his own turf. They protect their own here. It's a very exclusive club that runs this country. Less than a hundred men. And not one woman, I might add. Twenty bankers, twenty industrialists, a dozen lawyers, and so forth, and we Swiss all know their names. Zimmerli is one of them. So is my father. So is my boss, Dr. Wettstein. If one of them decides to go after you, they all will."

"Okay, Sabine. I think I've got the message. But I think you've got one little detail wrong. I am not here to upset Zimmerli and his pals. I am here to work *with* him."

"Then why do his friends in Germany have you on the list?"

It was a good question. To which we did not find an answer that evening, because I dropped Sabine at her house on Nadelberg and went back to the Euler to get some sleep—alone.

But the thought never really left my mind that evening: Why *did* the Germans have me on their list?

6

AT SEVEN-THIRTY the next morning Dr. Amadeus Zimmerli was waiting for me behind his desk in his office at Dufour-strasse 24. There was nothing fancy about anything in the place. Not that it was cheaply furnished; it was just not done to impress. It reeked of frugality.

Zimmerli had apparently decided to be affable. He had coffee and croissants waiting for me. *His* breakfast consisted of a series of Gauloise cigarettes. He puffed and I sipped for all of three minutes, and then got down to business. Or at least, Zimmerli got down to business.

"I think," he began, "that I should perhaps explain the problem as it was explained to me last night by our mutual friend Herb Patterson on the telephone. Then, if we agree on what the problem is, I shall suggest some approaches that might lead to a solution. Is that agreeable?"

It was.

"*Gut.* Now, as you perhaps know, I, my law firm, and a 'sister' organization were involved with similar problems in the past, specifically the marketing of the MDC Falcon missile. You are aware of that."

I was.

"*Gut*. Now, as I further understand it, you have tried to gain support for your ground-launched cruise missile in NATO without our assistance. And have suddenly run into problems. Is that correct?"

It was.

"The problem is that you think one of your competitors may have bribed someone, or more probably, a number of people, and you have not. Does that correctly summarize the problem?"

"Maybe. We have no evidence of any bribes on this thing. That's precisely why I'm here. To get your help in making such a determination."

"I think I may have an answer to that. But first let me ask you something. You are the president of Missile Development Corporation. You are their financial man. Is that correct?"

It was.

"Your European sales have always been handled by a Mr. Bob Lee. He knows everyone in NATO involved in this business. Why are you here and not Mr. Lee?"

"Because this matter is of extraordinary importance to the corporation. And because Mr. Lee, and all of our sales people, have been given very strict guidelines under which they must operate in regard to the promotion of foreign sales, guidelines in keeping with the Foreign Corrupt Practices Act. Mr. Patterson and I both felt that the situation may call for more flexibility than those particular guidelines, when strictly interpreted, might allow."

"I understand," replied Zimmerli. "And I agree with your reasoning. *Gut*. Now I will tell you what I have found out. I think that there has been massive bribery. And I think that the key to it lies in Belgium. Because the key man is a Belgian. Do you want to know his name?"

"Why not?" I replied. For having taken step one with that statement regarding my attitude concerning that ridiculous Foreign Corrupt Practices Act, I decided that I might as well go on to the next one.

"Prince Léopold. The youngest brother of the King."

This time I sounded a silent whistle.

"How sure are you?" I asked.

Zimmerli shrugged. Then: "Ninety percent."

"How did you find out?"

"Through our man in Belgium, René Van der Kamp."

"Who is he?"

"Minister of Economic Affairs. Liaison man between the Belgian Cabinet and the Royal Family," replied Zimmerli.

"And how does he know?"

"I think you will have to ask him that in person. There are limits to what one can do on very short notice over the telephone. I think you will agree that I have done rather well."

I did agree.

"Who's paying them?"

"I think we should consider 'upping the ante,' as you say in America."

"How much 'ante' do we have available?" I asked.

He picked up a large, dusty dossier from his desk.

"These are the documents you requested yesterday. Mr. Patterson, in our phone conversation last night, instructed me to release the dossier to you. However, it must not now or ever leave this office. You understand that?"

I nodded.

He handed over the dossier and said, "The current financial status is summarized where the red tab is."

I opened it there, scanned the page, and then said, "This is goddamn amazing!"

Normally I don't use such language in a business context, but I was truly astounded. I not only was president of MDC but had been brought in by Patterson to become the company's resident financial genius, and here was over eighteen million dollars that the chairman of the board of my company had managed to squirrel away in Switzerland and I had absolutely no knowledge of it whatsoever. Amazing. And admirable.

"Where did it come from?" I asked.

"Iran."

"When?"

"Long time ago. Nineteen seventy-eight, to be precise."

"How?"

"We used Aeroconsult to serve as MDC's sales agent for its Falcon missile in Iran. We did the deal with that general who was running the Air Force for the Shah in the final couple of years. Forget his name. We overcharged by about ten percent on the deal. Maybe it was fifteen percent. I forget that also. The general kept half and kicked back the other half, which amounted to about twelve million dollars, if I recall. That twelve is now eighteen million dollars. Compound interest."

"How come nobody found out?"

"You mean when the Shah left and the Ayatollah came in?"

"Yes."

"Remember, Khomeini had about a dozen generals shot right after he took over."

"Yes."

"Our general was the second to go. They were in such a hurry that they shot him before he confessed."

"How do you know that?"

"We now have a general in the *new* Iranian Air Force."

Made sense. But there was still something that puzzled me. So I asked.

"How did you handle the ownership of Aeroconsult?"

"Strictly arm's length in every respect. Aeroconsult is an absolutely independent corporation. Its charter defines its activities very closely. It acts as a sales agent and technical consultant for aircraft and related technology. The chairman of the board is a member of the Liechtenstein Royal Family.

The capital was issued in the form of bearer shares. The shares are in the safe in this office. Our law firm would vote them if matters ever came to a vote, which they never do."

"But if they did?"

"As I said when we met, my dear Mr. Rogers: I am and remain your humble and obedient servant."

"And if both Herb Patterson and I should happen to get killed in the same airplane crash? What evidence would MDC have of all this, including its eighteen million dollars?"

"None. Absolutely none. And I think, Mr. Rogers, we all prefer it that way. Don't we?"

You've got to give it to the Swiss: they seldom beat around the bush, and they never let morality stand in the way of common sense where money is concerned. It is too bad there are so few of them.

"I think," Zimmerli went on, "that we may very well have to call on Aeroconsult for some assistance in this particular matter at hand. Although I doubt that we will need the whole eighteen million dollars, in spite of inflation. As I recall, when Lockheed bought Japan, it had to pay Prime Minister Tanaka only one point two million on the L-1011 deal."

"Maybe so. But we might have to buy *three* countries."

"Ah, yes, but two of them are small." And he actually grinned. "I have a conference room available for you, to go through that dossier, if you still want to," he said then.

I did want to.

"Unfortunately," Zimmerli continued, "I must spend the rest of the day in court. So I will leave you. . . . And I leave you once more with the reminder that none of the contents of that Aeroconsult dossier can leave the premises."

He left, and I moved over to the conference room. And I can tell you right off, there was nothing new or startling in that dossier. Most of it dealt with the "marketing" of the MDC air-to-air Falcon missile, how much went to whom for what, under constantly changing and ridiculous code names.

Perhaps the most interesting section was the one right at

the very beginning, one that had quite obviously not been compiled by Herr Doktor Zimmerli or anybody in his office but by some anonymous outsider probably hired as a consultant by Herb Patterson. This report essentially addressed itself to the amazing relationships which the law office of Zimmerli, Zimmerli and Lutz had developed over the years with some of the most prominent arms manufacturers and dealers in Western Europe and customers in the rest of the world. It essentially endorsed the law firm as an ideal agent for any company, such as MDC, that was trying to sell weapons in the international marketplace. Most interesting from my viewpoint was the description there of the evolution of the relationship between the Swiss family Zimmerli and the von Amsburg family of Germany.

To a person unfamiliar with the details of twentieth-century European history it might seem peculiar that a German family engaged in arms manufacturing should be on such obviously familiar terms with lawyers in neutral Switzerland. But such a situation was, in fact, fully in keeping with the way things have been done for quite a while.

For most Americans, the anonymity—perhaps "cover" describes it more aptly—available in Switzerland because of its peculiar laws relating to bank secrecy and corporate and industrial espionage is a fairly recent discovery. For most individuals and corporations, the beginnings of their hanky-panky in Zurich or Geneva usually date back no earlier than the 1960s. But not so for the Germans. Not necessarily because the Germans were any smarter than the Americans in catching on to a good thing. In fact, the necessity for the Swiss connection had already been forced upon the Germans in the 1920s, in the aftermath of their having unfortunately lost World War I. The Treaty of Versailles put them out of the arms business permanently, or so it said. If they wanted to begin rearming, they needed to do it clandestinely and to operate through fronts. In the 1930s, as they began preparation for their revenge, the need for such fronts to mask their activities became ever more important.

In both decades, the Swiss—for a fee—were more than ready to act for them. They were natural allies. The majority of Swiss spoke German. They shared a frontier from Basel to the Austrian border. They shared a common legal system. They even held common military maneuvers as late as 1912. And they also shared a common contempt for the rest of the world, especially the Anglo-Saxon world.

Thus, in good part, the development of weapons outside Germany, and their testing in Spain, was financed through Swiss fronts. But the zenith of German–Swiss cooperation was reached in the 1930s, when the prime industrial force behind Germany's preparations for World War II and the architect of the gas chambers of Dachau and Buchenwald, I.G. Farben, decided to use Basel as its Swiss front for all its delicate international activities.

The law firm that, beginning in 1934, worked things out for Farben was no less than Zimmerli, Zimmerli and Lutz. The two Zimmerlis were the father and uncle of Herr Doktor Amadeus Zimmerli. What the Zimmerli brothers put together was a holding company called Interhandel, domiciled in Basel. All the shares of I.G. Farben's strategic international participations, especially its ownership of a major American chemical company, General Aniline and Film, were transferred to Interhandel. Then, mysteriously, the ownership of Interhandel was transferred to an obscure Basel bank called the Sturzenegger Bank, and *voila!*—all of a sudden I.G. Farben had disappeared from the scene.

Come 1942, the U.S. Government of course seized General Aniline and Film and all the other I.G. Farben properties in the United States as enemy-owned. And after Germany unfortunately lost a second world war, the U.S. Government, through its Justice Department, which was charged with the administration and disposal of enemy property, took steps to sell said properties. At which time Zimmerli, Zimmerli and Lutz stepped in. They went to the Swiss Government and screamed that the Americans were selling off good neutral Swiss assets which they had illegally seized during World War II. The Swiss Government, which has really only one firm and steadfast belief, and that is in the sanctity of Swiss property, protested to Washington. And one of the great legal hassles of the century was off and running. Everybody knew the Swiss were lying like hell, but every time the Americans tried to get at the documents deposited in the Sturzenegger Bank which would prove that, the Swiss Government invoked the Swiss bank-secrecy laws. And every time the Americans tried to get at the documents lodged with Zimmerli, Zimmerli and Lutz, the Swiss Government screamed industrial espionage.

The legal impasse lasted for almost twenty years. Then the Swiss engineered one of the dirtiest financial coups of the century. One today thinks of Robert Vesco as the guy who stole the most money in a single corporate heist in the twentieth century. Not so.

What happened was this: Switzerland's largest bank, the Union Bank of Switzerland, got interested. It bought up—very quietly—a very substantial percentage of the Interhandel shares in circulation—meaning those not locked up in some ex-Nazi's safety-deposit box in Argentina. You could buy the shares for a song, because who wants the shares of a company whose assets have been frozen by the U.S. Government? Then the chairman of the board of the bank, the good Dr. Alfred Schaefer, went out and got himself a consultant: Prince Stanislaus Radziwill—husband of the sister of Jacqueline Kennedy, but more important in this case, also an in-law of Robert Kennedy, Attorney General of the United States and, as such, boss of the Justice Department, which was in charge of the administration and disposition of seized enemy properties.

Well, Schaefer sent in his prince, who did his thing—and

miracle of miracles, in an astounding turnaround the U.S. Government recognized the Swiss claims in the United States; the properties were sold and the proceeds "repatriated" to Switzerland, to the great joy of a bunch of old Nazis, the Union Bank of Switzerland, Dr. Alfred Schaefer, and of course, the law firm of Zimmerli, Zimmerli and Lutz. It was rumored that its total legal fees, starting with I.G. Farben in 1934 and ending with the settlement in 1964, totaled $8.6 million.

By the way, the dossier included one of the old photos of the board of directors of I.G. Farben in 1934. You could see the picture and name of Graf Ludwig von Amsburg. He was standing next to Dr. Hermann Abs, who later became chairman of the board of the Deutsche Bank. Von Amsburg's son, of course, ended up as Minister of Foreign Affairs of the new Germany in 1985, while Amadeus Zimmerli had inherited the law firm that had handled all I.G. Farben's "business" in Switzerland.

So it was quite natural that the two men worked together. Because in 1962 or 1971, as in 1934 and in 1925, the problem for Germany was the same: to find a front for its international military activities. For West Germany had, first, been prohibited by the Allies from engaging in any international arms trade following World War II. And then to prove what good guys they were, the German Parliament in 1961 passed a law called the Kriegswaffenkontrollgesetz, or War Weapons Control Law, which precluded German industry from exporting arms to anybody but NATO allies or friendly democratic neutrals—like Switzerland.

So in 1962, while Zimmerli, Zimmerli, and Lutz were still working things out for I.G. Farben's Interhandel, the third Zimmerli in the firm, Amadeus, set out to establish a new front for the Germans commissioned by Otto von Amsburg, whose family owned the Von Amsburg Lastwagenfabrik—a maker of trucks, tractors, and tanks for the German Army. The company wanted to sell tanks to South Africa. It was

49

banned from doing so by the 1961 law. So the vehicles in question were sold to a Swiss company domiciled at Dufourstrasse 24 in Basel, the address of Zimmerli, Zimmerli and Lutz, which in turn sold the vehicles to Israel, which in turn sold the tanks to South Africa. And that little transaction, involving just over $195 million in 1962, set the pattern for a whole new generation of Swiss–German cooperation for the good of mankind.

Zimmerli, Jr. and von Amsburg, Jr. became thick as the thieves they were. They were essentially partners in the new Swiss "re-export" corporation, although the German was a very, very silent partner indeed. The next big coup Zimmerli pulled was in the reverse direction. And that was where the Missile Development Corporation, and its chairman, Mr. Herb Patterson, had become involved.

All those nations which had bought the Lockheed 104 as the mainstay of their air defense for the 1960s and 1970s were in the market for an air-to-air missile. Naturally, it would have to come from the United States. And everybody from Lockheed itself to Hughes to Boeing was trying to make the sale. MDC was also in the running, with its Falcon missile. And somehow the Chairman of MDC got wind of the special talents and connections of Zimmerli, Zimmerli and Lutz. The dossier I was reading never did explain that. But it did explain, in devastating detail, almost everything else. In summary, MDC paid massive bribes to the *then* Minister of Defense of West Germany, who will go very definitely unnamed here, as well as to the Minister of State of the Kingdom of Belgium, René Van der Kamp, to opt for the MDC Falcon missile. The German swung his Danish counterpart, and Van der Kamp made sure that both the Netherlands and Luxembourg, Belgium's Benelux partners, also went for MDC. With dollars—Aeroconsult dollars.

Total bribery cost: less than $10 million. Total value of the NATO contract: $476 million. Cheap. Then came the Iranian deal. Then some minor ones with South Korea, Pakistan, and

Egypt. The Falcon missile was now obsolete. But during its lifetime, MDC, through Aeroconsult and its Swiss lawyers, had developed sales of just under $1 billion around the world. Without the Liechtenstein/Swiss connection, our international sales would probably have been *nil!*

Now, as you know, this MDC approach to foreign arms sales was hardly unique. Lockheed, Northrop, Boeing, and the rest were all doing exactly the same thing. We had to. Because if we hadn't, how could we have possibly competed with the French? Or Swedes? Or the Italians? Look, Dassault would do *anything* to sell the Mirage aircraft and the Mistral missile. And the French Government would *let* the company do anything. Would in fact encourage it. The French Government made special rulings creating exceptions to its foreign-exchange-control laws so that Dassault could transfer money to Switzerland to bribe potential buyers all around the world. Could we, or Lockheed, or Northrop just sit on our hands and watch them take over the business? Obviously not.

The public perception, of course, is that we had no choice after all those investigations in the late 1970s, when Lockheed and Northrop and Boeing and just about everybody got caught and, it was assumed, had no choice but to fold up their "offshore" operations which had handled such matters.

Well, let me perhaps suggest that the public perception in this matter, as in so many such matters, was not entirely correct. Sure, they folded up those offshore operations where they had been *caught*. But what about the rest of them? I mean, there are some places where you get caught and some where you don't. If you were dumb enough to set things up in the Bahamas, or in Panama—in fact, anywhere in the Caribbean—you *deserved* to get caught. But have you ever heard, even once, of a Swiss-based "offshore" operation like that being shut down? Of course not. And believe me, we at MDC were not the only ones who had a big Swiss operation.

The thing is, MDC had stuck to Switzerland, and never

fooled around in other, less secure tax havens. So MDC never got caught even once. Thus there was no need to change anything. It was just prudent to lie low for a while. Until there was no other choice.

To be sure, an operation like Aeroconsult, with a front like Zimmerli, Zimmerli and Lutz, was just about perfect from a business standpoint. But what started to bother me, as I went through that dossier, was this: If von Amsburg had to make a choice between his American "clients" and his German "partners," which way would he jump? As Sabine had pointed out, Zimmerli was into very heavy things indeed. But what the hell—what was good for the cruise missile and NATO was good for MDC and the United States. Right?

After about two hours I gave up on the Aeroconsult dossier and went back to the Euler, leaving most of those thoughts behind. No use getting worked up over phantoms. What I was involved in was simply bribery as usual. No big deal.

But then why were the West German police tracking my movements?

When I got back to the hotel I called my wife, to explain that I was in Switzerland, not London. She remained monosyllabic during the entire two minutes. No comments, no questions; just "Yes," "Uh-huh," and "Good-bye." I probably sounded guilty, when there was not one goddamn thing to feel guilty about! Sure, I had seen Sabine, but at her instigation. And absolutely nothing had happened. Then why did my wife make me feel so guilty? The more I thought about it, the madder I got. So I called Sabine at the office and asked her to lunch.

We met at the Bottminger Schloss, a small medieval castle in the suburbs of Basel. It has good food and a fairly nice moat with drawbridge. I took Hans-Peter and the Mercedes. Just as we arrived, Sabine pulled up in her little runabout— a Ferrari, no less. We barely pecked each other on the cheek, and headed across the drawbridge.

"They must pay D.A.s rather well in Switzerland," I commented.

"You mean the Ferrari? It was Father's idea," she replied.

"Does he know we're seeing each other?"

"Of course. And if he does, so what? He's hardly going to go tattle to Nancy, is he?"

Somehow I always seemed to get involved with women who had such a wonderful way with words.

"I've found out a little more about who put through the request about you from Germany," she said.

"Oh?"

"If you're not interested, I won't bore you further."

"Okay, okay, I'm interested."

"The West German Ministry of Foreign Affairs."

"Anybody in particular there?" I inquired.

"Yes—in fact, very particular. The Foreign Minister himself, Graf Otto von Amsburg."

"I thought it was Doktor von Amsburg."

"It is. It is also Graf. It is also Herr Minister. Take your choice, dear."

"Aren't we being just a slight bit snippy today?"

"Perhaps we are. Shall we just stand here, or should we perhaps accept this gentleman's offer of a table?"

The gentleman in question was the headwaiter, who was staring down Sabine's décolletage.

"For how many?" he then asked, his eyes rising reluctantly to mine.

"*Zwei*," I replied, demonstrating my perfect fluency in German to the supercilious bastard.

Sabine, in Swiss dialect, ordered two dry martinis the moment we were seated.

"Thanks for remembering," I said.

"I remember a lot more" was her reply.

"Such as?"

"Such as the first time we slept together in Istanbul."

Which came fairly directly to the point. And she knew full well that while I liked doing what she had just mentioned, I hated to talk about it. Especially in public. And I knew full well that if I did not stop her right away she would probably start going into lurid detail in a loud voice just to make me squirm more.

"All right, Sabine. Now please cut it out. And please tell me what's bugging you."

She sat silent for a while on that one. Then she said, "All this big act of yours."

"What act?"

"Pretending you know nothing about your big friend Graf von Amsburg."

"What the hell are you talking about? My big friend Graf von Amsburg! For Christ's sake, I've never even met the man."

"Oh, really?" she replied.

"Yes, really."

"Not according to Father, my dear."

"Go on."

"Father likes you, you know."

"I know. Go on."

"He says that you are getting involved in a highly dangerous arms deal with Germany, and that if you know what's good for you you will get on the next plane back to California."

That slowed me down slightly.

"And how does your father know all this?" was the best reply I could muster.

She just shrugged. But then she said: "He hates the Germans. And he's been saying often during the past two years that we've got to watch out again. As long as Willy Brandt and Helmut Schmidt were running the country, okay. Although he also had his doubts about Schmidt. But what's got him worried is what happened in the last election when Franz Josef Strauss and his pals in the C.S.U. and C.D.U.

took over. Pals like your friend Dr. Otto von Amsburg. They hate the Russians, he says. But they hate the United States almost as much. And he cannot understand how Americans like you can be stupid enough to deal with Germans like this new crowd. Or naive enough. He likes you, Frank, so he believes you are naive and being used. But he says your boss, Mr. Patterson, is neither naive nor stupid. He is evil and he is using you and you should go back to California and stop this nonsense, whatever it is."

"Terrific. Now I have to submit to sermons from the Swiss, for God's sake. Who the hell was selling antiaircraft guns to Hitler right up until about five minutes before the war ended? You Swiss, and you know it full well. Who sent thousands upon thousands of Jews back over the Swiss–German border, year after year, lest they offend their business partners in Berlin? You Swiss. And you are telling me about doing business with the Germans? Why? Because some pal of your father's in Zurich wants to sell missiles to the Germans instead of us? Maybe Herr Binder? Come on, Sabine."

Well, at that point she just got up and walked out of the restaurant, and thirty seconds later came the roar of a Ferrari taking off from the parking lot.

That evening, Dr. Amadeus Zimmerli and I took the eight-o'clock Swissair flight to Brussels.

7

THE FLIGHT TO BRUSSELS from Basel on the old DC-9 did not take long—just over an hour. But it was sufficient for Dr. Amadeus Zimmerli to tell me a rather interesting story.

"The King of Belgium," he began, "has two brothers. Prince Albert, who is a nice man, and Prince Léopold, who is not."

Léopold, explained Zimmerli, took after his father and namesake, who had collaborated with the Nazis and, as a result, had been dumped from his throne after the war. The Swiss remember King Léopold well—because his wife had been killed in a tragic automobile accident on the road bordering the Lake of Lucerne. Every time a Swiss Sunday driver passes this spot he points to the monument and tells his family for the umpteenth time that good Queen Astrid was killed there. The Swiss love royalty, and Astrid was the only one who was killed in their country in modern times. All this according to Zimmerli, who seemed to have a rather highly developed sense of the macabre buried beneath his deadpan expression.

But back to Léopold, Jr. Although he took after his father where character was concerned, he could hardly be termed a collaborator—no hanky-panky with the Russians or Albanians or anything like that. Léopold's preoccupation was not with ideologies, geopolitics, or alliances. His problem was simply money. Being third in line (after two very healthy brothers) to a rather minor European throne was not easy to begin with. But it had become especially arduous for Léopold because the present King and Queen—an austere, religious woman of Spanish origin—kept him on a very short string, financially speaking. And Léopold, like some of his royal counterparts in other northern European countries, had expensive tastes.

For instance, in the 1960s and early 1970s he used to run around a lot with Prince Bernhard of the Netherlands, which raised a few insider eyebrows where both were concerned. Because Bernhard, like Léopold, was also kept on a short financial leash in spite of the fact that his wife, the good Queen Juliana, was probably the richest woman on earth, nosing out her counterpart in England by a good billion dollars or two. Juliana, Zimmerli pointed out like a good Swiss, was by far the largest shareholder in Royal Dutch/Shell, which alone was worth a lot more than most countries.

However, despite the poverty which had been thrust upon them by their families, Bernhard and Léopold used to travel the world in style. The Dutch prince seemed to always have a large private jet at his disposal, loaded with caviar, champagne, and women, in which he made his regular rounds from Paris to Rome to Rio to Hong Kong. Ostensibly, and also ostensively, it was to promote the World Wildlife Fund. Actually, it was to provide an escape from the boredom of the Netherlands and the clutches of a nice but dumpy wife who spent most of her time with her fortune-teller—according to Zimmerli, who probably had the soothsayer on Aeroconsult's payroll.

Anyway, Léopold of Belgium, having miraculously managed to avoid marriage, was a perfect traveling companion for the affable Bernhard. Some nasty types said that he was nothing more than a royal pimp. But, again according to Zimmerli, this was purely out of envy. Not that any of that mattered, since the B&L traveling circus came to an ignoble end in 1976 when the Church committee of the United States Senate unearthed the fact that the source of the Dutch Prince Consort's *richesse* was none other than the Lockheed Corporation of Burbank, California. The Prince, who was also a general in the Dutch Air Force, had been, as we all now know, on the take. The Dutch Government bought Lockheed aircraft and the Prince lived in style. But after the disclosure, naturally, no more jets, caviar, blondes.

"Tough luck, Bernhard," I commented at this point in Zimmerli's story.

"Ah, yes. But tougher luck, Léopold" was his reply. "For you see, don't you, my dear friend Rogers, that through no fault of his own Prince Léopold was also grounded, his lifestyle in ruins—all because of what was, in retrospect, a very minor bribery incident."

To a Swiss as to a Belgian, the fuss that was made over this affair was incomprehensible. Puritan ethics of both the Dutch and American varieties had never taken hold in either country, although their absence was probably more pronounced in Belgium than in most places. For as Zimmerli explained, half the Belgian Cabinet was always on the take, everybody knew it, and nobody cared.

"But that was ten years ago."

"Right. The trouble is that five years ago another scandal got going, this time involving Léopold's brother Prince Albert."

"I thought he was supposed to be a good guy."

"He is, believe me. I've tried to approach him on various occasions, and got absolutely nowhere," replied Zimmerli, which was probably as great a testimonial to his integrity as Prince Albert of Belgium would ever get.

"So what happened?" I asked.

"Well, there's a huge financial conglomerate in Belgium that essentially owns half the country, the Société Générale."

"Zimmerli," I interjected, "I used to be a banker here in Europe, so let's not assume I'm totally ignorant of what goes on over here."

"All right. Then surely you must have heard of that scandal involving Eurosystem Hospitalier?"

"Vaguely," I answered, which was partially true.

"It rocked the entire financial community of Belgium right down to the foundation. What happened was this. Eurosystem Hospitalier, which was a wholly owned subsidiary of the Société Générale, had contracted to build a hospital complex in Saudi Arabia for a price of one point two billion dollars. When the job was about three-quarters completed, it went bankrupt. Nobody could understand it. Where had all the money gone? Well, the government investigated and discovered that the reason the Société Générale got the contract in the first place was that it had paid secret 'commissions' amounting to no less than two hundred and eighty-two million. Now, that's what I call bribery!"

"Jesus!" I agreed.

"But," continued Zimmerli, "that was excessive even for Belgians."

"So how was Prince Albert involved?" I asked.

"Well, that did not exactly all get explained to the public. But it was well known throughout Europe that it had been Prince Albert who had headed the Belgian business mission which got that contract from the Saudis in the first place. It was, naturally, suggested that he might have gone beyond the normal call of royal duty."

"So what happened?"

"Prince Albert survived. But what I am trying to explain is that, once again, Léopold suffered a serious setback. First he had to suffer for the sins of Bernhard and then for those, real or imagined, of his brother Albert."

"And so he felt, no doubt, that it was time he got a shot at some of the goodies."

"Exactly," answered Zimmerli. Then he explained further. "It was not a question of willingness, but rather one of opportunity. For after the Prince Albert–Société Générale scandal, everybody inside Belgium proper was being very careful, bribewise. And the traditionally largest external source of bribe money, the American aerospace companies, were now also being forced to lie low. The Lockheed–then Northrop, then Boeing–scandals had been bad, but not so bad that they would not have blown over in a couple of years, after which bribery as usual could have been resumed.

"The real problem," Zimmerli said, "was that you American people put that Boy Scout in the White House in 1977. Even before he assumed office he was blabbering on about human rights, government morality, corporate honesty, even the Old and New Testaments, for God's sake. And now what is he? A Baptist missionary in Africa!"

What a way for a President of the United States to end up. Disgraceful. But he had left behind something we all had to live with: the Foreign Corrupt Practices Act, which made it a crime for American corporations to bribe officials of a foreign government to obtain or increase business. It also prohibited falsification of accounting records to cover up overseas payoffs. It was the only law of its kind among civilized nations. It was, in the eyes of Zimmerli and of the Belgians in general and Prince Léopold in particular, a joke!

But moral crusades, as the world has found out in every single instance in recorded history, have a very short lifespan. By the early 1980s this particular one was already dying. The business of America is, after all, business. Thus not one corporate executive was ever sent to jail under this act. And after 1982 not one executive was even cited. Thus by 1985 the American aerospace industry was once again ready, even eager, to use a man with Prince Léopold's rather dubious ambitions, though unquestionably solid connections. And Léopold, after lying low for so long after the Prince Bernhard/Prince Albert affairs, was also ready to make his move. His connections—aside from those from the old days in the Netherlands—were most solid where the aristocracy was concerned: the counts and dukes and papal princes of Denmark, Italy, Norway, and, of particular importance, Germany.

"For instance?" I asked at this point.

"For instance Graf Otto von Amsburg, Minister of Foreign Affairs of the Federal Republic of Germany" was Zimmerli's reply.

"So the road to Germany *is* through Brussels," I concluded.

"Exactly. Just as I tried to point out to you from the very beginning. It seems that this time it is not Lockheed but either Boeing or General Dynamics that has found itself a prince, and thus has sold a missile system. Our job will be to convince Léopold that he is dealing with the wrong party or parties."

"And the road to the Prince?"

"You will meet him in exactly ten minutes."

Baron René Van der Kamp was waiting for us as we deplaned at the Brussels airport. He was at least six feet five inches tall, elegantly attired in a fur-collared cashmere coat, and flanked by a uniformed chauffeur.

"Ah, my good friend Amadeus. So very, very good to see you." He removed one glove to shake hands.

"And you are Mr. Rogers," he continued. "Welcome to our little country."

With a wave of his hand we were sent through Police Control and Customs to the waiting Jaguar sedan.

"I have arranged for you to stay at the Amigo. I trust that will be satisfactory." Then: "You of course know Brussels, Mr. Rogers."

"In fact I do. I have had extensive dealings in the past with a number of your banks here. The Société Générale, Banque Lambert in particular."

"But of course. Baron Lambert has mentioned your name. But you are now in the missile business."

"Yes. But as you know, our business needs a lot of money. And my job is to make sure that we have it. So as you say, *Plus ça change, plus c'est la même chose.*"

"Ah, you also speak such excellent French! It is such a pleasure to meet a civilized American like you. I know we shall get on very well."

And that was my introduction to René Van der Kamp, the second member of the unholy trio of Zimmerli–Van der Kamp–von Amsburg—the Swiss–Belgian–German combination that eats naive Americans for lunch.

Or so they thought.

When I checked into the Amigo together with Zimmerli, there were various messages waiting for me. Five were from the same party, asking me urgently to return his calls—the treasurer of my company, Russ Egan. I had brought him with me from my old bank, so if I had anything resembling an alter ego at MDC, it was Egan.

Van der Kamp offered to take us out for a drink or something, but it was obvious he did not really mean it, so both Zimmerli and I declined and went our separate ways to our suites for the night. We agreed to meet again in the lobby at noon the next day.

It was almost 10 P.M. in Brussels, which made it just after lunch in California, and I knew that Egan usually took lunch at his desk when I wasn't around. He took his job very seriously.

I got him in thirty seconds.

"Russ, it's Frank Rogers."

"Frank! Glad to reach you. We've got a problem."

"Okay. Who?"

"Citibank. They somehow got wind of the strong possibility of our losing out on the ground-launched-cruise-missile contract."

"That's impossible!"

"I would have thought so too," replied Egan. "The fact is that *I'm* not even aware of anything like that in the wind." Egan paused. Then he asked, "Is it true, Frank?"

And without a split second's hesitation I replied, "Of course not."

"Then we've got no problem, I guess" was Egan's relieved response.

"Well, let's first pursue what they wanted."

"What they wanted was not very good. In fact, if they follow through it will be catastrophic. Because they said they have immediately suspended any further action in regard to the added two-hundred-fifty-million line of credit. And as you know, Frank, if we don't get the first fifty million of that within thirty days, we are flat out of money."

"Those goddamn sons-of-bitches" was my initial response.

"They laid it right on the line, Frank. They want more collateral, which we don't have, or convincing evidence—they spoke of a verbal type of reassurance from the Western German Government that we still had full NATO support for our cruise."

"I don't believe this," I said.

"It's a pity you're not here, Frank" was his lame comment.

"What did Herb Patterson say when you told him?" I asked.

"I haven't told Patterson. I thought I should first have a word with you, Frank. You know Patterson. He might go off the deep end with Citibank, and then we're *really* in trouble."

"You did the right thing."

"If you want my opinion, Frank, I think this calls for an emergency board meeting. We're talking now about rather deadly serious alternatives. If we are in trouble on the cruise-missile contract, well, we're going to have to go for outside help."

"You know full well, Russ, that Patterson won't stand for anybody even mentioning the possibility of a merger."

"We've capitalized well over a billion dollars of the development costs of the cruise missile, Frank. If we have to write it off, our net worth is going to be less than zilch. You know that. So that's the end of Missile Development Corporation unless Patterson listens to reason. McDonnell Douglas would—"

"Jeezus, Russ! You know full well that Patterson would go down with the entire ship, crew and all, rather than talk merger with McDonnell Douglas."

"I've told you my opinion before, Frank," continued Egan. "We'd fit each other perfectly. McDonnell Douglas has been making billions, supplying both Boeing and General Dynamics with their TERCOM guidance system. But that system is out of date, and they know it. What we've developed here is exactly what they need—not only to stay in the cruise-missile business, but a lot more. With our technology and their money we could jointly make monkeys out of both Boeing and General Dynamics, now and forevermore. McDonnell Douglas would pay a hell of a price for MDC, Frank. So even our shareholders would stay happy. It's a natural, Frank."

"Forget it, Russ. And I *mean* it." And those words were spoken a lot more sharply than was my usual practice—especially where Russ Egan was concerned.

"All right, Frank. You're the boss."

"Now, let's not get touchy. And Russ, don't let those goddamn bankers push you around. Do you *really* believe that Citibank is going to cut us off? When they and their friends have three-quarters of a billion dollars with us already? Do you really think they have any choice but to throw some more good money after the bad?"

"You have a reassuring way of putting it" was Russ's response, and he chuckled while he said it. So we were at least past the panic stage.

"Who called from Citibank?" I asked.

"Dillon."

Dillon was the president. We knew each other fairly well.

"Maybe I'd better give him a call and straighten him out."

"I think that's a good idea. Hell, if everything's still hunky-dory with the Germans, there's nothing to worry about."

"Exactly."

"And Frank, I think it's best you also call Mr. Patterson."

"I agree. In fact, I was going to call him in a few minutes anyway."

"When will you be back?" was his last question.

"If everything works out, no more than ten days."

"Glad to hear that. This company needs you, Frank."

"Okay, okay, don't worry. Let's have a beer together when I get back, Russ."

"Great."

And we hung up.

My next call was to Dillon at Citibank in New York. His secretary told me he was in conference, she clearly expected him to remain that way more or less forever until I explained that I was the president of Missile Development Corporation, after which she asked me to hold. Dillon was on the line in less than ten seconds.

"Good of you to call, Frank" were his first words. Then: "What's this I hear about your cruise-missile project?"

"What *did* you hear, Clay?" was my response.

"That you're out of it. That NATO's changed their minds."

"And who told you that?"

"Doesn't matter. Point is, I was told it came right from the horse's mouth."

"Which horse is that?"

66

"Herb Patterson."

"Come on, now. Do you really think Patterson would admit such a thing even if it were true?"

"Good point. No doubt Patterson would offer his mother as collateral if his goddamn company was at stake. So what *is* the truth, Frank?"

Careful, now, I thought.

"The truth is that I'm in Europe right now. And that I am going to be meeting with the Belgians tomorrow and the Germans two days later. And that I will be able to give you an absolute assurance about the status of our cruise-missile project after that. In person in New York, if you want, Clay."

"Yeah. Well, I don't want to put you out, Frank. But I think that would be helpful. In fact, very helpful. We've had a few calls today about this whole thing from some of our friends that are with us in our loan package to you. They're very worried. I think I'm going to have to have something rather concrete this time, Frank. Otherwise—"

"Come on, Clay. Let's not start that sort of shit."

"Look, Frank. This is no bluff. We've got very definite requirements in our loan agreements with you regarding your maintaining sufficient tangible net worth. If this cruise-missile thing collapses, we're going to move in. And you and Patterson are going to move out."

"I suspect your pals at McDonnell Douglas would like that," I replied.

"It has nothing whatsoever to do with our so-called pals at McDonnell Douglas. It has to do with three-quarters of a billion dollars of our money that you guys have pissed away on a missile system that nobody wants. Well, if you don't know how to run a missile company, McDonnell Douglas does. And if the solution to this thing is to merge MDC with them, that is what's going to happen," Dillon said.

"I can see that this is getting us nowhere," I said. "I tell you what, Clay. You calm down your friends for a few days,

67

okay? Otherwise the word is going to start making the rounds on Wall Street, and then everybody is going to get into the act, including the SEC, and I don't think any of us wants that. Right?"

"I agree," replied Dillon.

"This is Tuesday. Let's make a firm date. Lunch next Wednesday in New York. That's December fourth. I'll have what you need with me. And then I want that new credit line activated right away."

"Look, if you produce, we'll produce. The way we always have, Frank. Let's meet at my office at noon. All right?"

"Agreed."

"And Frank—good luck!"

"Thanks."

I could hardly blame Dillon for taking the tough line he had. Look, I had been a banker most of my life, and frankly, if I had been Citibank I would not have lent Missile Development Corporation one more nickel. However, let's face it: the world had once again changed dramatically during the first half of the 1980s. What used to be a totally unacceptable risk for a bank had now become one of the better types of loan available.

For the name of the game was to recycle petrodollars. At the beginning of the decade, with the price of crude petroleum at $30 a barrel, and with the OPEC countries exporting just under 30 million barrels a day, their total income had been about $300 billion a year; they had spent about $200 billion, which left $100 billion to be invested, somehow. Part of it they put into government bonds and notes: those of the United States, Britain, Germany, and Japan. But most of it they simply lent to the world's big banks—Citibank, Chase, Deutsche Bank, Union Bank of Switzerland, and so forth. These banks all had ready customers in the Third World:

Brazil, Chile, China, India—the list never ended. And they had lent them almost everything they took in from OPEC, taking the front-line risk that the OPEC nations themselves did not want to take.

But then in 1982 Turkey went to the brink of default, as did Bolivia and Zaïre. In 1983, Zambia and Sudan. In 1984, Jamaica and Poland joined the ranks of unacceptable risks.

So suddenly the flow of money to the Third World began to slow. But the OPEC surpluses had not. By 1985, OPEC sales had sunk to 25 million barrels a day, but the price had risen to $60 a barrel. With income now in excess of half a trillion dollars a year, the annual surplus had risen to $140 billion a year, and any loan, and I mean *any*, to a large industrial corporation of the capitalistic world was snapped up by the New York banks, even if it smelled to high heaven.

For, the argument went, no government on earth in the mid-1980s would let a company like MDC go belly up. Not that it had always been that way. In fact, in the 1970s, at least where the U.S. Government was concerned, it was sometimes a very tough call. Penn Central, for example. It was said that the Federal Government would have to step in. If it allowed Penn Central to default on its outstanding commercial paper, the entire New York financial market would go into a panic, and that could be the end of us all. Well, Penn Central went bankrupt and nothing happened. The opposite occurred, of course, where Lockheed was concerned. The government stepped in and bailed out Lockheed with loan guarantees, and the entire affair had a happy ending; Lockheed survived very nicely, and it did not cost the taxpayers a penny. The history of Chrysler was much messier, and left a bad taste in a lot of mouths.

But all that was ancient economic history. By the mid-1980s, with the never-ending energy crisis, precedents had lost their meaning. Now if a "strategic" corporation went to the brink, Washington, or Bonn, or Tokyo really had no choice but to bail it out, even if it went against all prior economic logic. It was "social" logic that now prevailed. The word was no longer survival of the fittest but simply survival.

For what choice did one really have? In prior eras, when growth was an ever-present phenomenon, one could let the inefficient die, because new, vibrant, innovative entrepreneurs would take their places. The world was always getting bigger and better. But no longer. In the 1980s not only had there been essentially no economic growth, but by 1985 the standard of living of an average American was no higher than it had been ten years earlier. Why? Because of energy. All economies are basically a very simple input–output machine: you put in energy, and you get products out. The only way output can stay the same if the energy input sinks is if productivity increases. America during the 1980s had, however, experienced the worst of both worlds: decreasing physical availability of energy, and decreasing labor productivity. Nothing startling had yet occurred, except for a few countries' going to the brink of bankruptcy. Rather, it had been a decade of never-ending economic "malaise"— zero real growth accompanied by an average annual rate of inflation of over 10 percent.

Not much fun for anybody.

But at least there was no mass unemployment. For now government ensured the survival of even the unfittest, if the employment of a sufficient number of people was at stake. MDC directly employed 36,000 people, so we were safe. Safe from collapse. But *not* safe from forced merger. What would happen was that the government would lean on Citibank; Citibank would lean on us, which it could do at any time as a result of the various covenants built into its loan agreements; and whether or not anyone liked it—shareholders, board of directors, or management—MDC would be merged with a stronger company. In our case it would no doubt be McDonnell Douglas. The banks would then finance McDonnell Douglas indefinitely, the government would guarantee the loans, and everybody would be happy—the banks, the labor unions, the Pentagon, and McDonnell Douglas.

What had happened to our company to bring it into such jeopardy? Basically, two things. We had gotten out of the civilian aircraft business in the late 1960s and even changed our name to Missile Development Corporation to reflect the change. That was a bad mistake. We—and I use the word "we" even though I had nothing to do with MDC at that time—had believed the projections that told us we were approaching saturation levels where civilian air travel was concerned: that all that would be left was the replacement market. Well, neither Boeing nor McDonnell Douglas, nor Lockheed, for that matter, believed the same projections, and although all had had very close calls, financially speaking, during the past two decades, in 1985 all were sound financially.

The other problem—I will not call it a mistake—was Salt II. That treaty, even though it was never ratified, had essentially stopped new missile development except for two cases: the MX missile and the cruise missile. This left MDC with three options: to go after the MX; to develop a cruise missile; or slowly to get out of the missile business altogether and try building refrigerators or TV sets instead. MDC had chosen to go the cruise-missile route, and we had bet essentially everything we had on coming out on top. Sure, we still had all kinds of other missile business, both old and new. But nothing that even faintly came close to the scope and promise of our ground-launched cruise missile. We had bet $1.5 billion on it, and if we lost, we were finished as an independent company.

It had nearly happened before; in fact, it had nearly happened before in California, and I had, unfortunately, been involved, since our bank had been one of the lead banks serving Rockwell International. Rockwell in the early 1970s had decided to go for broke on the B-1 bomber, just as MDC had decided to go all out for the ground-launched-cruise-missile contract. Rockwell spent five years and $3.8 billion dollars on the B-1.

On June 30, 1977, Jimmy Carter cancelled any further production or development of the B-1 bomber.

Rockwell survived, barely. MDC would not. We would end up a division of McDonnell Douglas. As somebody once put it, a military contractor is like a giant with a glass jaw: one sock and—out.

Dillon and Citibank knew these facts as well as anyone. But the man who would be affected most would not be Dillon or even me. It would be the man who had put his entire life into Missile Development Corporation: Herbert Patterson.

I decided I might as well bite *that* bullet right away too, so I picked up the phone again and asked the operator to get me Sunnyvale, California.

"Herb, I'm in Brussels" were my first words when he answered.

"How's it going?" he asked.

"Too early to tell. Should know more by tomorrow night."

"What's your feel?" he then asked.

"I think we're on the right track."

"Good."

"Now, Herb," I continued, "something pretty serious has come up with the banks."

"What do you mean?"

"Citibank has gotten wind of our problem over here."

"How the hell did that happen? Have you been talking to somebody?"

"Actually, Dillon said that it was you."

Which stopped the old bastard for a couple of seconds.

Then: "Me!" At the top of his voice. "I'm going to get that son-of-a-bitch on the phone right now and—"

"Herb, for God's sake don't make things worse. I just got

finished talking to Dillon, and I told him I'd stop by for lunch next week on the way back. With the reassurances he wants. Otherwise they're going to cut us off."

"Goddammit," Patterson said, "they all hit you at the same time!" And suddenly he sounded like an old man.

"Look, Herb, don't worry. I'm going to work this thing out over here. One way or another."

"I tell you, Frank, this company owes you a lot. And it's time everybody knew it. At the next board meeting I'm going to put you up for chief executive officer."

"Now, let's not get—"

"I'm not getting anything. I'll stay on as chairman, but you're going to run the show, Frank. I mean it. Now get that job done over there and come home and we'll work out all the details."

And that was that. Amazing.

Next I called home. No answer. I tried Sabine's number in Switzerland. Also no answer. Here I was about to become the head of a multibillion-dollar corporation, the boss of 36,000 people, and nobody even answered the phone when I called.

So I went to sleep.

The Villa Lorraine is situated in a park on the outskirts of Brussels and is the best restaurant in Belgium. Baron René Van der Kamp was well known there. They seated the three of us in a glassed-in alcove which provided both a view of the winter forest and privacy.

No one took an aperitif, and none of us did more than just sip the white wine—an excellent white Bordeaux, I recall. We all ordered Steak Diane. And then the awkwardness of the situation seemed to have become simultaneously apparent to all. It was Van der Kamp who finally decided to get things moving.

"I think, Mr. Rogers, that I should perhaps explain my posision. I have a true split personality. Half of me belongs to the public sector, where I have served as minister in five different cabinets. My other half belongs to the private sector, where I serve as a consultant to industry. To Belgian industry, but also to American industry. I like to believe that both halves complement each other. I have brought at least a dozen American companies to Belgium, a number of them large companies, and they have made an important contribution to employment in Belgium. As a consultant, I show them the advantages of my country and arrange for them to meet the right bankers, real estate people, and so forth. As a minister, I make sure that sufficient tax advantages are provided. So you see, my one hand washes the other hand. For the mutual advantage of my friends. You understand, Mr. Rogers?"

"I do. It's quite clear, Baron."

So far Dr. Amadeus Zimmerli had just been sitting there, looking impatient. Now he decided to say something. "René, could you tell Mr. Rogers what happened at the NATO meeting last week?"

"Yes. My colleague Monsieur Beekens—our Minister of Defense, Mr. Rogers—told me the following: As a result of considerations which he did not choose to confide to me, he temporarily—and I stress temporarily—withdrew the Belgian endorsement of Missile Development Corporation's ground-launched-cruise-missile system. The Netherlands did the same. And, of course, the Germans."

"Who made the first move toward 'temporary' withdrawal of endorsement?" asked Zimmerli.

"The Germans," replied Van der Kamp.

"So the order of withdrawal was first the Germans, then Belgium, and then the Netherlands."

"Yes, according to my colleague."

"Good. And the other members?"

"Said nothing. But all agreed to table any definite action on the weapons system."

"Then there was no endorsement of either the Boeing or the General Dynamics system?" continued Zimmerli.

"No."

"You're sure?" I asked, for the first time getting into the dialogue.

"I am positive" was Van der Kamp's reply.

"Do you have the feeling that either Boeing or General Dynamics played any, shall we say, role in this new situation?" asked Zimmerli.

"Perhaps."

"Why do you say that?"

"Herr Schleyer, I am told, was in Brussels last week."

"Herr Schleyer," interjected Zimmerli for my benefit, "is a German, resident in St. Moritz, formerly with the I.G. Farben operations in Paris, and known to have acted in prior situations as a 'consultant' to both Lockheed Corporation and Northrop, among other notable names. Senator Church's investigators tried to get at him a few years ago in St. Moritz. The Swiss Government told them to cease their efforts or they would be thrown into prison. They left Switzerland. Schleyer stayed."

"I see" was about the only answer I could muster. Obviously Schleyer and Zimmerli were in competition.

Zimmerli now began a new line of questioning.

"René, is your friend aware of the fact that we are here?"

"Yes."

"Does he feel that he might be able to be of some help?"

"That depends."

"On what?"

"On how you present your case. It is not just a question of . . . how should I put it—"

"Money," interjected Zimmerli.

Van der Kamp did not think this remark at all amusing, so, ignoring it, he continued.

"Let me perhaps put it another way. Prince Léopold is a man of high principles, as are the rest of his family. He, and they, will have absolutely nothing to do with any person or persons who might sully their reputation, deliberately or by accident."

"And if the Prince feels that there is no risk of that?"

"I think the chances are very good that he could be persuaded to be of help."

"How quickly? Time is of the essence in this matter. Either he can help us before the next NATO meeting, which takes place on December second, or we are all just going to be wasting our time."

"We can determine that immediately," replied Van der Kamp.

"How soon is immediately?" I asked.

"My friend would be willing to meet with you this evening. If all goes well, you could very well have your answer by tomorrow afternoon. Perhaps," replied Van der Kamp.

Zimmerli again looked to me for guidance. I nodded.

"Fine, Baron. Where this evening?"

"At my summer place. Outside of Knokke. In Het Zoute. You know the place?"

"I've heard," interjected Zimmerli. "At what time?"

"I would suggest nine tonight. I will meet you at my place. My friend will be with me. I'll give you directions as to how to get there. You will drive your own car. Yes?"

"Yes," said Zimmerli.

"You will be very careful. Yes?"

"Yes," said Zimmerli again.

"Now tell me, Mr. Rogers," continued Van der Kamp, "what do you think of your new President? We Belgians"— and so forth, as if nothing untoward had happened between us. Just another lunch between a visiting American corporate executive, his Swiss lawyer, and the Belgian Minister of Economic Affairs. An exchange of views.

At two thirty we left the restaurant. By three o'clock I was back at the Hôtel Amigo. I took a nap.

8

I REMEMBER THAT EVENING as well as I remember any evening of my life. It was the twenty-third day of November of 1985, and the weather in Belgium was miserable to a degree almost beyond belief. As we drove through the darkened streets of Brussels, I could not help remembering that city in the pre-Christmas days of old. It was known throughout Europe for its spectacular decorations, which had turned that eternally drab city into a winter delight. Days of old! That sounds like decades ago. In fact, those old days had ended just five years before: 1980 was the last year of the good old days, the year that energy had caught up with us all.

The streets of Brussels had always been full of potholes, but as governments were running short of funds everywhere and on all levels, their number was obviously setting new records. I had rented one of those German Fords, a Taunus, with a stick shift, which got forty-three miles to the gallon and rode like a 1935 Model A Ford. Symbolic, perhaps, of the direction in which our quality of life was heading, or had already arrived.

The traffic was sparse in the city, what with the stringent rationing system in effect, but once we had left the suburbs it became almost nonexistent. The drizzle was right on the edge of freezing. As we moved northwest, the winds from the North Sea started to pick up and occasionally rock the car. Zimmerli sat beside me in total silence. The car had no radio; the heater was weak. It was a depressing situation.

Why? Why was I doing this?

I'll tell you in a couple of different versions. The one that I was having myself believe that evening was that I was doing nothing more nor less than any top corporate executive would have done in a similarly critical competitive situation. It was us against them: Missile Development Corporation against Boeing and General Dynamics. It was a very big game, and I was playing it to win. The stakes were at a new high in my personal experience, and they had just been raised by Herb Patterson: my becoming chief executive officer of one of the most important aerospace companies in the world. For a guy still two years short of fifty, not bad, huh? Not bad at all! And if winning meant playing dirty, bending the rules, even breaking the goddamn law, well, okay. Frank Rogers was a big boy now. And he could play hardball with the rest of them. And if the game required associating with a bent lawyer like Zimmerli, and a slimy politician like Van der Kamp, in order to bribe a crooked Belgian prince, well, Frank Rogers was more than ready and willing and able to do just that.

In other words, tough guy plays tough game—and wins.

The other version was maybe closer to the truth. Maybe the real thing that was making Frankie run was fear. Because Frank Rogers had bet all his marbles on Missile Development Corporation. He had abandoned a twenty-year career in banking to take over the presidency of a company in a field

78

in which he really had no technical competence. He had traded in a $150,000-a-year job for one that paid almost $300,000 a year. He had a million-dollar house in Woodside —not even a third paid for; a $200,000 "yacht," meaning a glorified sailing boat, moored in the Bay and 20 percent paid for; a wife who needed at least $30,000 or $40,000 a year spending money. And if the cruise-missile project went down the tubes, so would Missile Development Corporation, one way or another, and Frank Rogers would be out of a job. And then a yacht. And then a house. And probably at the end, also a wife.

Because 1985 was not 1975 or '65. It was a world where the name of the game was survival. It was a world as unforgiving as that of the 1930s. One mistake, and you went from banker to bum; from Montgomery Street to Mission Street; from a Learjet to the Muni. And I was goddamned if I was going to let the phony Europeans do that to me!

If I recall correctly, it took us a little more than an hour to get to the seaside resort of Knokke, a real dog of a place. All it has to offer in summer is sand in the form of wide beaches and the grassy dunes behind them. The place would never have been built in the twentieth century, because the water is icy and polluted, the weather lousy, the natives (Flemish) inhospitable and speaking in a tongue known only among themselves, the architecture primitive, and the food ordinary and fattening, the highlights of local meals being beer and *pommes frites*. But before airplanes were invented, allowing Belgians to get a taste of the real thing, Knokke was the Nice of the north—being to Brussels what Atlantic City used to be to Philadelphia.

So much for tourist information. The point is, if that is what Knokke was in the *summer*, at its glorious peak, you can imagine what it was like on the twenty-third day of *November!* Bleak would not begin to describe it. Not that there was that much visible in the headlights of the car. For in Belgium, as all over northern Europe, the winter days are short. By nine o'clock we had already had five hours of darkness. If the idea was to take advantage of the cover of night for our little clandestine meeting, it was working out terrifically.

In Knokke there was not a single car moving; most houses were shuttered for the winter; every single beachfront hotel was closed, as were all the gas stations and all the restaurants. But at least there was a sign at an intersection indicating that if we took a right we would be heading toward Het Zoute.

Het Zoute is where the rich people of Brussels have their summer homes. Like the Parisians, whom the upper-class citizenry of Brussels ape in every possible respect, well-to-do Belgians must disappear totally during the month of August, and it is to Het Zoute that a lot of them flee, where they then proceed to spend most of the month attending cocktail parties, lunches, and dinners with the same people they were supposed to be escaping from in the first place. In many ways, the behavior of so-called European society is so predictable, boring, and unimaginative that for the life of me I cannot understand why so many Americans still suffer from feelings of inferiority when dealing with them. Now, where royalty is concerned it's something different. And thus I felt constrained to ask:

"Tell me, Dr. Zimmerli, just exactly how does one address a member of the Belgian Royal Family?"

"What do you mean?" he asked.

"I mean what am I supposed to say when we're introduced?"

"Oh. Just say, *Enchanté, Monseigneur.*"

"Monseigneur, huh?"

"*Ja,*" replied our Swiss legal adviser.

And then what? I asked myself. I mean, how the hell do you go about bribing a prince whom you haven't even met before?

"You just passed it," Zimmerli said.

"Passed what?"

"The Rue Royale," he answered, which I thought was kind of funny. "That's where Van der Kamp's house is."

So I took a U-turn, which involved as much risk as taking one in the middle of the Sahara, and then hung a right on the Rue Royale. At the third house, Zimmerli gave the signal to pull through the open gates into a driveway that wound around a sand dune. Perched on top of the dune was a long bungalow. There was only one car at the main entrance—Van der Kamp's Jaguar. So we obviously had the right place.

Outside, the wind had become a gale and was whipping icy particles of surf over the dunes. Van der Kamp must have heard us coming, since he opened the door before we even rang. We all murmured nothings as we shook hands. Van der Kamp took our coats and hung them in the closet himself. Obviously there were no maids or butlers hanging around the haunted house that night.

The living room was a good eighty feet long and dominated by an immense fireplace in which a huge fire was burning. And beside the fire stood a tall man in his mid-forties. Van der Kamp introduced me.

"*Enchanté Monseigneur,*" I said.

And he said, "Delighted to meet you, my dear Mr. Rogers. Now please let us dispense with the formalities. I shall call you Frank and you shall call me Léopold. I'm afraid that Léopold is not a very commonplace name in California. In fact, on one occasion in Malibu they started to call me Leo. but I must say that I found that even worse. Now René, you must get Frank a drink. Something rather strong, I would think, considering the climate outside."

An absolutely charming man!

The drinks appeared in the form of crystal water glasses half full of Chivas Regal, with a touch of water. The Prince took two, handed one to me, touched my glass with his, and said, "We welcome you as a new friend, Frank. I am sure this is just a beginning."

All the time, my hotshot Swiss lawyer was standing off to the side with Baron Van der Kamp, both saying nothing, just watching.

The next move was obviously to be mine.

"Prince Léopold," I began, awkwardly and not sure where exactly I was heading, "I am truly honored, and convinced that this is indeed just a beginning, not just for us but also for our two countries. I am not sure just how much you actually know about my mission here."

"I know quite a bit. You are trying to persuade NATO to back your ground-launched-cruise-missile system. Am I correct?"

"You are."

"Baron Van der Kamp has told me a lot about you. I think you should know that you are not the only representative of an American aerospace company who is trying to do the same thing."

"I am quite aware of the fact that both General Dynamics and Boeing have an enormous interest in accomplishing the same end where their cruise-missile systems are concerned."

"Yes. There is a man by the name of Manfred Schleyer. Herr Manfred Schleyer. He is a German, but he lives in St. Moritz now. You must know him, Zimmerli," he then said, turning toward the Swiss lawyer with a rather contemptuous look.

Zimmerli said nothing.

"Do you or don't you know him?" Léopold then demanded of him in a new tone of voice.

"I know him," admitted Zimmerli.

"Well?" asked the Prince.

"I know that he used to work for Northrop. And also for Lockheed."

"Yes. Lockheed. Between 1958 and 1974, to be exact. And

when the time came in 1975 and 1976 for him to step forward to tell the truth and clear the name of my good friend Bernhard, what did he do?"

Again no answer from Zimmerli.

"I will tell you what he did. He completely disappeared. And a couple of years later, when both Senator Church's committee and the Commissie van Drie in the Netherlands had finally completed their witch-hunts, only then would the Swiss admit that he had been hiding the whole time in St. Moritz, with their obvious knowledge. Church's investigators suspected that, but when they tried to go to St. Moritz to find him, the Swiss Government threatened to imprison them for espionage. Imagine! These people actually were staff counsels to the United States Senate, and the Swiss were going to throw them in prison, just to protect their banks. Do you know what I think of Herr Schleyer and you Swiss, Zimmerli?"

The good Prince Léopold made a very rude French gesture.

"And two weeks ago this Herr Schleyer actually had the nerve, the audacity, to ring me up. Said he was in Brussels and wanted to visit with me. He said that he represented a very, very large American defense contractor, that it was neither Lockheed nor Northrop, that they were willing to talk about *annual* compensation well into *seven* digits—seven digits in dollars and not, of course, Belgian francs. Imagine! I told him to get off the phone or I would have him thrown out of the country!"

"Monseigneur," exclaimed Baron Van der Kamp, "this is new to me. You should have called me immediately. I would have had the Ministry of Justice put him on the next plane!"

This from the good Belgian Minister of Economic Affairs who had called my good Swiss legal counsel no more than three days before to tell him that Schleyer had gotten to the Belgian prince, but he was not sure whether Schleyer had been representing Boeing or General Dynamics, and he was also not sure whether Léopold had been bought completely or was still open to a better bid. Obviously it was the latter. But who had sponsored Schleyer?

"I assume it was one of our "friends" in California who put this man Schleyer up to it," I ventured, joining the game.

"He actually did not say," answered Léopold.

"Perhaps because he did not know, Monseigneur," interjected Herr Doktor Zimmerli suddenly.

"Don't be ridiculous. How could he not know?"

"Perhaps he first wanted to have your commitment, and then he would have played one off against the other for your services, Monseigneur," replied Zimmerli, my bribery consultant, who was now, obviously, demonstrating his expertise in such matters, and at the same time insulting Prince Léopold to his face.

"My commitment?" the Prince screamed. "This man Schleyer was trying to set me up. I am convinced of that. They are trying to destroy our family. First my brother Albert, who was only trying to help our poor nation's exports. Now me. Next it will be the King."

The Prince was making a bit of an ass of himself at this point. But what he was saying convinced me, absolutely convinced me, that Herb Patterson's suspicions had proven, as so often, to be justified. I simply could not ignore the possibility that our competition was throwing very big money around Europe. Either we had to up the ante, or we could be out.

As if by magic, the flow of Léopold's conversation suddenly shifted in a direction that led to Herb Patterson.

"Now," he said, "I want to know exactly with whom I am dealing. I want no more of this Schleyer type of business."

"All right," I said. "You know our company—Missile Development Corporation. Mr. Herbert Patterson is the chairman and I am the president. That's it."

"And who else?"

"Who else?"

"Who else is involved from your company?"

84

"No one. Absolutely no one. You have my word. The only people involved in any way whatsoever are Mr. Patterson and myself in the United States, and Dr. Zimmerli and Baron Van der Kamp here in Europe."

Léopold's eyes remained on me for a full ten seconds after I had finished the last statement. Then he turned to René Van der Kamp and motioned very slightly with his head, and the two men left the room, leaving Dr. Amadeus Zimmerli and me alone by the fire.

"What's this all about?" I asked my Swiss counsel.

"Well, we seem to have reached what I believe you call 'the point of no return.' They are no doubt deciding whether to go beyond it."

"How'm I doing so far?" I asked.

"Extraordinarily well. But if they decide to go forward, you are going to have to commit yourself and your company all the way. You understand that? Otherwise Léopold is not going to put himself at risk. I can understand him, frankly. First his pal Bernhard gets destroyed; then his brother Albert got into that trouble. The King was extremely upset about the latter business, believe me. Baudouin is a very upright man. If Léopold gets caught doing something, Baudouin will probably kick *him* out of the country."

"But can he produce?"

Dr. Zimmerli shrugged. Then he answered: "Maybe. Maybe not. But whether we like it or not, Rogers, he's the only prince we've got at the moment."

"What about the technical details, assuming we proceed?" I then asked.

"My suggestion is that you leave that part to me. I've just got to know one thing. How much? And how much now?"

"You're the expert," I replied.

"All right. I think the parameters have already been established," said Zimmerli. "In the words of the Prince: 'Well into seven digits.'"

"I agree. So let's figure it out. We are essentially talking

85

about a three-country deal: Belgium, the Netherlands, and Germany. How much did you say we had available in Liechtenstein?"

"Eighteen point one million dollars equivalent."

"Okay. Let's see," I said, doing a quick calculation in seven digits. "How about a million on account? Another million five when he delivers Belgium. Ditto for the Netherlands. Double that, or three million, if he can deliver Germany. No. Hold on. That's not going to work. Without Germany the whole deal is shot anyway. So reverse the order. Three million if he delivers Germany. Three more million if he also delivers Belgium and the Netherlands—but like a bonus. No Germany, no bonus."

"He won't buy that," stated Zimmerli flatly.

"How do you know?"

"I know. 'Deliver'? What is that supposed to mean?"

"Just what it says. Votes in the NATO Council for Missile Development Corporation's ground-launched-cruise-missile system for European deployment. Very, very simple."

"He won't go for that. Do you recall what Van der Kamp said over lunch? Belgium and the Netherlands, yes. But Germany would be a big problem. Léopold and Van der Kamp are not going to go for your bonus plan, that I can assure you. They are going to want to get paid for each vote, separately. And they are going to want half in advance."

"Half in advance, just for *trying?*"

"That's right."

"And how will we know if he's really trying?"

"I think you can leave that to me," replied Zimmerli. "And remember, Lockheed paid Prince Bernhard for just trying. In fact, one time Lockheed paid Bernhard for *not* trying."

"Come on," I countered.

"True story. In 1968 Lockheed was trying to sell the Dutch Air Force—of which Bernhard was Inspector General—its P-35 Orion naval patrol aircraft. The Dutch Parliament preferred the French Breguet Atlantique. Carl Kotchian, who was then president of Lockheed—I guess he was almost exactly your counterpart, Rogers—offered Bernhard a half-million dollars if he would try to turn around a couple of key men in Parliament. It was really no big deal—it involved maybe thirty aircraft, at a couple of million or so apiece. Anyway, Bernhard refused the money because he said he probably could not deliver. Kotchian was so impressed with his honesty that he arranged for him to get a hundred thousand anyway. Through Switzerland, by the way."

"How through Switzerland?" I asked.

"Well, as usual they all tried to cover their tracks, so what happened was this: Lockheed, California, authorized the issue of a cashier's check in the amount of a hundred thousand dollars payable to a certain "Victor Baarn"—not too clever, that name, in my judgment—who was described as a Swiss lawyer who had been providing services to Lockheed abroad. A little bit like me, I guess, except that I never worked for Lockheed and I'm real," said Zimmerli.

"Unfortunately," I murmured.

"Well," continued Zimmerli, undeterred, "Lockheed, Burbank, told Crédit Suisse, Geneva, to issue a bearer check and to hold it until 'Victor Baarn' turned up to collect it and cash it."

"So what happened?"

"Somebody did just that. Except that when Bernhard was asked about it later on, he could not remember a thing. Nor could Crédit Suisse. When Senator Church's staff went to Europe and tried to get at Schleyer in St. Moritz, the Swiss Government threatened to throw them in prison. I don't know where Léopold got his information about this, but believe me, he's right."

"And what's the point of the story?" I asked.

"Two points, I guess," replied Zimmerli. "One—that local princes are rather spoiled where bribery procedures are concerned. And two, that Bernhard is still a prince in good standing and Crédit Suisse is still a bank in good standing. The only party that stands totally discredited is Lockheed, and the only guy who is gone is the man who was Lockheed's president, Carl Kotchian. Which facts provide the moral of this story, if you need one: namely, that it is better to be bribed than to bribe, in case something goes wrong down the line."

"What's that last crack supposed to mean?"

"That you, my dear Mr. Rogers, have also reached the point of no return" was Zimmerli's answer.

At which point in time Léopold and René Van der Kamp returned to the room.

"Mr. Rogers," said Baron Van der Kamp, "I think that we have come to a decision. We are willing to further pursue with you the matter of your company's cruise-missile system and its future role in Europe. Prince Léopold has expressed his willingness to give total support to your project, not just in Belgium but in other NATO countries where his influence can be brought to bear." Then he paused. And continued with the very deliberate words "Provided we can agree on the establishment of the necessary conditions."

"And they are?" said Dr. Amadeur Zimmerli, now assuming the role of spokesman. The entire matter now seemed to have risen to a professional plane—that of a profession in which he and Van der Kamp were no doubt charter members.

"I do not feel," said Van der Kamp, "that it will be necessary for Prince Léopold to be bothered with such details. I believe that he has a further pressing engagement."

Léopold nodded, royally.

"But I can assure you that Prince Léopold can give you a very definite agreement in principle to devote his full attention to this matter, immediately, should such details be ironed out by us this evening. Is that not so, Monseigneur?"

"It is," agreed Léopold. He stepped forward and shook my hand. And then turned to leave. As did Van der Kamp.

"Gentlemen," said Van der Kamp, "if you will excuse me

for just a few minutes. I must drive Prince Léopold to, ah, another place. Quite close, I assure you. Please help yourselves to another drink."

"What's all that?" I asked of Zimmerli when the front door had closed behind them.

"Léopold must have a car stashed somewhere close. They're very careful. And I must say I like that. None of us need any trouble, do we?"

Dr. Zimmerli then fixed two more Scotches.

Less than five minutes later René Van der Kamp was back. "I see you have helped yourselves," he said. "I will join you."

He went to the bar and upon his return lifted his glass with the words "To success. To Europe." And we all three drank.

"And now," continued Van der Kamp, "I think we should move over to my study, if we are to proceed in a concrete fashion. I assume, Mr. Rogers, that it is your intention to do so?"

"It is," I said.

Van der Kamp's study was, naturally, lined with bookshelves and had the usual French-style desk with red leather inlay. It was a cheerful room, very well lighted and airy. Van der Kamp waved Zimmerli and me to a sofa at the far end of the room, and instead of sitting behind his desk, drew up a chair on the other side of the coffee table.

"No," said Zimmerli, for some reason.

"What do you mean?" asked Van der Kamp, visibly puzzled.

"You sit here beside Mr. Rogers on the sofa. You are, after all, the two principals. I am merely here to give advice if called upon. By either principal." Which rather neatly established his position of Swiss neutrality. So Van der Kamp and he switched positions. And we began.

"What," I asked, "have you and Prince Léopold decided?"

"Belgium and the Netherlands," Van der Kamp replied, "will be no problem. The problem is Germany."

"Without Germany," I stated, "there is no deal."

"But you did not say that before," said Van der Kamp, his voice rising.

"I know. Perhaps I should have. But it does not matter. I repeat: no Germany, no deal."

"Do you realize who will be making that decision in Germany?" Van der Kamp asked.

"It will go right to the top, I assume," I replied.

"Do you know what that would cost?" he then asked.

"No."

"Do you realize whom you are talking about?"

"Franz Josef Strauss," I replied.

"Exactly. But not the old Franz Josef Strauss. You are talking about the man who now rules Germany and wants to stay in that position for a long time. Even in Belgium, Monsieur Rogers, political parties need a lot of money these days in order to survive."

"I realize that. I will tell what we are prepared to make available: a total of ten million dollars. For Belgium, the Netherlands, and for Franz Josef Strauss. But for that we expect a full, irrevocable commitment by all three governments of support for Missile Development Corporations' ground-launched-cruise-missile system within NATO." Which I thought rather admirably summed it up.

"It is not enough," said Van der Kamp quietly. And after a pause, he continued: "I know you feel that ten million dollars is a great deal of money, but I have the feeling that you underestimate European requirements today in such matters. The risk for all parties is not what it used to be. It is very, very high. Extremely high. We are talking about arrangements that involve the Chancellor of West Germany and his political party; a brother of the King of Belgium; and the chief of staff of the Belgian armed forces, who, obviously, must agree. We also have two very high-placed personalities in our neighbor to the north, the Netherlands, whom I have agreed not to name. Prince Léopold has required this of me.

However, I can assure you that the Dutch vote will be absolutely forthcoming in NATO should our arrangements be completed. And you also have me. To be sure, I am 'just' a minister of the Belgian Government; nevertheless, this is my entire livelihood and my entire life. I would not care to risk all this"—and his hand waved around the room—"without sufficient insurance."

"How much for everybody?" I asked.

"Twenty million dollars. Half now. Half after the vote is taken in NATO. And that is my first, and final, offer."

More or less just as Zimmerli had predicted.

"I believe that twenty million would amount to less than a tenth of one percent of the ultimate contract value of your cruise-missile project," continued Van der Kamp. "Lockheed and Northrop at times paid a ten-percent commission, based on actual sales value."

He was right. And with only nine days to go before the final NATO vote, how could I possibly develop an alternative course of action? So why haggle?

"You have a deal, Van der Kamp," I stated. And got up, and stuck out my right hand. And Van der Kamp took it in a gesture that was also quick and firm.

"Good," said Amadeus Zimmerli, who, as the agent for this deal, could not help demonstrating a sense of pride in what was being achieved.

"Okay," I said then to Zimmerli. "You're the expert. How do we wrap it up, procedurally?"

"Where do you want the twenty million?" Zimmerli asked of Van der Kamp.

"Swiss Bank Corporation, Basel," answered the Belgian minister, without hesitating an instant.

"In dollars?"

"Yes. It's a dollar account. Here is the number."

Van der Kamp reached into his pocket, pulled out his agenda, paged around a bit, tore out a page, wrote down a number, and handed it to Zimmerli.

"Who is the manager who handles it?"

"Rudolph Kaiser."

"A good man," commented Zimmerli. "His brother's a judge."

"Yes. A good team, I hear," said Van der Kamp.

"Well, let's say this: the Swiss Bank has not had too many judgments going against it in Basel courts."

They both chuckled. It was nice to know that one lived in a world whose key institutions, such as banks and courts, worked in harmony for the good of society. And it was especially good to know that Switzerland always stood ready to put its institutions at the disposal of its European neighbors to serve the ends of free enterprise and just government.

"Am I to assume you are going to handle the secondary distribution?" Zimmerli then asked.

"Yes, of course," answered Van der Kamp.

"And how are we to know whether . . ." Zimmerli's voice faded.

"Whether the various parties receive their due?" said Van der Kamp.

"Precisely. As you know full well, René, in the past many such a commission got stuck in the pipeline."

"I fully realize that, Amadeus. The point is this: all you care about is the result: three votes in NATO for MDC. Right?"

"Yes."

"How I produce this result is my business."

"Fine. But we will want it in writing, then."

"From whom? Strauss? From Léopold? Are you crazy?" Now Van der Kamp was really worked up.

"No. Not from Strauss and not from Léopold and not from Bernhard, nor from any of your generals or theirs. From you, my dear Baron," replied Zimmerli, with a smirk on his face. "And before you ask again, I will tell you why I want it in writing from you. Because I, and my law firm, plan to be in

92

business for a very long time. And we do not want, at some future date, to stand accused of failing in our fiduciary duty in this matter. By anybody! By that I mean we do not want Strauss, or Léopold, or, for that matter—in fact, in particular —Missile Development Corporation, especially Mr. Rogers here and Mr. Herbert Patterson back in Sunnyvale, accused of failing to transmit to you the full amount arranged for: that is, ten million dollars now and ten million dollars when you and your 'clients' fulfill their obligations, Monsieur le Baron Van der Kamp."

A rather longish statement, but the meaning was fairly clear: Zimmerli wanted to keep Van der Kamp's hand out of the cookie jar. And Van der Kamp's flushed face showed that he did not like the implication one little bit.

"My dear Dr. Zimmerli, sometimes your Swiss lack of manners is more noticeable than usual. I thought we all understood that these were to be gentlemen's agreements?"

"To be sure, they are, they are," replied Zimmerli. "Except that in your case, it will be in writing."

"What will be in writing?"

"Don't worry. Just this: 'Received from Mr. Frank Rogers, twenty million dollars.'"

"Oh, no," I said quickly. "No 'Mr. Frank Rogers.' 'Received from Dr. Amadeus Zimmerli twenty million dollars.'"

This time it was Zimmerli who turned red.

"What do you mean, Rogers? It is Missile Development Corporation that is spending the money and receiving the services for it, not I."

"It is you, Dr. Zimmerli," I replied, "who are being paid a very handsome annual fee by Missile Development Corporation to handle these matters in a manner acceptable to the senior officers of Missile Development Corporation. And this is the way I want this matter handled."

"Anything else?" asked Zimmerli, with as much sarcasm as he could muster.

"Yes, there is," I said. "I also want 'acknowledgment' from every recipient in the 'secondary distribution,' as you so nicely put it."

"Don't be an idiot," said Zimmerli, his total dislike of me now completely out in the open. "Only an American would be stupid enough to even think of such a thing, not to mention actually saying it."

"Really?" I replied. "Then I am afraid that we are not going to do business together after all."

And to the shock of the two men, I got up and started to head for the door of Van der Kamp's study.

"Wait, wait!" called Van der Kamp from behind me. "Let us not get excited. I am sure this can be worked out."

He hurried to my side and put his hand on my shoulder. René Van der Kamp is almost six and a half feet tall, and has hands to match. So he made an impression. I nodded, turned back, and resumed my spot on the sofa.

"What did you have in mind?" asked the Belgian baron.

"Nothing fancy," I replied. "In fact, what I want is very, very harmless. No receipts. No agreements. No mention of cruise missiles or NATO, or anything like it."

Amadeus Zimmerli appeared puzzled. Was there possibly something in his particular line of business that he might have overlooked?

"All I want is that each party write a simple letter of inquiry about services being offered by the payor."

"The payor?" asked Zimmerli, obviously not quite getting what a payor was. His English was almost perfect, but not 100 percent in times of stress, and this was definitely a time of stress.

"Our little Liechtenstein company."

"Aeroconsult," replied Zimmerli, the light slowly dawning in his squinty eyes.

"Exactly. Aeroconsult, A.G." I said. "Harmless. Completely harmless. And I will go one step further. I do not want these letters. Nor do I even want any copies. They are to reside in the famous safe of Zimmerli, Zimmerli and Lutz on Dufour-strasse in Basel, Switzerland. Do you understand? I want to see them. That's all. And know that they are there. Just in case, someday, it is my word against theirs, whoever 'they' may be. Understood? I am not about to become, my dear Dr. Zimmerli, another Carl Kotchian."

"And when do you want them?" asked Zimmerli, ever practical.

"Against them, and only against them, do we pay the initial ten million dollars. Plus Baron Van der Kamp's receipt. I am sure that your Herr Kaiser at the Swiss Bank Corporation in Basel is quite familiar with this type of transaction. I believe the German term for it is '*Zug um Zug*'—the *quid* being the letters of inquiry and the receipt of the Baron, the *quo* being ten million dollars now and ten million dollars later. I understand, of course," I continued, "that you, Baron Van der Kamp, will deduct ten percent from each 'secondary' payment, of two million dollars."

"I think," said Van der Kamp, "that these arrangements can be made."

Amadeus Zimmerli looked very sour indeed.

"I don't like it," he said.

"Why?" I asked.

"Because it won't work. Do you really think that Léopold or Strauss is going to send Aeroconsult such a letter? And sign it?"

"No," I answered, to his surprise. "But some staff person in their offices will. Without having any idea or clue, now or later, about anything. Because Aeroconsult will never reply, and that will be the total end of that. Just a simple letter of inquiry—a low-level letter of inquiry. Nothing more. I don't care. All I do care about is that I receive some small measure of insurance, very small in this case—insurance related to the current but especially future fidelity of my partners in this unusual bit of business."

"*Ja*," said Zimmerli, reverting for an instant to his native tongue, "*dä Saukaib het ebbis do.*" Which roughly translates from Schwyzertütsch into "Yeah, the son-of-a-bitch has got something there."

"When?" he then asked.

"Today's the twenty-third; let's say the twenty-ninth. We'll meet in Basel. We shall make our respective deliveries to Herr Rudolph Kaiser at the Swiss Bank Corporation. And then make our respective collections after Herr Kaiser has exchanged our *quids* for your *quos*. Butter for guns. Or at least, votes for the proper type of guns. Our guns."

9

THE SWISS BANK CORPORATION's worldwide headquarters is situated at the corner of Elisabethenstrasse and Aeschenvorstadt in Basel. It's a gray granite structure with small windows which gives a solid, stolid impression. Like a prison.

On the morning of Friday, November 29, at eleven o'clock, I walked into the main lobby, told a man in a dark suit that Dr. Rudolph Kaiser was expecting me, was escorted to the elevator, was escorted up in the elevator, was escorted to an empty conference room, and was told in no uncertain terms to wait there. I would be attended to shortly. About half a minute later, in came Dr. Zimmerli accompanied by Baron Van der Kamp.

"Well?" I asked.

"Everything is done," replied Zimmerli.

I looked to Van der Kamp. He nodded his head very, very slightly. And began taking off his gray suede gloves.

"*C'est parfait,*" he then pronounced.

Let me tell you, as I heard those words I was experiencing a feeling of both relief and triumph probably never matched before in my life. It had been six days since our meeting in Het Zoute, and during those six days I don't think my mind had ever left the matter at hand in my waking hours for more than five minutes.

There had really been no sense in hanging around Belgium, nor was there any reason to come early to Switzerland. So I had just bummed around northern Europe. I went to Stockholm for two days. It's a marvelous city in the pre-Christmas period. They have those special Christmas shops there where you are confronted with the most beautiful array of ornaments and under-the-tree figures and decorations to be found anywhere on earth. There is a gaiety in the winter air that is equally incomparable and totally unexpected among the otherwise dour Swedes. I stayed, naturally, at the Grand Hotel, which was in the process of preparing itself for the arrival of the 1985 crop of Nobel Prize winners. But the greatest thing about the Grand in December is the *smörgåsbord* put on in the huge buffet in one of its wings. There's another thing about Stockholm at that time of year. It barely stays light for more than a few hours. Thus one must really never have any qualms about drinking at any time of the day, since it is always either dusk or dark. On top of all that, the bar at the Grand makes the biggest and most powerful Bloody Marys in the universe, making the ones they used to dish up at the St. Regis, before Sheraton bought the place and ruined it, look like something you give children to go with their cornflakes. The net result was that I drank a lot in Stockholm, which took care of Sunday, Monday, and part of Tuesday.

Tuesday evening I went to Copenhagen and stayed at the Royal. I'd been there many times before—always with my wife—when we lived in London during my banking days. Nancy loved the Tivoli and I loved Danish beer and breakfasts. We always had a good time there.

I missed her right away, so about ten minutes after I checked in, I called her up. At first she sounded cheerful. She said that the temperature was in the 70s and that she was thinking of going into San Francisco to do some Christmas shopping before the rains started. You know, Nancy and I never did have any children, but nevertheless we have always celebrated Christmas as if we had: a big tree, lots of presents for each other, a turkey, the works. We always worked on it together, weeks in advance. This was the first time I could recall that I had left her completely on her own for so long at this time of year. And as we talked, it became very apparent that she was very lonely. After we finally said good-bye and I had hung up, I sat there on the bed with an empty feeling in the tummy that was definitely not caused by hunger.

It took a long time for me to get to sleep that night, and when dawn came I decided that Copenhagen had been a mistake. I went back to the airport and got a plane to Amsterdam. Upon arrival, I loaded up on English-language books at Schiphol Airport—there's a better selection there than at Kennedy—checked into the Amstel, and then proceeded to spend the entire rest of the day and evening in my suite there, reading and ordering things from Room Service. The next day I caught the afternoon flight back to Switzerland and ended up at the Euler again just in time for an early dinner. I called Zimmerli to tell him I was back, we briefly discussed a financial detail, and the week was over.

You might ask, Why all this travelogue routine? Well, I don't really know myself. I was a workaholic like every other red-blooded American executive. Normally I would have been chasing around Europe along the lines described above, but instead of drinking Bloody Marys by the gallon or holing up in hotel rooms for days on end just reading, I would have been lunching at the Enskilda Bank in Stockholm with the Wallenbergs, dining with the gentlemen of the Nordske Bank in Copenhagen, having breakfast with the Fokker Aircraft people in Amsterdam, and so forth and so on.

This time, except for the conversation with Zimmerli after

my return to Basel, between Sunday, November 24, and 11 A.M. on Friday, November 29, I had not had one single business talk. Well, one. That was a brief phone call to Herb Patterson at the beginning of the week. I had told him that all we could do now was wait and see. He had grunted, said that he agreed, and suggested that I go out and get laid. I told him I was getting too old and tired for that sort of thing—which caused him to grunt again.

And now, apparently, God was not going to punish me for my sloth. Instead, as I watched Zimmerli start to lay the papers out on the table in the conference room of the Swiss Bank Corporation in beautiful downtown Basel, it seemed it was all going to work out.

The first set of documents consisted of three letters. All were addressed to Aeroconsult, Vaduz, Liechtenstein. All had the same date. All inquired about the "consulting services" Aeroconsult was prepared to offer.

The first came from the office of the Chancellor of the Federal Republic of Germany. The second came from the secretariat of His Royal Highness, Prince Léopold of Belgium. The third came from the office of the Inspector General of the Royal Dutch Air Force. In none of these cases was the signature legible. Which mattered not at all. Collectively they represented my reinsurance. If somebody tried to scuttle my ship, I would take every one of the bastards down with me. My theory was that three letters like that, all with the same date, would be enough to get investigations going in all three countries immediately, should it come to that. I knew it, and there was no doubt in my mind that Léopold knew it, his pal up in the Netherlands knew it, and most important of all, Franz Josef Strauss knew it.

"Frankly, I was afraid that the time was too short for us to receive those letters," I said, after checking them out.

"You were almost right. Two came yesterday, the last with the morning mail in Vaduz. In Vaduz they deliver early. So

I had a helicopter bring them over. Rather appropriate for Aeroconsult, wouldn't you say?" This from Zimmerli.

I reached over to gather them in.

"No, no, no," said Zimmerli, now visibly agitated. "I am charged with fiduciary responsibility for these letters. That is what we agreed to in Belgium. Remember?"

I did. He was right.

"So what is the drill now?" I asked.

"When the proper time arrives, I will submit these documents to Herr Doktor Kaiser of this bank; he will, in turn, pass them to you when the money exchanges hands; and you will then give them back to me for safekeeping. That's what we agreed to. Remember?"

"Right again," I said, not particularly liking the idea now that I thought it over, but also not in a position to suggest any better, or more secure, arrangement.

The next actor to come onstage for our little amorality play was the good Dr. Rudolph Kaiser, one of the managing directors of the Swiss Bank Corporation. Surprisingly, he came directly to me.

"You are Dr. Frank Rogers, aren't you?" he asked. "Perhaps you remember me. We were at the University at the same time."

I didn't remember, but was not about to tell him that.

"But of course," I answered, and gave his hand a good Swiss series of pumps.

"We had coffee once together," Kaiser went on. "You were regarded as quite an *unicum*, you know: an American who spoke our dialect, Baseldytsch. The students respected you for trying."

"*I cha immer no a bitzli*," I responded. Which caused both Kaiser and Zimmerli to laugh. Somehow we Americans never come across as linguists.

"So, now what have we here?" continued Kaiser, indicating that the laughs were over, enough was enough.

"You know, of course"—and Zimmerli searched for the right word to describe René Van der Kamp, of Belgian aristocracy, cabinet minister, and confidant of the Royal Family—"our esteemed opposite in this transaction, Baron Van der Kamp."

"But of course," said Herr Doktor Kaiser. "He has been a valued client of our bank for many years."

The Belgian baron and the Swiss banker bowed heads in each other's direction.

Next move. Zimmerli made it.

"We have just entered into a consulting agreement with our friend the Baron. By 'we' I mean Aeroconsult, as you know, Rudy, from our phone conversations earlier this week concerning this matter," he said.

"Of course," replied the Swiss banker.

"Now to the first matter at hand. We want you to transfer, immediately, the sum of ten million dollars, U.S., to the numbered account indicated on this *Zahlungsauftrag*."

Zimmerli pushed the transfer order across the table to Kaiser.

"I would, however, like you to note on the *Zahlungsauftrag*, Rudy, that these three documents"—and Zimmerli now pushed the letters across the table—"have been deposited with you as part and parcel of this transaction with the instructions that they, in turn, be delivered to me, for which I, in turn, will give you a receipt. Here is that receipt. Everything clear, Rudy?"

"Of course." By Swiss banking standards this was an extremely simple transaction.

Kaiser examined the three letters, initialed them, examined the bank transfer order, initialed it, examined Zimmerli's receipt for the letters he had not yet received back, initialed it, picked up the phone, and barked into it. Seconds later a messenger appeared. Kaiser gave him the transfer order and then pushed the three letters over to Zimmerli. As the messenger started to leave the room, he was stopped short by Zimmerli's voice. "*Moment*," said Zimmerli. "There are a couple of additional payment orders which should accompany mine. Is that not so, René?"

Baron Van der Kamp nodded, reached into his very expensive briefcase, and extracted three duplicates of the Swiss Bank Corporation form that Kaiser had just handed to the messenger: the secondary distribution.

Zimmerli wanted to see them. Van der Kamp refused to show them.

"This is none of your business," he said as he handed them over to Kaiser.

"But this is," Zimmerli interjected, pulling out a receipt for ten million bucks. "You sign here." His finger pointed where.

Van der Kamp glared, hesitated, and signed.

Zimmerli retrieved it, looked at it, and then gave it to the Belgian again.

"You forgot to fill in the date. It's November twenty-ninth."

Van der Kamp could have killed him, but he again obeyed. Ten percent of ten million dollars was a full million. Even for a Belgian politician that was a lot.

Rudolph Kaiser, our resident gnome, now looked around at all the parties, gathered that a consensus had been reached, and sent the messenger on his way.

"Now, as I understand it, Amadeus, there is a further related matter which requires our attention."

"There is," replied Zimmerli, "namely, a second payment of ten million dollars from the Aeroconsult account, which is to be processed in exactly the same way."

"Quite clear," replied the banker. "There will also be an additional set of letters?"

"No," said Zimmerli.

"Now," continued the Swiss lawyer, "there is something that Mr. Rogers and I want to discuss with you in private, Rudolph, before we finalize this matter. I hope you don't mind?" asked Zimmerli of Van der Kamp.

"Of course not" was his reply.

"Perhaps we could go to my office for a few minutes," said Kaiser.

Which we did. And once there, Zimmerli kept right on going.

"It's about the one point nine million that we need. As you know, Rudolph," he said to the Swiss banker, "our account with you as of last Friday was $18,117,436.17. We need twenty million dollars exactly. I discussed this with Mr. Rogers last night on the phone, and his preference in the matter is that we arrange for a bridging loan from your bank for, say, thirty days—no more—for the amount. We would leave the terms up to you."

"I discussed the matter with my colleagues at our meeting this morning," said Kaiser, "and we would be more than happy to grant you the accommodation on an overdraft basis. However, as much as we respect and value Aeroconsult as a client, I think, gentlemen, you must agree that in essence Aeroconsult is not in a position to offer any collateral whatsoever for such a facility. And after all, it is almost two million dollars. So what my colleagues and I would like to suggest is that we receive a guarantee from another party. Such as your company, Mr. Rogers."

I nodded.

Zimmerli then proceeded to extract a single piece of paper from his briefcase. It looked very familiar, and with good reason. The letterhead was that of Missile Development Corporation of Sunnyvale, California.

"I have prepared just such a guarantee, Rudolph, along very normal lines. I trust it will be satisfactory."

Kaiser looked at it.

"Fine," he said. "As far as we are concerned, it just requires your signature, Mr. Rogers, as president of the corporation."

Actually, it required a bit more than that. According to the MDC bylaws it required the signatures of two senior officers plus a decision of the full board of directors . . . which Patterson and I often got after the fact. You cannot run a company like ours in slow motion. Maybe a food-processing company, or shoe manufacturer, but not an aerospace company.

So I signed.

"Any reason for us to discuss this any further with Van der Kamp?" I asked.

"Actually not," said Kaiser. "But there are two things I must have from you. When will this second ten million be released to Van der Kamp? Who will give me the instruction to proceed with the release?"

The NATO meeting was scheduled to start at noon. The vote would no doubt be in by one. Everybody would be out of the meeting no later than two.

"The funds will not be released before three o'clock on the afternoon of this coming Monday—the second of December, isn't it?"

We all looked at a Swissair calendar on Kaiser's wall. It was.

"And who will authorize the release?"

Sure as hell not I. This was a totally arm's-length transaction as far as Frank Rogers was concerned. At least, it had been so thus far, I had been careful of that, and it was going to remain that way. I was not about to become a martyr for MDC if, by whatever chance, something happened. So I said:

"Dr. Zimmerli will authorize it."

"I'll call you," said Zimmerli.

"*Ja*, but how will I know for sure that it is you?" countered Kaiser. And he was right. Anyone could claim that he was Zimmerli on the phone.

"Prearrange something," I interjected, slowly getting a bit tired of the bribery business.

"Good idea," said Zimmerli, who then lapsed into deep thought.

"I will call you, Rudy," he said after the delay, "and will say to you, in English: 'The Eagle flies!'"

Gawd! How corny could you get?

"And then I release the second *tranche* to Van der Kamp's numbered account?" asked Kaiser, making doubly sure.

"Exactly."

"But will he still be here to sign a second receipt?" Kaiser asked.

Good point, But not necessary. I gave an eye signal to Zimmerli.

"Not necessary," he told Kaiser. "Just make the transfer immediately."

We all stood up.

"Rudy, you will tell Van der Kamp how the second ten-million-dollar *tranche* is going to be handled?" Zimmerli asked.

"Yes, if you prefer," the banker replied.

"Why not?" I said.

So we shook hands; Zimmerli and I took the elevator down to the main lobby, went out onto the Aeschenvorstadt, shook hands again; and the deal had been done.

"Frank Rogers," I said to myself as I crossed the street and started to walk down the Freiestrasse toward the Rhine, "you have just pulled off one of the biggest arms deals in the twentieth century. And you are, therefore, about to become chief executive officer of the biggest and best manufacturer of cruise missiles in the world, and you are going to become very rich and very powerful and fairly famous. Now: should you call your wife, with whom you have spoken once in just under two weeks, which is stretching things a bit, or should you call your ex-mistress, who is closer at hand should one need some help, celebrationwise?"

I decided to call both.

Nancy sounded normal, even happy, when I told her that I would be returning to California on Wednesday evening. My ex-mistress sounded mollified after our rather disastrous last lunch together, and also happy when I asked her out for dinner Monday night.

I spent a lot of Saturday in the Basel Kunstmuseum, admiring once again the Holbeins and the extraordinary collection of Picassos, and most of Sunday reading in my room at the Euler. I like to spend weekends that way, and so does my wife.

Life was returning to normal.

10

ON THAT MONDAY, DECEMBER 2, I decided to have lunch in my suite at the Euler, since I knew that there would be a lot of telephoning early that afternoon and there would be no sense in getting trapped into a longish lunch in the restaurant below, even though the Michelin rated the Euler's restaurant among the very best in Switzerland.

I went through the *Basler Zeitung*, which was full of mostly local news that meant little to me; then the *Herald Tribune*, which had a small—very small—article on page three noting that a fairly important NATO meeting had been scheduled for that day, a meeting in which the ministers would be discussing the ground-launched cruise missile for the umpteenth time, although this time, the paper said, it looked as if the final decision would be taken.

Then I tried to turn on Swiss television, forgetting that Switzerland had no daytime television, since it was thought, somehow, corrupting. So I turned on Swiss national radio, Beromuenster, which offers, from noon to twelve thirty, a program of yodeling. At twelve twenty-nine and a half, the station tunes into an electronic time signal, which sounds a long beep when the half-hour has been reached. And then the news starts, listened to by at least half the German-speaking population, since at least that proportion still were going home for lunch in 1985. Sometimes when you spend a few days in Switzerland you have the eerie feeling that the clocks stopped back near the turn of the century.

There has been the same announcer on Beromuenster ever since I can remember, and he has a style that is certainly unique: no inflection whatsoever, slow, deliberate, calm. If Zurich, Geneva, and Basel all burned down the same night, I am sure that he would tell it the way he felt it: slowly, deliberately, calmly, and with no inflection.

About twelve forty-four he said, as he often said, and I still remember this from the days when I studied at the University of Basel: "This bulletin has just been handed to me." This time he went on to say—in German, of course, but I will translate:

"The NATO Council has just completed its meeting in Brussels. This meeting was called to select the type of ground-launched cruise missile that NATO will purchase and deploy, although the missile will remain under American control. In a unanimous decision, it was the missile developed by the General Dynamics Corporation of St. Louis, Missouri, and San Diego, California, that was selected. The Swiss Defense Ministry, which has been actively considering the potential of the cruise missile for Swiss defense purposes, will, no doubt—"

I remember exactly the words which I yelled out at that Swiss radio announcer at that point: "You dirty double-crossing European bastards!"

No more than five minutes later, the phone rang. It was Herb Patterson in Sunnyvale.

"You heard?" he asked without even saying hello.

"Yeah," I answered, and then started to repeat myself. "Those dirty double—"

"Leave it be for now. Now, listen carefully, Frank. Don't talk to anybody over there. In fact, don't even move. Got it?"

"I got it, but—"

"Do what the hell I say!" he yelled.

"For how the hell long?" I yelled back. I mean, this was hardly the time for Patterson to go totalitarian.

"Two days. Okay?"

"Why?" I asked.

Silence.

"All right. What about Dillon at Citibank? I promised to show up for lunch with him in New York the day after to-morrow."

"Forget Dillon for the moment. Just do what I say, Frank. Please?"

I guess the "please" did it.

"All right. But I'm going to have to tell my wife something. I promised to be home Wednesday night."

"As long as you keep it to that." And Patterson hung up.

I swear to God I sat there, just sat there, on the edge of my bed in the Euler, for two straight hours trying to figure out what he could possibly be up to. I mean, we were dead now. Dead! There was no way that he or anybody else could save MDC.

I had forgotten about Franz Josef Strauss.

PART TWO

11

GERMANY—DECEMBER 3, 1985. As the record later showed, at dusk on that date Graf Otto von Amsburg, Minister of Foreign Affairs of the Federal Republic of Germany, picked up Mr. Herbert Patterson of Sunnyvale, California, at the airport outside Cologne. Von Amsburg drove Patterson to a house in the countryside between Cologne and Bonn, and then proceeded another two kilometers to a small *Gasthaus* named Zum Sternen. In a private dining room in the rear, with direct access to the parking lot, four men awaited him.

They included, first, Herr Doktor Reinhardt Kreps, head of the Deutsche Bank, Germany's largest. He had been driven up the Autobahn in his Mercedes 600 at an average speed of 116 miles per hour from Frankfurt. Second in importance was Herr Direktor Doktor Josef Schmidt, who was, and still is, managing director of Siemens A.G., the largest electronics conglomerate in Germany. Schmidt had come from Munich in a Hansa jet—the stretch version. Then there was Professor Doktor Ernst Bosch, the scientist who ran Messerschmitt-

Bölkow-Blohm G.m.b.H., the company which, along with the Dornier Werke, represented West Germany's aerospace industry. He had taken the TEE from Stuttgart. The fourth man was General Lothar von Seefeldt, Generalinspektor der Bundeswehr, and thus commander-in-chief of the German armed forces. He had driven himself north from Bonn in his Opel Diplomat, and in his civilian clothes.

As you may have gathered by now, these men, together with Graf Otto von Amsburg, represented the elite of the military-industrial complex of the second most powerful nation of the West, the Bundesrepublik Deutschland. Now, it should and, indeed, must be stressed that the Chancellor of the Federal Republic of Germany, Herr Doktor Franz Josef Strauss, was not in attendance. I stress: *not!* Because it has been repeatedly said that it was *he* who personally orchestrated that entire evening. This is *not* true to the best of my knowledge, and there is no one who has a better knowledge of what took place that evening than I, except, of course, for those who had actually been physically present.

However, having said that about Franz Josef Strauss—and you may suspect that I have said this so that he will not sue me for libel, and you may very well be right—anyway, having said that, I do not wish to imply that Strauss had not provided the *inspiration* for that little conclave on the Rhine on that December night in 1985, because any fool could, and should, have figured out that once the Germans chose a man like Strauss as their national leader, what happened that night would have, eventually, *had* to happen. Karl Marx would have termed it a historical imperative.

For Strauss was the man who, alone—by virtue of his intelligence, his doctrine, his strength—was the prime mover of the massive political shift to the right in Germany, a shift that was to have—in fact, on that December night in 1985 *was having*—fundamental military consequences which, in the end, would amount to nothing less than a totally revised global strategic situation: just the thing the *prior* chief architect of the global strategic balance, Henry Kissinger, feared most.

Let me explain. Henry Kissinger was a result of what he had learned, what he had specialized in, what he knew best—which was not baseball.

The language Kissinger knew best was German. The area Kissinger knew best was Central Europe. And the history Kissinger knew best was the diplomatic history of the nineteenth century, which to a substantial degree was the diplomatic history of Central Europe, of which the most extensive analysis was, and is, in the German language. It all ties together. The nineteenth century, in the Kissinger view of things, did not begin at the stroke of midnight on the last day of 1800, but rather in 1815 at the conclusion of the Congress of Vienna. For that was when *Ordnung* returned to a world that had gone through decades of chaos brought on by the French Revolution and its inevitable product, Napoleon.

What Vienna meant was the restoration of legitimacy, the restoration of a world in which the nations who deserved to hold power actually ran things, and a world where the men who ran the nations which held global power were of one mind: to maintain the *status quo;* not to rock the boat. A key factor—no, *the* key factor—in the maintenance of the *status quo* was the maintenance of a military balance, a balance in which neither Britain, nor France, nor Russia, nor the Austro-Hungarian Empire, nor Prussia could establish a European, and thus a global, hegemony.

I know all this sounds boring as hell, but it serves two purposes. First to demonstrate that I, Frank Rogers, might at times—in fact, usually—sound just like tens of thousands of other businessmen: completely and exclusively immersed in business talk, having a very limited imagination, and as far as education is concerned, of the opinion that the pinnacle of scholarship is represented by the Harvard Business School. Well, that may be true of me much of the time, but not all of the time. True, I spent most of my working life as a banker.

117

And also true, I spent my best years as number two man at an aerospace company—a track record that would not exactly inspire Jane Fonda to make a movie of my life. But lest you forget, I also spent my most formative educational years at the University of Basel in Switzerland. And while there I did not just compare the monetary theories of John Maynard Keynes with those of Milton Friedman (concluding, by the way, that Keynes forgot more about monetary systems and theories than Friedman ever remembered). I minored in modern European history under Edgar Bonjour, and my specialty was nineteenth-century diplomatic history, with an emphasis on Central Europe, as taught in German, which was the language of instruction at the Basel university. This all just in passing.

The second reason, and by now you have probably forgotten that all of the above related to the first, is to draw a parallel between the situation existing in Europe *after* the Congress of Vienna in the nineteenth century and the one existing *before* that meeting in Cologne in the twentieth century; or to be more precise, between 1945 and 1985; or to be more precise yet, during the *Pax Americana* which Henry Kissinger was so much interested in preserving indefinitely, even if it did mean that at times he would have to support such crazies as the Shah of Iran to achieve that end.

So what was that pivotal (in the historical sense) meeting in Cologne on December 3, 1985, all about? It was about West Germany's cutting the puppet strings that had attached it to the United States since the end of World War II, and thus going independent in foreign policy, rejoining the ranks of the world's superpowers in the political sense, just as it already had in the economic and financial sense.

It is, in retrospect, almost incomprehensible that anyone was surprised by all that happened after that Cologne meeting. Did the world actually believe that American political and military hegemony over the West could last indefinitely, in spite of the fact that its economic and financial hegemony had been lost? Could anyone really have believed that those two "natural" superpowers, Germany and Japan, would remain dormant in their aspirations indefinitely, for never-ending decades, centuries, millennia? Did everybody really believe that Germany would always be run by good guys like Adenauer, Erhard, Kiesinger, and Willy Brandt—especially Willy Brandt?

The behavior of the fifth postwar German Chancellor, Helmut Schmidt, should have provided a tip-off that the winds of change were starting to blow through Deutschland. Schmidt had no qualms whatsoever about calling one American President a fool, a religious fanatic, a peanut farmer, and much worse. It was Helmut Schmidt who declared in 1979 that not only was Jimmy Carter hopeless, but every potential candidate on the American horizon for the office of President, Ronald Reagan included, was totally lacking in leadership qualities, and that whether Germany wanted to or not, it would slowly have to assume a leadership role in the West in the 1980s, to fill the vacuum developing because of the absence of American ability to lead. He was right in retrospect, of course. But it was not so much *what* he said back then that counted—it was *how* he said it; and that from a man who by comparison with his successor, Strauss, was a pro-American shrinking violet.

But after the landslide victory of the Christian Democratic Union/Christian Socialist Union coalition over the Social Democrats in the 1984 elections, Helmut Schmidt lost control of his party and disappeared. The German political landscape was now totally controlled by Strauss, leader of that right-wing coalition and Chancellor of the second-most-powerful nation in the Western world, the Bundesrepublik Deutschland. He had been around for a long time, Herr Strauss—in fact, so long that nobody really thought he would ever rise to the top in Germany. For Strauss had more than a few strikes against him.

First, he was Bavarian, and Bavarians are generally regarded by the rest of Germany as a bunch of uncouth beer-swilling, loudmouthed peasants. Well, Strauss more or less lived up to such expectations, since he did swill beer, was loudmouthed, lacked most social graces, was almost as fat as he was short, and spoke German with an atrocious Bavarian peasant's accent.

He also did not always keep the best company. In the mid-1970s, for instance, he was in New York—brushing up his image as an expert in foreign affairs, I guess—and staying at the Plaza Hotel. Although it was midwinter, Strauss—he later claimed—decided at 2 A.M. that he would get a breath of fresh air by strolling around the block on which the Plaza is situated.

Well, as you know, it's a big block. It is also a block that is not totally devoid of young or not-so-young women likewise seeking fresh air, or something, at all hours. Fate led Strauss to approach one of these clean-air advocates, or vice versa; and while it is not known whether or not either party gained any satisfaction from the brief encounter, what is known is that the young lady gained possession of Strauss' wallet and passport—in fact, cleaned poor Franz Josef clear out of all his money and identification.

So there he stood, on the sidewalks of New York, alone and broke, stranded on a foreign shore, all because of his friendliness toward natives. Strauss made the mistake of asking the New York P.D. for help in the matter—with the result that, naturally, he got no help but reams of publicity back home: the Bavarian rube caught in the big city with his pants down. Of such material are leaders of nations not normally made. Although in retrospect it might not have hurt our American nation if Jimmy Carter had . . . no, no, that's not nice.

The next big strike against Strauss was of a more serious nature. It was felt that perhaps he might not have a total respect for the constitutional rights of others if they chose to disagree with him too often and too strenuously. The organ that got him in trouble this time was, in contrast to his New York experience, a press organ—namely, that German newsmagazine whose format was a direct steal from *Time* and *Newsweek*, *Der Spiegel*, which was founded and was run by a certain Herr Augstein, a man of the left, who had been searching from the very beginning of his magazine for a way to destroy Strauss, the man of the far right. When Konrad Adenauer appointed Strauss West Germany's Minister of Defense in the early 1960s, Augstein's paranoia took on new dimensions in the fear that Strauss would succeed Adenauer as Chancellor and that Germany would sink back into rightwing radicalism. In almost every issue *Der Spiegel* took Strauss apart, piece by piece.

In 1962 Strauss retaliated. From his position as Defense Minister he accused *Der Spiegel* of revealing German military secrets, and summarily tossed some of that magazine's top executives into jail. It was as if Nixon had thrown Ben Bradlee of *The Washington Post* and Abe Rosenthal of *The New York Times* in the clink because they had published excerpts from the Pentagon Papers—something Nixon no doubt would have loved to do, but even in his most enjoyable dream would never have dared.

The backlash against Strauss because of this act was so vehement in Germany that within a very short time Adenauer had to fire him from his Cabinet post, and it seemed to many observers that this incident signaled the political end of Franz Josef Strauss. But not so—proving that the man, and what he stood for, had a much larger and much more powerful constituency in Germany than anyone would have believed. For Strauss essentially stood for putting an end to the subservient posture of postwar Germany. "A country that has pulled off an economic miracle in the fashion that Germany has done should not have to apologize about Auschwitz anymore." That was the type of statement which brought German audiences to their feet when Strauss, a brilliant orator, made speech after speech, year after year, organizing his comeback.

Some of his other statements tell us more about the man.

For instance: "I stand for German nationalism and demand unconditional obedience."

Or: "One thing should be asked of Herr Brandt: namely, What were you doing during those twelve years abroad? We who stayed home know what we were doing."

To be noted is that "those twelve years abroad" is the period during which Willy Brandt chose to live in exile in Norway and Sweden rather than stay in Germany under Adolf Hitler as Strauss did.

Or: "I may come to power, but then I am not about to go."

In the 1984 election, Franz Josef Strauss did come to power, to the total astonishment of a very large body of political analysts.

For the final—and in politics, at least, biggest—strike against Strauss was the general feeling that he was a loser, that he would never be able to win the big one. The big one for people of that opinion was the election of October 1980, when Strauss had sought the chancellorship of West Germany for the first time, and lost big. That, they thought, was finally the end of Franz Josef Strauss.

But those who thought that way were obviously not students of recent American history. Or else they had already forgotten the lessons they should have learned from the career of Richard Milhous Nixon. He was also a man of the right. He also had less than total respect for constitutional rights. And he also came from an area not exactly held in total respect by the rest of the country—Southern California. And he also had lost his first attempt to gain the American presidency, in November of 1960. After he tried for the governorship of California a few years later and failed, everybody, and I mean everybody, had said that that was the end of Richard Nixon. Well, all those people underestimated the tenacity of the man, convinced as he was that it was his *duty* to try again. In 1968 he did try again, and won by a substantial margin. So also, in 1984, with Strauss.

And contributing to his victory in a major way was the fact that the key plank in the platform upon which he stood was the commitment that Germany would develop its own independent military deterrent. And it was precisely to this Straussian declaration of independence that Graf Otto von Amsburg, Strauss' Foreign Minister, referred as he stood up to address the four other men who had gathered around him that evening in that Cologne restaurant.

"Meine Herren," he began, *"heute abend ist das Neue Deutschland endlich geboren, und dieses Ereignis ist nur einem Mann zu verdanken: unserm Bundeskanzler, dem neuen Führer des Deutschen Volkes, Franz Josef Strauss. Zu seinem Wohl!"*

With one motion, the four other men rose to their feet, and with their glasses full of Niersteiner Spätlese toasted the man who was indeed their new leader, and was in fact behind the birth of the New Germany, Chancellor Strauss.

Amsburg then continued: "I repeat—tonight the New Germany is finally being born, because it is on this evening that I can assure you that the new German doctrine of strategic military independence is on the very edge of becoming technologically feasible. We will once again be able to destroy the Soviet Union. Then, gentlemen, after forty years of subservience we will again be able to hold our heads high in the world."

The five men raised their glasses and collectively drank to the new object of their toast, as expressed in one word by Graf Otto von Amsburg: "Deutschland!"

To those unfamiliar with modern Germany all this ritual probably sounds overly dramatic, something I cooked up for effect. One can hardly imagine a similar group of Americans or British, not to speak of Italians, behaving in such a way. But not to know Germany and its ways can prove, in

123

the long run, fatal. To scoff at the Germans for either their formality on such an occasion as the one in Cologne or, by contrast, to sneer at them when they behave like barbarians during Karneval time or the Oktoberfest is a big mistake. Modern Germany—West Germany, to be exact—is a nation with awesome latent power poised for release. It is a nation of over sixty million, but what a sixty million! The population is almost totally homogeneous, endowed with a blend of intelligence, education, technological skills, entrepreneurship, pride of workmanship, frugality, obedience to authority, ambition, ethnic pride—and thus a sense of superiority. Despite two devastating setbacks in the first half of the twentieth century, the German people and their leaders have always been endowed with a sense of unfulfilled destiny. The nation that produced Goethe, Beethoven, Bismarck, and von Braun is, they feel, indeed an elite race whose time, with patience, will come.

Now, lest fingers be wagged, this is not to imply in any way a return to Germany of the racist attitudes fostered by Hitler and especially Himmler. Nor, in total contrast, has it anything to do with the Jeffersonian concepts of democracy vis-à-vis the Jacksonian variety. In other words, neither racism nor political theories enter into it in any major way. Modern German elitism of the 1980s variety had as its strongest component a belief in the inherent intellectual and cultural superiority of the German people relative to the intellectual and cultural status of those two superpowers which then dominated the world, the United States and the Soviet Union. It was as if all that General de Gaulle stood for, and expected of France, were coming true instead in Germany. Not that de Gaulle would have been surprised: he was a great admirer of things German, and in fact, German was the only foreign language he could handle with any facility whatever.

Graf Otto von Amsburg epitomized the finest flower of Germanic Gaullism. In fact, he had been a very good friend of de Gaulle's son during the latter's tour of duty in Baden-Baden. As such, and as a man from a family with a great military tradition, von Amsburg had no illusions that intellectual and cultural superiority counted for anything whatsoever in geopolitical-power terms. What counted was military might, and the will—or at least, the *apparent* will—to use it, even under conditions the more faint-hearted might consider suicidal. Graf Otto von Amsburg realized that for a nation to really count in the twenty-first century it would have to possess three essential military and political components:

1. Nuclear warheads.
2. The means of delivering such warheads over long distances.
3. Leadership, with the will to pull the trigger.

By mid-1985, conditions 1 and 3 had been met.

But hold on, you say: Since when had Germany possessed nuclear warheads? Answer: essentially since the late 1950s! For since that decade, dozens, hundreds, in fact *thousands* of American-built nuclear warheads have been stored in West Germany and have been essentially under the *joint* authority of the American/German high command in that military theater of operations. That is the reason the Soviet Union stopped fooling around with West Berlin—not because its leaders believed for one minute that one American drop of blood would be sacrificed for Berlin, in spite of the bombastic Kennedy oratory: *"Ich bin ein Berliner,"* and so on. No, because they knew full well that there were two fingers which had access to the nuclear trigger in the Central European war theater, and that one of those fingers was pure Aryan. To be sure, the nuclear weapons that could be triggered by that German finger were strictly tactical in character—that is, with a maximum reach of a few hundred kilometers. But that reach was enough to destroy in totality any first-wave ground attack force of the Soviets.

Not that the West Germans had any need whatever to

rely upon those tactical American warheads stored in their country. They could manufacture all the warheads they would ever need for tactical, strategic, or whatever deployment. For in the 1970s, they had already gone right to the fore in the *world* in regard to nuclear technology. Not only were there dozens of nuclear reactors operating on German soil, but the German nuclear industry had begun to dominate export markets. In fact, one of the biggest flaps that developed between Helmut Schmidt and Jimmy Carter, when both were running their respective countries, was over the issue of German exports of advanced nuclear technology to the Third World. The West German industry, composed of no fewer than *four* nuclear giants—A.E.G., Brown Boveri, Siemens, and the Kraftwerk Union—had negotiated a $5-billion contract with Brazil to build not only a number of power reactors, but also a reprocessing plant for the spent nuclear fuel. Carter vetoed that program because if the Brazilians were to couple the German-built reactors with the German-built reprocessing plant, they would have been in a position to produce enough plutonium to build an atomic bomb a month. The Germans eventually backed down.

What no one seemed to realize at that time was this: If the Germans had that much "spare" nuclear technology available for export, what was their *domestic* nuclear capacity? If they possessed technology which the United States considered a major threat to world peace if given to the benign Brazilians, just what was Germany's domestic capability—latent capability, to be sure—in regard to the manufacture of nuclear warheads? Answer: At least equal to that of France. Probably vastly superior to that of the United Kingdom. The best guesses around the world were that it would take Germany about three months to tool up for such nuclear-warhead production, and that it would have sufficient plutonium available, on an ongoing basis, to produce at least one hundred high-yield warheads per month thereafter.

So much for condition number one.

Condition number three, the credibility of German leadership in regard to the use of military force, was, of course, totally lacking between 1945 and 1984.

Up until the end of the 1950s, West Germany was in every respect a satellite of the United States.

During the 1960s it was no longer a completely subservient client state of America, but as a nation it was interested in only one thing: making money, getting rich, having a car in every garage, a television set in every other room, and one German per square meter of every Mediterranean beach between June and September.

During the 1970s, having achieved these goals under the Christian Democratic leaderships of Adenauer, Erhard, and Kiesinger, the German people decided to turn socialistic and pacifistic under Willy Brandt. But they soon found out that being rich and pacifistic gets boring. Germany wanted a leader who would finally flex a little muscle. Helmut Schmidt, though also a Socialist, was arrogant enough as an individual to fill that need for a while. But he was more interested in flexing Germany's financial and economic muscles than in building up military strength. His idea of a bid for international leadership was the creation of the European Monetary Union, a highly complicated monetary arrangement within the Common Market whereby, essentially, all the other major European currencies were to be tied to the value of the German mark. Thus the mark was to join the dollar and to succeed sterling as one of the world's two key currencies.

It was the first time since 1945 that Bonn had taken a political step directly against U.S. interests. Well, that was heady stuff for Schmidt, but pretty damned boring for guys in the beer halls of the Ruhr. They wanted some real action that they could understand.

Which brings us back to our old friend Franz Josef Strauss. He failed in his 1980 bid for the chancellorship, but by 1984 Germany was ready for him. He won that election in a landslide because he was thought to be the man who could deliver—deliver a world leadership role once again for Germany; deliver on the development of a truly independent—even *nuclear*—military capability, if that was what was necessary to impress the world regarding the seriousness of Germany's new global role. Strauss, therefore, ideally met the requirements for leadership defined under number three above.

Which left lacking just one element: a strategic missile capability—the means of delivering nuclear warheads to the airspace above Moscow. The responsibility for achieving that capability had been delegated by Strauss to the man who, in 1985, was as close to the Chancellor as any man in Germany—Graf Otto von Amsburg.

By ten o'clock, the five men in that Cologne restaurant had finished their dinner—*Rehrücken mit Preiselbeeren und Spätzle*—and coffee had been served, along with a large shot glass full of Kirschwasser in two cases and Steinhäger in two others, the lone abstainer being von Amsburg.

After the last waiter had left the room, it was again von Amsburg who began addressing the group, and this time he remained in his chair. It was a round table, but the Graf was clearly the *primus inter pares*, even though his guests included the most powerful banker in Germany, the most powerful industrialist, the nation's leading military man, and its leading scientist—who likewise headed the German aerospace industry. The organizations they represented—the Deutsche Bank, Siemens A.G., the Bundeswehr, and Messerschmitt—epitomized the enormous strength and depth of Germany, 1985. Von Amsburg intended to redirect those capabilities.

"I will come to the point, gentlemen. We are here to complete arrangements for acquisition of the technological capability to produce an all-German cruise missile. To be more precise, we shall be acquiring the capability to produce and deploy ground-launched cruise missiles with a range of three thousand kilometers at Mach two cruising speed when equipped with a nuclear warhead with a ten-kiloton fission yield, with or without enhanced radiation capability."

"From whom?" asked Herr Direktor Josef Schmidt, head of Siemens A.G., the largest electrical-equipment and electronics manufacturer in Germany.

"From Missile Development Corporation of Sunnyvale, California," was von Amsburg's answer.

"I do not understand," interjected General Lothar von Seefeldt, commander-in-chief of the German armed forces. "It was under your direct instructions, sir, that yesterday we withdrew our support of their cruise missile within NATO. That is my first point. My second point is that the United States has given an irrevocable commitment to the Russians that if and when ground-launched strategic cruise missiles are deployed in Western Europe, such missiles will remain totally and absolutely under American control, and that such deployment and control will be subject to on-site Soviet inspection and verification."

"*Und?*" asked von Amsburg, obviously put out by the general's answer and attitude.

"*Und?* Well, there is no '*Und*.' That's it. There is no way whatsoever we Germans can gain access to the cruise missile that has been developed in Sunnyvale, much less get a license to actually *build* it here."

"Finished?" asked the Foreign Minister.

"*Jawohl, Herr Minister,*" replied the general.

"Good. In fairness, gentlemen," continued von Amsburg, looking around the table at the three civilian guests, "all of what the general has just said was true. I stress: *was* true. No longer."

"Excuse me," said Schmidt of Siemens, "but am I to understand that you expect somehow to gain complete access to all the know-how required to actually manufacture the guidance system for the MDC cruise missile here in Germany?"

"Yes," replied von Amsburg. "And we would, naturally, expect that Siemens would undertake such production. Unless you have something against it, Herr Schmidt? In which case we would talk to Telefunken."

"No, no," interjected Schmidt. "You misunderstand my hesitancy. It had nothing to do with our willingness to undertake such a project for the Ministry of Defense. We not only would do it with great pleasure, but would give it the highest priority within our corporation. I am sure you are fully aware of the fact that we at Siemens, or at least, those of us who count there, are fully in agreement with Herr Doktor Strauss in regard to the development of our own German strategic nuclear capability. The question, and the only question, bothering me is: How? How could you possibly get total access to their guidance system?"

"I will come to that in a minute," replied von Amsburg.

"I assume from what I have been hearing that you will likewise have access to the technology of the MDC engine?"

This came from Professor Doktor Ernst Bosch, head of Messerschmitt, the one and only German manufacturer with a capability in the manufacture of both airframes and jet engines.

"That is correct. We are going to have full access to the MDC cruise-missile system—in its entirety. And Herr Professor, it is to your company that we will turn in regard to the manufacture of the MDC engine as well as the airframe."

"But what do you mean by access? Do you have a complete missile, fully operational? Or do you have total access to the blueprints, production procedures, test—"

"Excuse me for interrupting, Herr Professor. The answer to all your questions is: 'Yes.'"

"Das ist ja unglaublich!" exclaimed Professor Bosch.

"Not unbelievable," answered von Amsburg. "Just astounding, I would suggest."

"And what does the American Government say about this?" asked General Lothar von Seefeldt.

"The American Government knows absolutely nothing about this, my dear General. And will not know anything about it for quite a while. And by that time there will be absolutely nothing the government can do about it except keep quiet."

"How can this be kept quiet that long?"

"We have kept secret similar industrial developments in the past for long periods of time. You, General, should especially remember all that I.G. Farben managed to do in secret in the 1930s—the buildup of tremendous capacity in regard to the production of both synthetic rubber and synthetic fuel. And no one outside Germany, except perhaps the people at the top of Standard Oil of New Jersey, was even remotely aware of what we were doing.

"In fact," continued von Amsburg, "the people at Standard Oil, at our insistence, did not develop a synthetic-rubber capability in the United States in the 1930s, even though they shared the technology with us. To this day the U.S. Government does not know the details. You should be aware of this, General, since your father was on the board of I.G. Farben until 1944."

"I am fully aware of what you are talking about, Herr Minister," replied the general, this time with his Prussian chin thrust slightly forward. "I was not concerned about *our* ability to maintain secrecy in this matter. What I am concerned about is our partners in the United States. For it is quite obvious that such partners must be involved. And since you have brought up the example of synthetic rubber in the 1930s and the role of Standard Oil of New Jersey, I can only assume that in this case it is the top management of Missile Development Corporation which is involved; I can only further assume that it is without the knowledge of the full board of directors of Missile Development Corporation —since, if I am correctly informed, a former head of the Central Intelligence Agency is a member of that board."

"You amaze me," said von Amsburg, and there was no doubt whatsoever he meant it.

"You forget, Herr Minister, that I have visited Sunnyvale and Missile Development Corporation on two separate occasions in the past to familiarize myself with its cruise missile, because its version of that missile is precisely, but precisely, what Germany needs. I took the opportunity then to familiarize myself also with the corporation itself. Thus my fears about leaks on the American side, should this transfer of technology actually take place as you are suggesting it will."

"I am not suggesting, Herr General. I am telling you," stated von Amsburg, "that it will take place. Provided that we, and by we I mean all of us here—my ministry, the Bundeswehr, the German electronics industry, the German aerospace industry—gain the cooperation of our friends at the Deutsche Bank. In particular we will be looking to you, Herr Doktor Kreps."

Herr Doktor Reinhardt Kreps was Generaldirektor of the Deutsche Bank of Frankfurt, that most powerful of German financial institutions, revived after World War II by a certain Dr. Hermann Abs, also formerly of the board of directors of I.G. Farben; then confidant of Konrad Adenauer; then confidant of John J. McCloy; confidant of David Rockefeller, grandson of the creator of Standard Oil, which had been the partner of I.G. Farben in matters of war technology in the 1930s. Again matters had come full circle. To be sure, I.G. Farben and Hermann Abs and Konrad Adenauer and John J. McCloy were all gone, but their spirit lingered on in the person of Dr. Reinhardt Kreps. If Bundeskanzler Franz Josef Strauss called upon him in the name of Germany, he would listen. To be sure, Strauss was not there that evening, but if there was anyone who was his alter ego, it was Graf Otto von Amsburg. So Kreps looked around the table and then said, "Gentlemen, I am at your service. The Deutsche Bank and Deutschland have always served each other. What is good for Deutschland is good for the Deutsche Bank."

"Excellent," commented Graf von Amsburg.

"However," continued Dr. Kreps, "we at the Deutsche Bank must first be thoroughly convinced that what you are talking about is indeed good for Deutschland. Our bank, as you gentlemen know, is deeply involved in the United States. We have a large branch in New York; we have a major participation in a very large investment-banking group also in New York. We have as our clients scores of multinational corporations based in the United States. We have managed loans and bond issues for them that by now must total well over one hundred billion marks. In fact, our institution is the largest foreign supplier of capital to U.S. corporations. The largest. Therefore, we will not under any circumstances become involved in any type of 'adventurism' that might in any way imperil those relationships."

General Lothar von Seefeldt then spoke up: "My dear Herr Doktor Kreps, I must clarify something at this juncture. I have perhaps indicated a certain amount of skepticism this evening about what has thus far been discussed. I must emphatically stress, however, that such skepticism was not an outgrowth of any thoughts whatsoever that what was under discussion amounted in any way whatsoever to 'adventurism.' What bothered me, and continues to bother me, was how this transfer of technology could be kept secret until it was a *fait accompli*—after which it would not matter."

"I can assure you, General, and you also, Herr Doktor Kreps," said von Amsburg, "that we have recognized the problem of maintaining secrecy during the critical period of the transfer of technology proper, and that we have a solution. But I am not going to go into detail about *that* solution until we have a viable project here. And we do not have a viable project unless and until the Deutsche Bank cooperates. Of course—and no offense is meant here, Herr Doktor Kreps—there are other banks. The Dresdner Bank, the Bank für Gemeinwirtschaft, the—"

Now Kreps broke in. "I can assure you, Graf von Amsburg, that you will be faced with the same reservations at each of those institutions. You will have to convince them just as you have to convince me."

"Of what?" asked von Amsburg, visibly peeved.

"Of the importance of this cruise missile to the future of Germany."

Again General von Seefeldt spoke: "Herr Kreps, I must assume that you are not familiar with this new weapons system?"

"I am not, although I know what it is. Essentially a drone. An updated version of the V-1 or V-2 buzz bombs developed by von Braun for us in World War II. If that is all it is, I hardly feel that it is worth the risk of alienating our American clients."

"I think, sir," von Seefeldt continued, now addressing Graf von Amsburg with the demeanor expected of a general addressing the Minister of Foreign Affairs, "that if you agree, and if you allow me, I should describe in some detail the capability of the cruise missile to Herr Doktor Kreps. Then perhaps he will understand how our possession of this weapons system can fundamentally alter the geopolitical position of West Germany in the world, and how, most probably, our possession of this weapons system will, in the longer run, enhance, not diminish, the stature of the Deutsche Bank in the eyes of its American clientele; in fact, in the eyes of its clientele everywhere."

"Please do, if Dr. Kreps is willing to listen," replied von Amsburg.

"I am not only willing, Herr General," replied Kreps, "I beg you to proceed."

The general got to his feet.

"First, Herr Doktor Kreps, I want to say that you are completely correct in your assumption that this American cruise missile is essentially nothing more than, as you put it, an updated version of the V-1. I stress V-1 and not V-2, for the cruise missile is not a 'rocket,' but rather a simple winged vehicle propelled by an air-breathing engine and capable of sustained aerodynamic flight."

The general saw eyes beginning to glaze over, so he decided to switch vocabularies for the benefit of the civilian audience.

"In plain German, gentlemen, the cruise missile is basically just a small pilotless aircraft, as originally designed by von Braun way back in the early 1940s. The difference is that today's version of his V-1 can travel immense distances—up to three thousand kilometers—at very low altitudes—less than one hundred meters—and guide itself to the ultimate target with phenomenal accuracy. To be precise, one launched outside Cologne this evening would strike within less than thirty meters of Stalin's tomb, if that was the desired target."

The smiles that crossed the faces of his audience of four indicated to the head of the Bundeswehr that such a target was probably rather high on the desired list of those present.

"Historically . . ." continued the general. Tracing history, he well knew, was a *sine qua non* in an address on *any* subject to a group of German academics; and in contrast to their typical American counterparts, this was indeed a group of academics, since each and every one had a doctorate.

"*Historisch gesehen,*" repeated the general, "the modern cruise missile became possible only because of major breakthroughs by American scientists and engineers in three different areas.

"First"—and the general now began to sound like a lecturer at a military academy—"there was a breakthrough of major proportions in the field of jet-engine technology. The feasibility of the cruise missile depended upon the development of an engine that would be vastly superior to anything man

135

had yet devised in terms of compactness and efficiency. The Williams Research Corporation [he pronounced the W, of course, as a V] of Massachusetts, I believe, did precisely that about fifteen years ago. Essentially, it developed an engine that would propel a one-and-a-half-ton vehicle a couple of thousand miles, and yet it weighed only seventy-five kilos and was only one meter long and forty centimeters wide. Herr Doktor Kreps, it was a bit like an engine in your grandchildren's toy train powering your Mercedes 600."

"*Sehr interessant,*" replied the banker, in a tone that suggested that he would not terribly mind if the general cut things a bit shorter.

"*Der zweite technische Durchbruch,*" continued General von Seefeldt, "was in the area of cartography—yes, making maps. Immense and unique American computers built by IBM were used to enhance and define the images of the earth's surface provided by American satellites to a degree almost beyond imagination. One thing we must all admit, gentlemen, is that in the fields of aerospace and computers the Americans have accomplished things we Germans can only admire."

A few grudging nods, because all those present knew full well that without von Braun and Debus and a few other Germans kidnapped in the summer and fall of 1945 the American space program would have gotten nowhere.

"But it is in the area of microelectronics that the Americans have produced true miracles," said the general. "In this instance, McDonnell Douglas developed an incredibly small but incredibly complex missile-guidance system, known in its original form as TERCOM, which stands for 'terrain contour matching.' What happens is this: the microcomputer on board the missile, the heart of the TERCOM system, is programmed with those remarkably accurate computer-enhanced maps of the ground features of the terrain along the planned flight path. As the cruise missile flies, it uses its radar altimeter to measure alterations in the height of the land below relative to sea level as the terrain changes from hills to valley to lakes to mountains. Its flight path is programmed to match the earth's contours on, say, a line between Düsseldorf and the Kremlin. The critical point is this: that line would by no means have to be straight. A zigzag or any other pattern of flight can be equally programmed. This means that unlike the ballistic missile, whose path is perfectly predictable from the second it is launched, the cruise missile can wander, literally wander, all over the sky, following a flight path that is predetermined but absolutely unpredictable. Is that not true, Herr Professor Bosch?" asked the general, with a deep bow of his head in the good professor's direction.

"Absolutely. We at Messerschmitt are fully aware of this weapon's capability. The fact is that at present, it is almost impossible to shoot down. Since its path is unpredictable, the enemy must be able to track it continuously by radar if it is to take effective countermeasures. But you try to do that. Is that not so, Herr Direktor Schmidt?"

The ball was now in the court of the head of Siemens A.G., the largest producer of both primary and secondary radar in Germany.

"Up until now, yes," replied Schmidt. "You must understand, Herr Kreps, that even the best radar which we at Siemens produce, and I believe we produce the best in the world, has enormous difficulty picking up a six-meter-long flying object that is moving only eighty meters above the ground. Why? Because there is simply too much ground clutter that fogs radars at such low altitudes. And even if such a missile were picked up, its profile on the radar would be no larger than that of a sea gull. *Eine Möwe!*"

"Exactly," said the general, who was slowly orchestrating his entire audience. "So the attack strategy which was developed by the Amis, and which is currently in place, is that hundreds, even thousands of such cruise missiles will be released simultaneously from mother aircraft far from the enemy's borders, and that as they move in they will collectively simply overwhelm the opposition's air defense system."

"If I may, perhaps, add something here?" asked Professor Bosch.

"But of course."

"The engineer J. R. Utterstrom, whom I know, and who was in charge of the original cruise missile developed by Boeing, made a comparison to a swarm of rats carrying the plague. 'You get them all,' he once told me, 'or you're dead.'"

"Ja, ja," interjected Schmidt. "But Utterstrom, whom we at Siemens also know well, was, in our judgment, seriously overstating the case for the cruise missile."

The general, still standing, did not like this remark in the least. Was Schmidt going to screw up the entire show?

And if the general was disturbed, the Foreign Minister was even more so. Von Amsburg needed the support, the total blind support, of the Deutsche Bank in this venture, or else . . .

"My dear Direktor Schmidt," said von Amsburg, "I think we must ask you to clarify that last statement."

"Of course. First of all, I do not think that there is any sense in referring euphemistically to the 'enemy' or 'opponent.' We are talking about the Soviet Union, so let us not beat around the bush.

"We at Siemens are fully aware of the countermeasures that the Soviets have been developing in regard to the cruise missile, as are you, Graf von Amsburg. So we know, as you know, that already back in November of 1978 the Soviets tested their SA-10 surface-to-air missile on what amounted to a mock version of the Boeing cruise missile. It shot the missile down in five out of five cases. We know this exactly, since each operation was monitored and recorded by the American tracking stations which then still existed on the Iranian–Soviet border. The SA-10 has been in full production now for three years. It is as cheap to manufacture as the

American cruise missile—less than a million rubles a unit—and the Soviets are currently in the process of mass deployment of these missiles. The entire program will eventually cost them fifty billion rubles."

"But—" said the general.

"Later," said the Generaldirektor of Siemens A.G. "Now, the SA-10 would be useless without another parallel Russian technological development—namely, the successful installation of a 'look-down, shoot-down' radar system. Such a system has no ground-clutter problem. It works like this: the Soviet plane—it could be either the MIG-25 interceptor or the larger radar-surveillance plane, the Soviet counterpart of the American E-3A, which Boeing also builds . . . Anyway, Soviet radar projects a beam downward at a point in its patrol area—say, in Eastern Europe over Poland, or in northeastern Russia itself. Normally this would create all manner of interference on the plane's radar screen with the radar blips of buildings, hills, and other earth-based objects, all of which would tend to obscure the blip made by the cruise missile. But the Soviets now have an on-board computer in their surveillance planes which senses only that one object which is *moving*, and erases the *static* 'clutter' of ground-based interference from the screen. Within a fraction of a second the cruise missile's position is relayed to the ground stations, which can then fire the SA-10s with deadly results. The MIG-25s would even achieve a very high kill rate by simply firing their heat-seeking air-to-air missiles, provided they were close enough to the cruise missile they were targeting. I think that Herr von Amsburg can hardly disagree with any of this."

And Herr Schmidt fell silent, as did the room. Had he just shot down Franz Josef Strauss' bid for a global role for the new Germany?

At this moment—and it was now about eleven o'clock, Central European Time, on that December 3, 1985—a waiter knocked on the door of the private dining room. Graf von Amsburg went to answer it, murmured a few words, and then addressed the group from the now open door.

"Gentlemen, let us adjourn for a few minutes. I have an extremely important telephone call waiting for me. I will return shortly with, I think, good news."

The waiter proceeded to take orders for a new round of refreshments, while von Amsburg hurried to the restaurant manager's office.

"Von Amsburg hier" were his first words once he had picked up the phone.

"Ja. Und Amadeus Zimmerli hier."

"Where are you?" asked the German Foreign Minister.

"Hôtel Amigo in Brussels," replied the Swiss lawyer, "and I am sure that the line is perfectly clear. I know the hotel operator here."

"How did it go?"

"Perfectly. You can tell Mr. Patterson that he will have nothing to worry about in regard to Mr. Rogers."

"Do you have it documented?"

"Yes. It is all on videotape. I have just come from René Van der Kamp's place. He ran parts of the tape on his machine, and they reproduce perfectly."

"Excellent."

"I'm going back to Basel on the next flight. I'll be there if you need any help with Rogers."

"You are convinced that he won't try any tricks?"

"That's why we have all gone through this, isn't it? He tries to double-cross us now, and we throw him to the wolves. This sort of bribery attempt would mean a couple of years at least in Belgium, believe me. And also in the United States."

"Well, let's hope it never comes to that type of threat," said von Amsburg. "When I talked to Patterson yesterday on the phone, he said he was convinced that Rogers will go

140

along with the deal voluntarily, with no reservations whatsoever, when he hears about the package we are offering."

"You are probably right. Rogers does not strike me as a person any of us have to be afraid of. Bright, yes, but not exactly built of the stuff we are, if you know what I mean."

"Flabby?"

"Exactly. A typical flabby American," replied Zimmerli. "Precisely the type we Europeans are not going to put up with anymore, telling us how grateful we should still be because they won World War II."

"I know, Amadeus. That will now, finally, be a part of the past. All right. Then I shall proceed here. With Patterson. You can expect to hear from me right after our meeting is over tonight. In any case, bring Rogers to Bonn tomorrow. No, not Bonn. Some place much less open."

"Why not the Black Forest?" asked the Swiss lawyer.

"Where?"

"Sankt Blasien."

"That old inn?"

"Exactly. We stayed there years ago, when we were hunting wild boars. I'll call Rogers now and tell him we'll be leaving in the morning."

"Agreed. I must go."

And that was when the conspiracy passed beyond the point of no return.

12

HERB PATTERSON WAS SITTING in the living room of the country home provided by von Amsburg, rereading for probably the tenth time the proposal he had prepared, when the Graf stepped through the front door at about a quarter past eleven.

"Put on your overcoat, Mr. Patterson. My friends are expecting us back immediately."

"The financial arrangements have been agreed to?" asked Patterson.

"In principle, yes," replied von Amsburg, with something less than total candor. "Kreps—you know him, I assume— wants to be assured that your cruise-missile system is worth the risk."

"Worth the risk? Whose risk? Do you know the risk that I am undertaking just being here? I refuse to—"

"Please calm down, Mr. Patterson. And do put on your overcoat. It is cold out."

Patterson did as told and climbed into the car waiting outside. Von Amsburg took the wheel. It was snowing lightly.

"Now, we shall be there in just a few minutes. I suggest you do the following, Mr. Patterson. First, explain the merits of the MDC missile, as compared with what Boeing and General Dynamics have produced. Then, if you agree, Mr. Patterson, you might present your proposal. I am sure that Herr Doktor Kreps will be in a position to respond immediately."

"I hope so. I think I made it perfectly clear that either we make a deal immediately, or it's off. Permanently."

"You made it quite clear, Mr. Patterson."

"Have you heard from the Swiss lawyer yet?"

"Yes. I have indeed. I think your—or should I say our—problem with the president of your company will be resolved."

"Without his agreement, this whole thing simply will not work. He is the man who has total responsibility for our company's finances. If this deal works here, and if the financing becomes available, he would ferret out what happened in a matter of weeks, perhaps even days. So it's essential that he comes in and stays in. The technical side I've already taken care of. I don't need anybody there. I built up this company from scratch, and there's nobody in the industry who knows more about goddamn missiles than I do. Understand?"

"I certainly do understand, Mr. Patterson," replied Graf von Amsburg, who thought Herb Patterson just about the most obnoxious, coarse, loudmouthed, opinionated, and conceited American he had ever met. And he had met such standouts as John Connally, Hamilton Jordan, and even Muhammad Ali in his time.

Von Amsburg did not waste a second once the two men had entered the private dining room of the Gasthaus Hirschen.

"*Meine Herren,*" he said to his fellow Germans, "be seated.

I present to you Mr. Herbert Patterson, who came from San Francisco this evening to be with us. Mr. Patterson is chairman of the board of Missile Development Corporation. His company is the leader in the world in cruise-missile technology. Mr. Patterson has been, singlehandedly, responsible for this technical leadership. He is also a friend of Germany, and an admirer of Herr Bundeskanzler Strauss. Mr. Patterson."

It sounded somewhat like a nominating speech at a political convention. And Patterson loved it.

"It's an honor," he began. "I'm sorry Franz Josef is not here. I like him. He makes sense. In San Francisco we've got a men's club, the Bohemian Club. The club owns about two thousand acres north of San Francisco on the Russian River. We call it the Grove. Every summer we get together up there for a couple of weeks, to eat and drink with each other and our guests. Everybody who is anybody has been there. Strauss was there last summer. He knows how to drink with the best of them. Schmidt was also there a few times. Never did like the man. Strauss is—"

At this point von Amsburg broke in. The man was making a fool of himself, and it had to stop.

"Mr. Patterson, if you will allow me this interruption. The Chancellor has asked me to give you his most sincere regrets that he could not attend this evening. Unfortunately, a crisis of some sort arose in Bonn. Now I hope that you will tell us about your cruise missile."

Patterson—somewhat flushed in the face, since he had downed more than his share of booze on the Lufthansa flight from San Francisco—knew full well that he'd been cut off, but shrugged off the insult.

"All right, I will. I hear that some of you here are skeptical about the capabilities of our cruise missile. Okay, let me clear up any misconceptions you might have. First, our missile is in no way comparable to the cruise missiles developed by either Boeing or General Dynamics. They might be able to

145

con NATO into believing so, but that is NATO's problem. They are first-generation; we are second. Now let me tell you the difference. Boeing and General Dynamics—their cruise missiles are essentially twins. They are too big, too slow; and most dangerous of all for those who might rely upon them— as NATO seems to want to do—their guidance system, produced by McDonnell Douglas, is a turkey. It is not reliable. Now let me tell you about our missile. Here's a picture of it."

Patterson had brought his briefcase with him, and fished out a package which he gave to von Amsburg, who opened it and passed around copies of the sketches of the MDC cruise missile.

"Okay," he said, "look at the size. Not six meters like Boeing's, but only four meters—less than fourteen feet. Why? Because we developed our own engine which is vastly superior in fuel efficiency. You can see from that sketch that most of the bulk of the missile is necessary merely to store fuel. Save fuel, save space. That's what we did. But more important is that Boeing and General Dynamics have relied exclusively on a turbofan engine, the Williams. The Russians still use turbojets in their cruise missiles, for God's sake. Well, how fast can you go with a turbofan or turbojet? Not very. So everybody tried a ramjet engine. So they went fast, but not very far, since ramjets suck up fuel like nobody's business. We came up with the solution. The MDC Hybrid Engine, which incorporates the fuel efficiency of the turbine and the thrust of the ramjet. Our missile can *cruise* at Mach one point four."

Both Professor Bosch and Generaldirektor Schmidt let out an audible response of awe. And Patterson lapped it up.

"Surprised, aren't you? You ought to be. We reduced the size of the fuel-storage space by thirty-five percent and have virtually doubled the cruising speed, and we have *retained* —no, *increased*, gentlemen—the cruising range to three thousand kilometers."

Again Bosch and Schmidt looked at each other.

"Now, you people know about the Soviets and their countermeasures—specifically, their marriage of the SA-10 and the look-down radar surveillance system. Well, when that anti-cruise-missile defense system is fully in place, and it probably will be in about four years, our calculations indicate that with our size and our speed, over half—fifty-two point seven percent, to be exact—of MDC cruise missiles will penetrate that defense system and hit their targets deep in Soviet territory."

"So Utterstrom was right," commented Bosch.

"Utterstrom was only right, sir, because I developed not a swarm of rats, but a swarm of superrats. Which brings me to our guidance system. Schmidt, you must know this. But I'll tell you anyway. As far back as 1977, Professor Kosta Tsipsis from MIT told everybody who wanted to hear it that the guidance system used by both Boeing and General Dynamics—TERCOM—could not work over water, marshland, or very flat terrain. Right, Bosch?"

And Professor Doktor Bosch—who of course knew Patterson, and who did not particularly like being addressed as "Bosch" in public by a crude American of Patterson's ilk—nevertheless nodded.

"But any of you who have traveled extensively in the Soviet Union know that a good portion of the northern reaches of that country is made up of just such terrain. Right? So up there, over the most natural approach path to the majority of Soviet targets, you know what's going to happen to General Dynamics' missiles? They are going to get lost, that's what."

And Patterson chuckled. He could almost visualize their goddamn cheap missiles going in circles over the fucking tundra.

"But not ours. Oh, no. Why? Because we use a *laser* altimeter in our guidance system. TERCOM, at best, can resolve objects on the ground that are three meters wide and thirty centimeters tall from an altitude of two thousand meters. Am I right, Bosch?"

Again the head of Germany's leading aerospace company nodded.

"Okay. Our system, and we call it TERTRACK, yields resolutions of objects significantly smaller than twenty *centimeters* in width and five—yes *five*—centimeters tall. Got it? You could maybe lose our missile over the Atlantic or Pacific ocean, or the Great Lakes, but sure as hell not over Russia."

Now Patterson glared at his audience. "Convinced?" he demanded.

Von Amsburg turned to Bosch and Schmidt. "Gentlemen?" he asked.

Both scientist/industrialists actually got up and came around to shake Patterson's hand. And when Germans shake hands, they really shake.

"I think," said Bosch, "I can speak for my colleague Herr Doktor Schmidt in saying that Mr. Patterson has developed a weapons delivery system against which there will be no effective defense in this century. Our congratulations."

Patterson actually got tears in his eyes upon hearing these words. Somehow the hand of God which had helped him all of his life had once again led him in the right direction—to this group of Germans who had a true appreciation for the contribution that he, Patterson, had made to progress for all mankind.

"Now," continued Patterson, "you are no doubt asking yourselves, 'What is Patterson doing here in Germany?'"

And his audience was impressed. Very much impressed. The man was asking the right questions and, so far, giving the right answers with almost Germanic directness and efficiency.

"I will tell you why. And the reason goes back precisely six and a half years, to June of 1979, when the biggest jackass we have ever had as President, Jimmy Carter, signed the

148

Salt II agreement in Vienna. It was not the contents of the treaty itself that were so insidious, but what was in the attached protocol. And there was nothing anybody could do about it, because Carter, that ignorant piss-ant"—and that was a new word for everyone present—"said that he did not care whether the Senate ratified that treaty or not, he was going to abide by it in any case. Jeezus, if only he had stayed in Georgia!"

Everyone in the room nodded his head to that one.

"Now, you gentlemen no doubt all know what was in that protocol, but I'm going to refresh your memories anyway. In it the United States Government promised the Russians that it would not deploy any ground-launched cruise missiles with a range of over six hundred kilometers before January 1, 1983, at the earliest. Absolutely suicidal! Worse—that understanding has been *extended every year since*. Why? Why would the American government do such a stupid goddamned thing? Our missile—and when you are talking about a long-range strategic ground-launched cruise missile, you are talking about the MDC cruise missile, make no mistake about it—is the *only* new weapons system available to the West that could *immediately* neutralize the strategic military superiority which the Russians currently have. Why"—and now Patterson was starting to speak in a tone that was just this side of a yell—"why would the American Government, in cahoots with the Russian Government, ground it indefinitely?"

He glared at everybody.

"Because of you, gentlemen. Because of Germany. Because Russia is still scared shitless of Germany. Not of the United States—or at least, not anymore. Because they think we've gone soft. And goddammit, they're probably right. We are even too scared to stand up to that fucker Castro. Imagine! We even let *that* hairy faggot push us around. The Russians know full bloody well that if ground-launched nuclear-tipped cruise missiles were deployed on a massive scale in Germany, they would be caught in the old vise, between Germany in the west and not Japan but China, this time, in the east. Because with cruise missiles, Germany could just as easily stand up to Russia tomorrow as it did yesterday—in 1941. Now, don't get me wrong. I don't approve of what happened after 1941 in this country. All I'm saying is that the strategic military balance between Russia and Germany would be restored following the introduction of nuclear-equipped long-range cruise missiles in this country. Am I right?"

This time he looked at Graf von Amsburg.

"You are absolutely right." And while the Graf answered, his eyes were on Herr Doktor Reinhardt Kreps, head of the Deutsche Bank—potentially the pivot man in the German team that was going to acquire that missile for Germany.

"And the Russians have conned the Americans into believing that it is in our *mutual* interest to prevent this from happening. That in the end the United States would have as much to lose as Russia if a once again independent Germany emerged; that the *only* sure defense against a World War III is the maintenance, forever, of global cohegemony by Russia and the United States. You notice who now comes first in that so-called partnership: Russia. Why? Because they can now destroy the West with their missiles, and survive. That's why. And one of these years, they are going to let all of us in on their little secret, and blackmail us in a fashion that would make what OPEC and the Arabs are currently doing to us look benign by comparison. What I am talking about, gentlemen, is the end of Western society as we know it."

The audience was spellbound.

"But I, Herbert Patterson, do not intend to let that happen. With your help, gentlemen, the MDC missile will soon be part of the Western arsenal—in time, I hope, to stop the Russians at least until the end of this century. I pray to God it will be so."

On that religious note, the man from Sunnyvale sat down.

And perhaps to their own amazement, the five leaders of West Germany applauded. Franz Josef Strauss himself could not have put things into perspective more ably than had this crude American engineer.

In Germany it was now almost twelve thirty, a half-hour into December 4, 1985. Von Amsburg called for a second pause in the proceedings, and as the men rose, he immediately grabbed Dr. Kreps by the arm and took him well aside from the remaining group, talking intently the entire time. Patterson, Schmidt, Bosch, and General von Seefeldt, a group representing the multinational military-industrial complex at its very best—an engineer, an industrialist, a scientist, and a general, all brothers in the arms business, regardless of nationality or political bent—just sat together, silently, content in the knowledge that they were sharing a historic moment.

The politician and the banker did not take long. Their discussion in the corner lasted at most three minutes. It was the banker who now spoke, after the Foreign Minister had once again requested that the meeting reconvene.

"Mr. Patterson," began Dr. Reinhardt Kreps. "Before you spoke, I was extremely skeptical concerning this entire matter. I am no longer. I believe you have a proposal to put to us."

Patterson removed a series of papers from the yellow envelope he had with him.

"I do," he said. "But first here is our balance sheet, here is our profit-and-loss statement, and here are the details of our debt. You will notice that a high percentage of it is short-term."

The German banker's eyes slowly went down the first sheet, then the second, then the third, and then went back to the first.

"What do you yourself put your current net worth at, sir?" he asked.

"You can see that we have capitalized our input into the

151

ground-launched-cruise-missile project at one point five billion. I would say that after the NATO decision, which essentially has cast us into the role of a subcontractor to General Dynamics, about one-third of that represents real value. In other words, we must immediately write off one billion dollars."

"How much else?"

"Well, to tell the truth, probably another half-billion. A lot of now useless equipment, some very high-priced inventories, layoffs that will now be necessary are going to cost us another hunk, for which we have no reserves. All in all, as I said, another half-billion."

"Which would leave your tangible net worth at what?"

"I really would not like to say. But let's put it this way: it is probably close to nil."

"Liquidation value?" the banker then asked, pursuing Patterson, it seemed, relentlessly.

"Companies like Missile Development Corporation are not liquidated," Patterson replied, now sounding a bit testy. "We are too essential to national security."

"But to be perfectly honest, Mr. Patterson, when I look at your debt schedule and what is coming due at the end of this year, you will be put into receivership at that time, beyond any doubt. You are out of money. You really have no assets that you can readily sell to raise any money. You cannot borrow any more money, since, according to my very quick analysis, your tangible worth is not even nil, it is negative."

Kreps stopped there. Patterson remained silent.

"My dear Mr. Patterson," Kreps then continued, "I am not saying this to humiliate you. I am merely trying, for the sake of myself, my colleagues here, and also for your sake, to clearly establish your current financial situation. If we agree, then we can move on, perhaps, to a more constructive analysis."

"All right. Everything you say is correct. However, and

this is a very important point, the fact that we have not been chosen as the prime contractor for the ground-launched cruise missile does not mean that my corporation is at a dead end. We've still got our engine, which *every* builder of cruise missiles, whether air-, sea-, or ground-launched, is going to have to use eventually. That means both Boeing and General Dynamics: Boeing for its bomber-launched cruise missile, General Dynamics for its sea-launched Tomahawk missile, and now the NATO missile. The same thing applies for our guidance system. Everybody is eventually going to have to replace the TERCOM system with ours. There is no question of that."

"How long will it take before all this happens?" asked Kreps.

"Two or three years. Come fiscal 1988, MDC will be a viable concern well into the black and able to service all this debt. The problem is . . ." And his voice faded. Once again Patterson was starting to show his age. And no wonder. He had just flown five thousand miles and without a minute of sleep was here involved in the fight of his life for the survival of his company in a strange land among strange people in the middle of the night.

"How much bridging finance will you need?" asked the head of the Deutsche Bank.

"My president, Frank Rogers, is the financial man in our company," Patterson replied. "He's brilliant, and in the past his estimates and forecasts have proved to be unbelievably accurate. It is he who is going to have to give you the precise numbers, and the explanations for them. But he and I have, naturally, discussed this matter. And we agree on what we in the States call 'a ball-park number.' And that is one billion dollars.

"But let me finish. Our lead bank, which is Citibank, would want to be taken out if we went this route. Their solution to our problem, and thus their problem, will be a merger with McDonnell Douglas. Unless they are taken out, under the terms of our loan covenants with them they could *force* the merger. And as you correctly analyzed the situation, Dr. Kreps, they could start that merger process by first throwing us into receivership on January second after we were unable to meet the financial charges due at the end of this month. All right? Well, as you can see on that third paper, we owe them and the banks in their loan syndicate another three-quarters of a billion dollars."

"So we are talking about one point seven five billion?" asked Kreps.

"As I said, give or take something like ten percent. Frank Rogers will be able to give you the precise figure."

The men around the table were used to talking big numbers, but even for them this was a lot of money.

"It's too big for one bank—that you know, Mr. Patterson," stated Kreps.

"Of course," answered Patterson.

"So if we do step in here," continued Kreps—and now he was obviously addressing himself to the entire audience, not just the American—"we are going to have to do it on a completely normal market-conform basis, because we are going to have to invite a lot of other banks in on this thing."

"What's 'normal' right now?" asked Patterson.

"Well, 'normal' right now is that nobody would lend MDC a dollar—at least, no lender here in Europe. Inside the United States that might be different. But here in Europe we look to assets, real assets, in deciding whether or not to lend to a company. In your country, Mr. Patterson, the banks are often willing to look the other way in regard to tangible collateral and lend against earnings or the promise of earnings."

Kreps was beginning to wander. Surprisingly, it was not von Amsburg who stepped in to get things moving again, but rather the head of Siemens, Dr. Josef Schmidt.

"Reinhardt, I think we all know that. But if the Deutsche Bank puts its name on it, nobody else is going to really bother about the details. So what would be market-conform right now?"

"The maximum term would be three years. The interest rate would be variable, and adjustable every three months at a full point above the London interbank Eurodollar borrowing rate. That's thirteen percent right now, so the starting rate would be fourteen percent," Kreps replied.

"We're only paying eleven percent to Citibank right now!" exclaimed Patterson.

"Mr. Patterson," said Kreps, now in a very dry tone indeed, "I am not about to bargain with you or even discuss terms and rates. I am *telling* you what current conditions are." His eyes turned to the Foreign Minister for help.

"Mr. Patterson," von Amsburg said, taking up the signal, "it seems to me that we may be getting slightly ahead of the problem. Because unless *our* conditions are met, and that almost immediately, I am afraid that there is really no sense in *any* further discussion of a German financial package for your company."

"I can deliver my end, don't you worry," said Patterson, now getting testy again. "And I can deliver it before Christmas. But let me tell you, I am not so sure whether *you* people can deliver by then. I've been through this sort of thing before with bankers. They fiddle around and—"

"Not German bankers, Mr. Patterson," said Kreps. "If my colleagues here are satisfied that you can accomplish the transfer of technology within an agreed-upon time framework, I can absolutely guarantee that the Deutsche Bank will be in a position to totally refinance your company before December thirty-first of this year. Is that clear?" There was now a sharp edge in the banker's voice.

Von Amsburg, noting both the tone of voice and the time, and realizing that further negotiations under such conditions could suddenly turn counterproductive, decided to cut matters off right there.

He rose.

"Gentlemen, I think we have taken the matter as far as we can this evening. We all quite clearly agree in principle. We all also agree that time is of the essence. I would like to add one further factor: secrecy concerning this matter is paramount. So I definitely do not think it advisable that we meet again here as a group tomorrow. But wherever we agree to meet for renewed talks, I think it now will be appropriate if we split up into a technical working group and a financial one. I suggest that Dr. Bosch and Dr. Schmidt take care of the technological transfer arrangements with Mr. Patterson, and that Dr. Kreps and I then try to finalize the financial aspects of our new partnership with him."

Von Amsburg then shifted his head toward General Lothar von Seefeldt, Generalinspektor der Bundeswehr.

"Perhaps then, Herr General, you will join us all for the final session, should th working parties reach agreement. I say that because I am afraid that there will be no military implications involved unless such prior agreement is reached."

"I will stand by and be at your disposal, Herr von Amsburg," replied the general, who normally would then have clicked his heels, but was not in a position to do so efficiently this time, since he was sitting down.

"Where?" now barked the head of Siemens A.G., who was obviously growing impatient. "And when?"

"Both you and Bosch are in the south of Germany," replied von Amsburg, "so we might as well meet there. But I do not think it would be advisable to meet in either Munich or Stuttgart. And certainly not Frankfurt. In fact, I think we should avoid all large cities. And there is a further matter to consider. I believe, Mr. Patterson"—and the mention of his name roused the American, who was now badly in need of sleep—"that you would like the president of your company to be present at some of these meetings. Where is he right now?"

Von Amsburg asked this as if his pal Zimmerli had not told him just an hour before on the telephone.

"In Basel," answered Patterson, after thinking a moment.

Although it was late, and everyone present, not just Patterson, was fatigued, this little revelation managed to raise a few eyebrows. Why would the president of this California-based aerospace company be in Switzerland, of all places, at such a crucial juncture?

"How handy," continued von Amsburg, as if Basel were the most natural place in the world for anyone to be spending a little time. "That should make it easy. Let's meet in the Black Forest, then. There's nobody there right now. The fall tourist season is over, and the winter one has not yet begun. In fact, I don't think there has even been any snow there to speak of yet this year. How about Sankt Blasien? At the Gasthof zum Hirschen. You gentlemen all must know it. It's right across from the church with the *Zwiebelturm*."

Everyone but Patterson nodded. All the Germans present knew the church with the onion tower.

"Mr. Patterson and I should be there by noon tomorrow," said von Amsburg. "I shall arrange for all your accommodations. There will be no need for any of you to register. You understand?"

They understood.

13

HERE I MUST BACK UP. Not far. Just one day. Back to December 2, when the NATO axe fell on MDC and when Herb Patterson had called immediately thereafter ordering me to just stay put and lie low in the Hotel Euler in Basel for two days.

"Leave it to me," he had said.

Well, I sent a cable to my wife telling her that my return to California would be delayed a few days. Just that. And began lying low.

But then Sabine von Lathen called to remind me that we had prearranged a date for that evening to celebrate something or other, and that all she was calling about was to confirm that everything was still on, except that if I agreed, the arrangements would be a little different than I had perhaps anticipated.

Knowing Sabine's way of approaching awkward matters in an oblique fashion, I decided to cut right in right there.

"Sabine," I said, "I am in a very difficult mood right now. So please just tell me what you've arranged and then I'll tell you whether or not I'm coming."

I mean, after my career, my financial future, my God-knows-what had just been blown out of the water, I was not about to play kiddies' games with an ex-mistress.

"Having your period, dear?" she said.

"Come on," I said.

"Well, I thought you should get out and mingle a bit," she went on. "I noticed that you've gone a bit provincial."

"Continue."

"Well, Father likes you, you know. And he suggested that you might find it interesting if he invited a few of his friends over for dinner, and that we join him."

"This evening?"

"This evening."

"A bit late now to send out invitations."

"Well, actually, that has already been done. You see, I told Father that I was sure that you would come, because after all, you and I had agreed to spend this evening together in any case. You invited me, remember?"

"But not your father and all his golfing partners."

"This is Switzerland, dear. One does not dine with one's golfing partners. One barely golfs with them. One—"

"Sabine!"

"Yes, dear. Now, would seven at Father's place be all right?"

Lying low and staying put that was not. But it was about as close to it as one could get.

"All right. Seven is fine."

"Good. That will give you time for a nice long nap."

Now, at this point you may be saying to yourself, "This guy Rogers is a bit of a shit"—if you will pardon my use of

160

a word that normally puts me off quite a bit, especially when used by women. What I'm referring to is the fact that I was even considering going out again with my ex-girlfriend when I had a perfectly nice wife at home, one who obviously cared for me, worried about me, missed me, and all the rest. You are wondering why I did not phone Nancy more often, especially after that long talk I had had with her from Copenhagen during which her loneliness had become so apparent. You may also be wondering what kind of pushy type Sabine von Lathen was, acting as she did while being fully in the picture about my marital situation and the promises I had made to Nancy three years earlier.

Well, all this is not easy to explain. First, perhaps I should tell you a little bit more about me. I am not a ladies' man and never have been. Sure, I am well over six feet tall. I used to have a lot of rather blond hair. I used to play football at college. I did rather well scholastically, not just during my graduate years in Basel but also at the School of Foreign Service at Georgetown prior to that. I tell you this not to give you the impression that I am some kind of undiscovered intellectual Robert Redford—which, now that I am getting toward the fifty-year mark, would be a lie of rather substantial proportions, what with most of that blond hair gone, and a tummy that tends to protrude more than a little bit when I forget to suck it in—but to explain that I have not been a ladies' man not because women somehow found me abhorrent owing to ugliness and/or dumbness, but simply because I *chose* to lead that sort of life. To put it very bluntly: I have always enjoyed drinking and kidding around with the guys more than fooling around with the girls. Okay?

Now for my wife, Nancy. She looked like Jennifer Jones when I married her and she still looks like her today. No kidding. She plays a mean game of tennis. She has a nice sense of humor. She is very intelligent. She hates crude people. She won't abide social climbers. She refuses to go to dinner parties unless she knows whom she is going to have to sit beside. I guess when you come right down to it, she is a bit of a snob. But she has the credentials, both family and educational, to support such an attitude. I'm a bit of a snob myself and find nothing wrong with it. The point I am trying to make in a very oblique fashion—oblique because I *hate* this analytical sort of crap—is that *both* of us approached each other and our marriage in a spirit of being equals and in a sense of mutual respect. And since 1959 we have never, either of us, changed our minds. I might have wavered a bit a few years ago, but that was all. We still like each other a great deal and, I guess, also love each other in our own ways.

Then why Sabine? I really don't know. She just happened. I think I have already explained when and how. But I never did get to the why. Well, let me try now. But very briefly. Sabine has the same level of family and educational background as Nancy. In fact, it would be fair to say that there is more than just a bit of aristocratic blood flowing through the von Lathens' veins. So a cheap girl she definitely is not, to put it mildly. But where Nancy is serious, Sabine is playful. Where Nancy likes to waltz, Sabine likes to disco. Where Nancy *never* discussed our private life, not even with her mother when she was still alive back in Virginia, Sabine flaunts her sexuality.

Sabine giggles a lot. She loves to speak Italian. She drinks beer. She is also, by the way, a very strikingly beautiful girl: leggy, Italian-looking. But for reasons which she never expressed, she had never particularly liked men. Ninety-nine times out of a hundred, she often told me, she preferred to stay home reading or listening to music or going to visit her father to going out with some fool who expected her to jump for joy when he put his hand on her leg after buying her a lousy 100-franc dinner. Equally mysterious is the fact that she really liked me from the moment we set eyes on each other, and I really liked her. I still do. Very much. Because she is definitely more fun than kidding around and drinking with the boys. But for me, it was very much the same thing, if you can understand that. Sabine added a dimension to my life that is unique, and I would not have wanted to do without it for anything in the world.

The funny thing is—and I'm getting way ahead of the story again—I was wrong about Nancy's attitude in this whole thing. In the past three years we had talked, now and then, about Sabine in a neutral sort of way. And I sensed that Nancy was more than just curious, and she definitely was no longer jealous. She seemed to have developed an admiration for the Swiss lady, peculiar as that may sound. Thank God she did, as things turned out.

But I did not really know that at the time. The result was that I had an increasingly bad conscience about how things were redeveloping with Sabine. That was why I cabled Nancy about coming home late, instead of phoning. Because I knew that later that day I would be together with both Sabine and her father.

Rich Swiss tend to be very rich indeed. There is a myth, started and propagated by the Swiss, that wealthy as they may be, they hate to show it. That's about as big a whopper as the myth spread by the British about their politeness, when they really are among the rudest people on earth; or the story spread by the French that they are really the only people who understand and cultivate art as a natural component of their everyday lives, when they have managed to build some of the ugliest cities on earth; or the myth spread by the Swedes that they are lethargic, easygoing, nice guys, when in fact they can be some of the shortest-tempered drunken boors on the face of this earth.

Now, whom have I left out? Nobody that counts. So back to the Swiss. You may have noticed now and then that I do not particularly care for them, since I think the word "hypocrisy" was probably invented to describe their most notable trait. Well, the above is to prove that I dislike a lot of other people just as much. Now on to Sabine von Lathen's father, who was very Swiss, very rich, and flaunted both.

I took a cab to his place in Arlesheim, the suburb of Basel that is the Bel-Air of northeast Switzerland. The home was situated on about ten acres of lawn and shrubs; it resembled architecturally the old Douglas Fairbanks mansion in Beverly Hills, occupied for many years by a onetime Swiss resident himself, Bernie Cornfeld—a comparison and a fact that would have proven doubly odious to many rich Swiss, convinced as they are of the singularity of their good taste. A butler answered the door, a maid was waiting to receive my coat after the butler had removed it, while another maid was standing by one of the doors leading from the hall indicating the direction in which one should next proceed. I had been there before, when daughter Sabine and I had been rather thick, but never had Papa rolled out all the artillery like this. It must be the rest of the guest list that had brought this on, I reasoned.

And my reasoning was proved correct almost immediately. My host, after greeting me very warmly indeed—Sabine was right: for some odd reason he really did like me—made the introductions.

The first man was the son-in-law of the founder of Binder Maschinenfabrik, and currently boss of its largest subsidiary, Contraves, which was the prime producer of sophisticated weaponry in Switzerland, its manufacturing range including missiles of the antitank, air-to-air, and ground-to-air varieties.

The second man was the president of the Union Bank of Switzerland—the bank, if you remember, that had put Prince Radziwill on the payroll for a while when it was in the process of springing I.G. Farben's properties from the greedy grasp of the American Government.

The third was Professor Juergen Neuhaus, head of the Department of Economics and Political Science of the Uni-

164

versity of Basel and simultaneously rector of that institution, now 524 years old; academic guru, one knew, to Switzerland's ruling clique.

My host, as head of Hoffmann–La Roche, the world's biggest pharmaceutical company, and as such one of the most powerful industrialists in the world, was in no way catered to by his Swiss guests. Obviously all three of them—the arms manufacturer, the banker, and the professor—regarded themselves as fully his equals. To tell you the truth, I was extremely flattered that von Lathen had seen fit to gather them together in my honor. I could not help wondering if he would have done so had he been aware of what had taken place in Brussels that day and what it would mean for my future.

But that little thought came and went in a hurry, since Sabine made her grand entrance at that point. And grand it was! Her décolletage was the second thing one's eyes were drawn to, after the initial total body scan. Her bosom was deep, full, and magnificent and almost chaste, since it was constantly struggling against its ever-threatening escape from the enveloping folds of what had to be a $5,000 Givenchy special.

Sabine was on a "*du*" basis with everybody present except, of course, the professor. She was especially effusive when she greeted me—a greeting that ended with a very possessive taking of my arm, after which the two of us led the parade to the dining room, where I assumed the place of honor on Sabine's right. Her mother had been dead for at least fifteen years, so as the only child, she had grown up, essentially, as lady of the house—a function which she handled with sureness and grace.

What was to me strange but, I must say, impressive is the way in which upper-class Europeans handle the issue of the mistress. Everyone present that evening was no doubt fully aware that I was a married man of long standing. Yet everyone found it fully acceptable and natural that Sabine and I had been and probably still were lovers, companions, and friends. Our European president had *two* such open relationships, besides his elegant wife. Which goes to show that there is always someone who has advanced even further in man's eternal quest for perfection.

The dinner was upper-class Swiss: smoked trout followed by venison accompanied by marinated black cherries and—it was December, remember—Belgian endive and cheese, and St.-Honoré tart for dessert. The white wine was an Aigle, the red a Dole. And when the cheese arrived, the conversation turned to me. And it was the rector of the university who set the theme and the tone.

"Herr Rogers," he began—it being customary that among graduates of the University one dropped the "Doktor" title, since it was self-understood, or at least, used to be—"you are one of us and at the same time an American. Thus you are singularly well placed, from our point of view, to explain what is happening to the United States of America. Goethe, as you know, said, '*Amerika, du hast es besser.*' I fear that in this instance if Dr. Goethe were with us tonight he might express a second opinion."

Funny—for Basel. So we all laughed at his little joke. But then came the serious question.

"What has gone wrong?"

What indeed? It was hard to explain even to oneself, not to mention a group of foreigners.

"I don't know exactly," I began, "but something very basic has gone very badly wrong. We bandy about such phrases as the 'moral fabric' of a nation, or the 'faith in their own destiny' of a people, and the 'will to exercise power' of a nation's leadership. Well, that fabric today is badly torn, that faith is rapidly dwindling. And that leadership has been absent, now, for how long? Well, my opinion would be since 1973, the start of Nixon's second term, when he was already dead in the water and probably knew it and therefore went into paralysis. And we have really not had a President since.

166

First it was a peanut farmer; then an old burnt-out actor. The present man? He's only been in for a year, but he sure as hell looks just like more of the same. And we Americans strongly suspect that it is highly probable that this unhappy state of our leadership will continue.

"Raymond Aron, whom you, of course, all know, was convinced that the current American political and electoral system makes it inevitable that mediocre Presidents, lacking prestige and authority, will continue to succeed one another until a drastic overhaul of the electoral process is undertaken. The American President today must be an expert in public relations, not in the art of statesmanship. Thus it is next to impossible that an American President will ever have either the culture or the competence of a German Chancellor or a French President.

"The decline of the U.S. Presidency no doubt coincides with the decline of our country. And perhaps the most disturbing element of this decline is that for the first time in our history, we have totally lost our momentum as a nation. And momentum was the key, I believe, to the success of the United States. It always had to be heading somewhere, its people had to believe that that somewhere was good and part of our nation's manifest destiny, and they had to further believe that God would grant them leadership which would lead them into that promised land safe and sound because, as Goethe perceived, America indeed always did have it better."

I paused.

"I guess that sounds childlike, but that's America. Or should I say, that *was* America. Right now we are floundering as never before, preoccupied with the fact that our economic growth has stopped; sick and tired of inflation, which is robbing us all of our future; sick and tired of OPEC, which relentlessly keeps putting it to us year after year; sick and tired of the Russians, who get more bellicose every day, especially after they got away with Yugoslavia. And sick and tired, most of all, of the fact that nobody is *doing* anything to stop or reverse all of these processes. It is very frustrating to be an American these days."

"I believe you. But where does this leave *us*?" And for the first time it was the banker who had spoken up.

"Leave whom?" I asked, not facetiously, but not quite sure whom he meant.

"We Europeans. We Swiss," he answered.

"What do you mean?" And again I wasn't sure what he was driving at.

"You know full well that in spite of all the complaining we do, we all, all of us here at this table, look to the United States as the final salvation. The final refuge. The nation which, if it comes to that again, will bail us out. Even the French share that feeling. But *will* you bail us out now? *Can* you?"

It was starting to become a little clearer why this dinner party. These guys were getting worried—even the gnome of gnomes from Zurich. Because now he was worried where *he* was going to put *his* money. Funny, really. All those members of the doom-and-gloom end-of-the-world club in the United States thought they were clever as hell because they kept their last-last-gasp nest eggs in Switzerland. How dumb could you get? Without the protection of the United States, without the American military umbrella over all of Europe, the banks and currency of Switzerland would be about as safe as those of Latvia and Lithuania had been—should you still remember those little Baltic countries, before they were integrated into the ruble bloc.

The guy from the Union Bank of Switzerland obviously knew that. And so did my host, the pharmaceutical king.

"Frank," he said, he being the only one with whom I was on a first-name basis, "are you by any chance acquainted with a book by an old acquaintance of mine, Graf Otto von Amsburg?"

168

Uh-oh. Be careful, I thought. Now, why is *that* fellow's name coming up? Hardly our old friend coincidence. So there was a *lot* more to this evening than I had thought.

"Who?" I asked.

And now it was Sabine who did a double take. He was the German, she had claimed, who had put me under international police surveillance—hardly a name I would have forgotten so easily. In fact, she had been convinced that I knew him personally. But the evening had become too interesting for her to point that out and, perhaps, ruin the game that was being played. So she just said, in a sweet and slightly patronizing voice:

"He is the Minister of Foreign Affairs of West Germany"— and after the slightest of pauses added, "dear."

"Of course," I said, "but I'm afraid I am not familiar with his book."

"You must read it," Sabine's father continued. "But since you have not yet been able to do so, let me perhaps explain what it is about, and why I have brought it up." For some reason he looked down the table to the man who ran Contraves, and it seemed to me that he got an almost invisible nod of approval.

"Its title is *Deutschland am Ende des zwanzigten Jahrhunderts: Führer-Nation, oder Sklave.*"

"Catchy," I said, purely for Sabine's sake, but got no snickers even from that corner. This evening was getting *serious*.

"Von Amsburg's thesis is quite simple, and quite direct," continued her father. "With rather clear Teutonic logic he hypothesized that unless Germany moves to fill the leadership vacuum being left in the European theater by the United States, by the end of the twentieth century Germany, both West and East, will move irrevocably into the Soviet orbit. First, he claims, will come the 'Finlandization' of West Germany; then a type of 'confederation' with East Germany; finally, total 'reunifaction' under the Hammer and Sickle."

He paused, expecting, perhaps, some comment from me, but got none, so he went on.

"The United States, von Amsburg further reasons, moving as it is from energy crisis to energy crisis, from leadership crisis to leadership crisis, will continue to be so involved with its domestic chaos for at least another decade, and probably longer, that it will have no choice but to feebly stand by as Germany is slowly lost to the West—by default. As were Iran, Afghanistan, and most lately Yugoslavia. All were lost without one drop of American blood's being shed in their defense. It would be the utmost folly, he further reasons, to suppose that one drop of American blood will *ever* be shed for Germany."

That got unanimous nods.

"Of course," continued Herr Doktor von Lathen, "von Amsburg openly admits that such a process would not be possible were it not for the tacit acceptance of such a fate by German leadership. At least, *past* German leadership, meaning the Social Democrats; meaning the Willy Brandts and the Helmut Schmidts—the better-Red-than-dead crowd."

"But that crowd is now out," I interjected.

"Exactly. And getting them out was the real purpose of this book. It came out two months before last year's election in Germany. And in it, von Amsburg—not exactly unexpectedly, of course—states unequivocally that the only alternative to the end of West Germany as an independent nation would be the return to power of the party that restored Germany to greatness after World War II; the party of Konrad Adenauer, of Ludwig Erhard: the Christian Democratic Union. The only man fit to assume the cloak of greatness that had been worn by these giants of modern Germany was, in von Amsburg's scheme of things to come, of course, Franz Josef Strauss. Now, bear with me; none of this so far is exactly new or startling. But hear what comes."

Our host got up; went over to the nearby buffet; picked up a book with a red-and-black jacket, obviously von Amsburg's; returned to his chair at the head of the table; opened the book; and said:

"*Ja*, here it is. On page 197. I quote: *Um aus historischer Notwendigkeit unabhängig zu bleiben, muss Deutschland Atomwaffen besitzen und zwar genug solcher Waffen um Russland total zerstören zu können. Die Russen müssen wieder Todesangst vor den Deutschen bekommen. Nur dann werden wir als Nation das zwanzigte. Jahrhundert überleben.*"

"There it is," he then said, "black or white. Strauss and von Amsburg intend to arm West Germany with nuclear weapons in sufficient quantities to be able to *annihilate* Russia. That's their road to German survival."

Von Lathen then looked at me, as did everybody else around the table.

"Are you going to allow that, sir?"

We had suddenly gone formal. And we had suddenly directed at me what I considered to be a totally absurd question.

"I am afraid," my answer began, "that I have nothing whatsoever to do with whether or not the Germans go nuclear. You've got the wrong guy."

"Really?" asked the head of the Swiss missile company, Contraves. "Well, I, for one, am *not* convinced that we have 'the wrong guy,' as you put it. But before I say even one more word about that, let me point out that neither I nor, I believe, any of us here this evening are by any means necessarily condemning, or even disagreeing with, the theses and the conclusions of Herr von Amsburg. Therefore we are also in no way condemning you, Herr Rogers."

Things were getting confusing. Condemn *me* for *what*? But that was not yet to come out.

"Let me explain further. The Russians now have an overwhelming military superiority in the European theater. Absolutely overwhelming. They have twenty-one thousand tanks to NATO's seven thousand. They have four thousand military aircraft to NATO's two thousand. They have two soldiers to NATO's one. Of course, they have *always* had such a measure of superiority in terms of *Panzers* and manpower, but we—and I think I can use that term, because I have always thought of our Swiss Army as more or less an unofficial adjunct of NATO—relied upon the fact that we had such an overwhelming technological superiority, in terms of aircraft, missiles, nuclear warheads, warning systems—the entire technological gamut—that we were at least their equal in overall capability and that a balance of terror thus also existed on a theater level in Europe."

"We all know that," grumbled the professor. "Get to the point."

"The point is that the Soviets now have their SS-20 medium-range missile with nuclear warheads and a range of 2,750 miles fully in place, allowing them to destroy any part of Western Europe they choose. And none of us—NATO, France, Switzerland—none of us has any means of retaliation or any means of countering the SS-20 threat with a similar threat of our own. Either you Americans are prepared to risk your homeland for us by firing your intercontinental ballistic missiles at Russia, should Russia fire its SS-20 missiles at Europe, or we will all, eventually, go the way of Afghanistan or Yugoslavia or Finland."

"The point, the point!" exclaimed the professor.

"The real point is this: I think that we Europeans are now faced with a choice between protectors: the Americans or the new Germans. Which way should we go, Herr Rogers?"

This was not only getting serious. This was getting *deadly* serious.

"Let me put an additional question," continued the man from Contraves. "If we rely now on West Germany to shield us from the Soviet Union, will it be able to deliver?"

"Hold on right there," I said. "You are searching for solutions to problems that simply do not exist. Let's go back to the basic reasoning that was just thrown out on the table—

namely, that we have lost our technological superiority in the European theater. You forget something, gentlemen: our ground-launched cruise missile! The Russians may have their SS-20, but Europe has, or at least, will have, our medium-range nuclear missile which is, frankly, vastly superior. So there will be, once again, a balance."

"No, there will not," interjected the Zurich missile man, and it was now in a voice with bitter overtones. "I will personally have to see one of those missiles deployed and ready to launch before I ever believe it. Look, the United States has been promising Europe cruise missiles since the late 1970s. Here we are at the end of 1985 and there are still none deployed. Assuming I believed what you have just told us, Mr. Rogers, it will be at least two years before the General Dynamics missiles will be produced in sufficient quantities to be ready for deployment. But I must tell you quite frankly that I very seriously doubt whether they will ever be deployed. So where are we today? Just where we have been for the past six years. The Soviets can destroy Berlin or Bonn or Hamburg and, yes, Paris, London, Rome, and Zurich with their SS-20s, and with impunity. There is not a missile system in place anywhere in Europe that could retaliate by destroying anything of significance in the Soviet homeland.

"You Americans," he concluded, "by agreeing to this, by your eternal stalling, have betrayed Europe, sir."

The man was essentially right. Not about the "betrayal" crap, but about the missile situation.

In the protocol to SALT II the U.S. Government had agreed not to deploy ground-launched cruise missiles until January 1, 1983, and had subsequently agreed to extend this commitment should the Soviets keep up their end of that protocol, despite the nonratification of the SALT agreement itself. The White House was satisfied that the Soviets were complying, so the commitment was formally extended for two years in 1982 and for another two years in 1984. This was not a result of the "weakness" or the "senility" of any of the Presidents involved in the process, but was rather the outgrowth of the power of the bureaucracy that controlled the SALT process in both the Soviet Union and the United States.

Ronald Reagan had come into the White House in 1981 convinced that he would be able to totally renegotiate SALT II, and maybe even reverse the entire SALT process and reestablish American absolute military superiority over the Soviets. But as in regard to so many other things, he was forced to change his mind by the bureaucrats. If the SALT process were ever reversed, they argued, World War III would become an inevitability very soon. No one in the White House, whether hawk or dove, Republican or Democrat, whether Carter or Reagan, nor any of the Soviet leaders in the Kremlin, wanted to be responsible for that. So the protocol lived on.

To be sure, the American Government kept putting up smoke screens masking the policy. For instance, in December of 1979—almost six years to the day prior to that fateful NATO meeting of December 2, 1985—the United States had proposed, and most of the NATO members had accepted, the idea of our installing some medium-range ground-launched missiles in Europe sometime in the 1983–84 period, should the "understanding" with the Soviet Union on this issue break down.

Involved were 108 Pershing II missiles, built by our old friend General Dynamics (nothing more than updates of the old Pershing I missiles which had been lying around Germany for a decade and were just very short-range tactical support missiles—about as harmless as missiles come) and 464 ground-to-ground missiles built by the Martin Marietta Corporation with a maximum range of 1,200 miles—which were real dogs, if you will pardon the criticism. They were so slow that if even two of them had ever penetrated the Soviet defense system the guys who *built* them would have fainted—had they ever been deployed, which they never were. Not because first Belgium and then the Netherlands continually opposed their deployment, but because the United States never intended to deploy them if it could possibly be avoided.

So in 1984 the protocol was renewed yet again. But now, just a year later, further renewal no longer came into question. After the Soviet incursion into Yugoslavia there was no question whatsoever in my mind at least that the United States was finally going to install the General Dynamics cruise missiles. But—and it was this "but," I guess, which had the man from Contraves so aroused—even when deployed it was going to be solely an American finger that would or would not pull the trigger on the missiles. For *that* policy was the key to America's continuing hope to retain nuclear cohegemony of the world in concert with the Soviet Union—despite Afghanistan, despite Iran, and even despite Yugoslavia. To share tactical nuclear weapons with our allies, fine. But *never* strategic. Because if some third power had the ability to attack the Soviet Union, it might try to do so at some point and provoke a blind massive response that would destroy Western civilization.

So, to sum it up, we did not "give" the Western Europeans strategic nuclear weapons because we did not trust them. They had caused two world wars. That was enough. I said just that, in those words, to the men around the table.

And they agreed with the reasoning, if not the conclusion. As the professor then said:

"My dear Mr. Rogers, that was all fine and good as long as *we* could trust *you*. But we no longer do. We trust neither your intentions nor your will."

This coming from a Swiss academic!

"Do you feel Germany is more trustworthy?" I asked, incredulous.

"We are in the same boat," he answered.

"And we have just been outflanked by the Russians in Yugoslavia," added the banker.

"And as you put it yourself, Mr. Rogers," added our host, the good Doctor von Lathen, "the United States is today— 'floundering as never before' I believe were your exact words."

"So"—and it had gone back to the professor—"we Swiss must find someone to trust. Against all of our better judgments, against all the lessons of history, and against all of our emotions—because, as you know full well, Mr. Rogers, we thoroughly dislike Germans—nevertheless we seem to have no other choice. The sad truth is that you Americans have brought this not only upon yourselves but also upon all of us here."

I'm afraid that I simply had no ready response to that point. And so the man from Contraves again filled the void.

"Now I think it proper for me to return to what I was driving at a few minutes ago," he said. "And I think that now you will realize how extremely vital your answer will be to all of us here, not as individuals but as representatives of our Swiss nation."

He seemed then to search for the right words.

"Go on," I said, now slowly getting angry, not the least at Sabine, who had gotten me into this corner and who was just sitting there, saying absolutely nothing, just watching them put it to me.

"Is it true, sir," the missile man now said, "that the West German Government is going to acquire from your company the technology that will allow it to mass-produce, in Germany, a ground-launched cruise missile with a range of over three thousand kilometers, a speed of Mach one point four, and a capability of carrying a five-hundred-kiloton nuclear warhead?"

Jesus Christ Almighty!

"That is just about the most preposterous thing I have ever heard in my entire life!" I exclaimed.

Quite obviously, my vehemence had an effect.

"My dear Frank," interrupted Sabine's father, "let me assure you that we did not mean to imply any impropriety on *your* part. Nor, and you can rely a hundred percent on this, will any of us here tonight discuss this matter outside this room. You have the assurance of each of us. Is that not so, gentlemen?"

And the three other men nodded vigorously.

"However," continued von Lathen, "this possibility was brought to my attention over the weekend, and I found it of such extraordinary importance for all of us that I called together this dinner party to explore its possible ramifications for our country, and, indeed, for Europe. I do hope you will forgive my subterfuge. It was not meant to be harmful."

What could I say after that elegant disclaimer? There was no sense in just playing the insulted patriot. So I decided to again try logic.

"I'm afraid"—and I was addressing this to the Contraves missile man—"that your basic supposition does not even make sense. Why Missile Development Corporation and *our* technology? Look, if I were the Germans and wanted a cruise missile, I'd go after one that has been in business for a while. Like the Boeing air-launched version. Hell, our government gave them a contract for 3,418 of them way back in 1980 and they've built at least half that number already. They work. Or why not the people at General Dynamics, who build the sea-launched cruise missile, the Tomahawk? Also already built and proved in quantity. What's so special about ours? There are only a dozen prototypes in existence. You're a missile man. So you know the risks involved in something like that."

The man from Contraves was quite ready with his answer: "Indeed I am a missile man, as you put it, so I think the answer is obvious. Bombers like the B-52 are needed as launching platforms for the strategic version of the Boeing cruise missile—as you must know. And a navy is needed as home for the Tomahawk sea-launched cruise missile. Germany has no B-52s; in fact, it has no long-range bombers at all. Nor does it have any navy to speak of. Thus Germany needs a long-range strategic cruise missile that can be launched from a railroad car or, better yet, from a truck trailor, a *camion*—a semi, as I believe you Americans call it —in any case, from a mobile unit that can be parked in, say, the Black Forest; or should I say, hundreds of such units. That's what we need. And that is exactly what Missile Development Corporation now has."

He paused for a moment, expecting someone to interrupt. When no one did, he continued.

"And there is more than just the ground-launched aspect that makes your missile so interesting for the Germans, or for anybody else, for that matter. Sure, it would be possible to modify the Boeing ALCM for ground launching. Our company could do that easily. But the Boeing missile represents an already outdated weapons system. What MDC has developed is quite obviously a true second-generation cruise missile, with your new engine and your new guidance system. Both Boeing and General Dynamics have tried to keep pace with you, but in our judgment both have failed. The new guidance system of General Dynamics is a dud; that's why so many of its prototypes have simply gotten lost."

It was obvious from what the Contraves man had said that so far the Swiss intelligence people had not missed a bet.

"And when Boeing tried to develop a new engine to match yours in terms of both range and thrust, look what has been happening: they've been crashing all over the state of Washington!"

Right again.

"The only ground-launched cruise missile in existence today that meets all criteria in regard to its ability to deliver nuclear warheads on top of almost any desirable target in the Soviet Union is the MDC one. And that, sir, is why we all came to dinner this evening when the possibility of your making that missile technology available to the Germans was mentioned to our mutual friend Dr. von Lathen."

I was not going to go over all that again. His knowledge of the cruise-missile business was complete and essentially irrefutable. But his conclusion about what MDC would, or even could, do was simply bananas.

"Look," I said, "granting that all you said about the relative merits of our missile is correct, how could we transfer the technology of such a complex weapons system without half the world finding out? Even the thought is ridiculous."

I noticed the professor nodding his head as I was speaking and thought that finally I had turned the conversation around. Until the Swiss missile man started talking again.

"Have you ever heard of a man by the name of Alfred Frauenknecht?" he asked.

"No," I replied, "but apparently I should have. What has he got to do with all this?"

"Directly—nothing," replied the head of Contraves—and now I finally remember his name: Schmiedheine, Werner Schmiedheine—"but indirectly a great deal. It happened about twenty years ago, but that means nothing, since the technology involved has really not changed that much since, except for the introduction of much more advanced semiconductor devices. At the time, the Swiss Air Force was in the process of reequipping for the 1970s and '80s. It needed a new fighter-bomber. The government decided to go for the French-designed Mirage III, and had further decided to have it built under license in Switzerland by a competitor of ours, Sulzer Brothers A.G. in Winterthur."

"The point, the point," said the professor, and this time I must say I was rooting for him.

"The point is going to have to wait a minute," replied Schmiedheine, and then went on, undeterred by the heckling. "The Israelis had also decided to use the Mirage III

179

as the mainstay of *their* air force. Not a bad decision, as it turned out. For they won the Six Day War in 1967 essentially because of their technological superiority in the air, and this superiority was based on the Mirage III. In spite of that, quite a few were lost in battle. But when the Israelis wanted to replace them, de Gaulle—for reasons known only to himself, and he has taken them to the grave—blocked the further export of these planes. The Israelis had made the fatal mistake of trusting the French—buying them directly from France instead of building them in Israel under license. So what to do?"

"Go on, go on," urged the professor.

"Steal the technology and start building them. Okay—they got to this man Frauenknecht at a conference in Paris. He was a very run-of-the-mill engineer at Sulzer. They paid him a couple of hundred thousand dollars, if I recall correctly. And this simple engineer—he was really nothing more than a technician, since he had never gone to university—single-handedly managed to transfer the entire technology of the Mirage III to Israel, including the most complicated components of the plane, not the least of which was the highly sophisticated engine capable of propelling the Mirage at Mach two point two. Total weight of the blueprints: *almost three tons.* So how did he do it?"

Now we were playing Agatha Christie over a dinner table in Switzerland on a cold December night.

"I recall the incident completely," said our host, "so you will have to leave me out."

"So do I," said the banker. "It was, in fact, the most despicable act of treason this country had endured since World War I. I never did understand why the Supreme Court gave him only four and a half years. He should have gotten life. Or the firing squad."

Bankers in Switzerland, as everywhere, have hard hearts.

"I remember the incident, but I must confess I forget how he did it," said Professor Neuhaus. "However, I think it is

180

fairly obvious. He must have been able to microfilm the plans somehow?"

"I agree," I said.

"Close," said Schmiedheine; "in fact, very close. But too obvious.

"The key to success was access. To get access, Frauen-knecht came up with a truly brilliant idea. He correctly pointed out to the managing director of the company that there was only one full set of backup plans in Switzerland for the Mirage, and if something happened to them, fire or whatever, it could be catastrophic for the production schedule. Secondly, and this was the original part: knowing the policy of frugality practiced at Sulzer Brothers, Frauenknecht had figured out that if the plans were microfilmed and even if now two copies were kept in separate places, not only would one gain reinsurance against the effects of a fire, but the space, and thus cost, required for the storage of the plans would now be infinitesimal compared with the space and cost required to store the full blueprints. Frauenknecht had figured it out exactly: 50,000 Swiss francs per annum.

"Well, the general manager of Sulzer, being Swiss, could hardly say no to that. Frauenknecht, of course, volunteered to supervise the job personally, and, of course, got the assignment."

"So he made three sets of microfilm instead of two," I persisted.

"No," said Schmiedheine. "That would have been impossible. Sulzer was, and is, very security-conscious. All microfilming in the plant is under constant surveillance and the strictest of controls. So how did he do it?"

Well, now it was slowly becoming interesting. Not very interesting, but at least modestly challenging.

"I give up," said Sabine, joining the conversation for the first time and rolling her eyes slightly at me after she said it.

I think Schmiedheine noticed the eye action, since he glared at Sabine—though not long at her eyes, since at precisely that moment one of the maids slipped a Kirschwasser under her bosom, causing the Swiss arms manufacturer's attention to move a foot or so south to the décolletage that gaped just inches above the white liquid in the tiny glass. But he was not to be deterred by licentiousness.

"I will tell you," he replied. "It was really a type of sleight of hand. Security, naturally, required that once microfilmed, the original plans be destroyed. The logical place to do that was at the town incinerator. Frauenknecht insisted on personally taking care of that also. However, on the way to the incinerator he dropped off the plans at a garage he had rented. In that garage he had stored three tons of old blueprints—scrap blueprints which he had acquired from the Swiss patent office in Bern, which was required by law to dispose of such plans once they had reached the fifty-year limit. Switch accomplished, he proceeded to the incinerator and burned the wrong blueprints. Once a month he would load up a van with the original plans and transfer them to another garage near the Swiss–German frontier, where they would be picked up by an Israeli agent, who would take them to a private airfield in south Germany, where an Israeli aircraft would be waiting to take them to Tel Aviv."

"Nice," I said. "So how did he get caught?"

"Someone opened the garage door by accident one day and noticed the blueprints—the real ones, not the substitutes."

"And?"

"Unfortunately, each blueprint was stamped in red with *Streng geheim!* Top secret! The guy called the police, and Frauenknecht—when he came in with the final load—was trapped."

"And the Israelis?"

"They used the plans to develop their own aircraft—the Kfir, or Young Lion. It is still one of the world's hottest aircraft even today."

"The point?" interjected the professor, who had sat through the entire monologue with growing impatience, mollified only by the fact that the maid had, by now, slipped the third glass of Kirschwasser in front of him.

"The point is that if a simple low-level technician like Frauenknecht could accomplish the total transfer of the technology of one of the world's most advanced military aircraft to Israel, how much easier will it be for the chairman of the board of a company, such as yours, Mr. Rogers, to transfer all the plans and know-how related to the construction of your cruise missile to West Germany—especially since your boss, Mr. Patterson, is known as a bit of a tyrant whose instructions are to be followed, immediately and totally, or else. Am I right, Mr. Rogers?"

"Half right," I replied. "I am not a technical man. I must admit that I thought the secret transfer of advanced technology, especially of an entire highly sophisticated weapons system, be it an aircraft or a missile, was somehow essentially impossible. That it was in any case beyond the capability of one man. So I was wrong.

"However—and gentlemen, I really do not think that there is any sense in further discussion of this subject beyond this point—we are not dealing with a matter that hinges on technical feasibility. What you gentlemen are talking about in regard to Missile Development Corporation and the chairman of that company, Mr. Patterson—and indirectly, whether you expressly state it or not, me—is that we are involved in an act of treason. That like your Frauenknecht, we are betraying our country. That we, for reasons not one of you has stated, are in the process of giving a historically irresponsible nation, Germany, the means by which it could start World War III and destroy us all. No one would do that without an absolutely compelling reason, without an overwhelming motivation. That is where your whole scenario falls apart. Why should we do such a thing?"

I had thought I could stop things right there, close the matter out with that rhetorical question. But the banker from Zurich did not consider the question rhetorical.

"Why?" he repeated. "I can give you not *a* reason but *the* reason: that your company is bankrupt as of this afternoon."

Sabine actually gasped at this revelation. And the faces of the men around the table suddenly turned stony.

"How do I know that?" he continued, now looking not at me but at his compatriots around the table. "Because some of our clients are shareholders in Missile Development Corporation. Thus our trust department automatically tracks the performance of your company. I checked with them before leaving the bank. They told me that today you lost out on the NATO contract that you had so desperately been counting on. They further told me that, given the financial condition of your company, without that NATO contract you are finished. Except—and now this is my opinion—except if someone like the Germans helps you out.

"So I am afraid that our 'scenario,' as you described it, does not fall apart because of lack of motivation. What we are now talking about is the ultimate motivation: self-preservation. And it was precisely that same motive, self-preservation, which induced us to come here tonight. That being so, I think the evening was very well spent. For we all now seem to agree that we Swiss can no longer depend upon America to defend us. What was left to determine was whether our neighbor to the north is going to be *able* to assume the protector role, that of guardian of Europe against the Russian bear. We now know that the answer to that question is yes. With the help of your missile, Mr. Rogers."

As far as I was concerned, that was now enough. The conversation had gone from amusing speculation to a dangerous, absurd, and totally unsubstantiated accusation.

"Somebody has been lying to you," I said, and the Zurich banker turned crimson at these words. "Not," I then said to him, "about our financial condition, nor about the extremely grave consequences which the NATO vote will have upon the future of our company. Your information in that regard was absolutely correct." His complexion began to return to its normal gray.

"What I am referring to," I continued, now addressing the entire table, "was your information about a deal with Germany. I can guarantee that no one at Missile Development Corporation—no one: not its chairman, its president, no one —has ever had any discussions whatsoever with anybody in Germany regarding any possible deal regarding our cruise missile and its technology and its possible transfer in return for help in solving our financial problems. On that, gentlemen, you have my word as a colleague in the Swiss academic fraternity."

Then I pushed my chair back from the table.

Sabine's father, visibly embarrassed by my show of emotion, started to say something, but was stopped by a move of Professor Neuhaus' hand.

"Herr Rogers," he said, "we accept your word. And we apologize for any innuendo that might have, inadvertently, reflected upon your honor."

"Hear, hear" was then murmured around the table, though it was not exactly voiced with anything resembling convincing fervor.

Sabine's father then rose, signaling that this very strange dinner was at an end. Nothing more was really said as all filed toward the door. Coats were donned, hands shaken all around. The three Swiss visitors—the professor, the banker, and the arms maker—disappeared into the December night, and the host withdrew to bed. Sabine offered to drive me back to the hotel, but I declined, suggesting instead that she call a cab. We stood there in the hall saying nothing until it arrived. Then I walked out into the chilled air numbed not by the sudden cold but by the realization of what had transpired during the final five minutes at the dinner table. I got into the cab, gave the driver his instructions, and then my mind began to work.

Conclusion number one: the whole thing had been a setup. Conclusion number two: its purpose had been to give me a signal, a very strong signal, that something very big was in the works, that the Swiss military/political/financial establishment knew that something very big was happening and had concluded, subject to verification, that it would have a profound effect upon Switzerland's future. Conclusion number three: Herb Patterson was behind whatever was going on, it no doubt involved the Germans, and it was some kind of deal that was designed to resolve our financial crisis.

So?

I hadn't managed to solve our problem, so why shouldn't Herb Patterson take a crack at it? So what if he had to cut a deal with the Germans? They were our allies, weren't they?

For God's sake, Patterson would never in a million years work out a deal unless he had the approval of everybody from the Pentagon to the State Department to the Oval Office.

Right?

So why all the drama this evening?

Because maybe the Swiss want in on whatever deal Patterson is trying to cut with the Germans. Hell, their Swiss francs are as good as any German marks. But that doesn't make sense either: the Pentagon would never allow any deal to be cut with a neutral like Switzerland involving a weapons system like the cruise missile. The only way the Swiss could be dealt in would be if Patterson were trying to do a deal here in Europe all on his own. If he were, naturally Contraves would like to get into the act in order to gain the technology; the Union Bank of Switzerland would like to be the lead bank on the financing; the professor would be there to convince the politicians about the merits of the deal. So the evening did make sense.

Except that it would involve treason.

And it was at that point that I found myself back in front of the Hotel Euler. I paid off the cab, walked into the bar, ordered a Chivas and plain water on the side, drank it, ordered a second, drank that, paid for the drinks, took the elevator up to the third floor, walked into my room, undressed, went to bed, and went to sleep.

It was too dangerous to think anymore.

14

I SLEPT FOR THIRTEEN HOURS, ordered a sandwich in the room, and took a four-hour walk from the hotel to the point where the Swiss, French, and German borders converge. By the time I arrived back, the latter half by taxi, it was getting dark. It was almost exactly the same time on that December 3 that Patterson's plane had landed in Germany.

I did not want to just let things lie where they had been left the prior evening. I wanted to talk out my fears and suspicions, I guess. Nancy would have been the ideal partner for this, but . . . I called Sabine. She had to stay late at the office, she said, but could probably make it over to the hotel between nine and ten. She turned up at nine thirty, I remember, and we went across the street to that restaurant downstairs in the Bahnhof—the one that has the best Café de Paris steak sauce of any eating place on earth—and arrived back in my room about a quarter after eleven just as the phone was ringing. It was, of course, Herr Doktor Amadeus Zimmerli with the news that he had just talked to Mr. Patterson and that we were going to be departing for Germany the next day, to meet with him there—exact destination unknown. He said he would call me reasonably early the next morning before he came to pick me up.

Sabine had been sitting in a chair by the window, leafing through a *Time* magazine—and listening to every word, of course.

"Who was that?" she asked.

"You know who," I answered.

"You are going with *him* to *Germany?*" she then asked, very rhetorically.

I shrugged.

"Is your boss, that Patterson man, also going to be there in Germany?"

I shrugged again.

And then she got mad, came over to stand right in front of me, and started to wag her finger in front of my face while she spoke.

"My father warned you. Remember? He told me to tell you that the Germans and that man Patterson were using you, and that if you had any sense left in your American head, you would get out of here and go back to California. So you're going to Germany instead! Well, if you do, believe me, I'm not going to have anything more to do with it, nor with you. You are absolutely hopeless." And she started walking toward the door.

"Wait just a minute," I said. This getting-up-and-walking-out routine of Sabine's—which was not new by the way; she had pulled that at least twenty times during our so-called relationship—anyway, it was getting on my nerves. Another thing getting on my nerves was receiving advice, second-hand, for the second time, from her sainted father.

"Before you disappear this last, final time from my life, just tell me what kind of act your family put together last night."

"What do you mean, act? And what is with the family

thing? Didn't I warn you—don't start on my father!" Now she was mad as hell.

"And why not? First I'm supposed to believe that he is the world's most ardent anti-German. I can recall the words that you were kind enough to pass on to me during our romantic lunch a week ago at the Bottminger Schloss. 'He cannot understand how Americans like you can be stupid enough to deal with the Germans.' That's what you told me. Right?"

She was still at the door, but at least she had now shut up. For the moment.

"So tell me, dear," I went on, "just how come he now thinks it so wonderful that the German military seems intent upon replacing the Americans as the defender of Switzerland? And while we're on the subject, just who the hell told him that Patterson and I were going to give the Germans our wonderful little missile for the sake of our financial security, our pensions, and all the other little goodies that were not spelled out in detail by your father and his pals?"

"You fucking well know who told him," she screamed. "Your pal Amadeus Zimmerli."

"Why would he do that?"

"How should I know? But if you want me to guess, just tell me."

"Guess."

"Because if the Germans are going to be able to make a deal with your boss on that missile, why not the Swiss too?"

"You forget one thing. Zimmerli works for us. The attorney–client relationship would never allow—"

"Frank!" she said. Then she sighed. "Frank," she repeated, "you should never have left the Midwest."

The mere fact that I happened to have been born in St. Louis and stayed there until the ripe age of four, when my parents moved to California, did not exactly affect my attitude toward life forever. But Sabine had this fixation. So why argue?

"I agree. I was so happy there," I replied. "But let's not get off the subject, which was Amadeus Zimmerli."

"Look," she then said, "I told you."

"What did you tell me?"

"That Zimmerli is a crook."

"Well, not exactly in those words."

"Come on, now, Frank," she said. "You just didn't want to know. And then there is your other friend—or maybe better said, your ex-friend—von Amsburg."

"Jeezus Christ, Sabine," I yelled, "Can't you get it into your noggin that I have never in my entire life met von Amsburg? Why do you keep coming back to it? I don't know the man. Period."

"That's not what my father thinks."

"Well, your father is wrong. Possibly for the first time in his life."

"All right. That makes it even worse," she said after a moment's pause.

"Makes what worse?" I asked.

"Do you really want to know what I think?" she asked, and then added, "Now."

"What's the 'now' mean?"

"It means that I accept what you say about von Amsburg. And it also means that I accept what you said at the end of the dinner last night—that you never were involved in the setting up of any deal with the Germans."

"Hold on right there for a minute," I said. "Do you mean that until now you didn't believe that? That is just a bit too much!"

"You are getting worked up, dear. So just calm down a minute. And then tell me this: Are you interested in what I now think or not?"

"Go ahead."

"First answer one question."

"Maybe. You are now playing Staatsanwalt. Right?"

"In regard to whatever you were and are involved in with

Amadeus Zimmerli, did he ever at any time tell you that he would bring you into contact with von Amsburg? For his assistance, or whatever?"

"This is off the record?" I mean, after all, she was a goddamn prosecuting attorney.

"Yes, dear," she answered.

"Okay. The answer is yes."

"Next question: Did your boss, the now famous Mr. Patterson, by any chance ever indicate to you that *he* knew Graf von Amsburg?"

"Also yes."

"Third and final question: Am I correct in believing that Amadeus Zimmerli had given you good reason to believe that the Germans, and thus NATO, would vote for your missile yesterday?"

"Again, yes."

"So we can now, I think, reduce things to two hypotheses: Either Zimmerli and von Amsburg and consorts, because there must be others involved, have been leading both you *and* Patterson down the garden path with the ultimate objective of creating a panic situation—like the pending bankruptcy the Union Bank referred to—hoping that you, or Patterson, or both of you would jump right into their laps. Okay? Or that Zimmerli, von Amsburg, and Patterson have been working together from the very beginning trying to set you up. For exactly what I don't know."

"Scratch the latter."

"Meaning the former has some merit?" she asked.

"I'm afraid that it might," I answered.

"Do you think Patterson may have sold out to them?"

"Maybe. I'll find out soon enough, won't I?"

"Only if you are stubborn and stupid enough to go to Germany with that crook, Zimmerli," she said.

"All right, now I'd suggest that *you* calm down. And this time I'd like *you* to answer a couple of *my* questions. Okay? And watch the language."

"Really?" And she pronounced it "Rilly."

"Your father and Zimmerli are friends, right?" I continued, ignoring her smart-ass behavior.

"I never said that," she answered. "What I *may* have said is that they see each other now and then because they both belong to the clique that runs this country."

"Let's back up slightly. You have implied that it would be reasonable to assume, as part of a working hypothesis, that your father got his information, about our so-called deal with the Germans regarding the transfer of the cruise-missile technology in return for a financial bailout, from Zimmerli?"

"I did not imply that. I said it."

"Good. Now, Miss Prosecuting Attorney, would you please tell me why your father, who must also know that Zimmerli is a crook, and who, one is led to believe, hates the Germans—why your saintly father would go along with whatever Zimmerli and von Amsburg might have cooked up with Patterson?"

"What do you mean?" Sabine asked.

"I mean why didn't he just blow the whistle on them? Go public. Tell Dan Rather."

"Who's Dan Rather?"

"Sabine, for Christ's sake. Why didn't he? If he had, instead of staging that crazy dinner party, this entire discussion would be superfluous. The deal would be dead."

"All right, I'll answer you," she said. "But I am sure that you are too American, my dear, to understand what I'm going to tell you."

I just let that one go by without comment.

"You see, the Swiss, or more precisely, Swiss men, put their country first, last and always—above anything, and I mean anything, else: wife, children, mistress, dog, you name it. When a majority decision is reached affecting Switzerland, there is no more debate. They close ranks, regardless of what their prior positions have been, and present a monolithic image to the rest of the world, the rest of the world being the enemy."

"Fair enough so far."

"Well, that's what seems to have happened in regard to your cruise missile, the Germans, Mr. Patterson, Switzerland's potential vested interest in all this—and you."

"That's too complicated for my Midwestern American mind."

"Let me try it again. Father tried to warn you, to allow you time to get out of this whole affair, because he likes you and hates the Germans."

"You're repeating yourself."

"I know. When you failed to take the warning, and when Contraves and the Union Bank of Switzerland and the rector of the University all decided that what was good for Germany was now also good for Switzerland—well, that was the consensus. And now my father has no choice but to close ranks with the rest of the establishment. And that leaves you, my dear, on your own."

"And the question is whether or not I am a big enough boy to cope with all of this on my own?"

"Exactly."

"Well, I am. And I will. Tomorrow. In Germany."

"What are you going to do?"

"I don't know," I answered, and that, unfortunately, was the truth.

"May I come along?" she then asked.

"No." And she did not argue this time.

"May I stay the night?"

"Yes."

About three in the morning, for some reason, we both woke up at the same time.

"Frank?"

"Yeah."

"Are you sorry?"

"No. And yes."

"Well, don't be. It was my fault."

I said nothing.

"Are you worried about Nancy?"

"Not worried. It's just that sometimes I wonder if I should not have let her lead her own life, of which she is very capable."

"And what would you have done without her?"

"Maybe married you."

"Don't be an ass, Frank. Go back to sleep."

"No. Why not?"

"Because women like me do not marry Midwestern Americans."

"Then what are you doing here?"

"I'm here because I like you and because I also love you."

"But not enough to marry me?"

"Frank, now, listen. Nancy is obviously a very terrific woman. She needs you. You need her. You obviously like each other a lot. So don't rock the boat. I do not want to marry you. I never did. I never will. If you ever walked away from Nancy—by the way, and now that you've brought up the subject—you could forget about me. Immediately, absolutely, permanently."

"I never could figure you out, Sabine. If you didn't want to marry a Midwestern American, how come you didn't at least try to settle down with a nice Swiss husband from Bern or Luzern?"

"I've tried that. Twice during the last three years."

"Tried what?"

"To 'settle down with a nice Swiss husband,' as you so nicely put it, dear."

"Look—I'm not trying to pry, for God's sake. You don't have to tell me anything. It's your business—"

"Shut up, Frank, for God's sake. First you want me to get

196

married, and now you can't stand the idea that if I ever did, it would have to be to someone of the male gender."

"Did you live together?"

"Once, yes. The other time, no."

"Who were they?"

"Number one was a doctor. Surgeon. The other was with the Swiss Foreign Office. In Bern, by the way. How clever of you to know that."

"So you lived with a doctor."

"Just for two weeks. He was three years younger than I."

"Don't tell me any more."

"Oh, no, we don't stop here. You brought it up, buster. What I am trying to tell you is that I have now found out, finally and irrevocably, that I cannot put up with a situation in which I spend day after day after day with somebody who expects me to hang on his every dull word, admire his every dumb gesture, put up with his stupid antics in bed just because he's a man. Uh-uh. Not me. I want my peace and quiet. I like to be alone. I intend to enjoy my life my way. If that makes me selfish and egocentric, so be it. Some women are not meant to end up as wives, and I am definitely one of them. Got it?"

I said nothing.

"I want you in my life, Frank, and I'm going to try very hard to keep you. But on my terms. So no more talk about marriage. Okay?"

"It's a deal," I mumbled.

Then: "Frank?"

"Yeah."

"Do you think that one day the three of us might get together?"

That jolted me upright.

"In bed? Of all the crazy—"

She giggled.

"No, you silly man. Although—"

"Absolutely not!"

She giggled again.

"Come on, Frank. Don't be such a prude. I was just kidding. What I meant, and I meant it very seriously, is that I would like very much to get to know your Nancy better. She sounds like the kind of person I could get along with."

"I'm not sure that would work out."

"Would you mind if I called her sometime?"

"Look, Sabine, I don't want Nancy to get the idea that we're playing some sort of game with her. She is a very proud woman."

"I know. That's the very last sort of impression I would want to create. But still. Maybe someday it will all fall into place. I'd like that."

Then after about two minutes:

"Frank?"

"Yeah?"

"If I ever got sick, really sick, would you come?"

"Jeezus, Sabine," I said, feeling suddenly cold all over, "is something wrong?"

I turned on the light and looked at her.

"No. Of course not. It's just that I've got you back, in a way, and I don't want to ever completely lose you again."

"I'd come so fast, Sabine, you wouldn't believe it!"

"Sure?"

"Sure."

She reached over and put out the light again.

"Would you hold me until I go back to sleep?" she asked.

"Yes."

And I did.

PART THREE

SECTION TEN

15

WEDNESDAY, DECEMBER 4, 1985. Sabine and I had a subdued breakfast at seven. She left for the office at seven thirty. She also left four phone numbers, written on a Hotel Euler scratch pad, in my passport. When we hugged good-bye, I must say that I had some rather deep feelings for the girl— or woman, I guess you have to say now. She was a smart-ass beyond any doubt, and she tended to be a bit talkative and loud, and she also tended to mind my business a bit too much. But she was a good person—maybe a bit too good for me.

At eight thirty, my hotshot crooked double-crossing Swiss lawyer called, and asked if it would be convenient if he picked me up at ten. I said it would. He said that I should probably pack everything and check out. I asked why. And he said because I would not be coming back. Exactly in those words. Which sounded just slightly ominous. But what the hell: Sabine had gotten me so riled up with her various underworld theories that anything Zimmerli said would no doubt have worked me up.

A few minutes later, Russ Egan called from the plant in Sunnyvale. Now, *he* was *really* worked up. Said he had called at least thirty different hotels in Europe trying to track me down. Finally Patterson's secretary had suggested the Hotel Euler in Basel—which, I reflected, no doubt meant that Patterson would soon have a new secretary.

Egan's problem? Clay Dillon of Citibank had called and had sounded very, very nervous. Dillon had said he was expecting me to show up for lunch today. To be more precise, I had promised to meet Dillon in his office at noon. Was that right? Egan wanted to know. It was right, but it would be a little hard for me to make it, I explained, unless I were just about to board the Concorde from London, which I was not. So what should Egan do? Call Dillon, I suggested, and say that I would be a bit late. By, say, a couple of days. And what if he asked about the cruise-missile project? Stonewall, I said. I had never used that expression before in my life, because it had never seemed to fit any situation I had yet come up against. It fitted now. Egan had a further question: Did I by any chance know where Mr. Patterson was? Dillon had mentioned that he would like very much to talk to him. No idea, I replied. Stonewall on that too.

Following instructions, I then packed and went down to the lobby to check out. Amadeus Zimmerli showed up right on schedule, driving a Peugeot. Once my bags were in the trunk, we both got into the car quickly, since it was starting to get really cold outside. When I mentioned the change in weather, Zimmerli, as always, had a ready answer.

"Santa Claus comes in two days. It is always cold then."

In Switzerland Santa comes a bit earlier than he does in America—namely, on December 6. He shows up with a black book from which he reads off the list of sins committed by the junior members of Swiss families. He also comes armed with a switch made of branches, since crime and punishment

202

still go very much hand in hand in Switzerland. Once the threats are over, Santa reaches for the third object he has toted in with him, a burlap bag, and simply dumps its contents on the floor, rug, or whatever is down there—candy, nuts, mandarins, and of late, plastic toys. One final note: according to the Swiss, Sankt Nikolaus lives in the Black Forest.

When I started to mull all this over, searching for symbolic meaning, I started to—I guess the best word for it would be "giggle." Here I was, president of an American aerospace company in the cruise-missile business being driven by my double-crossing bent Swiss attorney to the Black Forest to see—well, certainly not Santa Claus. But the question was Who? And would it be the switch or the bag of goodies?

It was snowing when we entered the outskirts of Sankt Blasien, and so the village looked just the way a village in the Black Forest should look: chaletlike houses; the monastery and the old church with the onion tower; the confiserie with, naturally, *Schwarzwälderkuchen* in the window—and old people in the streets. Funny thing that. When I was studying in Basel, we used to go over to the Black Forest fairly often—sometimes to ski on the Feldberg in the winter, and often to just walk or hike around Titisee and Sankt Blasien in the summer—and it seemed to me that the only young people one ever saw were visitors or tourists like ourselves. Not only were the locals all old, but the women still dressed in either long black dresses during the week or, on Sundays and religious holidays, in the Black Forest *Tracht* composed of long blue polka-dot dresses, white blouses with puffed sleeves—the sort of thing one identifies with Snow White.

Snow White it was not, however, who was awaiting us—by chance, no doubt—as we drove up in front of the Gasthof zum Hirschen. Nor were there any of the seven dwarfs. Both men were well over six feet tall. One I knew, and I had fully expected and hoped that he would be there: my boss and mentor, Mr. Herbert Patterson. He was dressed as if he had just stepped out of his office in Sunnyvale, California. The man beside him looked as if he were about to set off for a tramp around the woods: *Lederhosen*, for God's sake, green stockings, laced boots, and even a hat with a feather in it. But ridiculous he did not look. In fact, at second glance he appeared to be, at the very least, Bürgermeister of Sankt Blasien and at the very most a stray member of the Habsburg clan, which still has a few castles in the region. The moment we stepped out of the car, Patterson came rushing over. Not to me, but to Zimmerli.

"Amadeus!" he gushed. "How good to see you again. It's been a long time."

"About seven years," replied Zimmerli. Then he turned to the man in the *Lederhosen*, who had also approached us. To my amazement, Zimmerli actually bowed his head—ever so slightly, but nevertheless giving a clear sign of subservience: just about the last thing I ever expected to witness in our hotshot Swiss lawyer. The man shook his hand without a word, then turned to me.

"You must be Mr. Rogers. My name is von Amsburg. Welcome. I shall try to ensure that your stay in this part of our country is as enjoyable as possible. Do let me help you with your bags."

Patterson, who had put a hand on my shoulder as his only greeting, had no choice but to join the Foreign Minister of West Germany in toting our bags into the hotel—no doubt the first time he had ever had a suitcase in his hands in many a year. When I approached the desk in the lobby in order to sign in, von Amsburg told me that it would not be necessary, handed over my bag to the elderly bellman, told me that I was in room 14, and said that they would be expecting me in the bar in about fifteen minutes. It was quite obvious who the man in charge was—and who it was not: Herb Patterson obviously belonged to the latter class.

Fifteen minutes later I entered the bar, although it was really not a bar, but rather a *Bierstube*—lots of antlers mounted on lots of wood, and full of locals having their first brews of the day.

"Will you also have one?" von Amsburg asked after he had waved me over to the table at which he and Patterson were sitting. No sign of Zimmerli, who had disappeared to a room down the hall from mine. By "one" he meant a stein of rather foamy beer. He and Patterson each had one in front of him— no doubt another first for my boss, who had touched nothing but hard liquor and expensive wine since I had known him. But it seemed to be follow-the-leader today, and if our German leader drank beer, we Americans also drank beer. After all, we were in his country.

"Now," von Amsburg said, once I was settled in, "let me start to explain, and from the look on your face, Mr. Rogers, I have the feeling that you are of the opinion that an explanation is rather long overdue."

"In that assumption, sir, you are absolutely correct," I answered, and halfway through it I looked right into the eyes of Herb Patterson. And saw nothing. So back to the German.

"Well, let me begin," continued von Amsburg, "by explaining how Mr. Patterson and I first became acquainted. And I am going to tell you this, Mr. Rogers, not to just make some conversation: the circumstances of our getting acquainted have a very direct bearing upon why we are here today. You know the Bohemian Grove, of course."

Of course I did. But let me explain in case you might not. "The Grove," as members refer to it, is the summer adjunct of the Bohemian Club situated in downtown San Francisco— the city's number two club, since it ranks, of course, behind the Pacific Union Club up on Nob Hill. It has about two thousand members, including most of those who count in

Baghdad-by-the-Bay, plus a lot of young lawyers and stock-brokers who would like to think they count.

The Grove is located about fifty miles north of the city, on the Russian River about ten miles from where it empties into the Pacific Ocean. It consists of a magnificent grove of pri-meval redwoods and includes a lake, a natural amphitheater that can seat thousands, and a swimming hole on the river. But the centers of activity are the "camps," which are really nothing more than clusters of large wooden cabins, or chalets, or whatever, with lots of bunks for sleeping, kitchens, dining tables, and, most important of all, bars, since the time mem-bers spend up there is mostly spent drinking, usually until two or three in the morning. They periodically piss on the nearest tree, and then go back to drinking. No women al-lowed, not even hookers. For those you have to go outside the grove proper, to the adjacent town of Guerneville.

The two big weeks at The Grove begin in the middle of July. The entertainment ranges from lectures by Nobel Prize winners, of whom dozens are members, to music provided by the likes of George Shearing or Benny Goodman.

But the real attraction of The Grove in the second half of July is the opportunity to rub shoulders with the big-name members and honorary members, who start with Presidents and former Presidents of the United States, Secretaries and former Secretaries of State, the heads of the top hundred of the Fortune Five Hundred, the heads of the twenty largest banks in the United States—and include special guests who come in from all corners of the world: kings, princes, shahs when there were still shahs, premiers. They fly into the Santa Rosa airport in their jets, ranging from small Lears to the 707 that Kissinger used to come in on when he was running the State Department. There is still a picture of it in the lobby of the Santa Rosa airport.

The camp of camps, where the Jerry Fords and Prince Bernhards and Henry Fords and Helmut Schmidts and An-thony Edens—the list never ends—would stay, is the last camp on the left as you walk down the main trail which dead-ends at the river. It is, for example, the camp where Eisenhower and Nixon met for the first time, in 1950 if my memory serves me correctly. To be sure, the place where the Nixon-Eisenhower partnership began would probably merit only a very small footnote in some obscure history book produced under the pressure of publish or perish. However, something much more momentous occurred at the Bohemian Grove eight years prior to that, in 1942, an event that deserves at least a full paragraph in any history of the modern world. And that was the incident to which von Amsburg referred.

"You remember," he said to me, "what happened there during the war. It resulted in victory for the democracies because it led to the defeat of the fascist powers—Japan, Italy, and, of course, ourselves. Well, I do not want to exaggerate, but I feel that the result of my having met Herb Patterson at the Bohemian Grove in 1965 may very well now be leading toward an equally important historic result."

I said nothing, but the old mind was working. And not liking. For that reference to that incident in 1942, and the parallel that was being drawn, were, to put it mildly, ominous.

Because in September of 1942 it was Ernest Lawrence, James Conant, Arthur Compton, Robert Oppenheimer, Edward Teller, and eight others who had gotten together there. Do these names ring a small bell?

For me they definitely do. One night I sat between Reagan and Teller at some dinner, whose purpose I've forgotten, and afterward I told Herb Caen, the San Francisco columnist, that it had been a little scary sitting between Eddie who was going to make 'em and Ronnie who was going to drop 'em.

Well, that did not exactly make points with Ronnie. But so what? This was 1985, and Ronnie was just a memory. But what happened in 1942 at The Grove, though also just a memory, was not exactly one that was also eminently insignificant. For it was those men who put together the program that led to the production, testing, and dropping on Hiroshima of the atomic bomb.

Why at the Bohemian Grove? Because if the critical mass of Oppenheimer, Conant, and Lawrence had ever been known to come together in one place, then the people in the physics departments of the universities of Göttingen and Tübingen and Tokyo would have known, instantaneously, that the atomic age had dawned in America. But the last place anybody would have looked would have been the River Clubhouse in that Bohemian Grove of Decadence on the Russian River in California.

So the world got the bomb. So what? If no one can deliver it, why worry? The Pakistanis and the Indians and the South Africans and the Israelis have the bomb now. How can they deliver it on targets that count? They can't.

But what if they could? That, my friends, is really what separated the nuclear men from the nuclear boys in 1985: the delivery system. And at the Bohemian Grove in 1965, Graf von Amsburg had met his future supplier of just such a delivery system: Herb Patterson. But that is getting slightly ahead of the conversation that day in the *Bierstube* in the Black Forest. But just slightly.

"Who introduced you?" I asked the German Foreign Minister.

"I was with Franz Josef Strauss," he replied. "Both of us were guests of———."

Von Amsburg told me whom they were guests of, but I am not going to mention the name here; and believe me, this is the one and only time that I am going to censor my own story. The point is that the gentleman involved had absolutely nothing—I stress *nothing*—to do with the conspiracy that began at The Grove that summer. So why drag him into this?

"So was Larry Metcalf," von Amsburg continued, and when he said that name, both his and Herb Patterson's eyes seemed to squint. As well they should have. Larry Metcalf, as you all know, is now the man closest to the President of the United States, is the current White House Chief of Staff, is what all modern Presidents seem to need—a guy who fixes things. Eisenhower had Sherman Adams, Nixon had Haldeman, Carter had Ham Jordan, Reagan had Ed Meese. And so forth.

"Metcalf liked Strauss' ideas a lot." He paused . . . and added: "Larry might join us a little later."

"I see" was my only answer. I waited for one of them to continue. But nobody did. Both just sat there waiting for me.

"So what is all this about?" I asked.

"It's about two things, Frank," Patterson said. "Two very important things—namely, the survival of our company and the survival of what the goddamned West is all about."

"How's the company going to survive?" I then asked. "No cruise-missile project, no money. We're broke, Herb."

"Not anymore. Or at least, we won't be after today. I've been working damn near without interruption for the past three days putting together a deal, Frank. We'll be getting one point seven five billion dollars to tide us over until we've developed something to take the place of the cruise missile."

"Who's giving you that amount of money?"

"*They* are," Patterson answered, his eyes shifting first to von Amsburg and then back to me.

"I see," I said.

And right then the seventy-two-year-old bellman came in to tell von Amsburg that he had an urgent phone call. From Bonn, he added. Von Amsburg said it would take only a few minutes, and left.

Leaving Herb Patterson and me alone for the first time since this whole unbelievable thing had started.

"All right, Herb, just what is going on here?" I said, and I said it harshly and probably bitterly.

"Not what you think, Frank," he answered.

"You set me up from the beginning, didn't you?" I proceeded.

209

"That is exactly what I thought you would say," Patterson replied. "And you are wrong. Now shut up, for Christ's sake, and let me explain before that goddamn German comes back."

"It had better be good, Herb."

"It is, and it isn't. But it's true. When I sent you off to Europe to try to swing that vote in NATO it was absolutely genuine. I thought that with the help of our man in Switzerland and his friends in Benelux and Germany we could get that NATO contract."

"They took the money, Herb," I answered.

"I know they took the money," he said. "But they double-crossed us."

I had never expected Patterson to say *that*.

"Hold on," I then said. "Do you mean to sit there and tell me that they also double-crossed *you?*"

"Of course."

"How?"

"I got a call from von Amsburg. He said that there was no way that he could find to influence the vote in our direction, as much as he wanted to. The generals and bureaucrats had decided to go for General Dynamics and that was that. It was the bureaucrats who crossed us up. Double-crossed us, if you like. And von Amsburg couldn't do anything about it."

My look of deep skepticism kept him talking.

"Look, Frank, the same thing could have happened in our country. Everybody overestimates that real power a Secretary of Defense or Secretary of anything has over his department. Ninety percent of the decisions he makes are really nothing more than *faits accomplis* fed to him by the people in the Pentagon who were there before him and will be there after him. It's the same here."

"So you were saying that you got a call from von Amsburg," I said.

"Exactly. Right after the vote; and Frank—I called you in Basel right after I talked to him. Remember that."

"I remember."

"All right. What von Amsburg proposed was this: his government and some of their friends in finance and industry would perhaps be interested in bailing us out."

"With one point seven five billion dollars," I said.

"Well, the figure was not mentioned then. Just the principle."

"All right, I track you so far. Now answer me this, Herb: what exactly did von Amsburg suggest as the *quid pro quo* for that not-yet-mentioned one point seven five billion?"

"Our cruise missile," he answered, and to his credit, he was not exactly beating around any bushes. "The entire technology of our missile, including a few prototypes."

"Hold on right there. I want to clear up a few minor points that still puzzle me before I get to the big ones."

"Go ahead," Patterson replied.

"Are you really saying that the Germans—von Amsburg and his pals Dr. Amadeus Zimmerli, René Van der Kamp, Prince Léopold—led us all the way down the garden path on the NATO vote, then double-crossed us, and then—knowing the absolute vulnerability of our situation—proposed this so-called bailout?"

"That's the end result," answered Patterson. "Whether it was all planned that way I don't know. We'll never know."

"But this is incredible," I said. "If these bastards did that to you, why in hell are you here?"

"What's the alternative?"

"Bite the bullet. Work out a merger with Boeing or General Dynamics or even McDonnell Douglas."

"No, Frank." And that was it as far as Patterson was concerned. MDC was his baby and it was going to stay his baby. Regardless.

"Look, Herb," I said. "*You* may still be able to 'do business' with these people, but count me out. It's just not worth it. I mean, for God's sake, you are blandly suggesting that we essentially go into partnership with a foreign government that allowed itself to be bribed, took the money, and then double-crossed us, and that we just overlook such petty details and go on from here because the survival of MDC is more important than even the most basic of principles?"

"Easy, Frank, old boy," Patterson replied. "I'd suggest that you go just a wee bit lighter on the principle angle. I mean, who was the prince among men who bribed that foreign government—make that governments—in the first place?"

"Let's leave that be for the moment," I said.

"I'm afraid that we cannot 'leave that be' for this moment or any moment. That's now a fact of life, Frank."

And when he looked at me now, that slight hint of embarrassment which had been present in his general appearance and conduct since we had met here in the Black Forest was now totally gone. After all, we were birds of a feather, partners in crime.

"But that's only half the story," Patterson said. "I think you had better hear me out on the other half before you jump to any wrong conclusions, and especially before you seriously talk about 'counting me out.' I think you will see that you want to remain very much in."

"All right," I said. "Convince me."

"I am not going to try to convince anybody," Patterson said then, knowing that he was back in control of things and letting *me* know it. "You will have to convince yourself."

I said nothing.

"You must be wondering about Larry Metcalf," Patterson said.

"Right."

"Well, first let me tell you that if he comes he will not be here in any official capacity. He will come as a private individual. And if anybody ever asks, he was here to get a little rest at Baden-Baden, with a few side trips to the Black Forest."

"Just like the time Ham Jordan went down to Panama to work out things with the Shah."

"You're closer to the mark than you think, Frank."

"Why don't you just go on and tell me what Larry Metcalf wants here, and let me judge how close I am to any given mark for myself."

"Easy does it, Frank," Patterson said. "No use getting worked up. Okay. Let me tell you what happened. After I got the offer from von Amsburg about a potential bailout deal with Germany, I got to worrying a bit about the national-security aspects."

He paused and waved the waiter over to indicate that two more steins of beer were in order. They came right away, and Patterson then picked up where he had left off.

"I knew Metcalf had kept up his relationship with both Strauss and von Amsburg. And I'll tell you why. Because their thinking on where we seem to be heading in this world is very, very similar. And so is mine. And so is the thinking of one hell of a lot of other people—people who matter."

"For example?" I asked.

"Some of the true aristocracy of Europe. Baron Van der Kamp, for one. Von Habsburg, for yet another. Bernhard. Look, it's not just the Germans."

"Where did you guys get together to figure these things out?" I then asked.

"At the Bilderberg conferences. Or meetings of the Mont Pélerin Society. The Trilateral Commission."

"Come on, Herb. Don't bring up that old crap about the Trilateral Commission somehow running our lives as part of some big conspiracy and you are just acting as a messenger boy for David Rockefeller."

"I'm nobody's messenger boy, Frank. That much you fucking well ought to know by now. All I'm trying to tell you is that there has been a growing consensus among knowledgeable people of the international community that if things are allowed to continue to drift in the West, as they have been drifting under American leadership, then we are headed toward very big trouble very soon. Larry Metcalf shares our thinking. So does General Harms. So does Franz Josef Strauss. So do Graf von Amsburg and Prince Léopold and—"

"Okay. I've got the 'who' part. Now, what, just exactly, is the 'what.' What are you guys trying to do?" I asked.

"I'll make it fast, because von Amsburg is bound to be back in a couple of minutes. And I'm talking geopolitics. I know you sometimes think I'm just a crude old bastard, Frank, but every now and then I think a little.

"West Germany is the most important country in the world, by far, for the security of the United States. West Germany is 'our' protector of Europe. You mentioned Hamilton Jordan and the Shah. You were right. Just as Iran and the Shah were our protector of the Persian Gulf, West Germany is our guardian of Europe. The Shah was our policeman, we let him down, and look what happened: the whole of southwest Asia went to pieces. That was bad enough. But if Germany goes, then Europe goes and that's it.

"Well, Germany does not have to go. Strauss and von Amsburg are ready to take on the Russians—which is more than you can say, really say, about the United States these days. Strauss' German Army is at least twice as good as our army. If they're told to fight the Russians, they'll fight right down to the last man. You know our army, Frank. They are all so doped up they wouldn't know a war had started until it was half over. The Germans know what pitiful shape our military is in.

"And now I will come to the point. They know that if the Russians push, we have neither the will nor the means to push back. The Germans have the will. Now they want the rest of the means. Cruise missiles. And we agree they must have them."

"By 'we' you mean who?" I asked.

"I mean the White House. I mean General Harms. I mean Al Haig. I mean John J. McCloy. I mean Richard Nixon."

"You've talked to Nixon about this?" I asked.

"No. But he'd agree."

"You've talked to the President, then?" I asked further.

"I talked to Larry Metcalf. Which is the same."

"Uh-huh. Tell me a little more about Larry's response," I suggested.

"It was very straightforward. He feels that if we don't accommodate the Germans on this matter, they could make a deal with the Soviets. If you can't fight 'em, make as if you're joining 'em."

"I thought Strauss and his crowd hated the Russians."

"So did Hitler and his crowd."

"*Touché.* Go on."

"Well, the problem is that the American public is not ready for all this. They still think Germany is full of Nazis. Nor is Congress. Most of those dumb bastards wouldn't even be able to follow this conversation."

"So?"

"So if they're ultimately faced with a *fait accompli,* what are they going to do?"

"And Larry Metcalf is willing to assure Strauss and von Amsburg that the White House is not going to interfere. That the guys at the top would like to give their official blessing, but owing to political circumstances can, at least for now, only promise that they're going to look the other way.

"Well, he didn't exactly say it, but yes, Frank, that's my impression. I also talked by phone with General Harms in Baden-Baden yesterday, and Harms couldn't have been more supportive. Which is quite natural. As commander-in-chief of our NATO forces, he knows better than anybody that the only power that stands between the Soviets and the Atlantic are the Germans.

"So Frank," Patterson said, "I think that now, after you've heard who is involved in this . . ."

Von Amsburg was back.

"I'm sorry it took so long," he said. "It was the Chancellor. He asked me to extend his very best regards, Herb."

Patterson beamed at these words.

215

"He said that he got your invitation to join you at the Bohemian Grove next July as his guest. He plans to come."

Now Patterson was really pleased with himself. And I could not help reflecting on how the circle would close at The Grove, that idyllic spot which had given the world the atomic bomb and Richard Nixon and now was about to spawn a Franz Josef Strauss in command of a missile system that could destroy the Soviet Union. And all of us with it.

"Gentlemen," I said as I stood up. "I think my further presence here will really serve no purpose. You seem to have already worked everything out."

No beams from Patterson now.

"Sit down, Frank," he said. I guess the better word would be "ordered."

"Sorry, Herb."

"I think you had better sit down, Frank," said Patterson. "There are a few more details I really think you should know about before you leave—if indeed you really want to leave."

"It seems I've interrupted something," von Amsburg interjected. "I think it better I return a bit later." And left again.

"You can't walk away from this, Frank," Patterson said then, ignoring the German's exit.

"Why not?" I answered.

"Because we're not going to let you."

"We?"

"Yes, we. You are in this right up to your neck, Frank, and we've got it all in living color on videotape."

"What's that mean?"

"Your attempt to bribe three NATO governments. Your offer of twenty million dollars to the Belgian Minister of Economic Affairs. The works."

"Het Zoute."

"It's all in Zimmerli's safe in Basel. Where it will stay, believe me. Provided you cool off, Frank, and act sensibly."

"It won't work. If you pull that, everybody goes down with me."

"Like who?" Patterson asked.

I paused to think about that one.

"I am told," Patterson continued, "that the only people involved on the tape are Van der Kamp and yourself. I am further told that Monsieur Van der Kamp was acting upon instructions of the Belgian Ministry of Justice."

"Entrapment" was the only answer I could muster to that.

"Not in Belgium. Entrapment is a way of life there, I'm told."

"Look, let's be realistic," I said. "You try that on me and I'll blow the whistle on this whole setup here."

"Who's going to listen to a crook? Provided that crook would get a chance to blabber."

That last remark I did not like. In fact, I suddenly got a very funny feeling in the midriff. I had been standing the whole time. Now I sat down and thought very, very fast. Logic led to just one conclusion. Either I would play ball right now or I would disappear. Very quickly, very permanently, probably right here in the Black Forest, where whatever they did would occur under German jurisdiction, and that would be the end of that.

All right. Be careful. Go along with the Abscam-tape bluff of theirs. Don't give the slightest hint that you've thought it *all* the way through. Because even Patterson has obviously gone completely around the bend on this thing. Nobody and nothing is going to stop these guys now.

"Look, Herb," I said after almost a full minute of silence, "I don't like this business. I don't like what I've been hearing. But I'm not crazy either. I would never go public with all this. So why all the threats?"

"Frank, I didn't want to bring these things up. But—"

"What the hell," I said, interrupting him. "There's no use being naive. It's business. Right?"

"Exactly. It is also the right thing to do, Frank."

"Okay, I'll think it over."

"That's not good enough, Frank."

"What do you mean, Herb?" I asked.

"I mean you've got to make up your mind *now*," he answered. And when he said it there was a fanatical—yes, fanatical—look in his eyes that was goddamn scary, let me tell you. I was right. These guys would kill me!

"All right," I said. "I'm in. I'm damn reluctant—but I'm in."

"Are you absolutely sure, Frank?" Patterson asked me—those eyes, it seemed, penetrating right back into my brain. "There is no room whatsoever for any fun and games here. This is *extremely* serious business. You understand that?"

Boy, oh, boy! He almost said it out loud. Be very, very careful with this man, I thought. One little slip and it's going to be time for extreme unction.

"Of course I understand," I replied.

"If you're counted in, you are in forever. You understand that also?"

And how!

"Of course," I replied.

One more scan with the crazy eyes.

"Okay, why don't you drink the rest of your beer, Frank? I'm going to have a word with von Amsburg."

I'd passed the test. I drank. With a very shaky hand.

Patterson returned with the German less than three minutes later. I'd calmed down by then and was able to look von Amsburg right in the eye—his being icy-cold, not crazy—as one partner to another when he came up to shake my hand.

"I am so pleased that you have decided to work with us on this project after all. You won't regret it," he said. Then: "Some of the other gentlemen to be involved have arrived in the meantime. I shall explain our working procedure: we have decided to split into two working parties, a technical group and a financial one. The financial people are gathering in room 21, on the second floor, down the hall at the end. They are expecting you."

Patterson actually put his arm around me as the three of

us walked out of the bar together, side by side. Too bad there was not a little martial music in the background—music for fascists to walk to. We were now going to get to work making the world safe—not exactly safe for democracy: more like safe *from* democracy. And there I was, literally caught in the middle.

What a bloody mess. They had me by the balls. And the way things were going, they would soon have America by the balls. And then what would they do?

The answer to that was already becoming rather clear. These men on their white horses could suddenly start to dictate—and that's absolutely the right word: "dictate"—the course of Western foreign policy according to what they considered right, morally correct. What was really happening here was a major transfer of power from the United States to Germany. What was also happening here was treason: treason on a massive scale. They were going to try to do, in their bent way, what President Reagan had tried to do in a democratic way, and failed, because he had inherited a military situation and an economic situation that were *both* in such pathetic shape that *nobody* could have turned things around in four years. The logic behind what Patterson was doing, I guess, was that if Reagan couldn't do it, nobody in America could. Or would. So turn it over to the Germans! *They* would know how to take care of Russians.

But without Frank Rogers! I never did like Germans; I never trusted them; but that was not the point. I have *always* believed that morality *does* and *must* play a role in governmental policy, especially foreign policy. The United States, in spite of a few accidents like that of Vietnam, was the *only* nation that was able to maintain sufficient military power to stalemate the Russians indefinitely without using such power in an amoral fashion to subvert other nations to its will. That much I had learned at Georgetown, and that much I have continued to firmly believe all my life.

But how to stop these guys? If they got just one glimmer

of what was going through my head, there was now no doubt in my mind what they would do: have me shot and buried about twelve feet deep in the Black Forest. It would be so easy. Nobody even knew I was here. Except Sabine. But what could she do?

One thing was now totally clear: I had to get out of here pronto, before anybody came back to the subject of Frank Rogers and concluded that he represented too great a security risk. First get out, stay alive, and then see if somehow this could be stopped.

I'm not going to bother you with the details of the rest of that day in the Black Forest. I'll just sketch out what happened. I joined von Amsburg and the head of the Deutsche Bank in room 21, and believe me, I was put through the ringer. First, we checked out every number on our balance sheet, every footnote to that balance sheet, and every comment on every item and every footnote that had been made by our auditors. The upshot of the whole damn thing was that we reached the conclusion that with the cancellation of the NATO cruise-missile project, our tangible net worth per December 31, 1985, would be — $435 million—stress the negative.

We then picked up on the profit-and-loss statement. I was requested to quickly flesh out *pro forma* profit and loss projections and cash flow for fiscal 1986, 1987, and 1988, based on the assumption of an infusion of new capital of $1 billion. I made various assumptions about potential sales of both our advanced engine system and our guidance system to the rest of the aerospace industry and concluded that our cash-flow hemorrhage would most probably stop in the third quarter of 1987. But in the meantime, as our company adjusted to its new role as a subcontractor from that of a prime contractor, our cumulative negative cash flow would reach $1.6 billion. So it took hardly any genius to conclude that the $1-billion shot in the arm would not save the patient. We would need at least another $600 million, for a total German package of $2.35 billion, if the Deutsche Bank and its partners were to take out Citibank, and the three-quarters of a billion they had lent us.

Dr. Kreps shook his head when I put the final number on a piece of paper and showed it to him.

"We cannot swing that," he said. "Not with that kind of balance sheet you have. You look the way Chrysler did in 1981 and look what happened to them."

"That comparison simply does not wash," I countered. "Chrysler had to completely retool to get back into the car business, because it had fallen technologically so far behind the competition and the requirements of the market. Our problem is exactly the opposite. We are years ahead of the competition, and the market has not yet caught up with our products. It's going to take a couple of years for that to happen. But we are tooled up to produce now."

It was true. There was no doubt in my mind that during the remaining years of our century MDC would probably sell tens of thousands of engines and guidance systems to Boeing and General Dynamics and even Martin Marietta. The thing was, by the time they woke up to the fact that they needed our technology, we might no longer be there to supply it—at least as an independent company.

"You are probably right," said the German banker. "But it will be impossible to explain to our partner banks. They look at numbers. And there's something else. They all believe that there is safety in numbers. By that I mean, the more international banks involved in a deal such as this, the better. Because then if we need governmental assistance to bail us out should things go wrong, we have *all* major governments involved. The one true serious flaw in this package I now see is the fact that Citibank wants out. With them out, we all lose very significant influence in Washington—in fact, key influence—should something happen."

"The U.S. Government is not going to let Missile Development Corporation go belly up," I countered.

"Maybe not. But one cannot be totally sure. They came very close to letting Lockheed go out of business."

He was right.

"And if Citibank stayed in?" I asked.

"Is that a realistic possibility?" Kreps countered.

"Maybe. Maybe not. But what if?"

"Then we could manage it. In fact, that would mean that we would have to put together only one point six billion instead of the one point seven five mentioned last night by Mr. Patterson. *Ja.*"

"All right. Get me a phone," I said.

In Germany they do not *get* you a phone. You *go to* a phone, as God intended you to do. So I went to the phone, called the hotel operator, and instructed her to get me Clay Dillon, president of Citibank in New York. Dillon came on the line so fast you would have thought he was expecting the call.

"Where are you?" were his first words after I had introduced myself. I guess you could say that they were barked at me.

"Germany," I answered.

"Germany, huh?" No bark now.

"Yes, Clay. By the way, did Russ Egan call you apologizing for me about lunch today?"

"Yes, he did. Most thoughtful of you. What's happening in Germany?"

"I think we're solving our problem."

"Really? The only way my problem will be solved is when I get that seven hundred fifty million dollars, Frank."

"If you insist, Clay, I think it can be arranged before the end of the month."

"Let's be serious, Frank."

"I am."

"Who is going to come up with that amount of money— and give it to you guys, knowing where you are after NATO dumped your cruise missile Monday?"

"Some friends over here in the banking business."

"In Germany? Are you kidding? They wouldn't touch MDC with a barge pole."

"Want to bet?"

"Who?"

"Deutsche Bank."

"What are they proposing?"

"A recapitalization. They are willing to come in with one point six billion bridging money."

"Jesus Christ!"

Then: "Who are you talking to at the Deutsche Bank?" This time with skepticism back in his voice.

"Dr. Reinhardt Kreps," I replied.

"Jesus Christ!" And this time he really meant it.

"Why?" he then asked. And frankly, I did not quite know how to handle that one. But just then the door to room 21 opened and in marched Herb Patterson, followed by Larry Metcalf and General Harms.

"Tell you what, Clay: I'll let somebody else answer you. Herb Patterson and a few friends just walked in. Hold on."

I grabbed Patterson, explained who was on the line, what we were talking about, and what I was trying to achieve—namely, trot out the German refinancing deal and scare the hell out of Citibank: it was all of a sudden about to lose a very valuable client—one that was in the process of moving suddenly from hopelessly bankrupt to totally solvent.

Herb Patterson loved it. When he took the phone, instead of talking to Clay Dillon he asked where Walt was—Walt being Dillon's boss and the chairman of the board of New York's largest bank. Walt was apparently in a meeting. Herb told Clay to get Walt out of that meeting: it was important if Citibank still wanted to maintain a relationship with Missile Development Corporation.

Well, Walt was on the line in nothing flat. Herb told Walt that he wanted to talk to him in privacy, so he would be moving to another phone extension and that he should just hold on for a minute. Patterson laid down the phone and told von Amsburg to have the call shifted to his room. Von Amsburg said that only the telephone operator could do that, so Patterson told him to run downstairs and tell her. Von Amsburg hurried out of the room, Patterson grabbed Larry Metcalf and General Harms, and the three went out the door of room 21 having spent very little time there.

I was suddenly all alone in the room with Dr. Kreps. And neither of us really knew what to say. So I asked him if he knew a good restaurant in the vicinity that stayed open late. He suggested the Hotel Schwarzwald in Titisee, just a few kilometers north. He said the dining room overlooked the lake and served one of the best Sauerbratens in Germany, and he suggested I try a bottle of the local wine from Baden, a Riesling that was not great, but good, and was hardly available outside the region. He thought that I might get served as late as ten, which for Germany was very late indeed. But he suggested I call ahead to make sure. In fact, he said, if I didn't mind perhaps he might accompany me. He looked at his watch. It was about five o'clock. It was already dark outside. Our financial talks had been so intensive that none of us had noticed the time passing.

"If you agree, I will call over to Titisee now and make the reservation. For seven thirty, or maybe eight. I think there are still a few matters that Graf von Amsburg will want to cover this evening—provided things are now being worked out satisfactorily with your bank in New York," the German banker said.

He took up the phone, which was still lying there off the hook, but apparently now dead; jiggled the—whatever you call that thing you jiggle on phones; got the operator; and got the eight-o'clock reservation.

And just about then Herb Patterson burst back into the room.

"Who's been on that goddamn phone?" he bellowed.

Kreps looked at him as if he were some kind of ape that

had descended from one of the Black Forest's many trees. I didn't say anything but sort of nodded my head in the German banker's direction. Patterson calmed down.

"Of course. Sorry. Now I would appreciate it if you could pick up the phone again and talk to our bankers in New York, Dr. Kreps. We've got a conference call going here. Both the chairman and the president of Citibank are on the other end. I'll be on my phone down the hall. All you have to do is explain what you are prepared to do in regard to our bridging finance. I think Citibank will now want to stay in with their old credit facility."

Kreps picked up the phone; repeated in precise detail the status of our company's balance sheet, the *pro forma* projections we had arrived at in regard to the next three years' profit-and-loss and cash-flow situations in Missile Development Corporation, and the willingness of the Deutsche Bank to examine the possibility of putting together a syndicate to refinance our company to the tune of $1.6 billion on a three-year basis; and then listened for a while.

He then said, "We agree" and listened another minute or so.

"I think it would be better if one of you came to Frankfurt," he then said, followed by "perhaps exactly a week from today."

He listened again, said "Excellent," hung up, and turned to me.

"You were right, Mr. Rogers. They have agreed to stay in. So I have agreed to proceed with our refinancing. Mr. Dillon will come to Frankfurt next Wednesday, and we will jointly work out the conditions of the new loan agreement. He realizes that his loan must be subordinated to ours, so he will want to know our exact conditions. You understand that, of course. So, Mr. Rogers—we are now partners."

He stuck out his hand, and I took it.

One more step down the road to perdition.

Patterson burst back into the room, and there could really

be only one word to describe his condition now. Triumphant! He'd pulled it off once again. To the brink he had gone, yes, but now the future of his company, the legacy Herb Patterson would leave to the world, the best goddamn missile company on earth was assured.

He came right at me.

"I told you, Frank. I knew we could pull this off. And I'm going to repeat what I've told you twice in recent days: when we get back to Sunnyvale, the first thing I am now going to do is step down as chief executive officer. You're going to be the boss, Frank, and before this week is out. Let me tell you, the way you've handled yourself here makes me goddamn proud of you, boy." And Patterson had tears in his eyes and was not ashamed of it.

Von Amsburg was suddenly back in the room. And that meant the end of Patterson's moment of glory. For it was crystal clear that the Foreign Minister had played messenger boy for the American for the first and definitely last time in his life.

Von Amsburg went up to neither Patterson nor me but rather to Reinhardt Kreps, and to him he said the words "I have just spoken to the Chancellor. He has asked me to extend to you his thanks in the name of Deutschland."

And now Dr. Reinhardt Kreps got tears in his eyes.

Von Amsburg turned to us.

"Gentlemen, now that the financial side is settled, I think we should perhaps all get together in, say, an hour and meet with the technical people. I am told by Mr. Patterson that they have also had no difficulty in reaching agreement on the transfer of technology, and on a preliminary production program."

"That's right," said Patterson. "I think the only open question now is that of deployment. I for one would like to hear what your General Seefeldt has in mind. I've got our General Harms here, and I think he's got some pretty good ideas on the subject himself, and all of you should listen to him."

No mention of Larry Metcalf. I later found out that after Metcalf had had a long word with the chairman of the board of Citibank he had left as quietly as he had come. Mr. Fixit had fixed it once again.

One hour later we gathered on the main floor in the hotel's one and only conference room, which was small but sufficient in size to accommodate our evening session—the plenary session, I guess one could have termed it, of the German Cruise Missile Planning Committee—no, Joint Committee, in the American–German sense; or better yet, German–American, because we Yankees were a bit outnumbered, being only three. Herb Patterson, General Harms, and me—the arms producer, the general, and the money man. These were three of the essential components in the planning of any war, or threat of war. To be sure, the fourth, the political one, was lacking now that Larry Metcalf had gone. But he had no doubt left behind his assurances that the evening's proceedings would receive his blessing and therefore the blessing of the throne, the power behind which he represented.

The Germans had their strategic posts all manned, and well manned indeed. Von Amsburg was as close as you could get to the head of state without actually having Franz Josef Strauss physically present. Dr. Reinhardt Kreps represented the largest and most powerful bank on earth, the Deutsche Bank. His bank had overtaken the former world leader, Bank of America—an event that had gone largely unnoticed. If it had received wider publicity, perhaps the world, especially Americans, would have realized before it was too late that the German march to ascendancy was on the way to succeeding this time—after two abortive attempts during the first half of the century. But . . .

The military-industrial complex was, if anything, slightly overrepresented on the German side. For at six on the dot on that Wednesday evening, in filed, in this order: Herr Direktor Doktor Josef Schmidt, who ran Siemens A.G., the second-largest electronics concern on earth; Herr Professor Doktor Ernest Bosch, head of Messerschmitt-Bölkow-Blohm G.m.b.H., the firm that had a monopoly on the German aerospace industry; and finally General Lothar von Seefeldt, inspector general of the West German armed forces and their commander-in-chief.

Five Germans and three Americans who were in the process of changing the way the world was run.

Von Amsburg introduced Kreps, who reported on the outcome of the activities of the *Finanz* group. We had, of course, achieved 100-percent success.

Ernst Bosch told us all what the technical working group had accomplished. Or rather, what plan they had come up with.

Messerschmitt-Bölkow-Blohm G.m.b.H. would act as the prime contractor for the missile and also build the airframe. Siemens would produce both the engine and the guidance system. Von Amsburg's family firm in Bavaria—Nuremberg, to be precise—would produce the launching vehicles: very large *camions—Lastwagen, auf deutsch*—and later, specialized railroad cars—both equipped with launching ramps for the all-German ground-launched cruise missile.

The only item that could not be produced or reproduced from the plans to be flown over from Sunnyvale was the contour maps of the earth's surface, or at least that part of the earth's surface which would be of importance here: Western Europe, Eastern Europe, the Soviet Union, the Arctic, and just to be sure, Southwest Asia. Theoretically, one could direct a swarm of cruise missiles southeast from Bavaria and they could curve down through the Balkans, over Turkey, and even over Iran before they turned north to targets in the Asian part of the Soviet Union—specifically, the missile production and testing facilities down there.

Those maps could have been developed only by a nation with a highly specialized network of space satellites and the even more specialized contour-mapping equipment. The value of the finished product for the United States was such that when, in 1980, the British were considering trying to buy ground-launched cruise missiles from the United States to replace the outdated Polaris submarine-based ballistic missiles, one of the hang-ups was that the Pentagon refused to even consider releasing those maps to the British. In the end, the British opted for the Trident ballistic missile, at a total cost of about $12 billion, when they could, no doubt, have gotten a vastly superior system in the form of the cruise for half the price—had the American military trusted them with the advanced technology. But memories of Burgess and McLean have never died in America, and the strategic balance between the Soviet Union and the United States had become too delicate in the 1980s, in the opinion of the American defense planners, for them to take the slightest chance that their ace card, the cruise-missile potential, would be given to the enemy by even the most reliable of the few allies of the United States left in the world.

But Missile Development Corporation, naturally, had the maps. They were integral to the functioning of its guidance system. And to show his goodwill, and to accelerate the financial arrangements to the greatest degree possible, Herb Patterson had promised that one of MDC's air freighters would be landing in Frankfurt the following Monday with a full and complete working set of the maps built into the memory of our TERTRACK computer system.

How could Patterson do that? Simply by ordering that it be done. He ran Missile Development Corporation.

The rest was pretty easy. Siemens would be sending three men to Sunnyvale immediately to determine what blueprints, plans, manuals, and the like they needed to get into production. Likewise for Messerschmitt, which would be more interested in the machine tools and their plans in Sunnyvale than in end products.

Our electronic systems engineering would be the focal point of interest for Siemens, and in that regard one major hang-up had developed. There were a number of strategic electronic components that simply could not be produced by Siemens, since its lag in the production state of the art in the semiconductor field was still too great. Patterson said that Siemens should provide him as soon as possible with a list of those components, and he would simply order them directly from *his* suppliers in Silicon Valley—ostensibly for stocking against possible future production needs as a subcontractor to U.S. prime contractors—and simply transfer them to Siemens in Munich—at cost plus, naturally.

In regard to the launching vehicles, Von Amsburg's Nuremberg company would be on its own. Missile Development Corporation had no experience in that field. Von Amsburg, though not a technician, assured the group that his company could easily handle the task. It had built the launching vehicles for the Pershing I in Germany, so it was quite familiar with the engineering, which was basically quite simple.

There was, of course, one more component of the weapons system, and a rather important one: the warhead. To be more precise, the nuclear warhead. But for that the Germans did not need the help of the United States, or Missile Development Corporation, or anybody else. In this field they were perhaps the most advanced of any nation on earth, and everybody in that room knew it. Only a detail had thus far precluded them from applying their expertise to warheads: West Germany's signing of the nuclear-nonproliferation treaty in 1954. But that treaty was based upon the assumption that the two superpowers would be able to control their respective halves of the world. In 1985 that was no longer true. Thus the treaty now really represented nothing less than a mutual suicide pact of the signators. When such nations as India and Pakistan and Israel and South Africa and, now, Libya with the help of Pakistan had nuclear weapons, there could hardly be any question any longer that the 1954 pact was as obsolete as the Treaty of Versailles.

Thus the matter of nuclear warheads was covered that evening by two sentences spoken by Ernst Bosch of Siemens: "I have talked with some colleagues in our company and they assure me that once they know the technical parameters —weight, displacement, and so on—it will take them less than three months to tool up. They further assure me that we have more than sufficient weapons-grade plutonium potential available from the new reprocessing plant in Mannheim to meet almost any reasonable production schedule we might establish."

So there we were. The technical people stopped talking shortly before seven o'clock. Which left, really, only a couple of open questions. Timing—when could deployment begin? And the second, related question: how could such deployment take place and also remain secret?

General von Seefeldt, who, among other credentials, had an advanced degree in engineering from the Technische Hochschule in Stuttgart, and who, as already mentioned, had taken various trips to Sunnyvale to acquaint himself with our technology, and who, further, was quite familiar with the development and production capabilities of the German armaments firms present, Siemens, Messerschmitt, and Von Amsburg A.G., was introduced as the man most capable of answering these queries.

And he did, very succinctly.

"We shall need two thousand cruise missiles ultimately," he began. "But with only three hundred in place we will already have a credible deterrent as far as the Soviet Union is concerned. Why? Because in the initial stages of our deployment they will not have had time to develop any defense system whatsoever. Later, of course, penetration will become more difficult. Although it is really not of any military significance," he continued, "it might be worth noting that at present the Soviets have about 275 SS-20 medium-range missiles already deployed—with triple warheads, I might mention—and continue to deploy further missiles at the rate of about one per week. I mention this because, politically, some semblance of balance, or the appearance of balance, between the number of German and Soviet missiles *in situ* may be of importance. The one thing that one should never try to do is achieve the appearance of overwhelming superiority over the Soviets. The only time Russians fight well is when they feel they have been driven into a corner."

I noticed that our General Harms nodded very vigorously at these last words. Obviously both considered themselves more than a few cuts above the run-of-the-mill general.

I also noticed Patterson glancing at me now and then. Was he having second thoughts about my loyalty? Was he worried about my being in this room hearing this? What would happen to Nancy if they . . . I couldn't call her now. I should have done that from Basel. Brother, what a mess. What would she do if I suddenly just disappeared? Whom would she call? Patterson, of course, and she'd get a lot of help there! And then, maybe, Sabine.

"All right," General von Seefeldt was now saying, "what production schedule can be anticipated and when can deployment begin? Absolutely precise nobody can be at this point, but I anticipate that within twelve months we shall be in a position to be able to begin producing seven units a week, rising gradually to a peak output level of eleven per week after another twelve months. That means that we should have our target initial level of three hundred missiles available for deployment in about twenty-one months, or September of 1987."

He paused. No one seemed to want to ask any questions, so he went on.

"I have really just one point to cover: deployment. I feel that we should not involve ourselves in a program of gradual deployment. The chances of detection by the East Germans and thus the Soviets would be close to a hundred percent. I'm afraid that if that happened the Soviets would deliver an ultimatum, and that would be the end of this program. And perhaps more. No, deployment must occur literally overnight. So that *we* will be in a position to match any Soviet ultimatum with a fully credible counterultimatum. You agree?"

He had directed this question at General Harms, our commander of NATO, who had continued in the thinking-general tradition of General Haig. In fact, he was a protégé of that former assistant to Richard Nixon, who had run the United States very efficiently during the final Nixon months, had been rewarded with the post of Secretary of State under Reagan, and thus served as a model for thinking generals everywhere—especially the two with whom I was sharing a conference room and conspiracy in the Gasthof zum Hirschen in the heart of the Black Forest.

General Harms had the good sense to just nod and not say a word. Somebody might be running a tape. No doubt he'd learned that from his mentor, Haig, also.

And that was that! The meeting was over. The plot was set. Every character knew the role he was expected to play. And it was exactly 7 P.M. on the evening of Wednesday, December 4, 1985, when the countdown started.

Herb Patterson came over to tell me that he and von Amsburg and General Harms had a few things that they wanted to discuss further with General von Seefeldt on the know-how transfer procedures and scheduling and would I mind if I were left on my own for dinner? Maybe, he suggested, we could get together for a drink later on. I told him not to worry, that I planned on dining with Dr. Kreps, during which time we would also be attending to some of the financial details, and suggested that probably both of us would be rather pooped, especially Patterson, since he had been going for almost four straight days now, and that the prudent thing might be to get some sleep and get together first at breakfast. He agreed and we decided on eight o'clock the next morning over *Kaffee und Kuchen*.

"I'm going to book us back to San Francisco on a flight

later tomorrow," Patterson then said. "And on the way back we are both going to drink a lot, Frank, seeing as how you are about to become Missile Development Corporation's chief executive officer. We've both got something to celebrate. Right?"

He looked at me carefully when he said that, and I swear to God, that crazy look was back in his eyes. *He* might be going back to San Francisco on that plane. But would I? Get the hell out of here, Rogers, I said to myself. Fast!

"See you in the morning, Herb," I said as we all moved toward the door. Then I thought of something and called after him, "Herb, maybe Zimmerli would like to join us for dinner. Where can I reach him?"

"Forget it. He went home a couple of hours ago. His job's done."

16

TITISEE LOOKS JUST LIKE a miniature Lake Tahoe: blue waters surrounded by tall fir trees on steeply rising terrain. In December at Tahoe the snows start to fall on the peaks of the Sierras in neighboring Squaw Valley or Incline; and likewise, on that evening, six thousand miles away, the first really heavy snow began coming down on the Feldberg, the highest mountain in south Germany, just a few kilometers to the north of the lake. By the time Dr. Kreps and I arrived at the Hotel Schwarzwald on Titisee, snow showers had also started there.

"*Schön*," he said, as we got out of his BMW 2000.

"*Sehr schön*," I replied. "*Und so friedlich.*"

Peaceful. It was almost enough to make you break out into a few verses of "Stille Nacht, Heilige Nacht." Christmas was, after all, just three weeks off.

But my mind, I am afraid, was full of highly un-Christian thoughts. Such as how to steal Dr. Kreps's BMW and get the hell out of there. I figured that if I got away, the rest *might* begin to fall into place.

The dining room at the hotel was exquisite, the local wine good, and the conversation stimulating. Reinhardt Kreps was a highly intelligent man and also a nice man.

At ten we drove back around the lake and down the hill to Sankt Blasien, both of us, we assured each other, ready for a good night's sleep.

"Damn," I said, as we stepped out of the BMW in the parking lot behind the Gasthof zum Hirschen, "I forgot my overcoat."

Which was true. I had hung it up in the foyer of the restaurant and forgotten to reclaim it on the way out. Kreps had not worn one in the first place and so had not thought of it either.

"Reinhardt," I said then, "I know you're tired. Why don't you go to bed? If you allow, I'll just borrow your car, drive back and collect my coat, maybe have a whiskey nightcap as long as I'm at it in the bar up there, and then leave the keys in your front-desk box here at the Hirschen when I return."

He agreed. Reluctantly, but he agreed. Europeans—all Europeans; even very rich Europeans like Kreps—love their cars beyond belief, and if not too many of them are willing to lay down their lives for their country anymore, the vast majority would unhesitatingly do so for their Peugeot, Volvo, or BMW. So they *never* lend *anybody* their cars. But Kreps was hardly going to risk offending me to such a degree that evening that it might have had some unknown effect, perhaps, on the deal that had just been put together. So he handed over the keys, and disappeared into the Hirschen.

When the motor started—I already had visions of it, for some reason, failing to do so—I glanced at my watch, and it was exactly 10:17 P.M. The tank was full. I turned on the heater, pulled slowly past the Gasthof zum Hirschen, and after about thirty seconds floored it.

I again drove north, past Schluchsee to Titisee, and

stopped in front of the Hotel Schwarzwald. Leaving the engine of the BMW running, I whipped in, got my coat, whipped out, got back into the car, and headed for the frontier.

I reached the German–Swiss border at 12:35 A.M.

I knew that I would be on the list there, and sure enough, after the green-uniformed Swiss border guard had taken my passport he went inside, and reemerged three minutes later. When he handed the passport back to me, he shined a flashlight directly in my face, the bastard, and, keeping it there, grunted, "Okay." He watched as I drove off.

The streets of Basel after midnight at midweek in early December are totally deserted. People don't leave for work at seven thirty there; they *arrive*. Which means they all go to bed early the night before. Would you believe nine o'clock for some of them? Ten for most? And eleven for the wild and crazy ones?

I knew where I was headed in Basel, but was not quite sure how to get there. It had been quite a while since I had lived in that city. But thank God, little had changed. I followed the black-and-white signs indicating STADT ZENTRUM, came to the Wettstein bridge spanning the Rhine, and suddenly knew exactly where I was. When I came to the headquarters of the Swiss Bank Corporation, where I had so recently been taken for $20 million, I drove down the hill to the Barfuesserplatz—named after the church where the barefoot monks used to display their poverty and humility, traits no longer considered *en vogue* in Switzerland. In fact, Christianity itself was generally considered passé, so the church had been converted into a museum displaying medieval art and artifacts—suits of armor and crap like that. The traffic light was red, and when I pulled up to wait a cop was standing right there on the corner, about ten feet—no, six feet—from the car. He looked at the BMW, and his head went down slightly as he tried to take a look at its driver—me. My peripheral vision is, I guess, normal under normal circumstances, but that night, as the adrenaline started to flow, I was probably able to cover 360 degrees without moving my head one inch. And as I sat there for what seemed an hour, waiting for the light to change, I did not even breathe, much less move.

For all I knew, Herr Doktor Reinhardt Kreps couldn't sleep for worry about having lent out his pride and joy to a foreigner and had gone down to the parking lot to check it out.

But when it finally turned green, and I pulled ever so cautiously across the wide intersection, it seemed to me, as I kept my eyes glued to the mirror, that the cop did not bother to especially check my license plate and for sure, did not take out any pad on which to write the number down.

I therefore concluded that Reinhardt Kreps had slept on, and so I had at least seven hours—until my 8 A.M. appointment with Herb Patterson—to do my thing.

Which was what?

I didn't know exactly, but I knew where I would start: at Nadelberg 27. I drove the BMW up the hill past the city jail, then took a right past the university's main building, and pulled into the small parking lot in front of the Peterskirche —a church that was still a church.

It was now growing foggy. The temperature was sinking rapidly. At least, I had my overcoat back. I got out of the car, locked it, and put on the coat. I went down the alley to the right of the church; turned onto Nadelberg; went past a house where Erasmus of Rotterdam lived for a while in the early sixteenth century and where he used to entertain Hans Holbein, among others; and two houses farther, right at the top of Imbergaesslein—an alley which is just a series of steep steps leading straight down to the center of Basel—stopped before a four-story yellow stucco building. I pressed the buzzer beside the "v. Lathen" metal plate, and about ten seconds later a voice came out of the loudspeaker mounted in the outside wall.

Sharply: *"Um Gotteswille, was mechtesi zu daere Zyt?"*

"It's me," I said. "And for God's sake, keep it down and let me in."

She pushed the door-opener buzzer immediately, and I was through it, up the two flights of stairs, and in front of her apartment door in about 7.6 seconds. She was there waiting.

"You look funny, Frank," she said, pulling back slightly to look at me. "What's happened?"

"Let's go in," I said.

Once we were inside and she had turned up the lights in the living room, she again looked at me, carefully.

"You should not have gone, should you?" she asked, knowing full well that she had repeatedly warned me to stay away from the Black Forest and to go back to California.

"No. You were—"

"What happened?"

I sat down on the sofa, and began. As I told her, she got out some cheese and a bottle of Gewuerztraminer. And sat across the low onyx coffee table, listening.

And when I had finished, she came over and knelt in front of me, took both my hands, looked straight at me, and said, "My dear, I'm going to be very straightforward with you, okay? All right. I'm afraid you've made three big dumb mistakes in a row. Coming here in the first place on that hare-brained bribery mission; then going to Germany and committing yourself to the whole treasonous scheme instead of walking out; and, it seems to me most stupid of all, to pick up and run, in a stolen car, for God's sake. I mean, Frank, where are your brains? What are you going to do now?"

"I think I slowly know what I'm going to do. In fact, I knew more or less all along. But now it's getting clearer. I'm going to go public with all this and simply stop it," I said.

"Then you're finished, Frank," she said. "For life."

"I know it."

"What about Nancy?"

It is really something! Girlfriends invariably, but every

time, find some way of bringing up your wife even when she has nothing, but nothing, to do with the matter at hand. So:

"What does Nancy have to do with this?" I asked.

"How are you going to support her?"

"How should I know?"

"Will she stay with you?"

"How should I know?"

"What are going to go public with?"

"With just what I told you," I said.

"How much documentation were you able to bring back with you?"

"What do you mean, documentation?"

"Frank, let's try a little harder. *Documentation!* Proof. Pieces of paper linking Franz Joseph Strauss and Herb Patterson and one and a half billion dollars together—and linking them collectively to the Germans' getting the MDC cruise missile."

"I don't have any."

Now she let go of my hands, got up, walked over to the bar that separated the living room from the kitchen, lit a cigarette—by 1985 only women still smoked—and said, "Then forget it."

"But," I said, "I know where to get it."

"Where?" she asked.

"The safe of Herr Doktor Amadeus Zimmerli."

"Are you sure?"

"Well, that's where he keeps the bribery files."

"How's that going to help you?"

"What do you mean? It's against the law to bribe people, you know. At least, in our country."

"Well, who did the bribery?"

"You know full well who did it."

"Yeah. You!"

"Yeah. But under whose orders?"

"Prove it."

"Look, there's a dossier in that safe of Zimmerli's with the whole history of the shenanigans that Missile Development Corporation and Patterson were pulling for years and years in Libya and Iran and Pakistan and—"

"What years?"

"What's that got to do with it?"

"What years?" she repeated.

"Well, up to 1977."

"The statute of limitations has long since run out. Not just that. As far as I know, it wasn't even against the law back then. I mean, the American law!"

"Doesn't matter. I'll throw 'em to the press. I'll ruin that Patterson via the media, and that's the end of the German deal. They now depend exclusively on Patterson to deliver. Now that I'm out."

"You know what the Swiss call the kind of information you intend to go public with, Frank?"

"What?"

"'Kalte Kaffi'—cold coffee. Yesterday's news. Nobody cares what Patterson did ten years ago if it wasn't even against the law!"

"They sure as hell will care when they hear about what he's trying to pull now."

"You may be right," she said then, "although you'll never be able to touch anybody over here with that stuff."

"I'm not so sure. I think Der Spiegel might be interested."

"Only if you have proof that will stand up in a German court when Strauss sues them for a billion marks for slander."

"We'll see. My guess is that there's a hell of a lot more in Zimmerli's safe about this whole matter than you and I could even dream of—stuff that will make Missile Development Corporation's bribery dossier look harmless by comparison."

"You may be right again." She lit another cigarette.

"So this brings me to a couple of questions, Sabine"—and while I said that I remember looking at my watch and noting that it was already well past two in the morning.

I hesitated.

"So ask them," she said.

"Okay. Will you help me?"

"Yes," she said with not even one millisecond of hesitation.

"Thanks. All right, I'll tell you what I'm going to try to do. Tonight."

"All right—tell me."

"I'm going to go and get Zimmerli, and I'm going to haul him down to his office on Dufourstrasse, and I'm going to make him open that safe, and I'm going to take everything in there that I can carry. Well, everything that seems to, you know, apply."

"How are you going to persuade Zimmerli to go along with this?" she asked.

"I am going to borrow your gun, if I may. Dear."

"Frank," she said, "you are also a dear, and I love you, but you know full well that you have never used a pistol in your life, you probably don't even know how to load one, and if you did you would probably shoot yourself in the foot. Don't talk asinine."

"I'm not talking asinine. I mean it!"

"You could never shoot anybody and you know it."

"I'm not going to shoot anybody, for Christ's sake. I'm just going to kind of wave it at Zimmerli."

"Like in the movies."

"Like in the movies, yeah. What's wrong with that?"

"So what if Zimmerli doesn't buy your bluff?"

"You want to know what?"

"Yes."

"I'll whack him one. With this." And I held up my right fist. I'm a fairly big guy and I'm in reasonably good shape, and I won't lie to you and say that I was a heavyweight boxing champion in college but I did play football. And she knew it.

But do you know what Sabine did? She laughed! Though nicely.

"You wouldn't even hit that bastard, Zimmerli," she said.

"Look," I replied, "you might be right under any other circumstances, but not this time. I mean it."

I did mean it, and she now saw that I did.

"Just out of curiosity," she said then, "how did you know that I have a gun?"

"I didn't," I replied, "but it was a fairly logical guess. I don't think Swiss prosecuting attorneys, even female ones, are any more popular in terrorist circles than they are anywhere else in Europe. It seems that your type gets kneecapped rather regularly in Milan. So I figured they must let you arm yourselves."

"Well, this time you were right. Although it happened only last year and after a long debate."

That I also understood. I had lived in the country long enough to know that guns are taken very, very seriously in Switzerland. The reason is that there is a very powerful weapon in essentially every household. Every male Swiss is in the Army between the ages of seventeen and fifty-three, and during that time he keeps his government-issued *Sturmgewehr*—the Swiss-produced automatic rifle capable of killing dozens of people from one magazine. By law, each citizen soldier must also keep sufficient ammunition at home. Yet despite this proliferation of weapons, the murder rate by gunshot in Switzerland is virtually nil. Nobody, but nobody, would even think of putting the *Sturmgewehr* in the closet to anything but military use. Furthermore, it is essentially impossible to get a permit to buy any type of handgun, and even permits for hunting rifles are very carefully registered. In the Swiss cult of everyday living, guns are absolutely taboo.

But this was different. I was in the process of saving mankind from the German revanchists. And for that, I needed a gun—Sabine's gun.

"Well?" I asked her.

"No," she answered.

"'No'!" I said—in fact, to be more truthful, I yelled. "Don't be so fucking Swiss! I need the gun, Sabine, so come on."

"No," she repeated. "I can't give it to you. And that's that."

I knew she meant it and that there was no point in arguing any further.

So now what? Try to put yourself in my position that night. Logic and self-preservation dictated that I get at the documents in our Swiss lawyer's safe. Logic further indicated that the only way this could be accomplished was through the threat, and maybe the use, of force. Now—I grew up in a normal family where people sometimes argued, but never dreamed of ever applying force or even vaguely threatening its use. I had played football in college, as mentioned, but that was truly just a game. I was too young for the Korean war and too old for Vietnam, so I had no military experience that might have helped me out that night. I had never been robbed; nobody had ever attempted to mug me. The only, but only, experience I had ever had with true violence was at the movies or on the television screen. There Sabine was right.

But I still had to do something.

"Bluff it," Sabine then said, reading my mind fairly well.

"With what?"

"It doesn't matter. Anything that has a point that might be that of a gun—as long as you keep it in your pocket."

"Come on, for Christ's sake. That went out with Humphrey Bogart."

"Look, if there is one thing the Swiss believe about Americans—no, two things—it is that they are a very violent people and that they are gun-happy. I read recently that in the city of Oakland—not so far from where you lead your protected little life, dear—that last year, 1984, there were 207 murders within the city limits of Oakland, almost all committed with handguns. We have not had that many murders in Switzerland during the last twenty years! And we've got a population of six million people, and my guess is that there can't be more than a million in Oakland."

"So what has all that got to do with me?"

"If you say you've got a gun on you and if you are mad as hell, as I suspect you will be when you come face to face with Zimmerli again, he'll believe that you've got one, and he'll even believe that you might use it."

"Because I'm an American."

"That's right. And there is another reason why Europeans have had enough of the Americans: they are simply too crude for our tastes."

"Thanks a lot," I said.

"Well, it's true. So take advantage of it."

It was now two thirty in the morning.

"You are absolutely sure about the gun?" I said.

"Absolutely."

"Okay. Have you got a big wrench or something?"

"You don't need a wrench."

"Psychologically I need a wrench."

"I have a toolbox in the bedroom closet. I'll look."

She came back with a fairly hefty wrench.

"Okay. Where does Zimmerli live?" I asked.

"On the Bruderholz," she replied, "and his wife died a few years ago, they had no children, so all you will have to worry about is whether or not he has a vicious dog. The address is Arbedostrasse 19. I have a map in the bedroom. She got it, and showed me the route I should take.

"Now, let's assume that it works, that I get the documents and—"

"What are you going to do with Zimmerli?" she asked, interrupting me.

"Right. What am I going to do?"

"Lock him in a closet in his office is what I would do," she said.

"That's a good idea. That's what I'll do. Then what?"

"Get out of Europe fast," she said.

"Right. But from where?"

"I don't know. It depends upon what your pals in Germany decide to do when they get the good news about you."

"Don't you think they will be very, very careful about creating any public stir whatsoever?"

"I do. But that does not mean that they won't try to have you arrested very, very quietly."

"For what?"

"I don't know. They'll cook up something."

"That will take time, I think," I said, not totally convinced myself.

"Maybe," she said, "but I think that when the deed is done, if I were you I would certainly get out of Switzerland permanently and ditto for West Germany. They can arrest you in either place for simple theft—one BMW in Germany and a safe full of documents in Switzerland."

"I *borrowed* the car," I said.

"I know, dear."

"All right. So I'll go to Paris and take Pan Am back."

"It will take you all day to get there."

"What's closer?"

"Luxembourg."

"Luxembourg! That's the last place they'll be looking, too. But won't I have to stop in Iceland on the way over?"

"So what?" she said. "If they haven't heard about you yet in Luxembourg, they sure won't be looking for you in Iceland. Let's not get paranoid. You'll only be in the transit lounge there, anyway. No one will know."

"Hold on," I said. "Forget everything."

"Why?"

"Because the moment I cross the Swiss border into France on the way to Luxembourg your police would know, and as you told me a couple of weeks ago, the word goes up to Bonn instantaneously. They will think of Luxembourg then."

"You're right. So I'll take you over the border to France," she said.

"How?"

"Leave it to me."

I got up, and believe me, I was hyper as hell, and the knot in my stomach that was going to grow to the size of a basketball before the night was over was already forming.

"Where will we meet?" I asked.

"Where are you parked now?" she asked.

"In front of the Peterskirche."

"Same place," she said. "When?"

"At four," I said.

"I'll be there in my car," she said.

"Why two cars?"

"Because," she answered. "Now, if something goes wrong, telephone."

"All right."

I put on my trusty overcoat, slipped the wrench into the right side pocket—still not quite believing that I was actually going through with all this—pecked Sabine on the cheek, and went out the door before I got the shakes and made an ass of myself in front of her.

It took me precisely twelve minutes to reach Zimmerli's home. I drove by it and circled the block. All was quiet, so I parked the BMW directly across the street from number 19. Speed, I thought, was more important than discretion.

There was a short walk of perhaps ten meters leading to the door. There was a street lamp almost in front of the house, so I had no trouble finding the buzzer. I pressed it for about three seconds. Almost instantaneously a light shone out from a window on the second floor immediately above the entrance and me. The window was pushed open and it was Zimmerli's voice that said, very quietly, *"Waer isch do?"*

I backed up, looked up, and just said quietly, "It's me— Frank Rogers."

"Some trouble?"

"Yes. Patterson sent me."

"All right. Stay there; I'll be right down."

The light from above went out. A few seconds later the front hall light came on, the door opened, and there stood Herr Doktor Amadeus Zimmerli in his dressing gown. He extended his hand, and I shook it, without speaking. He obviously did not suspect anything as far as I was concerned.

As I stepped in the door, he asked another question: "Is Patterson in Basel too?"

"No. He's in Germany. They're still working out the technical details of the transfer. They've run into a problem." Implying that he could probably solve it.

"Of course, of course. Let's go into the living room," he said, not realizing that the problem was going to be me—and that it was unsolvable.

Once inside, he flicked a couple of light switches; the living-room lights went on just as the hall lights went out. The draperies were fully drawn in the living room. We had our privacy.

"May I take your coat, Frank?" he said, beginning to extend his arms in the expectation that I would allow him to help me out of it.

"No," I said, and feeling like a fool and convinced that it would never work but having no choice now but to keep going, went on, "in fact, Amadeus, I would suggest that we go and fetch *your* coat. We're going to your office."

His arms stopped in midair, and he backed up two steps.

"One more thing, Amadeus, and I hate to bring this up, but I've brought a weapon with me and I've got it in my overcoat pocket, and I am in a state of mind to use it if you don't do exactly what I tell you. Understand?"

"*Bist du wahnsinnig?*" he asked, turning first red in the face, and then white when I moved toward him.

"Not crazy at all. Just extremely angry. Now get your overcoat, Zimmerli, or I'm going to start getting rough right here and right now." I made a move toward him, and he backed up another three steps to avoid any physical contact.

"Have you been drinking?" he asked.

"No. Cold sober. And fully in control of myself, Zimmerli. Overcoat. Where is it?"

"Don't get—"

So this time I moved right in on him, grabbed the lapels of his dressing gown, and nearly lifted him off the ground with my left hand.

It wasn't even play-acting. Now that I was face to face with the gold-plated son-of-a-bitch, I had a really strong urge to teach him a little lesson.

"Enough," he said, and now he was definitely scared. "I'll get dressed."

"Nope. You'll get two things: your overcoat and your keys. And I expect that among the keys you will have one to your office building, one to your office, and one to the safe in your office. Three keys." I held up three fingers of my left hand, my right staying in the coat pocket and hanging on for dear life to the wrench in there.

"All right, all right," he said.

"So move," I said.

He walked back into the hall, where he put on the light, opened a closet door, and drew out a gray overcoat.

"Put it on," I said, and he did.

"The keys are upstairs," he said.

"So up we go," and this time I gave the pocket a little nudge with the wrench.

"Don't get nervous," he said.

"I'm not nervous," I replied. "I just don't have all night."

The keys were on the dresser in the bedroom situated right above the entrance. He picked them up and started to walk back out.

"Nope," I said. "Close the window, and then turn out the light."

249

He did. Downstairs he turned off the hall light, and also locked the front door once we were outside. I gave him a little shove in the direction of the street, and then another shove in the direction of the BMW.

"Now, real quiet," I said, as we both got into the automobile. I started the car; glanced at the house, which was just as dark and quiet as when I had first driven up; turned the next corner; and started back toward downtown.

"What went wrong?" he now asked.

I just kept driving.

"What do you want?"

"A few things in your safe. To be specific, the file—no, all files, plural—related to Missile Development Corporation; Aeroconsult; the twenty-million-dollar transaction we did so very recently at the Swiss Bank Corporation, including especially the correspondence between Aeroconsult and the Chancellor's office in Bonn; and—"

"But why?"

"Shut up. Also your files related to Herr von Amsburg, René Van der Kamp, and assorted Belgian and Dutch princes." Here I was, of course, both bluffing and fishing. Whether he even kept records on his dealings with those guys was questionable—at least, records that would make sense to a third party—and even if he did, why should he admit that they existed to me?

"And some videotapes," I added, to keep him off balance.

Just then a slow-moving car loomed up ahead of us in the fog. Zimmerli recognized the situation at exactly the same time I did, and so I said, "Don't!"

It was a police car, and as we approached it more closely, it moved toward the curb and stopped. I drove by without changing speed or looking over. I kept going, knowing that the cops were no doubt checking out the German license plate on the radio. When they pulled away from the curb —now almost three blocks behind me—and turned right at the next intersection, I knew the BMW was still clean and would remain that way until morning.

"Don't expect that kind of luck to last," Zimmerli said. "We have probably the most efficient police force in Europe. And I might add—in case you have any illusions about the Swiss—that our police are more interested in getting results than in observing niceties. Just the fact that you have the stupid audacity to use a gun will mean very big trouble for you, Rogers."

"The gun is going to mean even bigger trouble for you, Zimmerli, if you don't shut up."

"One question?" he persisted.

"Ask it. Then shut up," I said.

"All right—and I suggest that you listen carefully. Why don't you tell me what is bothering you? If you do, and if you are reasonable, I am sure we can work things out to your complete satisfaction."

I just kept driving.

"I know it is not money. It is the principle of what is going on. Right? Of course, and I agree. This thing with the Germans is dangerous. And we must all be concerned about what might happen if something goes wrong. And that will require insurance, whether we want to talk about it or not. We took care of *our* insurance needs with that videotape. Okay? Well, I think I can already assure you that we can take care of all *your* insurance needs too, whether it's a million or even two million."

"Shut your bloody mouth, Zimmerli. Just concentrate on the files and the tapes, on where they are in that safe of yours, and on what is going to happen to you if I don't get my hands on them in about five minutes from right now."

"Have it your way," he said, with a cockiness that seemed to me to be misplaced. Had I missed something?

We were on Dufourstrasse in less than five minutes, and I parked smack in front of the building in which his office was located. Why not? This was going to be either quick and easy, or so complicated it wouldn't matter.

We got through the front door and into the elevator without turning on any lights. On the third floor we also managed to get into his office suite with the help of the tiny penlight he had attached to his key chain. Then I figured that we had to risk it, since the only way I could be sure I was getting the type of damning evidence I was looking for would be if I could read it. Right?

"Let's have some light," I said, and he turned it on. The light itself seemed almost to scream out, and I guess shocked both of us, since we just stood there for a few seconds after it came on. But the silence continued, unbroken.

"The safe," I said.

Well, I'll tell you what happened then, and it's the truth. He knelt down, took out his safe key—in Switzerland many safes are still on a key and not a combination, for what reason I don't know—put it into the lock, turned it, put both hands on the small wheel, turned that, opened the safe door, reached in—and came out with a goddamn pistol!

"Don't!" I screamed.

And at the same time, I pushed him. Hard, of course. That gun was right in front of my face!

He pitched backward. And his head hit the edge of the safe door as he went down.

And then there was total silence.

"Okay, Zimmerli," I said. "Let's get on with it."

I said it, but I think I already knew.

I then knelt down beside him. No motion. I picked up his right hand and checked his pulse. There was none. I checked again. Nothing.

Dead!

It was beyond any doubt the worst moment in my entire life.

17

THE SAFE WAS WIDE OPEN; Zimmerli's little Walther PPK pistol had fallen out of his hand and was lying beside his right leg. I picked it up and put it in my left pocket. Why I do not know to this day.

Kneeling, I looked into the safe. Right in front, blocking my view of anything behind it, was a small black suitcase. So I pulled it out onto the floor. Behind it was a stack of dossiers. Just what I had been after. I pulled out a dozen and began looking at the labels. The first said BRAZIL—H.U.F. The next: GUMMI A.G. Then: HAMMER—VADUZ. But no MDC. I took out another stack. Same thing.

I stood up, kicked the suitcase, and then saw it in small print right on top of the damn thing: AEROCONSULT—1985. In Switzerland, *Ordnung* requires that everything be labeled. I picked it up and it was fairly heavy. That meant the jackpot. Zimmerli had no doubt been in the process of transferring everything to an even safer place. Paper is heavy, and from the feel of it he must have put in not just Aeroconsult

—1985 documents, but the whole history of his and Patterson's seedy relationship dating back right to the beginning.

That was what I had originally come for. So I took it firmly in hand and headed for the door. I turned off the light as I left my former Swiss attorney's office, but then discovered that I could not see a thing in the outside hall. So I turned it back on, went to the elevator, got in, pressed the ground-floor button, got out, and headed toward the Dufourstrasse entrance. No one beside the car outside; in fact, no one anywhere. It was even foggier than before, and very, very chilly. I placed the suitcase beside me on the front seat of the BMW and began to drive off.

Suddenly I thought I would have to throw up. In fact, and I hate to have to put this in, I pulled over to the curb—right in front of the Swiss Bank Corporation, I might add with a slight touch of pleasure—fell more than stepped out of the car, and did just that.

I was sweating and freezing at the same time now, my arms felt leaden, and my legs were shaking. True grit, right? Well, dammit, I was not exactly used to killing people and robbing safes! I was a guy who had spent most of his life in banking and was now president of an aerospace company, earning a third of a million dollars a year, with a wife, a home in Woodside, and a yacht—well, at least, a large sailing boat—moored in San Francisco Bay. And here I was in Switzerland, at 3:45 A.M., throwing up in the street because although the mind was still willing, the body had decided to rebel against the utter unreality of the situation.

But it was already sinking in: I had actually ended a man's existence. There was not, could not be, any excuse for that. Sure, he had pulled a gun on me. But he could have been bluffing, just as I had been bluffing minutes earlier with the wrench in my coat pocket. Sure, it had all happened so fast. But why had I had to push him so hard? I remember saying out loud then, "God, forgive me. Please. I did not want this."

But that did not make it go away. I sat there, as motion-

254

less as the dead man in the building up the street, desperately trying to find a mental way out. But there was none. I had ended a man's life for no compelling reason. And that was despicable!

Now what? Why had I taken all that stuff out of the safe? What good would it do now? How would I ever get home now? They would be after me in droves within hours, three or four at most.

Maybe the best thing would be to go right now to the police and tell them the truth, tell them exactly how it had happened. That it had been an unfortunate accident—no malice, no forethought, not intended, not foreseen, deeply regretted. Would they accept that? No, they wouldn't. They would go with me to look at the body and then they would charge me. With what? Involuntary manslaughter? No, manslaughter. Or maybe murder.

Then what? They'd lock me up. And from what I had heard, they could lock you up for quite a while in Switzerland without having to tell anybody. I would simply disappear for a while. And then what? Maybe—no, for sure—those men in Germany would learn about it. Probably right away. And then, maybe, somebody would arrange for an unfortunate suicide. That, I had heard, was the way they dealt with terrorists in Central Europe. And I was now a greater danger to the powers that be in Central Europe than were terrorists, because I was now in a position to bring down governments, to cause a complete reversal of their grab for real power in this world.

But where and how could I now do that?

Would those men in the Black Forest not be able to reach out, directly or through their friends, and grab me from almost anywhere now? After all, there were extradition treaties between all civilized nations. Assuming I could get on an airplane to London or Toronto, wouldn't I just get arrested there and put right on a return flight to Central Europe? How, I wondered, did that whole extradition thing really work? I had read about the process in novels; but what do the guys who write them really know about anything—at least in detail, reliable detail?

Dead end there. But maybe not. Vesco had gotten away when everybody seemed to be after him. How? The name of the game now was to buy time to think. Anything was obviously better than immediate arrest in Central Europe, to be possibly followed by involuntary suicide. So get moving, Rogers, I told myself. Quickly!

Miraculously, or at least, it seemed so to me, there was still absolutely no traffic whatever in the heart of downtown Basel. But I decided not to go back to the Barfuesserplatz and risk having the same policeman standing at the same corner down there observing the same BMW with the Frankfurt plates cruise by for the second time since midnight. So I took a U-turn in front of the Swiss Bank Corporation and headed back in the direction of the late Dr. Zimmerli's residence. After a lot of circuitous routing, I ended up in front of the Peterskirche after having shared the streets with only three other vehicles—two taxis and an old beat-up VW with Austrian plates.

It was now seven minutes after four on that early morning of Thursday, December 5, 1985. Sabine was waiting, but not in her Ferrari. It was a VW Golf—property, she explained much later, of the Justice Department of the Half-Canton of Basel-Stadt, for which she worked as assistant prosecuting attorney.

"How did it go?" she immediately asked after I had parked the BMW and gone over to her car.

"Not good," I said.

"Police?"

"No, worse," I answered.

She looked at me and then said, "Later. Let's get going before people start leaving for work. Tell me later. Just follow at a bit of a distance."

I got back into the BMW and did just that. Sabine was

proving to be more loyal, frankly, than I would ever have expected or suspected, even when we had been very thick a few years before. Girlfriends, after all, are not exactly supposed to rank high in the loyalty category. These days, or so I hear and read, they go through men at the rate of one or two a year, at least in the big cities. I wondered what she would do, however, when she heard what had really happened. I also wondered what I would do. There was, after all, a limit, a very definite limit, as to how much further I could drag her into this. I mean, if she got caught with me now, it would mess up the rest of her life almost as much as mine was already fouled up!

Traffic was beginning to appear on the streets. There were no streetcars or buses, but I guess the people who would be driving them soon were now starting to go to the depots in their cars. It was very foggy, and once you were outside the range of the street lights—half of which had been, it seemed, permanently turned off to save energy—it was pitch black. As we hit the outlying parts of the city of Basel, Sabine's VW started to speed up a bit.

Now . . . in case you ever want to leave Switzerland and enter France without having to bother about such details as Emigration and Customs checks, I'll tell you how to do it.

If you are in the center of Basel, just look for a sign, black and white, that says ZOOLOGISCHER GARTEN—the zoo. It's about ten blocks from the heart of downtown. When you get to the main entrance go slightly up the hill and take a left. You are now on Oberwilerstrasse, and from here, as they say in Switzerland, you can't miss it. Just go straight ahead. After a couple of miles you go past our old friend the Bottminger castle on your left. Then it starts to thin out. You go through the village of Oberwil and now you are in the countryside. Next village: Biel, and then the smallest village of them all: Benken, population 155 souls.

As you pass through, you will notice a sign on the right that says ZOLL. There is a lane leading off into seemingly nowhere. Take it. After two kilometers you will come to a second sign saying ZOLL, and under it DOUANE. On the left there is a typical country Swiss house, in front of it is a flagpole with a Swiss flag on it, and inside lives the Swiss border guard, Customs man, Emigration authority, all in one. When he hears a car stopping in front of the house, he comes out to see who it is. Normally—in fact, almost always—it is a Swiss who is going a few miles down the road into France where he has an orchard, or a small vineyard, or a French relative who lives back there in splendid isolation. He is on a first-name basis with almost all his "clients." The whole arrangement is very un-Swiss, because it is so easygoing.

What is striking about this border crossing is that there is no barrier that can ever close it off, and most important of all, there is no French border guard there. In fact, on the other side of the invisible line separating France from Switzerland there is nothing—no houses, no farms—nothing but a dirt road leading into the Alsatian forest.

That night, or morning, at shortly before five, both our vehicles stopped about a half-kilometer short of that border crossing—also in the middle of nothing, but still Swiss nothing. Both of us had shut our engines off.

"Sabine," I began in a whisper once we had our heads together in front of the BMW, "before we get any further into this thing I want to explain what happened tonight at Zimmerli's office."

"Later," she replied. "It's getting late." By which she meant early.

"Now listen," she continued. "The border is half a kilometer down this road. After it you have about five kilometers of dirt road on the French side. When you come out of the forest you will be in Neuweiler. It's in France, but they still use only the Germanic name of the village. Now listen. When you get there, bear left in the middle of the village. Left! Because if you keep going straight ahead you hit a border crossing again going right back into Switzerland. Except that this one is manned by a French border guard."

"Don't worry. I'll remember. Bear left in Neuweiler. What I'm worried about is that border crossing just ahead. How do you know it won't be manned?"

"There are very low odds on that," she replied, not that reassuringly. "Sometimes these guards go out on patrol, usually with a dog. But so what? Just step on the gas if you see anybody."

"Okay. Then in France, what?" I asked.

"Keep going straight ahead. You'll go through Hueningen —in French it's Huningue—and you'll come to Neudorf— Village-Neuf. Involved is maybe ten kilometers for that stretch. On this side of Neudorf you will see a country restaurant called Restaurant du Canal. There is a lane leading off right beside it. Go over the canal and go to the first house on the right. There's a barn there. Put the car into the barn, close the doors. Somebody will come out and put you up in that house until we figure out what to do next. Her name is Hélène. Frau Hélène. She's my cleaning lady. First her mother, then she, have been with our family for forty years. She speaks only Alsatian dialect, but I think you'll be able to handle that. Okay. Tomorrow I'll come over and we can go up to Luxembourg together and get you out."

"Got it. But wait one minute, Sabine, because—"

We both heard a car about then, moving at a very high speed. The sound faded almost as soon as it came up. Obviously somebody headed through Benken, and then toward Basel. But it brought home the point that morning, and thus movement, was rapidly approaching. Just what I did not need.

She grabbed me around the neck, kissed me hard, and moved swiftly back to her VW. I had no choice but to likewise get going. She turned on her engine, then her parking lights, turned the VW around with some difficulty so that it faced the other way, and, I thought, she then waved. But I was no longer concentrating on Sabine. I now had the BMW engine purring; I then put the lights on full, and floored the son-of-a-bitch. I must have passed that house with the Swiss flag in front of it—that much I saw on the periphery— going about 120 or 130 kilometers an hour. The car hit the dirt road on the other side with a bang, swerved like hell, caught itself, and then we were in the forest. The road got bumpy, the BMW was rocking and skidding and bucking, but we were moving—man, were we moving—and I was out of Switzerland, and it felt so good that I let out one big "Whoopee!" and hit the accelerator once again.

The feeling of relief was indescribable! I'd beaten the system and left the bastards behind! France, to me at that moment, was the land of the free and the home of the brave. I went by the sign saying NEUWEILER and also its French equivalent, which I forget, and was concentrating on veering left fairly soon, as Sabine had instructed—when it happened.

The man, with a dog, just as Sabine had warned, was right there in the middle of the street. He saw me, and he dived as best he could out of my way, but . . .

There was a hell of a thud. Absolutely sickening. I'll never forget the sound. Ugh. Even now it's hard to think about it. Of all the stupid, impossible, rotten things to happen!

I stopped about fifty meters down the road. The tires screeched all the way. I got out of the car and looked back, and while I did it lights came on in three different houses. So there would be help. Immediately.

If help was needed. It was so dark and foggy that it was impossible for me to determine just what had happened. Perhaps, perhaps, the man had made it, and the thud had been the dog. Which, in itself, was sickening. Another two lights went on. The village was obviously aroused.

I got back into the car. The engine was still running, so I simply slammed the door and floored it once again. The

BMW still drove perfectly, so the front end could not have been seriously damaged . . . probably just hit the dog with the bumper. Running now at close to 150 kph, I went through the village of Huningue fifteen minutes later, and five minutes after that I saw the sign indicating the outskirts of Village-Neuf. I braked hard when I saw a building on the left that must have been the restaurant, turned carefully into the lane beside it, crossed the bridge over the canal, and just as Sabine had described it, pulled up in front of a house with a barn on its left, its door open.

As I very, very carefully closed the door behind the German car, the lights went on in the house. The back door opened, and a woman stood there with a flashlight.

"Sin se dr ami vo dr Madame Sabine?" she asked in that weird language of the Alsatian part of France which is a mixture of the primitive dialect of the Germanic tribe of the Alemannen and very countrified French.

"Ja," I answered.

"So kemme'se jetzt iine, Monsieur," she said. *"Vite—sisch froid."*

See what I mean?

I had nothing with me except the clothes I was wearing and the small black suitcase I was carrying. She led the way to a bedroom, indicated where the toilet was down the hall, and closed the door behind her. I put the suitcase on top of the dresser, then took off my overcoat, jacket, shirt, and trousers and climbed into bed and lay there and thought and thought and thought.

At about half past seven I was still awake and it was slowly getting light outside. In half an hour, I knew, all hell would start to break loose not that many kilometers to the east of where I was in France: on the other side of the Rhine up in the hills beyond in a place known as the Black Forest.

18

THE DAY STARTED OFF quite normally in the Black Forest. Herr Doktor Kreps, Generaldirektor of the Deutsche Bank, arrived in the breakfast room about seven thirty-five and had a leisurely meal while he read the *Frankfurter Allgemeine*. At seven fifty-five the American, Mr. Patterson, entered the room, and asked for just coffee. He told the waitress that he was expecting somebody else in a few minutes and would wait until he arrived before ordering. At precisely eight o'clock Herr Minister Graf Otto von Amsburg arrived, also with a *Frankfurter Allgemeine* in hand, and after nodding to the two other gentlemen, also seated himself alone. The scene looked more English than German, one of rather studied aloofness.

But that scene and that privacy were not to last for long. The first minor break came when the ancient bellman entered the breakfast room, approached Dr. Kreps, and spoke softly though urgently into his ear, after which the banker dropped his newspaper—without even folding it—on the table and rushed out. The second also seemingly minor interruption came when the girl from the front desk informed Minister von Amsburg in a rather loud voice from the doorway that he was wanted on the telephone—very urgently. This left Herb Patterson all alone in the room, a state of affairs that he decided not to put up with.

He had told Frank Rogers to meet him at eight o'clock, and it was now four minutes past the hour. Patterson's uneasiness grew as each further minute passed. Had he made a terrible mistake by letting Rogers get out of his sight last night? Better check his room. Right now!

As Patterson was approaching the house phone at the front desk, Dr. Kreps confronted him.

"Where is your colleague?" he demanded.

"What are you talking about?" replied Patterson.

"Your Mr. Rogers. I want my automobile."

Patterson had no idea what the silly man was referring to, and his blank expression must have shown it.

"The hotel was supposed to put my baggage in my BMW 2000 while I had breakfast, but I have been informed that my automobile is gone. I checked, and it is. I lent it to your Mr. Rogers last night."

Patterson's face was now no longer blank.

"That double-crossing son-of-a-bitch" were his next words. It was now the German banker who had no idea what the other was talking about.

"Where is Mr. Rogers?" he asked.

Patterson picked up the house phone, asked for room 14, and naturally, got no answer. He jammed the phone back at exactly the same time as Herr Minister von Amsburg came, white-faced, out of the telephone booth right next door—the one that housed the outside phone.

"*Er ist tot,*" he said.

Patterson, who did not speak a word of German, understood nothing, but the sight of the color of the German's face was enough.

"What's gone wrong?" he demanded of von Amsburg.

"Murdered. Zimmerli. They found his body just a few minutes ago."

"Who?" asked Kreps. He had never met or even heard of Amadeus Zimmerli.

"A Swiss," answered the German Foreign Minister, recovering very quickly. "Probably terrorists."

The ruling elite of Germany live in constant acute fear of their own peculiar brand of terrorists who seem intent upon bringing the "capitalistic" system there to the threshold of anarchy through a seemingly endless series of executions of politicians, bankers, and judges.

"Where are the police?" the German banker then asked. "They must get us out of here. There might be a bomb—"

"No, no. You don't understand. Not here. In Basel. Someone apparently kidnapped Zimmerli from his home, forced him to go to his office and open the safe, and then killed him," said von Amsburg.

Patterson, listening, stepped back as if someone had pushed him, or as if he did not want to hear what he had just heard.

Then he asked, "When did you give him your automobile?"

The question was, of course, addressed to Kreps, but von Amsburg thought the American was talking to him.

"What automobile? What are you going on about, Patterson? Don't you understand what—"

"Shut up," Patterson said, and von Amsburg seemed on the verge of actually striking the man.

"Forget terrorists. I'm afraid what happened has a much simpler explanation. Rogers, you see"—and he was now talking exclusively to von Amsburg—"seems to have taken Dr. Kreps's automobile last night and not returned it. I very much fear that he may have gone to Switzerland with it. And . . . well, you can figure it out from there. You heard part of our conversation yesterday."

Von Amsburg's head began to nod. It made sense. Without saying anything he went back into the telephone booth.

Less than a minute later he reemerged.

"Rogers crossed the German–Swiss frontier at Lörrach at exactly twelve thirty-five this morning."

Patterson's expression was one of "I told you so."

"But what has Mr. Rogers got to do with this Swiss?" the German banker wanted to know.

Von Amsburg just waved his hand at him. "Later," he replied; "I will explain later. I suggest, my dear friend, that you leave this matter to me. I will take care of it very quickly, you can be sure."

"Yes, but what about everything that we have done here? Is that now endangered? Do I proceed with the banking arrangements as we discussed? After all, it was with Mr. Rogers that we worked out the details."

"Proceed exactly as planned and exactly as scheduled," replied von Amsburg. And Patterson vigorously nodded his agreement.

"Mr. Rogers is essential to none of these matters, when you come right down to it," said Patterson. "It's now something that you and the Citibank people will be working out. Right?"

He looked at von Amsburg, who this time nodded his agreement.

"But what about the confidentiality of these matters?" persisted Kreps. "I thought that it was absolutely essential to success."

"It is," admitted von Amsburg. "We shall make sure it is maintained. If Mr. Rogers is involved in this affair in Switzerland, you can be absolutely sure that Mr. Rogers will be caught and will be arrested and will be held incommunicado. And will thus have no opportunity to talk to anyone about anything until such time as he can do no harm. I shall personally talk to the Swiss authorities within the next few minutes. We have jointly dealt with delicate matters of mutual interest in the past, and very successfully. I think that when they realize, when told however obliquely, that our mutual future defense interests may be at stake here, Mr. Rogers will disappear for a *very* long time indeed.

"May I suggest, gentlemen, that perhaps you return to your breakfast. I will let you know our future path of action very shortly. And if I may ask this of you both, please do not bother any of our other colleagues with this matter right now. None of them really knew Zimmerli, and what has happened in Basel may or may not involve Rogers"—and now he was talking directly to Kreps—"and even if it does, it has absolutely nothing to do with what we have been discussing here. It is purely a coincidence of timing."

Kreps knew he was lying, but von Amsburg was the Minister of Foreign Affairs of West Germany and Kreps was a German, and so if that was the way it was *supposed* to be, that was the way it *would* be. As far as Herr Doktor Kreps and the Deutsche Bank were concerned, Mr. Frank Rogers had ceased to exist.

"*Ich verstehe,*" he said, and started toward the breakfast room, but then turned back for one more query. "My BMW?"

"I'd suggest you get another one," replied von Amsburg, "and if any of the authorities contact you concerning the stolen vehicle, just tell them it was stolen by person or persons unknown to you. Understood?"

"*Jawohl,*" Kreps answered, and this time disappeared into the breakfast room with no further hesitation.

"So," said Patterson, "are you going to put your security people on this?"

"Absolutely not," replied von Amsburg. "No security people, no intelligence people, no counterintelligence agencies. Strictly the police and the pertinent people in the Ministry of Justice. All we have here in Germany is a stolen automobile. But what they have in Switzerland is a first-degree murder. And we have information that can no doubt be of great assistance to the Swiss police and the Justice Ministry of Basel in catching the man who did it. No doubt your man Rogers."

"But wouldn't the intelligence—"

"No," interrupted von Amsburg. "That would make it political. We do not want to make this political. This is a simple matter for the people who deal with common crime. We want no political complications. Do you understand, Mr. Patterson?"

He did, finally.

"Now I must make a few phone calls."

The first call went to Herr Doktor Wettstein, chief prosecuting attorney of the Half-Canton of Basel-Stadt; friend of the late Amadeus Zimmerli; friend also of a few other prominent Swiss citizens such as those who had been assembled for dinner just two nights earlier in the suburb of Basel known as Arlesheim. Von Amsburg very succinctly indicated that the German authorities had good reason to believe that an American by the name of Frank Rogers had been involved in the murder of Amadeus Zimmerli earlier that morning. In fact, the German authorities had had this American under surveillance for quite a time, since they had been tipped off that he was involved in some illegal arms trafficking. The local authorities believed that Rogers was traveling in a blue BMW with Frankfurt license plates.

The second call went to the head of Hoffmann—La Roche. It was also very brief. Von Amsburg said that he was imposing upon their acquaintanceship because he knew that they had had a mutual close friend, the unfortunate Dr. Amadeus Zimmerli. He wanted to indicate that not only he, but also his government had a vital interest in the Zimmerli case. That the man who had killed him was no doubt an American by the name of Frank Rogers, suspected of illegal trafficking in arms on a global basis. He, and his government, would highly appreciate it if von Lathen were to have a word with Dr. Wettstein, the chief prosecuting attorney of the Half-Canton of Basel-Stadt, indicating that when Rogers was arrested he should be kept incommunicado indefinitely. He, von Amsburg, would then like to meet personally with the

Swiss Defense Minister to further explain the background of this entire affair, and he would then appreciate it if Dr. von Lathen could discreetly arrange such a meeting, preferably on Swiss soil.

He assured the Swiss industrialist that what he and his country would receive in the way of reciprocity for handling the Rogers/Zimmerli affair as swiftly and discreetly as possible would represent a major contribution to the long-term national interests of Switzerland.

Von Lathen assured the German Foreign Minister that he would personally attend to the matter immediately and that he would, very tentatively, inform the Swiss Minister of Defense about this conversation.

The Central Europeans were closing ranks very rapidly.

During the next hour, the men who had met so secretly at the Gasthof zum Hirschen in Sankt Blasien left for their respective destinations completely unaware of the fact that everything that they had so carefully planned together was now in great jeopardy through the defection of one of them. The members of the "conspiracy" who were involved, or at least informed—von Amsburg, Patterson, and Dr. Kreps—were the last to leave, and they left together in a special Mercedes 600 which had been driven down from Stuttgart, from the Mercedes plant itself, at nearly the speed of sound after the Generaldirektor of Mercedes-Benz had received an urgent request for such transportation from the Ministry of Foreign Affairs in Bonn.

You see, the system works. The Old Boy net, whether in Britain, where it was invented, or in Germany and Switzerland, where it is emulated, serves its purpose well. In fact, that net perhaps best embodies what is so vaguely referred to as the "fabric" of a nation. For that net, that fabric, is real and functional. If the German Foreign Minister needed transportation, the head of Mercedes would provide it with no questions asked. If the Swiss Defense Minister thought he could get hold of the cruise-missile technology, the president of Hoffmann–La Roche and the chief prosecuting attorney of Basel-Stadt would do his bidding. And if an American got caught in this net—well, tough luck!

The special car left Sankt Blasien at about eleven that morning. Dr. Kreps was dropped off right in front of the Deutsche Bank skyscraper in not-so-beautiful downtown Frankfurt at about 1 P.M., after which the Mercedes returned to the Autobahn and crossed the main north–south artery, and the second passenger, Herb Patterson, got out in front of the massive terminal complex of the Frankfurt airport. An hour later he was on his way back to the United States.

The German Foreign Minister got to his Bonn offices shortly before normal closing time. He immediately called the head of the German Federal Police, the president of the Bundeskriminalamt in Wiesbaden, and asked to be informed within the hour of all the facts that had developed in regard to a murder case in Basel. He assumed Interpol would be fully informed. He gave no reason for his interest.

According to protocol, this request should have gone to Wiesbaden via the Minister of the Interior in Bonn, who is politically responsible for police matters in Germany. But von Amsburg wanted to keep the circle of the "informed" as small as possible. The men in Wiesbaden obviously understood this, because at six fifteen that evening Germany's chief cop arrived personally—by helicopter, it seemed—with some highly astounding news. According to Interpol and the Basel authorities, the BMW that Rogers had stolen was seen on the streets of Basel in the vicinity of Zimmerli's law office just minutes before the estimated time of the Swiss lawyer's murder. That was not unexpected. But what had later transpired added a new dimension, in terms of both urgency and geography, to the manhunt. That same blue German BMW with the Frankfurt license plates FR 78349 had run down and killed a French border patrolman who had challenged it near a border crossing on the outskirts of Basel.

The exact details were not known, but three witnesses had already come forward.

At present Mr. Frank Rogers was absolutely on the top of the wanted list of both France and Germany, wanted for manslaughter of a public servant in France and wanted for murder, grand larceny, and bank fraud in Switzerland. In the latter country it was a toss-up whether murder or bank fraud was considered the worst of the three crimes.

After the Bundespolizei chief had left, assured that he now had yet another very good friend in high places, von Amsburg lit up a cigar, the first in days. It looked as if the "Rogers problem" was already taken care of. He opened an "urgent" dossier which had been left on his desk. It appeared that the German Ambassador to Indonesia had been caught with the local Prime Minister's seventeen-year-old daughter *in flagrante* at a hotel in Jakarta. Von Amsburg decided to recall him for a firsthand report.

First Rogers, now this. Life is full of details that, unfortunately, divert one's attention all too often from one's primary mission. Von Amsburg looked at his watch. It was approaching seven. Franz Josef Strauss was expecting him for dinner at eight. He would be pleased when he heard what had been accomplished during the past two days. Germany was finally on its way back to the top. Where, this time, it would remain.

All thoughts but one of the American, Frank Rogers, disappeared as if the bothersome little man had never existed. The one fleeting reflection was one of pity: woe to the foreigner, especially an amateur, who was nailed by both the French and the Swiss for killing one of "their own." Von Amsburg actually shuddered ever so briefly.

19

IT WAS ALMOST FIVE when I woke up that afternoon. At first, I was totally disoriented. Then, unfortunately for my peace of mind, I realized exactly where I was, and why.

I got up and raised the shade, and although dusk was falling, there was enough light to allow me to see exactly where I was. Beside the house was a small canal; across the canal was the Restaurant du Canal. And all around were the fields, flat as could be, where the second-best asparagus in the world is grown. The best, of course, comes from the Calvados region in the South of France.

I knew Village-Neuf reasonably well. When I had studied at the University of Basel we used to come over the border to Alsace almost every weekend during the months of May and June for one—no, two—reasons: to eat and drink. That was back at the start of the 1960s. At that time, for 10 francs —and we called them *nouveaux francs*, since French currency reform had just recently taken effect—you could get a heaping platter of hot white asparagus, a *saucière* full of mayonnaise, almost as much country ham as you could eat, unlimited amounts of French bread, plus a bottle of either Edelzwicker or Kaefferkopf Riesling, all for the equivalent of two American dollars!

Dead. One Swiss for sure, and one Frenchman maybe. There was no getting away from it. Daydreaming could not change it. I was no longer that student with no problems any greater than a dissertation or a pending oral examination. I was a man of forty-eight years who had just done something that was so far removed from anything even remotely imaginable for someone with my background, my education, my . . . but it had happened.

There was an unsure knock on the door of my bedroom, and then it opened very tentatively, and a voice said:

"*Monsieur, sin'se wach?*"

"*Ja,*" I replied, and the woman now showed her head.

"*S'isch d'Madame, au telefon,*" she said.

"I come," I replied, to add further to the lingualistic confusion.

I pulled on my trousers, and the woman led me through the darkened house to a living room where a bright fire was burning in the wood stove. She indicated the phone lying on an end table near the fire.

"Hello," I ventured in a voice that was both weak and shaky, for I knew that whatever was going to come from the other end of that telephone connection was not going to be good.

"Frank! Oh, Frank!" was all she could say at first.

"Yeah. Not good, right?" was all I could bring out.

"You can't believe what's happening here," she then said.

"I believe. How bad is it? I mean, the man—the French one . . . ?"

"Also dead."

"Goddammit!" I said.

"He had four children," she said.

"Sabine, for God's sake, I did not exactly do it on purpose."

274

"Forgive me, Frank. I didn't mean it that way. But you cannot believe how worked up the people are. Not just the authorities. The press got hold of this, and your name, your picture, your everything is all over the place. What are you going to do?"

"Get the hell out of here, that's what I'm going to do."

"And go where?"

"South America, I guess. I mean, that's where they go, isn't it? Or Costa Rica."

"How?" she then asked.

"I don't know. But we've got to figure this out very quickly," I paused. Then: "That is, if you still want to."

Immediately: "Stop that, Frank. I want to. As they say, we are in this together. I was the one who sent you down that road last night. Of all the bad luck . . ."

"It happened. And it was my fault. A hundred percent. You had nothing to do with it. And if you want out Sabine—"

"I said to stop it. Now . . . listen, Frank, I'm coming over."

"Are you sure?"

"Yes. I'm home right now. I could not stand it at the office any longer. They know about our past history there. And my father—he called. He tried to make it sound as if he were being, you know, helpful, but I could not help feeling that he was fishing around. My boss, Wettstein, is personally in charge of you now. Even Bern has gotten into this thing, Frank. The French, Paris, Bonn—"

"Bonn?" I interrupted.

"The Germans were on the phone with Wettstein when I left the office. The President of the Federal Office for Criminal Affairs, no less."

"What have *they* got to do with this?"

"I think you are going to have to tell me that, Frank," she answered. "All I know is that the word is out that when they get you, be it here in Switzerland or in France or in Germany, you are to be held incommunicado and kept that way more or less forever."

"I believe you," I answered. This was just what Patterson and von Amsburg wanted. I had blown this entire thing completely, and handed those bastards my own head on a platter.

"Hold on," she then said. "Somebody's at the door. Look, I'm hanging up."

She did.

And left me standing with a dead phone in my hand in a strange house in the middle of Europe—with no place to go. Except—well, it had to be faced sometime. To prison. For a very long time. Unless I could get out of Europe and to a haven. But what haven? What country would afford me protection against the demands of the authorities of France and Switzerland? It was not as if this were a tax case, or fraud, or even some kind of politically motivated violence that was involved here. It was pure and simple: murder and manslaughter.

Maybe Brazil. But Brazil had slapped extremely tight controls on foreigners. You had to have a visa or they would not even admit you. Paraguay. That was a realistic possibility. Some of the biggest international crooks alive traveled on Paraguayan passports. Obviously they would take care of almost anybody, no matter how slimy. But that was a matter of price. In my case, my guess would be probably a million dollars minimum to the people around the General down there.

But that was all fantasyland. I had no million. I had no idea how to approach anybody in Paraguay. I had no idea how in the hell one could possibly even get out of the Alsatian province of France. Fly, naturally. Maybe up to Luxembourg and take Iceland air. Now, that was finally something!

But so I somehow got to Iceland. Then what? And the next stop was New York and the FBI and absolutely certain arrest now. That was the very last place. At least, in some airports you could hope that the authorities were so inefficient that you could get through the border checks and maybe disappear beyond. But not where the U.S. of A. was concerned. Sure, maybe you could get across from Cuba in a boat, or swim the Rio Grande, but you could hardly sneak by the people at Kennedy Airport. And even if you did, you would have to live like Patty Hearst thereafter. Always on the run, living in the underground. I was too old for that sort of thing.

But wait: Cuba. Now, that might be something! A very, very last resort, but not to be totally dismissed. How to get to Cuba? I knew an answer to that! Via East Germany. There were direct flights from Berlin—East Berlin—to Havana. I knew that. Those big old Ilyushins that could fly halfway around the world, it seemed, without refueling. I knew East Germany. I had once had dinner with Walter Ulbricht over there. True story. I had been at the trade fair in Leipzig, trying to work out some financing on a big trade deal, when I was still a banker in London, and Ulbricht had invited me to dinner. The last of the Stalinists, but so what?

For sure I was still on record there. They kept track of everybody.

But would even the East Germans want to have anything to do with me now? I mean, with two people dead? It was nothing political, at least as far as they knew. Cuba, I was sure, would be no problem. Okay. But how to get to East Germany? There was no way by air. And that was out anyway, since I could never get by a European passport check. They for sure had my number posted in red, white, and blue at every airport in Europe by now. So I could drive it. Not in the BMW. But maybe Sabine could arrange for another car. But that would mean crossing the width of West Germany, provided I first got through the passport checks on the French–German border, where *both* sides, apparently, were out for my blood.

It wouldn't work.

Okay. How about going out by sea? With a car I could reach the English Channel or the Mediterranean or even the Atlantic without crossing any border. Forget the English Channel. On the other side of that was England, and by now Interpol was certainly involved, and England was a full-fledged member of Interpol, so when they caught me in England I would be extradited back to either France or Switzerland so fast it wouldn't be funny.

So Africa. North Africa. Now, that was starting to make sense. Algeria, no. Morocco, no. Libya! Maybe that was it! Qaddafi would take *anybody*. And just imagine if he found out that I was Mr. Cruise Missile—goddammit, he might send a submarine for me. Pick me up in Marseille. I was starting to like the thought. It would be like a combination of a World War II movie and Humphrey Bogart in the casbah.

"*Monsieur.*" It was Sabine's cleaning lady.

She had a tray in her hands, and on the tray were a green bottle and a crystal glass. It turned out to be a Gewuerztraminer—a Hug—that was chilled just right so that the earthy, herby flavor was sufficiently subdued to make it one of the greatest drinks that mankind has ever created, in this case the men of two of the world's most imaginative nations—Hungary, which had originally supplied the grapes, and France, which had supplied the viticulturists and the oenologists.

Then she turned on television. She had one of the most complicated sets on earth, capable of picking up the programs of France and of Germany and Switzerland, even though the two areas used completely different broadcasting systems and even different color systems. The set was, of course, an old one which Sabine had given to her and which represented the *pièce de résistance* of that country Alsatian living room. It was six o'clock, and *I Love Lucy* was playing on the German channel, *The Rockford Files* on the French, and Walt Disney on the Swiss. They laugh at our culture, but they eat our hamburgers and watch our crappy sit-coms.

About half an hour later, Sabine's *Putzfrau* came in with a platter of pâté and ham and bread, and a big jar of corni- chons. Seeing that the first bottle of wine was empty, she returned with a second.

At seven the Swiss news came on. The first item con- cerned itself with Poland. The Russian occupation forces were under increasing attack, but no concessions seemed to be in the offing. The situation, the commentator suggested, in Russia in 1985 was coming increasingly to resemble the situation of the United States back in 1968 or 1969, when, as a result of overexpansion abroad, things began to fall apart at home. The second item was a train accident near Bern.

The third item was me. First my picture, a very recent pic- ture; then a picture of the blue BMW, with a close-up of the Frankfurt license plate; then an appeal: if anyone had seen either the car or the man, at any time, day or night, the police should be informed immediately. If—future tense— anybody spotted this man, he should not be approached. He had killed two men already, was most probably armed, and it was felt that he would have no qualms whatsoever about killing again. Then further details were given. The man was an American but could speak German and the Swiss dialect with great fluency. His French was thought to be fairly mar- ginal. He was nearly two meters tall, weighed about 80 kilos, had brown-blond hair, thinning, and was wearing, most probably, a suit and tie, American cut, and a blue overcoat.

Then they put on some film of the outside facade of the building in which Zimmerli's office was situated, then switched to some street scenes in the village of Neuweiler in France, right on the Swiss border. Body under blanket. Ugh.

I switched it off.

Madame came in about fifteen minutes later and switched it back on, this time tuning in the French number one chan- nel—obviously a nightly ritual. On came the news. I was the fourth item in France. Madame watched the entire sequence and quite obviously did not make the connection between the same body under the same blanket on the French news and the man who had done it, sitting in her living room.

At least, I hoped not.

About ten minutes later the phone rang again. I took it, and it was, of course, Sabine again.

"I can talk for only a few seconds," she said, "because I'm back in the office."

"I watched television," I said.

"Exactly. Now let me talk. I may be on to something. But it has to be a hundred percent."

"Paraguay?"

"Just listen, Frank," she said. "By the way, I had a long talk on the telephone with your wife earlier today."

"What?" That was about all I needed.

"She sends her love."

"Why drag her into this, Sabine?"

"Now listen to me, dammit," she replied. "I want you to get rid of that German car. And right now!"

"How?"

"There is a dirt lane that follows the canal. Follow it for two or three kilometers and then dump the car in."

"Won't they spot it in the morning?"

"Maybe. In fact, probably."

"Then the police will be swarming all over the place."

"You won't be there anymore," she replied. The adverb that would apply here would be "enigmatically," I guess, but I never use that word.

"How do I get back here after I dump the car?" I then asked.

"You walk, my dear. Walk. Remember how?" she said.

Smart-ass as always.

"Got that?" she went on.

"Yessir," I said.

"Good. Now listen. I'm going to pick you up at exactly eight thirty tomorrow morning. Be ready."

As if I needed the "be ready" bit. I would be so ready that—

"Now put Madame Hélène on the phone."

"Look, she has no idea who I am. Why involve—"

"Put her on, Frank."

So I waved the phone at Madame, who had been standing in the doorway leading to the kitchen, listening the whole time anyway. After Madame had taken the phone she listened, giggled a few times, and then hung up abruptly.

"Wait a minute!" I yelled. But the deed had been done, the connection broken, and I could hardly try to call her back at the office, which happened to be the Swiss equivalent of the district attorney's office—the center of the manhunt for a fugitive American wanted for two deaths plus assorted other crimes, major and minor, who just happened to be me.

Madame, the Alsatian cleaning lady, had disappeared into her kitchen and now reappeared with a very long flashlight, which she handed over to me.

The car. Or as we say in France, *la voiture*.

All of a sudden I was feeling better. I mean, it seemed that Sabine was onto something. In fact, it must really be something. Otherwise she would hardly have called Nancy. Right?

Maybe Nancy is going to meet me in Paraguay.

But how am I going to get to Paraguay? The mood was already starting to fade, so I got up, with the flashlight, and went to the bedroom for my jacket and overcoat.

When I returned, I noticed that the light by the barn *cum* garage was on and that Madame was in the process of opening the door. And there it was—just as shown on Swiss, French, and probably various other TV news programs that evening: a blue BMW with Frankfurt license plates—FR 78349, to be exact.

Now, Madame had seen the same program, with the same picture, as I had, and if she did not somehow start to put that car and me and a dead French border patrolman together pretty soon, then my name wasn't Frank Rogers. When I thought further of it, maybe it would not be the worst idea to start casting about mentally for a new name. I also thought it was time to jettison the blue overcoat, complete with wrench and pistol, so into the back seat it flew.

The BMW started immediately. I backed it out of the garage, went all of ten meters down the road, and then took a left down the dirt lane running exactly parallel to the canal. I could see that Madame had already turned out the lights outside her house. I did not turn on the car lights. At first it was difficult, but fortunately there was about a three-quarter moon that evening, and almost no cloud cover.

The whole thing proved remarkably simple. I drove about two miles, at which point the canal seemed to widen and, perhaps, maybe, even deepened. I stopped the car, jockeying it around so that it pointed directly into the canal, drove it to the very edge, and then stopped again, pulled the emergency brake as tight as I could and put it into park with the motor running. The thing was that although the front tires of the car were on the strip of cement, about a meter wide, bordering the rim of the canal, the rear tires were in one of the ruts in the bordering dirt road. It was thus impossible to just push the damn thing into the canal the way they do in movies that take place in Amsterdam. So how could I manage this without getting wet and perhaps drowned?

This is not the sort of problem that they teach you how to solve at the Georgetown School of Foreign Service.

I decided to turn the car around. After a dozen or so back-and-forths I now had the rear tires of the BMW on the cement rim of the canal. I put it back into park, left the brake off, got out of the car, slammed the door, put my arms through the open window, put the shift lever into reverse, and jumped back.

In she went without a murmur. But then the thing just sat there on top of the water. Miracle! No: as the beam of my flashlight indicated, just an air bubble. It took at least fifteen minutes for the thing to sink. But sink it did. The roof disappeared entirely. No doubt the car would be completely visible in its now underwater parking place in daylight, but somebody would have to either sail down the canal or walk immediately beside it in order for it to be spotted. Fair enough.

The walk back to Madame's house took twenty or thirty minutes, and in spite of what Sabine had implied, I found it invigorating—especially without an overcoat! Maybe I was not getting much action related to the solving of my little problem, but at least I was getting a great deal of motion.

Madame, the *Putzfrau*, was waiting in the living room for me. Now, maybe at this point I should be a little more detailed about this particular cleaning lady. It may well be that I have given the impression up to now that she was about seventy-five years old, wrinkled and gnarled. Well, that would not be 100 percent God's truth. She was probably in her mid-thirties, rather well endowed topside, fairly big-boned, and in fact rather tall and, when you came right down to it, handsome—rather like a rural red-cheeked version of a rough cut of Ingrid Bergman. Now, that's an exaggeration, but anyway—she was not the beast I have perhaps thus far implied she must have been. And I guess she liked me. Because when I now think back, there is no way she could not have known who I was. Or maybe it was just out of loyalty to Sabine. Anyway, what she did next really made her an accomplice, I guess you would call it, of mine.

She was there in the living room waiting for me, as I just said, sitting on the sofa with her apron still on, with a bottle of what looked like shampoo in front of her and beside that another, smaller bottle, both of which bore the brand name "L'Oréal." Beside her on the sofa was what looked like, and proved to be, a type of terry-cloth robe. She got up, handed it to me, and said:

"*Madame Sabine het mr gsagt, I muess ihre Hohr faerbe. S'il vous plait ziense das a ich mach das scho firse.*"

283

Rough translation: Madame Sabine has asked me to dye your hair, so put that on and I will do it.

Things were starting to look better all the time. Sabine obviously had not only an idea but a plan, one calling for me to become a master of disguise. Well, I would have been ready to do anything at this point to get the hell out of the grasp of the Swiss and the French, so into my guest bedroom I went, stripped, and was back in the living room in my knee-length bathrobe in about two minutes.

"Bit short," I said, after Madame Hélène had started to giggle at the sight of me.

"*S'isch mim Mann gsi*," she said. Her husband's.

"And where's he?" I asked.

She shrugged the French shrug which means Who knows and who cares?

"*Kemme se*," she then said, and this time led me into the bathroom. In front of the washbasin was a stool, and that was where she wanted me to sit for the moment. She filled up the basin, indicated that I should stand up and bend my head into it. She poured some shampoo onto my hair, and then grabbed—and I mean grabbed—my head, stuck it into the water, and started to give it the massage of the bloody century.

"Take it easy!" I yelled, but to no avail.

Then out came bottle number two, which was obviously some kind of dye or rinse or whatever they call the stuff that they use to color hair these days. It was applied with the same vigorous massage action. Madame Hélène was a strong girl! Then came a towel, which was expertly wrapped around my head, and since my eyes were still full of suds, it was only with her manual direction that I was able to find my way back onto the stool. Then she gave me a little pat, like the one you give an eight-year-old boy when he's behaved himself, and left me sitting there to ponder life's absurdities for the next half-hour until it "took."

She finally came back, removed the towel, and giggled

quite violently. I got up, looked in the mirror, and saw why: what greeted me there was a rather weird-looking dark-haired stranger with a two-day growth of blond stubble. I looked silly. We both just stood there for a minute—embarrassed for each other, I guess—and then I thanked her, shook her hand, and went to my room.

The woman must have noticed the stress I was under, because almost immediately there was a knock on the door, and when I opened it there she stood offering me another bottle of wine, this time a Riesling. She smiled at me, said *"Guete Nacht, Monsieur,"* and disappeared. I went to bed, drank the bottle, and was back asleep within the half-hour.

20

IN WHAT SEEMED TO BE the middle of the night I thought I heard the phone ring. But it could just as well have been a dream, since I had fallen into a sleep that was so deep it must have approached the edge of a coma. At seven thirty in the morning, however, there was no doubt that somebody was shaking me, gently, and that it was Madame Hélène. "*Se mien ufsteeh,*" she said. "*Vite.*"

She wanted me to get up quickly. She was dressed in a heavy dress, a wool sweater, and a shawl, so obviously we were going to move out.

I did take a shower in that bathroom, but a very quick one, since the temperature in the house must have sunk to the low 40s or high 30s. A peek outside indicated that frost had covered the entire countryside. She still had her husband's shaving equipment, so there was no problem there. I put on everything I had and appeared in Madame Hélène's kitchen to be greeted by hot croissants, fresh butter, and that wickedly dark French *café filtre*. Within less than five minutes Frau Hélène was in the kitchen, now wearing a sweater on top of her sweater and bearing what was obviously a man's ski parka and one of those small flat briefcases with a zipper on top. Both looked damned expensive.

She handed both to me, and pointed at the cuckoo clock —yes, cuckoo clock, on the kitchen wall; the cuckoo must have been gagged, since I never had heard the thing—and told me that we had to get going.

Get going. Sure. But where? And how? And where was Sabine?

Madame Hélène wasn't talking, and the way she kept pointing to the clock, I was not asking anymore. Maybe they had already found the car in the canal just down the stretch and were starting some sort of house-to-house search. I put on the ski parka—I was told later that it was an old one from Sabine's father's closet—grabbed the briefcase, ready to go, and then remembered: the little black suitcase, for Christ's sake! Back into the bedroom for that, and then out the door into the cold French morning I went, right behind Madame Hélène.

Leaning against the barn was the obvious mode of transportation: two bicycles, one bright red and new—hers—and a dusty old green one, mine. In this land of the Tour de France both were, naturally, ten-speed, and since I came from the land of the outdoors freaks, they were, fortunately, no mystery to me. The good wife and I had spent many an hour winding our way through the back roads of Woodside and Los Altos Hills on Sunday mornings, before we started to work on the Bloody Marys, either at somebody's place along the route or at home when the clock struck noon. My God, I thought, how remote all that was! I would probably never see Woodside again. Maybe I would never set foot in the United States again. And all because of that double-crossing Patterson and his German fascist friends. Then I remembered Somoza, for some very odd reason, or maybe not so odd. After all, he had also gone to Paraguay, but they

had sought him out and blown up him and his car with ba-
zookas. He had not gotten back to Nicaragua, but had made
it to America. In a coffin. He had wanted to be buried in
Florida. Anybody who wanted to be buried in Florida probably deserved being put away by a bazooka.

Madame Hélène put the briefcase in the carrier behind
the saddle of the red bike and the suitcase in the carrier of
the man's bike. We mounted, and off we went across the
canal. At the Restaurant du Canal we hung a right heading
back toward the main Mulhouse–St.-Louis highway. About
fifteen minutes later we had reached said road, but instead
of turning right and heading north, away from that den of
thieves known as Switzerland, we turned left in what I considered the wrong direction. A half-hour later, on the outskirts of the border town of St. Louis, we turned right again,
following the sign indicating the direction of the AERO-
DROME.

Aha! We were headed for an airport. To be more exact,
the Mulhouse airport, which is the twin of the Basel airport,
the two of them sharing a landing field, which is in France,
but having separate terminal facilities, which are completely
and hermetically sealed off from each other, at least on the
outside. It was the most peculiar airport arrangement probably anywhere on earth. Leading to the Swiss terminal,
through French territory, is a two-lane highway with a high
fence on either side which, like the onetime Polish Corridor,
leads extraterritorially to the Swissair departure gates. But
all that was not to concern me. I was in France and was no
doubt going to stay in France for a while. My best guess was
that somehow I was going to take the Air France commuter
to Paris, and then maybe take another internal French flight
down to Marseille, and then, perhaps, out of Marseille by
ship. And freedom.

My faith in Sabine at this point was supreme. And well it
should have been, for thus far all the arrangements—with the
exception of that unfortunate incident which had resulted in

the death of that French *douanier*—had worked out absolutely perfectly: the crossing of the border by stealth, the haven at Madame Hélène's, the dumping of the car, and now the exit from the territory where they would be searching for me via an internal French flight, which would not require my producing any passport.

Very, very good!

Well, it was exactly nine thirty when we reached the parking lot of the Bâle/Mulhouse airport. It had turned out to be an absolutely beautiful day: cold, crisp, not a cloud in the sky. A good day to be alive, and not in jail. There had been a good amount of traffic on the highways beside the bicycle paths, but no one had given the two of us even the slightest glance. Bicycles in France are still a means of transportation and not just there for recreation. We had, thus far, blended perfectly into the Alsatian scene. We were there where they were certainly not looking.

We went to the far corner of the parking lot and dismounted. I took off the parka and handed it back to Madame Hélène. She, in turn, gave me the expensive-looking briefcase with the zipper on top, which, together with the little black suitcase I had retrieved from the green bike, made me look like the typical businessman about to leave on an overnight trip.

"*D'Madame Sabine het mir gsagt, dass alles was se brueche, isch do drinne,*" she said. Everything I would need was inside the briefcase.

Then she reached over to me with her left arm, grabbed me around the neck, and planted one big, hefty kiss right onto yours truly. Our faces were both icy cold from the wind, but her lips were warm and full, and her eyes were blurry from now welling tears. It was damn nice of her to somehow express in such a beautiful way the camaraderie—and that is for sure the best word—that we had established within twenty-four hours. And then she turned around, took the right handle of the old green bike, led it over parallel to her bike, mounted, and started pedaling back toward the parking-lot entrance. She never looked back. And she disappeared from sight a few seconds later. I have never seen her since. But I often think of her when I am in a retrospective mood. She was in every respect a big girl: big hands, big smile, and a very, very big heart.

All right. There I was. Back on my own, with no more guides like Madame Hélène to lead me, led in turn by that invisible hand of the other Madame, Sabine.

But not quite yet, on second thought. That invisible hand would have to continue to operate, this time via the contents of that briefcase—I assumed. How had the briefcase gotten there?

I walked into the terminal. The check-in area was empty except for two girls behind the Air Inter counter, one man behind the Air France counter, and one girl and one passenger at the Swissair counter.

There were some plastic-covered chairs against the wall opposite the counters, and it was there that I sat down and opened the briefcase. The first thing out was a letter. Well, it was not exactly a letter. It was a typewritten message with no signature. More exactly still, it was a listing of the contents of the briefcase. They had been sealed in five envelopes.

1. One passport, French, in the name of Jean-Paul Mayer.
2. One empty envelope, prestamped, by which that passport should be returned. The address will be given later.
3. One confirmation of an airplane booking in the name of Monsieur Jean-Paul Mayer.
4. Two hundred French francs, to pay for that ticket.
5. Two thousand Swiss francs.
6. A telephone number to be called at exactly 11:15 A.M.

And that was it!

I looked at my watch. It was now nine forty. It was Friday. And it was December 6. So much for the general orientation. I will admit that I needed some orientation at this particular juncture, because the shock of being back in public view, back among people who might recognize me and call the police, who in turn would put me in prison for probably the rest of my natural life—well, that shock hit me right there and right then. So I just sat for a minute or two. I must have been white as a sheet. And I felt like throwing up on the spot.

I forced myself back to what apparently was going to happen. I had a telephone number for Sabine, and she wanted me to call her in exactly one hour and thirty-five minutes. If I was going to call her from Paris that soon, there must be a plane leaving any minute now.

Panic time! I struggled to my feet, ready to dash, and then realized I did not know where to dash to. Now the clerks behind both the Air France and Air Inter counters had disappeared. Was it too late?

The only person available for information was the girl at the Swissair counter. So I started to approach her—and then something, some second sense, held me back.

"Easy, easy man," I said to myself. And turned around, went back to the plastic-covered chair, sat down, and pulled myself together. I opened the zipper once again on the briefcase Madame Hélène had given me and opened envelope number one. I took out the passport. It was blue, it was French, it was in the name of Jean-Paul Mayer, and it had a picture of a guy about my age who had the same color hair as I now had—but a really close resemblance it was not.

Throw-up time was returning. But then I started to relax again. That passport would not be tested until later. After all, I was going to Paris, on an internal French flight, and you did not have to go through a passport check in the Mulhouse airport for that.

"So open the envelope with the flight confirmation," I said to myself, "and then we can get this show on the road."

292

I did that, and the slip indicated that Jean-Paul Mayer was indeed booked on Flight 49 leaving Bâle/Mulhouse at ten fifteen on December 6—but the rest of what was printed there was not to be believed: the destination of Flight 49 was Zurich, and the carrier was Swissair!

Let me tell you, the old heart started to really pump then! What kind of maniac plan was this? I had killed a man, for God's sake, getting out of Switzerland, and now my crazed girlfriend was going to fly me back in!

Easy, easy, I said to myself again. Maybe there is logic here. The last place they would look. Right? The *last*. It's like when you want to hide something in a room. Put it at eye level—right where nobody looks when searching for something that is supposed to have been deliberately hidden. We all learn that one as kids. Right? So the game plan must be to get to the international transit lounge at Kloten Airport in Zurich, and then get the plane to Paraguay. Or wherever.

Very, very clever!

And very, very dangerous, let's face it. It was now 9:52 A.M. My flight would leave in twenty-three minutes. I ripped open the envelope containing the French francs, stuffed them into my jacket pocket, put the passport in my other pocket, got up, picked up the small black suitcase, and walked over to the Swissair counter.

"*A Zürich,*" I said.

"*Votre nom?*" she asked.

"Mayer," I replied.

She punched the buttons on the computer terminal, and out popped the ticket a few seconds later.

"*Cent quatre-vingt sept francs, Monsieur,*" she said.

I handed her two one-hundred-franc bills. She gave me the change and the ticket.

"*La valise,*" she said then, pointing at my little black suitcase.

"*Je la porte,*" I replied. She handed me a carry-on bag tag

293

—Swiss *Ordnung* yet again. I duly attached it to the handle, and I was ready to go.

Next stop: the French *douane*. I walked across the waiting room and entered the "slot" between the two steel railings leading to a turnstile through which you passed to the international transit lounge—provided the French official standing there let you through. There was not one, but two of them standing there. They were talking. And laughing. I walked up, put my suitcase and briefcase on the counter, reached into my left pocket, took out the French passport, gave it to the one who stuck out his hand. They kept talking. He flipped it open and shut it so quickly and so nonchalantly that when he tried to hand it back to me I just stood there. Then I grabbed it, and pushed through the turnstile. They were still talking. Neither of them even looked at me. Like most people in the world these days, they simply didn't give a damn. Plus an element of the disdain of one Frenchman for another. Where had Sabine gotten this passport?

I went through the X-ray check, then through a door, and found myself in the huge international transit waiting room, with lots of chairs, a big tax-free shop, and almost no people —maybe a dozen in all, and, it seemed to me, all of them Swiss. They had come through the other wing of the terminal, the Swiss side, to take the local commuter flight to Zurich—the feeder line from the provincial airport of Bâle/Mulhouse to Kloten, Zurich's airport, which represented one of the hubs of international air travel, with flights to almost every major city on earth via the dozens of airlines that land there.

I started to approach the newsstand, out of habit, but then stopped, turned around, and retreated to a row of chairs completely empty. I could spot it from ten meters away: the *Herald Tribune* had my picture on the front page! Now the *Americans* were trying to do me in!

Less than a minute later Swissair Flight 49 was called,

the dozen or so people in the lounge lined up at the gate, I lined up behind them, and within another few minutes we were all inside the Swissair DC-9. I was the last in through the rear entrance, and took a seat in the last row, so that I would be the first out. Nobody was going to get too long a look at my face if I could help it.

The stewardess came around with the local paper, the *Basler Zeitung*, and a paper cup full of bitter coffee. She, like the men of the French *douane*, did not even look at me. I was just another member of the herd that airplanes shuttle back and forth. Their attitude: get the day over with; just hope that nobody causes any trouble or extra work or anything. My problem was not to overthink the situation, not to credit anybody with undue suspicion or unrealistic diligence. Who gave a damn about Frank Rogers? I was just a crook among many crooks on the run. Right?

I opened up the *Basler Zeitung* and I was right on the front page! So much for that type of reasoning. But at least there was no picture. European—or at least, Continental European—papers are not big on pictures. And they use such crappy paper that the ones they do use are fairly blurry. At least that was the new line of rationalization running through my head.

The flight from Bâle/Mulhouse to Zurich is so short— about fifty miles—that the plane never gets above a few thousand feet. If you sit on the right side of the airplane on a clear winter day like the one this December 6 was turning out to be, you can get a spectacular view of the entire north side of the Swiss Alps. I was sitting on the left side and, frankly, did not especially give a damn.

We landed exactly on time—at ten forty-five. I was the first to deplane. And suddenly was inside the transit lounge at Kloten, and it was packed: hundreds and hundreds of people changing flights. Zurich is to Central Europe what the Atlanta airport is to the southern part of the United States:

a passenger turntable, where one flight interconnects with many others. If you died and wanted to go to heaven in the South, it is said, you would still have to change flights in Atlanta. So also Zurich.

The problem with Zurich, as far as I was concerned that morning, was the fact that the town, its airport, and the hard stuff beneath my feet were very definitely Swiss territory. And on Swiss territory Frank Rogers was a much-wanted man. In fact, if they got him, my growing suspicion was that somehow Mr. Frank Rogers' life expectancy would be substantially below the norm for a healthy forty-eight-year-old American.

I sat down once again in an airport chair, put the *Basler Zeitung* in front of my face, and waited it out. I knew the number I was supposed to call at eleven fifteen, since I had had more than enough time to memorize it on the flight.

"Okay," I said to myself, "here we go." I went over to one of the public telephones at exactly eleven fourteen on the airport clock, put in 1 franc and 80 centimes, and dialed the number, and after just one ring, Sabine answered.

"It's me," I said.

"*Gott sei Dank*," she said, slipping back into her native language to thank the Almighty. "Frank—I've got very good news. But I have very little time. This is a phone booth on the street right downstairs from the office, and I can't stay here long. Now, listen."

"I'm listening."

"Send the passport back right away. I'll give you the address."

"Wait a minute," I said, "I'll get that envelope out of the briefcase." I did. Then: "Shoot."

"It's my father's address: Riehenerstrasse 217 in Arlesheim. Put my name on it."

I wrote it on the envelope. The envelope already had Swiss stamps on it. I put the passport in and sealed it.

"Okay," I said. "That's done. There's a mailbox not more

than ten feet away. In it goes when we're done here. Okay? Now where do I go from here?"

Then: "Wait a minute, for Christ's sake," I said, and it was in a much louder voice than I intended, but all of a sudden a few things were starting to dawn on me. "How the hell do I get out of here without that passport?"

"Just listen, Frank, don't think," she said.

"I'm starting not to like this," I said.

"There is no alternative," she said.

"All right, tell me," I answered.

"Go over to the Swissair ticket counter in the transit lounge. If I recall correctly, it is adjacent to the bank of phones where you are now standing."

It was.

"There is a Swissair flight—Number 100, if I am correct—that leaves every day at noon. For New York. Get on it."

"New York!" I screamed. Well, not exactly screamed; it was a kind of throttled yelp.

"Do what I say, Frank. Otherwise—"

"Wait a minute," I said. "What name do I give to Swissair?"

"Your own. And you also will have to show them your passport. You still have it, don't you, Frank?" The last question was asked with a voice that had a kind of desperate doubt in it.

I patted the left breast pocket of my jacket. It was there.

"I have it. But Sabine, they'll get me." Now it was my voice that was a bit off-key. If I want to be honest, it came close to a whine.

"They won't!" she yelled. "Those girls behind airline counters are the most mindless twits on earth."

"But why not just keep going with the French passport?"

"Because, you dumb bastard, a Frenchman needs an American visa in his passport before they will let him into the United States. And he must show that visa in his passport to the airline people; otherwise they will not issue him

297

a ticket, or in any case, they won't give him a boarding pass."

It made sense.

"Furthermore," she continued, "and it has nothing to do with what is feasible and not feasible, but I have to have the French passport back as soon as possible."

"Where did you get it?" I asked.

"He's in jail here. Monsieur Mayer. Fraud. He's over here at the Lohnhof awaiting trial. We always keep their passports in a special safe here. We have 113 foreigners in jail right now, which means 113 passports. His was the closest match I could find. But the sooner Monsieur Mayer is back in the safe, the better, if you know what I mean."

"How did Madame Hélène get all that stuff?" I asked, as if it really mattered.

"I telephoned her very early this morning and she came over on her bicycle and picked up the little briefcase. I simply could not risk personally crossing the border. They might remember later on, when this whole matter is investigated, and then—"

"What about the computer?" I asked.

"What computer?"

"The Swissair computer," I answered, "when the twit behind the counter punches up my name as a passenger on Flight 100 to New York."

"Why should it do anything? You are not wanted by Swissair and its computer. You are wanted by the Swiss police, the French police, Interpol—"

"Jeezus, Sabine!" Talk about rubbing it in!

"They found the car about forty-five minutes ago," she said, now in a soft voice. "You left Zimmerli's gun and my wrench in your overcoat in the car."

"Why not?" I said.

"No reason. I'm just saying that now they've got you absolutely dead to rights."

"So?" I said. "They had me anyway."

It was already eleven twenty-five, and Swissair Flight 100

was being called for boarding on the public-address system.

"You're right," she said. "It doesn't matter. Provided you get there."

"To New York," I said.

"Yes," she said. "In eight hours. Oh, Frank, I'm going to go home and just pray for you." Now her voice was a bit shaky.

"But will it really matter in the long run?" I asked. "Sure, I know that in the States I can get lawyers, and they can stall, but in the end I'll get extradited, and—"

"Frank, you don't understand," she said.

Then: "There is somebody outside the booth," she whispered. "I'm going. Just get to New York, Frank," she whispered with a hoarse intensity that was almost scary. "Get to New York!"

And she hung up.

I stood there with the phone in my hand and all I can recall feeling was an overwhelming sense of anticlimax. What kind of "solution" was this supposed to be? Even if it worked and I got back home, for how long? Why not face the music now and get it over with? This running away would no doubt only make things worse in the end.

Except, except, except—I was the only guy, the *only* guy, who could stop those bastards in Germany and those bastards in Washington and those bastards in New York and that bastard back in Sunnyvale. Give up now, and it would be bye-bye for Frank Rogers before he could say one word to anybody.

I'd been on the run so much since the Black Forest that I really had had no time to consider what all this was really about. Now it started to dawn on me: What was going on here was betrayal on the scale of Pearl Harbor! Patterson was not just selling us out to the Germans; he was starting an irrevocable process that would undermine the entire future of the United States!

You know, I hate those guys who exhibit their patriotism

with bumper stickers or flags in their lapels or by holding their hands ostentatiously over their hearts when "The Star-Spangled Banner" is played at ball games. But at that moment, *because* I knew that our country is the best damned country on earth, best by such a margin that it is not even funny, I also knew that I had no choice but to keep going.

But how could I stop these traitors the way things were now headed? Somehow I had been *sure* that Sabine would come up with *something*. Even Paraguay would be better than this. That would have meant a clean getaway, even though the life of a fugitive in Paraguay might not be exactly what my mother had expected of her son. But at least that trip would have had a temporary happy ending—would have given me ample time to "regroup." There I would have been free to walk around without knowing that one day I no longer could. What does it help a man if he gains a couple of years' walking-around time only to know during every one of those days that the end is coming nearer—and then back to Switzerland or France, in handcuffs, probably for keeps.

But to hell with it, I thought: You never knew. Right? And if I hung around Zurich any longer, there was no doubt whatever what would happen to me: into the slammer! And *subito!*

I hung up the phone, picked up the suitcase and briefcase, walked over to the mailbox, and dropped in the envelope. When it disappeared, it seemed to do so with a rather ominous finality. Then I disposed of the now empty briefcase in the trash can that was standing beside the mailbox. So there were no more tricks up my sleeve. Now it would be luck.

The second call to board Flight 100 came on the loudspeaker just as I walked up to the Swissair counter.

"Still got seats on the New York flight?" I asked.

"Do you have a reservation?" she asked, the twit in blue with the golden Swissair insigne in her lapel. If I had had a reservation, would I be asking that question?

"No," I said.

"Do you have a ticket?"

"No," I replied.

She looked a little dubious. They are not used to walk-on passengers in Zurich. You buy a ticket a month or two ahead of time, you make your reservation, and you get to the airport two hours ahead of time. That's how a good Swiss does such things.

"Let me check," she said. Then asked, "Which class?"

Knowing it was stupid, I replied, "First."

"Smoking?"

"No."

She punched the keyboard.

"We have space. Seat 7B."

"Fine."

"That will be one thousand three hundred and eleven francs," she said. "And your passport, please."

I counted out fourteen from my bundle of twenty hundreds, and then reached inside my jacket for my passport.

This was it.

"You're American."

"Yes," I replied.

She did not even open the passport! Why should she? Americans don't need visas to get back into their own country. Good thinking, Sabine, I thought—for at least the third time that morning.

She wrote up the ticket, tore out the coupon, and stuck it in the envelope that was my boarding pass. This she then gave to me, along with my passport. "Have a nice trip, sir," she said.

And that was that. No luck required.

So now all that was necessary was to get on the plane and off the ground.

In Switzerland they still retain a healthy respect for class distinctions, realizing that certain people are preordained to a higher status by an omniscient God. Thus first-class passengers in the Zurich airport board first—not women with babies or people in wheelchairs, but people with money—as it should be.

The lineup was short, but now that departure time was getting so near, all of a sudden I started to get nervous again. Sure, this was the international transit lounge. Sure, nobody had to look at your passport for you to either enter or leave the place. It was like neutral territory, a temporary nonnational haven for travelers. But I had been through this airport before, and I could have sworn that I had seen Swiss police in this transit lounge. It still belonged to them, and as far as I knew there was no law whatsoever against their coming in and hauling somebody off and out. I mean, this was not the U.N. building!

So every time the line moved up a person, I gave a glance back. And then I was inside the DC-10. I gave the steward, male, my boarding pass, and he pointed to his left and said, "Five rows up, sir," and then added, "May I take your coat, sir?"

After all, it was December, it had suddenly clouded up and was snowing very lightly outside, and who knew what the weather would be like in New York?

"No coat," I said.

Which produced the first really inquiring glance at me so far that day. My behavior was outside the norm. Airline employees don't like that. People whose behavior patterns are outside the norm can be dangerous, and it is drilled time and time again into airline people to spot them and keep an eye on them. El Al has this down to a complete science. Fortunately, this was Swissair. The steward turned to the next passenger, and I was free to walk up to row 7, to put my little suitcase in the upper rack, and to sit down in the aisle seat. The window seat was still vacant.

"Irish coffee, sir?" asked the stewardess.

"Yes, indeed. And quickly!" I replied. She smiled. No inquiring glance there. I relaxed. A bit.

What if, through some god-awful coincidence, they were just now finding out that I was somewhere in this airport? I thought. And came on board right now to get me? Wouldn't that be a pain in the ass?

She brought the Irish coffee, and it was strong and it was hot, and my hands were shaking a bit when I tried to drink it, but boy, did it taste good!

My seatmate arrived then. I seemed to have gotten the luck of the draw. It was female and not too old, or young, and not bad-looking. And when it said, "Excuse me" as it moved in, there could be no doubt about the American accent. Good. It might appear to the rest of the passengers as if we were traveling together—just a dentist and his wife from Rock Island coming back from the ten-day European special, a goodie but cheapie since it was off-season.

I was gaining confidence. But not enough to start talking to anyone. I was just going to sit, and wait, and maybe even pray a bit until we were off the ground.

That happened at exactly twelve oh two. Ten minutes later the seat-belt sign came off, and I went to the lavatory immediately. Inside I looked at myself in the mirror for the first time that day since leaving Madame Hélène's bathroom in the little house on the canal Alsace. I did not look terrific. The hair job did not seem to blend too well with the rest of my head, and upon closer examination was a little streaky. I looked a bit like a fading gay. When my good-looking seatmate found out that I was from San Francisco, she would conclude that there was little to be feared, or gained, from this particular traveling companion. Which was good.

The toilets in a DC-10 are right in the front, as you know, so that every time you have to go, the entire first-class cabin can watch you—which is a bit embarrassing if you are having trouble with the urinary tract, or have a case of something naughty caught in Paris, or are just a nervous type of pisser. In my case it was none of the above. But there was a guy sitting in the fourth row, in the middle, on the other aisle, whose face sure seemed to harden when our eyes met as I nonchalantly walked back to my seat.

Just acute paranoia, I said to myself as I sat down. But first it had been the steward because of the lacking overcoat, and now it was this guy who looked very Swiss and thus potentially very dangerous.

Why Swissair? TWA flew from Zurich to New York too. Sabine had made a mistake there. The Swiss fly on Swissair and almost never on another airline if they can help it. They are more chauvinistic than the Israelis or Irish in this respect. So this was the last place I should be. TWA would be full of young Americans smoking pot who couldn't have cared less about anything. This plane was full of Swiss patriots! And I was the guy who had just eliminated one of the leading citizens of their *Vaterland!*

"Going home?" she asked.

"Yes," I replied, hoping that my voice, which cracked a bit when I spoke, did not sound too nervous.

"So am I," she said. "And glad to get out of here."

Jeezus. *She* was glad!

"Why's that?"

"Can't stand the Swiss," she said.

"Me either," I said, "but that's a long story." Ha, ha. "What did they do to you?"

"Nothing. It's just their goddamn superiority."

"What do you do?" I asked.

"I'm a doctor. A gynecologist. Was at a conference here in Zurich. On tampons."

"Don't bother with too many details," I said.

She laughed.

"Would you mind giving me a medical opinion?" I then asked.

She looked wary, but nodded.

"Do I look a little peculiar?"

She laughed again, and then said, "Now that you mention it, yeah."

"Well, I'm not. I just dyed my hair. Same long story."

"I believe you," she said.

"May I buy you a drink?" I asked.

I waved the stewardess over rather regally—they hate that, since you are supposed to wait until they decide to do you a favor—and got two vodka martinis on the way.

"*Skål!*" my seatmate said when they arrived.

Ten minutes later she said "*Skål*" again, and by the time we had reached the Atlantic coast, yet again. I was so relaxed by this time that my hands had actually stopped shaking.

Then that Swiss sitting on the other aisle went to the lavatory, and when he came out he started walking back down *my* aisle, and as he approached row 7 he had eyes for just one thing: me. You talk about the evil eye!

Then he was past me, and although I dared not look directly at him, I could tell from my now very highly developed peripheral vision that he had circled behind the first-class cabin and was back in his seat in row 4, on the other side of the plane.

"Did you see that guy?" asked the good doctor beside me.

"Yes," I answered, now really worried if it had been so obvious.

"He seemed to know you," she continued.

"Probably did my hair sometime," I replied.

She laughed and said, "You're cute. What's your name?"

"Frank."

"Mine's Laura." We shook hands.

We must have been about an hour and a half out of Zurich when the crew started to make their motions toward mealtime. I hate to get trapped, so I started up toward the lavatory again—the result of the Irish coffee and the, come to think of it, three vodka martinis. On the way back I once again scanned the crowd up front. The Swiss on the opposite aisle was not in his seat this time. I kept walking. And there he was—at the rear end of the first-class section, talking to the steward and another guy in a rather intensive way. None looked in my direction. So what? Even if I were the subject of that little conference, what the hell could the Swiss do now?

Then the meal came, and it was actually a rather good one. I found out that the gynecologist was from Los Angeles—more precisely, from Holmby Hills; that she had a husband who was a surgeon, which explained how they could afford to live there.

She had a daughter going to Columbia, so she was going to stay in New York a few days before going home. When she asked me what I did and I mumbled something about having opted for early retirement, she gave me a bit of a funny look. But then we got off on skiing, and Sun Valley, and Gstaad, and had a good time together.

When the meal was over we had a Benedictine, then got some blankets and pillows and were ready for a snooze if the movie proved to be as lousy as most movies are on airplanes. Just as we were both snuggled in, she reached over and gave my left hand a little pat—the same sort of gesture that Madame Hélène had made after doing my hair in France the night before.

"Frank," said my new friend Laura, "you're a bit of a strange one, but I like your type. Don't let them get to you!"

I seemed to be bringing out the mother in everybody!

Well, the movie came on and it was a remake of one of the classic American films of the 1970s, *The Silver Bears*, starring a now older but even better Michael Caine and a somewhat chubbier but even sexier Cybill Shepherd.

By the time we got to Lugano in the movie I was starting to feel more than slightly mellow, thanks to the recent rather high alcoholic intake, when somebody tapped me on the shoulder. It was the steward.

He leaned down and in a very quiet, rather heavily accented voice said, "Would you please come with me, sir. Someone would like a word with you." The "would" was pronounced "vud."

What to do?

"Who?" I said, trying to think. It had not been very smart to drink like that, and it had been even dumber to sit in first class. Back in economy I would have been just one of the herd. Stupid, goddammit.

"Two gentlemen," he answered.

"Not interested," I said.

"I'm afraid they insist," he said.

"Tell them to bugger off," I replied, not sure whether he was familiar with the second verb in that sentence.

"What's wrong, Frank?" Laura asked.

"I don't know," I said.

The steward backed off.

"Go back to sleep," I said to Laura. "It's nothing."

Then another tap on the shoulder. It was very dark in the cabin because of the movie, but when I glanced back over my shoulder to really give the steward a piece of my mind I saw that it was not the steward but one of the guys from the cockpit, and from the look of the stuff on his sleeves, most probably the driver.

Trouble!

"Come with me, sir," he said. "I'm the captain."

I got up. He indicated that I should go up front ahead of him. So I did. In the space between the partition upon which the movie screen is mounted and the cockpit itself, where the stewardesses usually hang out, there were two men standing and obviously waiting for us. One was the Swiss from the other aisle, row 4. The other guy, also with a square head, held a newspaper.

"Let's make sure," the captain said.

He turned on a flashlight and pointed it first at the photograph in the newspaper and then right into my face, the son-of-a-bitch.

"*Das isch dr Gauner*," said the Swiss, "*gnau wieni gsait ha*"—indicating in the primitive Swiss dialect that I was the one, just as he had said.

Win a cigar!

"*Was mache mr jetzt?*"—this coming from the Swissair captain and addressed to the other squarehead, who, it turned out, was a lawyer from Basel, a colleague of the recently deceased Dr. Amadeus Zimmerli. This was a classic case of the wrong guy in the wrong place as far as I was concerned.

"What's going on here, for Christ's sake?" I now interjected, and in a loud voice, startling the two concerned Swiss citizens as well as the captain of their ship.

"*Passesi uf*," said the Swiss from row 4; "*er isch sehr gfaerlik*."

Which was a warning to watch out, since I was damn dangerous!

"Are you Frank Rogers?" asked the captain, finally getting to the point.

"That's right," I replied.

"The one in this newspaper?" he then asked.

"No doubt," I replied, without even looking at the paper.

"You have the nerve," the Swissair captain continued, pronouncing "nerve" as "nerff," "to come on this plane?"

"Nerff?" I asked. "What's that? I got on this plane with a ticket like everybody else, one that cost me about thirteen hundred Swiss francs. Which means, Captain, that you are working for me. So don't waste any more of your valuable time which I am paying for: state your business, and then I'll be going back to my seat to watch the rest of the movie."

When in doubt, attack! The three Swiss guys just stood there, all, by now, with faces in various shades of red, completely astounded by the continuing "nerff" of this crude American.

"That's enough," the Swissair captain said. "I am in command of this aircraft, and don't you forget it, Rogers."

Then to the two Swiss civilians: "I want you to keep him right here."

I to the two Swiss: "Touch me just once and you're going to get hit."

I to the Swissair captain: "I'm going back to my seat now. Don't try anything, Buster, or I'm going to put this entire plane into an uproar. You don't really want that, do you?"

He didn't.

I went back to row 7, seat B. Laura was sleeping.

Ten minutes later the steward returned.

"The captain would like to speak with you again, sir."

"Why not?" I said, and got up and followed him. This time he frisked me when we got beyond the front partition, and then he knocked on the cockpit door. It was opened from the inside, and I was asked to step in and sit down in the third seat, behind the copilot.

"Mr. Rogers," the captain now said, obviously having decided that even though I was a despicable killer, a crude American, and God knew what else, there was no sense in riling me up, "I have been in radio communication with our chief of operations in Zurich. He has been on the telephone with the criminal authorities in Basel. I have been asked to relay to you a number of messages and a request."

"Go ahead," I said.

"The chief message is this: Within the past hour you have been formally charged with murder by the Chief Prosecuting Attorney and Examining Magistrate of the Half-Canton of Basel-Stadt, Dr. Wettstein. An international arrest warrant has been issued, and I have been asked to act in accordance with that warrant and detain you, sir."

"I see," I answered.

"Furthermore, I have been asked to inform you that you have also been formally charged with manslaughter in France, and that an arrest warrant has also been issued for you in that country. Interpol has been informed by the Swiss authorities that you are aboard this aircraft, with the request that this information be relayed to the Ministry of the Interior in Paris."

"I see," I said again.

"I have been further asked to inform you that no jurisdictional problem is anticipated with the French since you are being detained essentially on Swiss soil, since this is, of course, a Swiss-owned-and-operated aircraft. Thus there can be no doubt that the authorities primarily responsible for you now are those in Basel and not the French. Do you understand all this?"

"I do. Indeed I do."

"We Swiss, as you must know, always like to do things in a fair and orderly and generous way. It will be greatly to your advantage, I am told, if you will now surrender voluntarily to me, acting on behalf of the Swiss authorities. I have been told to expressly inform you that such a voluntary surrender will be looked upon extremely favorably by the courts when your verdict is handed down. Do you understand this?"

"Yes. Most generous," I mumbled.

"I agree," said the Swissair captain, and he really meant it.

"Fortunately," he continued, "one of the men whom you met outside a few minutes ago is a Swiss lawyer, and he has volunteered to draft a document that will summarize the situation and in which you will agree to surrender voluntarily to the Swiss authorities to face the charges that have been brought against you. If you sign it, I think that will more or less take care of matters for the time being."

"Sounds just great to me. I do hope I'm not putting you to too much trouble. I mean, you've got to fly this airplane, and I can see that there are some clouds building up in front of us, and—"

"No, no," said the dumb bastard, "we've got it on automatic pilot."

"How silly of me," I said, brushing my hand across the top

of my streaky hair and wondering how I could possibly get out of this one.

"Where are we exactly?" I asked.

"Two hours, more or less, from Kennedy," he replied.

"So you are going in on schedule?" I asked.

"Of course," he said. Then: "*Ach*, you thought maybe we have been asked to turn back because of you? No, no. We carry only the minimum amount of fuel necessary these days. We can get to Kennedy plus one hour. France is now four hours back, Switzerland almost five. Impossible."

But they had thought of it!

"I see. So what's the game plan for us?"

"I think it's a bit early to go into all the details," the Swissair captain replied.

I'll bet it is, I thought. But it was also much too early for me to paint myself into a corner by getting offensive with these guys.

"When will that document be ready?" I asked.

"Oh, probably in ten or fifteen minutes," he said.

"I must say, I feel a bit faint," I said then, and tried to look as faint as possible.

"Perhaps a glass of water?"

"I think I should probably lie back a bit. And maybe take a shot of insulin. I'm diabetic, you know, and susceptible to diabetic shock when subjected to emotional stress."

Now the Swissair guy turned pale. He sure didn't want a premature corpse on his hands.

"Where is your insulin?" he asked.

"In my little suitcase in the baggage rack. Fortunately, the lady sitting beside me is a medical doctor. I'm sure she can advise me as to what to do."

They moved me out of the cockpit and back to my seat in a matter of seconds. They had me trapped, and could have kept me under wraps up there during the entire turnaround time at Kennedy. Swissair Flight 100 going from Zurich to New York turns into Swissair Flight 101 going from New

311

York to Zurich just two hours after landing, and I would be the only passenger making a round trip. And who knew that I was on this plane? One person: Sabine. She had gotten me on, but there was no way that she could get me off.

"Laura," I said, and shook her a bit. "It's Frank Rogers. I'm in rather big trouble," I continued, "with the Swiss authorities."

"I gathered something was wrong," she said, now totally alert.

"Let's get right to the point before they come back to get me again. They are going to try to keep me on this plane and take me back to Switzerland."

"They can't do that!" she exclaimed.

"I know that, you know that, but—"

"Right," she said.

"They had me trapped up front, so I told them I was a diabetic and going into shock because of the stress."

"Are you?" she asked, now looking directly into my face.

"No. My wife's diabetic; nothing serious, but I know enough about it to fake it."

"You want me to help you fake it even better," she asked.

"Exactly."

"Stewardess!" she said to the girl hovering in the aisle just behind us, obviously with instructions to watch me.

"Get two blankets, and two glasses of water. Right now. And help this man put his seat back."

Almost immediately I was half horizontal and packed into two blankets, and sipping water and almost choking on it from the glass being held by my seatmate.

"I said I had some insulin with me in the black suitcase in the baggage rack above. Can you fake that one?"

"I can do better than that," she said. She had her own little black satchel, as doctors always do, and with great ado got the stewardess to retrieve it, got out a syringe and swabs, and squirted some water, or something, into me.

"Don't worry, it's harmless," she said. "Maybe you might

312

consider groaning now and then. This is usually accompanied by rather sharp abdominal pain, heavy breathing, vomiting."

"I'll try," I said.

The people around us had remained unperturbed by all this, thanks to the movie. But then it was over, the shades were put up, and there I was lying in their midst, groaning ever so slightly now and then.

That sort of thing really makes people uncomfortable.

About ten minutes later the captain came up the aisle, this time carrying a legal-size piece of paper.

"How is he?" he asked my seatmate.

"Not good," she said.

"Can he read this?" he asked.

"Absolutely not. Do you want him to lapse into a coma?" she said.

I'll give the Swissair guy credit. He took one last look at me and there was more than a slight element of skepticism in it. This sudden attack had been a mite too handy.

"Will you help us deplane him at Kennedy?" he asked.

"I'll take care of him getting off and when we're inside the terminal," she volunteered.

"Thank you," he said, having now washed his hands of this dirty little man—me—and avoided getting involved in what was developing into a potentially very messy situation. There was no way they could keep me on the plane now, once it was on the ground in New York. The Russians had tried it a few times, and it simply would not wash legally when it was known that I was aboard. And it was obvious that I now had Laura available to make it known. But ten minutes later the pilot was back again for a parting shot.

He spoke to Laura, since I was still faking a semicoma beneath the two blue Swissair blankets.

"If he is well enough to hear it, you might let him know that I have spoken to the authorities in Switzerland about his case. They said that they had no choice but to inform the

FBI that he is aboard. He can expect to be met by them. I'm afraid *that* shock cannot be avoided."

He paused. "In my opinion," he added, "he would have been better off returning to Switzerland voluntarily. But as you Americans say: It's his funeral."

And after that nothing happened. We approached Kennedy, made our landing, pulled up to the gate; the door opened and I walked out, draped in a blanket, followed by my seatmate doctor, who was carrying two black suitcases —hers and mine.

The Swissair personnel lined up at the door to say goodbye never said a word as I passed. In fact, they managed to not even look at me. It had been embarrassing enough just to have had to mingle with a creature like me for so many hours. The Swiss from row 4 and his hotshot lawyer friend I never saw again. Ten steps inside the terminal I stepped to the side, unwrapped the blanket, brushed some of the wool from my jacket and trousers, got out a comb and ran it through my hair, and said to Laura, who was standing at my side, "I can't possibly express my thanks in any way that would match what you have done for me."

"We're both Americans," she said. "And I liked you the moment I saw you. I don't know what's going on, but I know a guy in big trouble when I see one."

Then the two men stepped up to us.

"Federal Bureau of Investigation," both said, and they both showed me their identification.

"Are you together?" they asked, looking at Laura.

"No," she answered, and immediately rejoined the line that was still coming out of the airplane and moving toward immigration control. Gone.

"We were contacted by Interpol about forty-five minutes ago, and they informed us that a certain Frank Rogers was on board this aircraft and asked us to detain him for questioning. They also relayed us a picture on the teleprinter."

314

He showed me a picture of me.

"Are you Frank Rogers?" the spokesman for the FBI duo then asked in a formal tone.

"I am," I replied.

"You are a citizen of what country?" he then asked.

"The United States," I answered, and for some reason, both of the men were somewhat startled.

"You are an American?"

"I am," I answered.

"Do you have your passport?"

"I do." And I got it out and handed it to him.

He glanced at his buddy and then said to me, "Would you mind waiting just a minute or two here with my associate, sir?"

His voice oozed politeness.

"Not at all," I replied.

The remaining two of us then just stood there, rather awkwardly, not really knowing what, if anything, to say to each other. What would you say to a man you were about to cart off to jail and then ship off to Europe to be locked up for God knew how long? So he said nothing.

About five minutes later his partner returned and handed me back my passport.

"They tell me it's valid, Mr. Rogers. Thank you very much. Sorry to have bothered you."

"What?" I said.

"You are free to proceed, sir. Again, I must apologize for any inconvenience we may have caused you."

"I thought Interpol had a warrant out for me?" I said, not quite believing any of this.

"The Swiss have an arrest warrant out for you, Mr. Rogers. And the French," he stated.

"Interpol—"

He cut me off. "The United States does not belong to Interpol, Mr. Rogers. The Bureau does, however, exchange

315

information with Interpol and acts on certain requests on a voluntary basis. In this particular instance both the Swiss and French governments put out a request for you through Interpol, Paris, and under certain conditions we would have honored that request to detain you. However, they left out certain very pertinent information, in this particular case related to your nationality. I have just spoken with our office and they have authorized me to tell you that we will inform Interpol in Paris that we have spoken to you, and that you are in New York. That is all. We are authorized to do nothing further. So again, Mr. Rogers, we do hope that we have not caused you any inconvenience. Goodbye, sir."

And they walked off!

I got into the lineup for Immigration and gave the official my passport, and he waved me on to Customs. There I realized that I had absolutely nothing to declare. The only thing that I *had* had, past tense, was the little black suitcase, and my seatmate, no doubt totally disturbed by what was happening and not realizing what she was doing, had walked off with it, just as she had walked off the airplane carrying it for what was supposed to be her patient.

Then she saw me and waved. And she had a big smile when she saw that I was alone. And she held up my little black suitcase. She was already through Customs. Since I had nothing to declare, I was also through Customs minutes later.

And then somebody else waved at me, frantically.

My wife!

The next few minutes were very mixed up. Nancy crying; Laura now totally confused, apologizing about the suitcase; explanations to wife regarding Laura; thanks to Laura by wife and myself for help given; picking up the suitcase; picking up my wife's suitcase; kissing Laura; walking outside the terminal with Nancy. And then my wife and I were in a cab and headed for midtown New York.

"You're safe, Frank" were the first words she said once we were alone in the back seat.

"I don't understand this," I said.

"Frank, you're trembling. Take it easy. You're safe," she repeated.

Now I started to not just tremble, but shake—the goddamnedest thing that had ever happened to me!

"Hang on, Frank," Nancy said, holding me as firmly as she could. "It's over."

"Everything all right back there, folks?" asked the cabbie, sensing something.

"Fine, driver, just fine," I said, and the shakes began to subside.

"It's getting better, isn't it," Nancy now said. "You're not going to get sick now, are you, Frank?"

"No, absolutely not."

"Because when I get you to the hotel and tell you some things, Frank, you are going to feel so well you won't believe it."

"I expected to be on the way to jail right now," I said.

"I know. I've talked to Sabine."

"Who put the fix in?" I asked, now beginning to grow paranoid. "Patterson!" And I yelled his name so loud that the cabbie started to look nervously at us in the rearview mirror again. "Those bastards have got me again!"

Sure. If they got me out of this, then what choice would I *ever* have but to go along completely, but completely and forever, with what they wanted me to do? *That* was why the FBI guys were apologizing all over the place. Hell, last-minute orders had come down from on high, probably relayed from Patterson, now back in Sunnyvale, to Larry Metcalf in the White House to the guy running the FBI to the New York office of the FBI: "Lay off. National security."

And they had me. This time completely.

"Frank!" And now Nancy's voice was way up there. "Cut it

out. Gawd, they've really gotten to you, haven't they?" And she started to cry again—something completely, but completely, out of character for Nancy.

"It's just that somehow I thought I might beat the bastards," I said.

She stopped crying immediately. "Frank, you have. You won't believe it. I can't believe it entirely yet. But I know there is no error. You've beaten them, Frank. Now all you have to do is ruin that bastard Patterson once and for all."

"How?" I asked.

"In the hotel," she said. "It's too good to tell quickly."

21

THE HOTEL WAS the New York Hilton. I remember staying once at the New York Hilton shortly after it opened. That had been it. But Nancy had made the reservation. And she disapproved of the Plaza and the Regency and the Carlyle and so forth because, she said, the rooms in all of them had fading wallpaper, dirty rugs, antique bathrooms, and outrageously bad room service—all for three hundred dollars a night. She preferred one hundred and fifty at the New York Hilton because, as at the Holiday Inn motels, one knew what one was getting.

"And after all, Frank," she had further explained, "we've got to start thinking about money, you know. Rich we are not." Only in America can one make hundreds of thousands of dollars a year, year after year, and end up not rich.

"I'm thinking of getting a job," she added. "You won't mind, will you?"

How could I mind? She had gotten her Ph.D. the same week I'd gotten mine. And she'd taught at Mills College for three years right in the beginning. But that was a long time ago. And she was not always in perfect health.

"Let's not think about that yet, Nancy," I said.

And then we were fighting our way across town on late Friday afternoon; it was a very mild day in New York for December; Park Avenue was, as usual, splendid with Christmas decorations; Fifth Avenue was even more splendid. I opened the window of the cab and breathed it all in.

You don't appreciate a lot of things until you come very, very close to losing them: the cliché of clichés, I guess. But to be home safe, in the U.S. of A., with Nancy, in the back seat of a rattly old New York cab, watching the traffic and the pre-Christmas mobs on the street—that was what I had almost lost, probably irrevocably.

She had splurged. We had a one-bedroom suite. The first thing she did when the bellman had left us was order four vodka martinis from Room Service—two for her and two for me. We had been married so long that her doing this was automatic.

"We're going to have to get you something to wear," she said, since the only things I had with me were the clothes on my back and that black valise from the safe of the late Dr. Amadeus Zimmerli. She had put that in the closet.

"They almost trapped me in that plane, Nancy," I said.

"Want to tell me?"

I did.

"You're lucky," she commented when I had gotten to the point where I was leaving the airplane in my blanket, followed by Laura, "that you knew about diabetes, and luckier that you had a seatmate like Laura."

"I agree," I replied. "But then came more than luck: two guys from the FBI approached me, asked a few questions, checked out my passport—and then backed off and disappeared!—Unbelievable!"

"All right," she said then. "You relaxed?"

The second martini was almost gone, and I was as relaxed as I had been for the last two weeks.

"Has it been two weeks?" I asked.

"More. You left on November twentieth, Frank. It's now the sixth of December. You've been gone sixteen days."

"You knew I should never have gone in the first place, didn't you?"

She shrugged. "On the plane back to San Francisco from Hawaii, I was going to ask you to resign right then and there. But I didn't. I figured you were a big boy and knew what you were doing."

"Yeah. Well, I was playing with a lot bigger boys, I'm afraid."

"That's what Sabine said," she replied.

"Look, Nancy, about Sabine—"

She cut right in.

"I'm going to say this just once, Frank. I don't want to know anything about Sabine. Nothing. All I know is that she has probably saved your life. And thus, to a good degree, also mine. That's all."

"Fine. But—"

She held up her hand. And that was that.

"Now, on a nonpersonal level: Sabine von Lathen is about the brightest girl I have ever dealt with. And quick. She shifts mental gears at a speed that makes even you, my dear, look like a clod."

Now it was my turn to shrug.

"She had to get you out of Europe, but to where?" Nancy continued. "What she needed was not just a temporary haven, a place where one bought time, but a permanent haven, and one in which your future safety was absolute. *Absolute!*

"I think she's still in love with you, Frank," she then said, herself breaking the ground rules that she had just established in regard to Sabine von Lathen.

"Then she remembered a case back in the early 1970s—at least, remembered hearing about it. She called the American Embassy in Bern, and they said the only documentation in Europe that might help her was probably in the library of the American Embassy in London—the only one of our embassies that has an extensive legal library: specifically, an exhaustive library of the treaties in which the United States has entered during the past two hundred years."

"You're not getting to the point very quickly, Nancy," I said.

"No I'm not, Frank. Nor do I intend to," she answered.

She deliberately took a slug of vodka and then resumed.

"Sabine could obviously not go to London—she was busy taking care of you. So she called me. I got the call at two yesterday morning in California, so she must have called around ten A.M. yesterday, local Swiss time."

That figured. I had gotten to Madame Hélène's house about dawn the previous day and then fallen into that deep sleep. Sabine had been in Basel, working this thing out. I had talked to her that evening on the telephone, right before watching the news on television, and I remembered now very distinctly that she had said that she was on to something but that it had to be 100 percent and that she had talked to Nancy earlier that day. It was coming together now.

"Go on," I said.

"She told me to go to Washington, immediately. And she told me exactly where to go. She would make an appointment for me by telephone at the law firm of Saxon, Ross and Dunbar on Dupont Circle."

"For what day?" I asked.

"Today," she answered. "This morning."

"How the hell did you get here, then?"

"I took the one-o'clock shuttle from National to La-Guardia, and took a cab out to Kennedy to meet your plane."

"So you knew I was coming on that plane?"

"Sabine said that if all went well you would be on it."

"But I thought she needed some documents before she could be a hundred percent sure about whatever she insisted upon being one hundred percent sure about. I got on that plane before she knew that. Right?"

"She had no choice, she said. She was ninety-nine percent sure."

As if it made a difference now. But it seemed to me, suddenly, that just about everybody these days was taking chances with my life.

"Okay. Now, goddammit, Nancy, let's get to the point finally."

"All right." She got up and went over to her suitcase, opened it, took out an envelope, opened that, extracted a document, and handed it to me.

"Read it," she said.

The first page read like this:

1900
EXTRADITION TREATY

Concluded May 14, 1900; ratified by Senate June 5, 1900; signed by President February 25, 1901; ratified by Switzerland January 21, 1901; proclaimed February 28, 1901.

ARTICLES.

I. Delivery of accused.	render to third state.
II. Extraditable crimes.	X. Extradition deferred.
III. Attempts to commit extraditable crimes.	XI. Persons demanded by third state.
IV. Special court.	XII. Property seized with fugitive.
V. Procedure.	
VI. Provisional detention.	XIII. Expenses.
VII. Political offenses.	XIV. Annulling prior treaty; duration; ratification.
VIII. Limitations.	
IX. Prior offenses; sur-	

The Government of the United States of America and the Federal Council of the Swiss Confederation, with a view toward better administration of justice . . .

"You can skip the rest of that page," she said, watching me read. "Go on to Article I."

ARTICLE I.

The Government of the United States of America and the Swiss Federal Council bind themselves mutually to surrender such persons as, being charged with or convicted of any of the crimes or offenses enumerated hereinafter in Article II, committed in the territory of one of the contracting States, shall be found in the territory of the other State: Provided that this shall be done by the United States only upon such evidence of criminality as, according to the laws of the place where the fugitive or person shall be found, would justify his apprehension and commitment for trial if the crime or offense had been there committed.

In Switzerland, the surrender shall be made in accordance with the laws in force in that country at the time of the demand. Neither of the two Governments, however, shall be required to surrender its own citizens.

ARTICLE II.

Extradition shall be granted for the following crimes and offenses, provided they are punishable both under the laws of the place of refuge and under those of the State making the requisition, to wit:

1. Murder, including assassination, parricide, infanticide and poisoning; voluntary manslaughter.
2. Arson.
3. Robbery; burglary; house-breaking or shop-breaking.
4. The counterfeiting or forgery of public or private instruments; the fraudulent use of counterfeited or forged instruments.
5. The forgery, counterfeiting or alteration of coin, paper-money, public bonds and coupons thereof, bank notes,

324

obligations, or other certificates or instruments of credit; the emission or circulation of such instruments of credit, with fraudulent intent; the counterfeiting or forgery of public seals, stamps or marks, or the fraudulent use of such counterfeited or forged articles.

6. Embezzlement by public officials.

7. Fraud or breach of trust, committed by a fiduciary, attorney, banker, administrator of the estate of a third party, or by the president, a member or an officer of a corporation or association, when the loss involved exceeds 1000 francs.

8. Perjury; subornation of perjury.

9. Abduction; rape; kidnapping of minors; bigamy; abortion.

10. Wilful and unlawful destruction or obstruction of railroads, endangering human life.

11. Piracy; wilful acts causing the loss or destruction of a vessel.

And there I stopped. And all of a sudden I was not feeling so good again. According to Article II, I was about as extraditable to Switzerland as they come!

"Honey," I said—and I was now choosing my words carefully—"are you and Sabine sure of what you're doing?"

"Positive," she answered.

"Yeah? Well, let me give you a preliminary box score on your husband. As I read Article II, I would fall under more than just one of these categories."

"Really?" she answered.

"Really! Number 1: Murder or manslaughter: guilty—one dead lawyer in Basel. Category 2: Arson—innocent. Category 3: Robbery, house-breaking—guilty as hell. Broke into lawyer's office, stole black valise from lawyer's safe. Category 4: Counterfeiting—innocent. Category 5: Alteration of instruments of credit. You might not know this one, but I signed a guarantee for a two-million-dollar loan by the Swiss Bank Corporation last week—illegally, since two signatures of Missile Development Corporation officers are required for such things; therefore, guilty."

"Do you want to go on?" she asked.

"Yes, I want to go on. Category 6: Embezzlement—nothing there. Category 7: Fraud—guilty. See category 5 above. Category 8: Perjury—innocent, so far. Category 9: Abduction—one lawyer from his home—guilty as charged. Categories 10 and 11: innocent."

"It doesn't matter." Nancy said.

I ignored her. "So count 'em up. Five out of eleven of the extraditable offenses they got me on."

"It doesn't matter," she said again. "But since you want to torture yourself, tell me—what exactly did happen with that lawyer?"

"He was trying to blackmail me with some videotapes he had in his safe. I made him go down to his office with me to get them. He opened the safe and pulled a gun. I pushed him. He fell and hit his head. And he died."

"That's awful," she said.

"Don't you think I know that?" I answered, getting testy.

"Easy, Frank," she replied, and then she pulled a second document out of the large envelope she was still holding. "Read this."

It was written under the letterhead of Saxon, Ross & Dunbar of 33 Dupont Circle in Washington D.C. It was dated December 5, 1985. It read:

Dear Mrs. Rogers:

We are pleased to render to you our opinion concerning the construction of the treaties of extradition between the United States and Switzerland and France. The United States Supreme Court has noted that the principles of international law recognize no legal right to extradition apart from treaty. *Factor v. Laubenheimer,* 290 U.S. 276 (1933). We have enclosed copies of both the Swiss treaty and the French treaty.

The second paragraph of Article I of the Swiss Treaty of 1900 provides:

"Neither of the two Governments, however, shall be required to surrender its own citizens."

You will note substantially similar language in the United States–French Extradition Treaty of 1909, namely:

"Neither of the contracting parties shall be bound to deliver up its own citizens or subjects under the stipulation of this convention."

(The distinction between "shall be bound to deliver up" in the French treaty and "shall be required to surrender" in the Swiss treaty diminishes further in the French version of both treaties—*"ne sera tenu de livrer"* as opposed to *"ne sera obligé de livrer,"* respectively.)

In 1936 the United States Supreme Court in *Valentine ex rel U.S. v. Niedecker,* 299 U.S. 5 considered this language. In that case France requested the extradition from the United States of two native-born citizens of the United States who were charged in France with offenses listed in the treaty. Following their arrest for extradition proceedings instigated by the French government they applied for *habeas corpus* contending that the President of the United States had no constitutional authority to surrender them to France because the treaty excepted citizens of the requested state. The Supreme Court agreed, holding that there is no legal authority for the U.S. to surrender its own citizens.

The Office of the Legal Adviser of the Department of State has informally advised us that they consider the language of the *Valentine* case to govern their interpretation not only of the French treaty but also of the Swiss treaty.

We conclude, Mrs. Rogers, that your husband, as a United States citizen, would not be extraditable by either France or Switzerland.

We enclose a statement for legal services in the amount of $5,000.

Sincerely,
Saxon, Ross & Dunbar

"Unbelievable!" was the only thing I could say.

"It is absolute," Nancy said, "just as Sabine thought it would be."

"What did those two guys do in that *Valentine* case?" I asked.

"Murder. Two murders, in fact. And absolutely no doubt about their guilt," Nancy answered.

"They killed two guys in France?" I asked, wanting to be very, very sure. "And that was it? Once they were back on American soil, because they were American nationals they were home free?"

"Exactly."

"Same applies for Switzerland?"

"Exactly."

I got up, went over to my wife, put my arms around her, and said, "Nancy, I'm home to stay. And I mean that in every possible way."

"I know," she said.

We both slept fourteen hours straight that night, and then spent a weekend on the town in New York. We bought me what I needed, saw two shows, ate Saturday night at the Four Seasons and Sunday night at Michael's, and by Monday morning both body and mind were back in shape. And I had my game plan ready.

By eight o'clock I was showered, shaved, and dressed, so I went down to the lobby to get the *Times*. Back up in the room, I retrieved the black valise from the bedroom closet, and then sat down at the small table in the sitting room, ready to prepare my campaign of putting one very big spanner in the works of Herb Patterson, Graf Otto von Amsburg, and consorts.

Nothing much on the front page that day, so I turned to the business section almost immediately. There it was: "MISSILE DEVELOPMENT CORPORATION ANNOUNCES SUSPENSION OF

Its PRESIDENT." Then there were three paragraphs. The first said that the suspension announcement had been in the form of a one-sentence statement issued Saturday by the chairman and founder of MDC, Mr. Herbert Patterson.

The second paragraph stated that the man involved, Mr. Frank Rogers, had apparently become involved in some very bizarre occurrences in Europe. It went on to say that the Swiss authorities had confirmed that a warrant had been issued for Rogers' arrest in connection with the death of one of the foremost international corporate lawyers in Switzerland. It was further alleged that Mr. Rogers was also wanted by the French authorities in connection with a border incident that had resulted in the death of a French official. No confirmation of this could be obtained.

The final paragraph stated that the present whereabouts of Mr. Rogers was unknown.

"Nancy!" I yelled, and then went into the bedroom to show her. She was still sleeping.

I let her sleep and went back into the sitting room. And picked up the phone. When I got the *Times*, I asked for the business editor, giving my name.

"Yes?" he answered.

"This is Frank Rogers," I said.

"Are you—"

"Yes."

"I see. Well, what can I do for you?"

"I'd like to see you," I said.

"Where are you?" he asked.

"Right here in New York," I replied.

"Let's say eleven," he said. "You know where we are?"

"Yes," I said.

"See you then."

All right. Now for the goodies. I picked up the black valise, laid it out on the table beside the telephone, and opened it. It was packed with large sealed envelopes. No videotapes, it seemed, though. Can't win them all, I thought.

Then I noticed. Each envelope had the emblem of the Swiss Bank Corporation on the left-hand top corner, the three crossed keys. Peculiar.

I lifted out the top two envelopes. I slit the top of one of them with a pen, carefully. I peeked, and then ripped it open. The envelope contained nothing but tightly packed stacks of money: five-thousand-franc bank notes. I ripped open the next envelope. Same thing.

There was a small envelope stuck between the stacks. I opened it. It contained a short letter addressed to Zimmerli by Rudolph Kaiser of the Swiss Bank Corporation, confirming that the Swiss-franc equivalent of $2 million exactly had been withdrawn from Account Number 76-48-73-2, the account of René Van der Kamp, over which Zimmerli also had signature rights.

Hold on, I thought. That must have been the account into which the two $10-million transfers were paid, and then out of which the two $10-million payments, less 10 percent, were distributed to our "friends" in NATO to make sure of the vote for MDC. Obviously the whole thing had been a charade —Zimmerli mistrusting Van der Kamp, wanting to ensure that the "secondary" payments were actually made from Van der Kamp's account, and so forth and so on. They had pre-agreed to share the 10 percent. And thus they shared signature privileges over the intermediary bank account at the Swiss Bank Corporation. The only thing was that Zimmerli, apparently, had decided to keep 100 percent of the commission, and to get it out in cash before Van der Kamp tried to do the same thing to him.

Boy, I had really gotten involved with a swell bunch of fellows over there. No. Correction: Herb Patterson had gotten me involved with this pack of thieves, who not only had double-crossed me but were double-crossing each other. No Boeing, no General Dynamics had ever been involved. Just a bunch of greedy European middlemen who had invented the whole deal.

So I now had the two million bucks. But I did not have one single document, or one single videotape. Nothing. Nothing but money.

Nancy walked into the sitting room right about then, smiling at me while wiping the sleep from her eyes. The smile stopped almost immediately when she saw my face.

"Now what?" she asked quietly.

"Look," I said.

There was money all over the place. She knew Switzerland—she'd studied there as long as I had—but she had never seen a 5,000-franc note before.

"Are they real?" she asked.

"They're real," I replied.

"So what's wrong?" she asked.

"That's it. That's all I brought with me. No documents, no evidence—just money."

Then: "I've got an appointment at the *Times* at eleven. To tell them the whole thing," I continued. "Here."

I handed her the business section, pointing to the article. She read it.

"Forget it, Frank," she said.

"What?"

"Forget the *Times*. They probably won't even listen to you. 'Bizarre,' it says here. They'll think you're crazy. They know you're a crook. It says so right here in their paper."

"They'll listen," I said.

I went at eleven. The man listened for fifteen minutes, his face saying nothing. Then he asked for some documentary proof. I told him that I had none. He asked me if it was true that I had killed the lawyer in Switzerland. I told him it had been an accident. He asked me if I had been involved in that other incident in France. I told him it had also been an accident. He suggested that I turn myself in. He also suggested I consult with a doctor. He said he was sorry. And he ushered me to the elevator. And he did not shake my hand when he turned his back to me and walked off.

We took the afternoon plane to San Francisco.

By seven that Monday evening we were back in our house in Woodside.

I never left that house for three months.

They'd won, as they always do.

22

THAT SAME MONDAY, the first shipment of blueprints, manuals, and maps and some electronic circuitry were loaded onto a 707 freighter at the MDC airport in Sunnyvale, and twelve hours later landed in Frankfurt am Main, where they were transferred into trucks, which took them to an extremely heavily guarded facility on the grounds of the Siemens A.G. industrial complex on the outskirts of Munich.

Another plane left four days later.

On Wednesday of the same week, Clay Dillon arrived by TWA at the same Frankfurt airport and was met by Dr. Reinhardt Kreps. The president of Citibank and the General-direktor of the Deutsche Bank the next day jointly agreed on the financial package designed to bail out Missile Development Corporation. It involved a $1.6-billion three-year loan, syndicated under the lead of the Deutsche Bank and conditioned by the agreement of Citibank to subordinate its currently outstanding credits to MDC of $750 million to the new lenders. On Friday, Herb Patterson was back in Germany together with MDC treasurer Ross Egan, and in quite a ceremony in the boardroom of the Deutsche Bank headquarters, all parties attached their signatures to the $2.35-billion package.

That evening, Herb Patterson had dinner, privately, at the home of Graf Otto von Amsburg in Bonn. Not even the German Foreign Minister's wife was present.

The two men were in an expansive, self-congratulatory mood. The Graf had laid on a 1979 Schloss Johannisberger Grünlack Spätlese, and as the two men sipped it the conversation turned to unfinished business, or at least what seemed so to the German count.

"And now what about your man Rogers?" he asked.

"Amazing chain of events, there," answered Patterson.

"He actually killed Zimmerli, you know," von Amsburg said.

"I am totally convinced it was an accident," answered Patterson. "I've known Rogers for too long to believe that he could have done it deliberately."

Von Amsburg shrugged.

"Anyway," continued Patterson, "it doesn't matter. The man is through. Last Monday *The New York Times* called me and said that Rogers had been in their offices that morning with some wild story about a conspiracy to leak highly secret missile technology to a foreign power."

"I don't especially like to hear that," commented the German.

"Not to worry," replied Patterson. "They listened to him for a while, asked for any kind of proof or documentation of such a conspiracy, and since Rogers apparently had absolutely nothing with him, they decided that he was somewhat unbalanced mentally. They knew about the deaths in Switzerland and France caused by the man."

"He can't be extradited, it seems," commented von Amsburg.

"Yes. Our legal department determined the same thing. Amazing, isn't it?" said Patterson.

"This sort of thing is more commonplace than most people realize," answered the German diplomat. Then: "Was that the end of it with the press?"

"So far. Obviously Rogers has realized he's finished and is not going to pursue the matter further."

"But what will be the reaction of the *Times* when they hear about the new financial package that has been put together for MDC by, of all banks, the Deutsche Bank?"

"I'm sure they'll call again," said Patterson.

"And what will you say?"

"I will say the obvious. West Germany is the most important ally, militarily and otherwise, of the United States. What's good for West Germany, militarily, is obviously good for the United States. And vice versa. What we have here is not a conspiracy but a further cementing of the key alliance in the Western World."

"Herbert," said von Amsburg, "I suggest we proceed with dinner."

PART FOUR

23

It was on January 17, 1987, that the first German cruise missile was ready for testing. The testing was done in a remote area of Zaïre in early February. It proved a complete success. A second test took place in March. It was also 100 percent successful. The second test involved a cruise missile that had been coated with a plastic substance designed to make it "invisible" to enemy radar—one major component of the "Stealth" technology developed by the United States during the 1970s and early 1980s. Missile Development Corporation had been deeply involved in this program from the very beginning. Mr. Patterson saw to it that Siemens A.G. got access to the pertinent technology. The German chemical industry—to be quite specific, Höchst A.G.: one of the successors to I.G. Farben, to round things out historically—came up with some rather dramatic improvements in the technology, with the net result that the German cruise missile was substantially—not completely, but substantially—immune to detection, even by look-down radar. It was judged that 71 percent of the missiles would now hit their targets in the Soviet Union.

Testing was stopped immediately, since now total continuing secrecy of the project was more important than any marginal improvements on the weapons system that might evolve out of a more extensive testing program.

On June 15, 1987, Graf Otto von Amsburg went to Moscow, causing more than a few raised eyebrows around the world.

Not that this was the first time a German Foreign Minister representing an ultra-right-wing regime had made a surprise visit to Moscow in modern times. Joachim von Ribbentrop had done precisely the same thing on August 23, 1939. George Kennan, who was attached to the embassy then, described von Ribbentrop as a "pompous, disagreeable man, a former wine merchant who had hitched his wagon to Hitler's star, a Nazi parvenu par excellence, bumptious, officious . . . servile toward the Führer, arrogant to everyone else."

Graf Otto von Amsburg was none of the above. He was an extremely well-mannered aristocrat, from a family that could look back on centuries of wealth and privilege, and although he had hitched his wagon to the star of Franz Josef Strauss, he was hardly servile to the man. Nor was Strauss a Hitler.

But there were, unfortunately, similarities between von Ribbentrop's boss and von Amsburg's boss. Rudolf Augstein, publisher of the German counterpart of *Time* magazine, *Der Spiegel*, whom Strauss had tried to put in jail more than once, was probably as well qualified as any German to judge the two men. And Augstein claimed that Strauss, like Hitler, was fully convinced that he was one of the "chosen"—a modern-day "Messiah." He was totally convinced, like Hitler, that he had a "mission." When asked once by the *Frankfurter*

Allgemeine Zeitung, the *New York Times* of Germany, who or what he would have wanted to be, had he had the choice, Strauss' answer was "Professor of history, or German Chancellor in 1932."

Well, when Strauss lost the election for the chancellorship in 1980, everyone thought the new German messiah was through. No one wanted to know that 45 percent of all Germans who went to the polls voted for him, giving him his country's largest bloc of votes. No one wanted to realize that Germany was entering an era of revived nationalism and xenophobia, whose primary external target was the United States. No one wanted to think that a Franz Josef Strauss would convince the German people four years later that he, and only he, could save the world, or at least Europe, or at the very least Germany, from a third catastrophe in this century, convince them that the new road to perdition lay in following any further the mindless, intellectually bankrupt leadership of the United States. Convince them that salvation lay in the political, economic, and military independence of Germany. Convince them that the prerequisite to independence from the United States lay in Germany's military strength, and that the corollary to a declaration of independence from the United States was a declaration of willingness to coexist with the Soviet Union.

Call it the Finlandization of Germany or whatever you like: the Strauss/von Amsburg objective was to achieve a state of armed neutrality, with the stress on the adjective "armed." Its symbol could very well have been the same as that of the American colonies: "Don't tread on me." Or else.

He only hinted at all this, sometimes in private meetings, sometimes very obliquely in television interviews in the 1984 election campaign. He did not have to shout it from the housetops: the German knew what he was getting at, and they knew he had to be cautious. So they voted him in. And even in his first two years in office, he had to be careful. For he still needed the military umbrella of the United States standing protectively over his Germany. He still needed the three hundred thousand American troops stationed in Germany to stand between his people and the Soviet tanks. He still needed the threat, even though the whole world knew it was as empty as any threat would ever be—namely, the "commitment"—that America would fight a nuclear war, even if it involved the American homeland, to protect its German allies and friends.

But in June of 1987, he knew that soon—very, very soon— he would no longer need the stupid, arrogant, inferior—yes, inferior—Americans.

So he sent Graf von Amsburg to Moscow to test the water there, just as Hitler had sent von Ribbentrop.

The difference was that von Ribbentrop and Hitler had been in a hurry. Because they were planning on attacking Poland exactly one week later. And they wanted to be absolutely sure that the Soviets would remain neutral.

To pursue any more parallels between the 1939 and 1987 situations would be misleading. For under no stretch of the imagination could anyone accuse Strauss of thinking in terms of starting a war! In fact, his objective was exactly the opposite: to stay *out* of a war; to jockey Germany into a position in which it was no longer doomed to be the first to be destroyed in any major Soviet–American military conflict. The Strauss/ von Amsburg position in 1987 was more closely that of Stalin and Molotov in 1939 than that of Hitler and von Ribbentrop: to obtain agreement to the status of their country as a nonbelligerent neutral in the face of a pending global conflict.

We really know nothing about the exact nature of those Soviet–German conversations in Moscow in June. Von Amsburg is completely fluent in Russian, so not even a translator was present. The count, like so many Germans, had learned the language while a guest of the Soviet Government from 1945 to 1947.

But in any case, we know that the Russian water tested very positively. For the Soviets knew that they had played the guns-for-butter game to the absolute limit and that if they pushed any further, in fact if they even kept it up at the current ratio for very much longer, something inside the Soviet system would snap. Paradoxically, Karl Marx had told his disciples that all they had to do was wait it out, since it was inevitable that the capitalistic system would eventually snap and blow up in one final explosive oscillation. The Soviets had thought the energy crisis was signaling that the final moment was near. But it had not happened. No Crash in '79 or '81 or '84. It never came. And in the meantime the Soviet system was the one that was approaching the breaking point. The Soviet Europeans were the poorest white people on earth—poorer than even the Poles and the Bulgarians and the Albanians. And they were not going to stand for it very much longer.

Von Amsburg represented the potential opening the Soviets had been hoping for. He presented the promise of that crucial geopolitical shift which would allow the Soviets to finally exercise the military power they had been building up for three full decades. The Soviet economic system might be approaching the breaking point, but the Soviet military had achieved a measure of superiority on a global scale that was unparalleled in modern times.

It was going to be the application of the doctrines of von Clausewitz rather than Marx that would, finally, bring prosperity to the Russian people through the establishment of global Soviet dominance. First the British had done it in the nineteenth century, then the Americans in the twentieth century. Now it was Mother Russia's turn, just in time for the twenty-first. Provided Germany now stood aside.

On the evening of his departure, the Russians almost drowned von Amsburg in Crimean champagne in their eagerness to please him. When he got back to Bonn the next day,

343

we know what he told his boss: "The Russians are ready to make a deal, Franz. Now all we must demonstrate is that we can enforce that deal."

That same June of 1987 was the beginning of what was going to prove to be the most glorious summer we have had in Northern California in the twentieth century: very hot days, well up into the 90s, followed by very cool nights back down into the 50s, week after week and month after month. By the end of June, everything seemed to be under control at the vineyard—and I'll come back to that subject just a little later—so Nancy and I had decided to escape the heat by spending a few days down at the lodge at Pebble Beach, golfing, playing some tennis, and just enjoying the coolness of the climate of the Monterey Peninsula at that time of year.

My wife and I normally tended to keep away from what had happened back in 1985. We both knew that there was nothing we could do about it, so we had agreed not to worry each other unnecessarily. But I think it was on the third day of that brief vacation that we broke the rule—or at least, Nancy broke the rule. We were having breakfast on the terrace, reading the papers together as we always do, when she handed me a piece of the West Coast edition of *The New York Times*.

"Read this," she said. "It is not to be believed."

It was the editorial page of the *Times* that she handed me. The lead editorial used as its takeoff point the NATO meeting which was convening that week in Washington. The first sentences told it all: "The Atlantic Alliance," it read, "has never looked more solid. What started out in 1949 as a protective arrangement—ten European states being shielded from the Soviet menace by an overwhelmingly powerful United States—is now a true partnership among equals. What is particularly gratifying is the coming together, once again,

344

of the United States and West Germany after so many years of strained relations under both Carter and Reagan."

Second paragraph: "The current Administration is to be congratulated on having found just the right attitude and tone in dealing with the man who is evolving as one of the best friends we have in the world, the German Chancellor, Franz Josef Strauss."

That was enough for me. I gave her back her newspaper.

"Can you believe this?" Nancy asked. "Doesn't *anybody* know what's going on?"

"I guess not," I replied. "Or maybe it all fell apart." I said it, but I didn't believe it.

I went back to my paper, *The Wall Street Journal*. Every day when I read it I was increasingly thankful that I was no longer part of the industrial or banking world. The economic and financial roller coaster America had been on since the beginning of the decade seemed never to end its trip. The prime rate had now hit 20 percent or more eight times since 1980. It was the same thing, over and over again: up to 20 percent, followed six months later by a recession. Back down to 12 percent, followed six months later by a new burst of inflation. So back up to 20 percent. And so on and so on and so on. Al Malabre had a piece on the front page rerunning this miserable history. I got to the third paragraph and quit. Who needed to get more depressed?

On the third page, where the *Journal*, for some reason, runs its big story instead of on the front page, it was IBM. It was also not to be believed: *IBM* was in trouble! It expected to run a *loss* in the second quarter! Maybe it would go as high as a billion-dollar loss for the year, the article said. It did not anticipate any cash-flow problems, however, since it had just concluded a three-year loan agreement with Saudi Arabia under which it could draw down as much as $3 billion. It did not say at what cost.

Right beside this article was another article explaining the reason behind IBM's troubles: Japanese competition, naturally. There were now some new names for us Americans to learn: Fujitsu and Nichidan-Toshiba. These two companies, combined, already had 19 percent of the large new computer market in the United States. But more ominously, the latest figures indicated that the Japanese share of the California market was already over 50 percent.

Next story, same page: Apple Computer. There are those of us who remember Apple Computer as the darling of Wall Street back in late 1980 when it went public. Now, almost seven years later, it was going into receivership. Those shares which started back then at $23 and went up to $98: you could have them now for $1.50. It seemed nobody wanted them. Apple had also been hit by a Japanese tidal wave of home computers—some more new names involved there: NEC, Sharp, Hitachi.

Page 4: St. Louis bankrupt. Page 5: The Yankees had just paid $7 million for a left-handed outfielder from Puerto Rico who had hit .300 only once in his life. Page 17: United California Bank had apparently lent Apple Computer a lot of money. The *Journal* was wondering how much, and what it might do to UCB's earnings in 1987. Page 23: Moody's announced that it had downgraded IBM's bonds from AAA to A. Their price was off an average of 300 basis points in one day.

I put down the paper for a moment and thought of that poor woman who now comes in to clean once a week. Her grandfather had left her a portfolio of blue-chip bonds when he died in the late 1960s with instructions that they were to be held to maturity in a trust fund which was to support her comfortably forever. Well, the market value of that portfolio was now 19 percent of its original cost. It was typical of the situation of so many older Americans: their savings had gone up in inflationary smoke and they were just left there, bewildered and poor. I grunted when I thought of it.

"What's wrong?" Nancy asked.

"Bonds," I replied.

"Oh, them," she commented. She knew what I thought of bonds. In fact, she naturally knew most of my opinions, and usually shared them. Such as how we continued to put up with a government that had promised to balance the budget every year for the past ten years and had never come close even once. How we continued to put up with those jackasses in Washington who had promised us energy "independence" every year since 1977, when we were no closer to that in 1987 than when the promise had first been given. How we put up with a labor force that was gradually refusing to do any work whatsoever. How we put up with officials who steadfastly refused to enforce the immigration laws, so that we were slowly sinking in a sea of humanity that did not even want to become assimilated to our culture.

I guess I'm starting to sound like a reactionary old bastard. Well, so be it. I knew that America had been drifting sideways and downward, in alternating stages, ever since Jimmy Carter, and that no end was in sight. And I was worried, worried sick, that one of these days one of our enemies—either a known enemy or one still lurking in the bushes—would take a crack at us in our weakened state. I was worried that nobody seemed to be aware of how vulnerable we had become as a nation.

The final straw that day, I remember, was when I turned to the *Journal*'s editorial page. I always read that page last because it is normally very good, good enough to be savored. Not that day. The lead editorial was headlined NATO: BASTION OF AMERICA'S FUTURE. The first sentence of *that* piece began: "Under the leadership of the United States and West Germany, the security of the West has never been more assured."

It sounded to me like the sort of thing Americans had probably been reading in the months and weeks prior to Pearl Harbor. I didn't show it to Nancy. I didn't want to worry her any more than she was worried already. And correctly so, as events soon proved.

Three months later, on October 21, 1987, just after sunset, a convoy of 327 cruise-missile launching vehicles, really nothing more than huge truck–semitrailer combinations, left the grounds of the Von Amsburg Lastwagenfabrik in Nuremberg and moved south on the Autobahn to Munich, taking the exit that led to the huge Siemens A.G. industrial complex. One by one they then passed through the gates, heading for the heavily guarded facility where the final cruise-missile assembly operations took place. The mounting of the missiles on the launch vehicles involved a very simple operation. The operations research people at Siemens had developed a computer model which, when put into practice that night, allowed all 327 missiles to be put on the trucks before dawn.

Each missile was tipped with a 500-kiloton nuclear warhead—one that would carry a nuclear explosive force equal to 500,000 tons of conventional high explosives. Each missile was pretargeted at a specific population center in the Soviet Union. The strategy was to kill 50 percent of the Soviet population with this one single wave of attack vehicles, this estimate of the "kill" being based upon the probability of 71 percent of the cruise missiles' evading both radar detection and countermeasures and actually reaching the desired target.

By the evening of October 22, all 327 launch vehicles were in place. They would move, by night, time and time again thereafter, to new launch sites, thus essentially precluding any preemptive strike that might catch them on the ground. It represented a cheap MX type of shell game. The operations research people at Siemens had also figured this one out.

On October 23, the East German intelligence network in West Germany, which essentially blankets the latter country, informed the Soviet Union that an unknown number of mobile ground-launch cruise missiles had just been deployed in the southern half of Germany.

On October 24, Graf Otto von Amsburg contacted his counterpart in the Kremlin, the seemingly eternal Andrei Gromyko, and suggested that it might be time for follow-up conversations on those subjects which had been broached in their bilateral talks in Moscow in June.

Gromyko, who already had the revised East German intelligence estimates in hand—they suggested that as many as 1,000 cruise missiles were already in launch position—came back to von Amsburg in less than an hour, suggesting that the following day would be most convenient.

On October 25, von Amsburg went to Moscow for the second time that year. Two days later, he and Gromyko had already hammered out the draft of a Soviet–West German nonaggression pact in which it was agreed that in case either of the contracting parties was attacked the other would remain neutral. In the attached secret protocol, West Germany agreed to withdraw from NATO and to immediately put the United States on notice that it had sixty days to accomplish a full withdrawal of its troops from German soil. In the same secret protocol, the Soviet Union agreed to totally withdraw its military forces from East Germany in exactly the same time framework—namely, sixty days from the signing of the pact. The Russians also agreed to release East Germany from the Warsaw Pact.

On October 28 of 1987, Franz Josef Strauss came to Moscow and attached his signature to the treaty. At noon Moscow time, a joint, very terse Soviet/German communiqué was issued.

To say that the United States Government was dumbfounded by the Moscow communiqué would be the understatement of the century. What von Ribbentrop had pulled off on August 23 of 1939 was back-page news by comparison.

The White House was more than dumbfounded when, two hours later, it received "notice" from Bonn regarding Germany's decision to withdraw from NATO immediately, coupled with its request that all American military forces be removed from West German territory within a maximum of sixty days.

A National Security Council meeting was called for nine o'clock that morning to help the President formulate a response. One of the President's aides thought the gravity of the situation called for the presence of the best possible minds familiar with the subject, and suggested that Henry Kissinger be invited to come over from Georgetown and sit in on the meeting. The President agreed.

The Council members were already seated in the War Room when Henry finally arrived—late as usual, but ensuring that he would be the center of attention. It worked, because it was to him that the President addressed the first question.

"Henry, what is going on over there?"

"Very big [he pronounced it "bick"] trouble, I'm afraid."

"But why, Henry?"

"Why what, Mr. President?"

"Why are the Germans doing this?"

"Because, Mr. President, they do not like us Americans. To be sure, they also do not like the Russians. We jointly destroyed their nation in 1945, then split it in two, and since then we have essentially been holding the two parts as our respective vassal states. Germans don't like to have to be subservient to anyone. Franz Josef Strauss is apparently in the process of trying to end that, and maybe get the ultimate revenge, all in one go."

"But Chancellor Strauss was here only a few months ago. We agreed on almost everything," protested the President.

"I'm afraid he led you down the garden path, sir," answered Kissinger. "Perhaps if I . . ." He let his voice trail off in a guttural sigh. Without him it had been inevitable that the world would get into trouble.

"But Strauss repeatedly said that they needed our troops

350

as a shield against the Soviets," continued the President, struggling a bit with the subject matter.

"No more, sir," interjected the Secretary of Defense at this point. "If you read our intelligence brief, sir, which was delivered almost an hour ago"—nods all around the table assured him that this was true—"then you know that the West Germans have installed between five hundred and a thousand nuclear-tipped cruise missiles, all of which seem ready to go. The Germans can now destroy the Soviet Union on their own if they are attacked. So they don't need us anymore, sir."

The President nodded. So *that* was what lay behind all this.

"So what do we do?"

"We don't panic," Kissinger said, "because that is exactly what the Germans would love [pronounced "luff"]. If we and the Soviets now started to lob intercontinental ballistic missiles at each other, over the Germans' heads, we would kill each other off and they would finally have won World War II after all. The only surviving major industrial powers left in the world would be Germany and Japan. Ironic, no?"

"But is this situation not intolerable?" The question came from the President's National Security Adviser, and seemed to be addressed to the room in general.

"What does 'intolerable' mean?" answered the Secretary of State. "If we tell the Soviets that we will not accept this new situation with the Germans, we risk exactly what Henry was talking about—the Russians will anticipate the inevitability of a showdown and will immediately launch a nuclear first strike against the United States."

No comments, so he proceeded.

"Well, this would then raise the question of whether or not we could suffer such a first strike and be able to respond with a nuclear counterstrike that would be effective enough to allow the United States to 'win' the war."

"Is there any likelihood that we would *not* win?" asked our nation's commander-in-chief.

The Secretary of Defense appeared very uncomfortable then, and even seemed reluctant to answer the question. But no one in the room that day was going to bail him out on this one. "I'm afraid there is, sir," he said, at length.

Deadly silence enveloped the War Room.

"I was never told that."

"No, sir. I guess because these matters are never really that clear-cut. From our viewpoint at the Pentagon it was really only a matter of time. When our MX system is in place and when our anti-ballistic-missile laser weaponry is functional up there"—and his eyes rose ever so briefly toward the satellites above—"well, no problem anymore. This thing has just come up a couple of years too soon, I'm afraid. Right now, sir, our counterstrike forces are extremely vulnerable."

More silence in the room. Now that the life of everyone present was also on the line, along with the rest of the citizenry, the truth was coming out.

"So what are our remaining options?" asked the man who was supposed to be running the Free World.

He looked at the Secretary of the Treasury, who had, wisely, kept his silence up to this point.

"One could, perhaps, hypothesize a conflict with the Soviet Union that would remain nonnuclear. We would take our troops out of West Germany by moving them east against the Red Army."

The head of the Joint Chiefs of Staff almost gagged when he heard that one. Here was this stockbroker from Wall Street trying to tell him how to fight the Russians!

The stockbroker continued: "But Mr. President, I'm afraid that that option is also limited. We are in no position to fight what could turn out to be a prolonged major conflict. We have only eighty-nine days' supply of oil in the country. Half of our Navy is under repair right now. We are essentially out of titanium. I'm afraid—"

"Balls," said the Joint Chiefs of Staff leader. "There is no such thing as a limited option, because there is no way that we can win a ground war with the Soviets in Europe. Period. So forget that crap."

"All right, Luther," the President said, addressing the general and also becoming visibly impatient, "what *can* we do?"

"You really want to know?" the general replied, and everyone in the room now cringed.

"Yes."

So the Pride of West Point let fly.

"It's very simple, and we don't need *him* here to tell us"—and his head jerked in the direction of Kissinger. The Pentagon, it seemed, had had enough of pointy-head professors. "*I'll* tell you."

The room braced itself.

"We have two choices: *either* we move first, preempt them, bomb the shit out of them, *level* them"—and a smile fleetingly crossed his face as he mentally envisioned the utter destruction—" *or* we get the fuck out of Europe."

He was not a man of elegance, no, but he did have a talent for the terse summing-up.

The President's eyes shifted back to Kissinger.

"Henry?"

"That's it. One way or the other we're going down the tube. The only question that remains open is which way."

As usual, Dr. Kissinger had the last word. At this point the President rose, signaling that the meeting was over. He then headed back to the Oval Office, alone, to make the choice.

24

THAT OCTOBER 28 fell on a Wednesday, and to this moment I can recall almost every detail of it. It started out warm and ended up hot, as had the days for almost five months in succession in Northern California. Ah, what an absolutely glorious year 1987 was!

Nancy and I had risen with the dawn and were in the highest of spirits from that moment on. For both of us were looking forward with immense anticipation to the arrival of our guest from Zurich, one who had promised to stay with us at the vineyard until Thanksgiving. Yes, it was, of course, Sabine von Lathen. She had called us just a week earlier and asked if she could come sometime—just like that, out of the blue, which was true to her character, to be sure. It was Nancy who had spent most of the time on the phone talking to her, reassuring her that the timing could not be better and finally persuading her to come right away.

When she stepped out of the little commuter plane that had brought her up from the San Francisco airport, it was the first time we had seen each other since that night on the Swiss–French frontier. She was the same: beautiful, intense, self-assured—but perhaps softer. There was now a new element there, one of fragility. Had something happened?

She and Nancy embraced right on the edge of the tarmac, and it was one of these rare cases of instant and lasting mutual approval. Nancy laughed, Sabine giggled, and they spontaneously linked arms and headed off toward the parking lot, leaving me behind, scarcely noticed, to shlep the luggage. The Santa Rosa airport is so small and informal that you just grab the bags as they're unloaded from the plane and off you go.

"Now, Frank," Sabine said when we got to the freeway, finally paying a little attention to me, "tell me about the vineyard and winery and everything."

"No," I replied, "I'll show you, not tell you. If you could wait this long to see it, you can certainly wait another twenty minutes."

Nancy said later that I was pouting, but that is, of course, silly. So the two of them, both in the back seat of the old Cadillac, returned to reviewing each other's respective lives as I drove north on U.S. 101 and then turned east on California 128.

We were there in less than twenty minutes. When Sabine first saw it, on the hill overlooking the lush Alexander Valley, she could hardly believe her eyes. Then, as we went through the gates, there were the vines, then the winery, and then the old white Victorian that was now our home. She loved all of it.

"It is not Bordeaux, it is not Burgundy. It is . . ." She could not quite find it.

"It is California, my dear," I said, "and welcome to it at last."

This time it was I and not Nancy who got the big kiss and

nstalled her in one of the upstairs back bedrooms and

suggested that she take a long nap. Nancy and I went out to the front porch, which overlooked our two hundred acres, just to sit and enjoy the early-afternoon sun. The harvest was in, our winemaster had done his tricks, and now there was really nothing more to do except wait to see if our immensely high expectations for the 1987 Château Nancy Cabernet Sauvignon would be realized. They were, I should add. It is today said that it will probably be known as the greatest Cabernet to come out of California since the 1977 Jordan. And that's saying something!

But now I must back up a bit to explain this rural scene and our pastoral life.

After Nancy and I returned to our home in Woodside in that December of 1985, I guess you could say that we went into a state of numbed suspension. Word, naturally, had gotten around before our return of my involvement in some peculiar events in Europe, even entailing violence. Nobody could figure out exactly why I was still free to walk around, but nobody seemed to want to get close enough to ask, either. Missile Development Corporation sent a salary check—one, covering the final month of 1985—by registered mail; it had my office belongings sent over by a delivery service, again surrendered only against signed receipts; it sent a lawyer over with an offer to settle my pension claims, which I had never made. I also signed that.

So my life, it seemed, was more or less over at forty-eight.

Well, I think it was the middle of January when Nancy kept disappearing for entire days on end. I really could not blame her, since about all I ever did was sit around the house reading and waiting for the six o'clock news to come on television. On that last day of that month I was standing in front of the set about to turn it on when she burst in the front door. Her cheeks were red with excitement.

"Frank, where is that Swiss money?" she demanded.

"In the safe. Where it is going to stay. That's dirty money."

"How much is it worth in dollars?"

"About two and a half million."

"Well, we're going to trade in those francs for a new life."

"Oh, no."

"Oh, yes. It's time you pulled out of it, Frank. So you listen to me for a change. Come over here and sit down!"

I came and sat, and she stood in front of me.

"Have you already forgotten what they tried to do to you over there? To put you in prison, to maybe even have you killed? For something *they* had cooked up. They considered you—no, present tense: they *consider* you to be absolutely expendable. A nothing. A throwaway. And look how your wonderful company has treated you since we've been back. They send messenger boys over and you sign. Nobody comes near you. They've made you a leper in our own community. Not just you. Also me. And I simply will not stand for it any longer. Not one more day!"

Boy, was she mad. It was all coming out now.

"But that money is tainted," I protested.

"That money is money and it belongs to you and me, fair and square. Get that through your thick head once and for all! Pull out of it, Frank! That amount does not even *begin* to pay for the damage that gang of thieves and traitors has inflicted on us."

Then she told me about the vineyard. She had been searching for one, and now she had found exactly, but exactly, what she had envisioned.

"We've both been wine freaks all of our lives, Frank," she said, "so why not go all the way? Thanks to Herb Patterson and his pals, we are now free to do what we want, live where we want."

The next day we went up to Healdsburg and met with the seller. He was an Iranian who had come out with the Shah and a lot of money, part of which he had stashed in a property in the Alexander Valley. Someone had taken care of it for him. Now he wanted to get out: quickly, cleanly, and, hopefully, without having to pay any capital-gains taxes. In other words, he wanted a cash-and-carry deal, after which he was going to return to the Middle East. When he saw our bundles of 5,000-franc notes, it was as if they were manna sent from heaven. Both he and Nancy insisted that we do the deal then and there, even to the point of going down to Santa Rosa to finalize the title transfer. By that evening, we owned a two-hundred-acre vineyard and a well-established winery. And I had not even seen the place.

Needless to say, it has been the joy of our lives ever since. I insisted upon renaming the place Château Nancy—for the obvious reason, but not only that. Nancy, after all, is the name of a reasonably well-known French city. Very few Americans, I reasoned, would know that it was famous for coal mining rather than wine and was situated in a valley that resembled the Ruhr more closely than the Napa. I was right. We charge $30 a bottle and simply cannot keep up with the demand. So at least I have made a small contribution to our family business. Also, I had "borrowed" the man I considered to be the best winemaker in California. We had the grapes, we had the facilities; all we really needed on top of that was the right man. He was. And the result was that 1987 Cabernet Sauvignon which I have already referred to: one of the best wines ever produced in the United States.

Nancy, who as you know has always had something of a medical history, seemed to bloom like a rose from the moment we got out of Woodside and moved into the old Victorian that came with the property. She was out in the vineyard every day, from spring to fall. Even her diabetes, which had been getting progressively worse, suddenly subsided to such a degree that the doctor took her off insulin. It was the exercise, he explained. I guess all this sounds like pretty dull stuff compared with what we had been doing. I'm often asked if I miss the action of the old days. My answer is always the same: Nancy and I now have more enjoyment every day than we used to get in a month. And one of our greatest pleasures is just to sit on the porch for a while in the afternoon, doing nothing, as we were on that late-October day in 1987.

Then the phone rang. I hurried to get it lest Sabine be awakened by the noise.

"Frank, turn on the radio. Something very peculiar is going on in Europe. Thought you should know." It was a neighbor.

I went into the kitchen and turned on the all-news station from San Francisco. All it said was that the Germans and Soviets had signed a nonaggression pact. Rumors of war were circulating everywhere. The President would be addressing the nation at seven, local time.

I went back out to the porch to tell Nancy.

"It didn't even take them two years," she said.

Then she added, "I'm scared, Frank."

I nodded. So was I.

"What can we do?"

"Nothing."

"Will there be war?"

"No."

Nancy decided that our guest would probably be famished when she woke up, so at five she was already in the kitchen, preparing the meal. Sabine came down about five thirty and was in a summer dress that was simply stunning. But so was Nancy in her blue jeans and white blouse, which set off her deep tan and accented her slimness.

I prepared one of my specialties, Mai Tais, which most of our guests claimed, after the third one, were even better than those served at Trader Vic's. That evening we stuck to two. After the second one, Sabine let us know that she had quit her job and had decided to leave Switzerland for a while. It was simply too repressive, too stifling. She said she couldn't breathe there anymore. She had to get out for a while. So could she stay? Perhaps even a bit longer than—

She could stay and stay and stay, Nancy told her. We were just in the process of starting to build a small guesthouse down on a little lake that she had not yet seen, at the foot of the property. It was a prefabricated chalet. It would probably be finished in six or seven weeks. It would be exactly right.

Sabine was so happy after that that neither Nancy nor I had the heart to tell her about what her fellow Central Europeans were in the process of doing. She had just left Europe, trying to leave it all behind, and now the bastards were even going to invade our tranquillity seven thousand miles away.

Nancy had cooked two pheasants and had concocted a deep red wine sauce to go with them. In honor of Sabine, she had also prepared some *Spätzle*. I had decanted two bottles of our 1985 Cabernet, and when the three of us sat down to the table it was to a joyous meal. But about ten to seven I felt that I had to broach the subject to Sabine of what was happening in Europe.

Her response was exactly the same as Nancy's had been: "So they are actually going through with it."

I sometimes forgot that these two women knew everything I knew about Patterson and von Amsburg and Franz Josef Strauss and cruise missiles. At the moment, I could not help remembering that it was also these two women who had made it possible for me to be there in the Alexander Valley that evening, with them, instead of being in a Swiss prison cell, alone.

Just before seven, I went to our bedroom to get the portable television set we kept there and brought it back to the dining room.

"I know it's tacky," I said, "but I think we must hear this, and I don't want to end the party yet."

Both Nancy and Sabine agreed. They cleared the table, and we were left with just cheese and bread and wine in front of us.

The President was on for only three minutes. He told us

that the Soviet Union and West Germany had signed a mutual nonaggression pact earlier that day in Moscow. He told us further that Germany had pulled out of NATO.

"We shall respect that decision," he continued. "In fact, it is now apparent that the times have overtaken the need for such military alliances. So we have decided to withdraw all American military personnel from German soil. We expect that to happen within sixty days. They shall return to the United States."

"So he isn't going to push any buttons," Nancy commented — "just as you said, Frank."

"So now they can do with Europe whatever they choose," said Sabine, always the realist. "But without me. I'm out, *Gott sei Dank.*"

The President droned on, not daring to look at the camera but keeping his eyes steadfastly on the written text: "It is increasingly apparent that *all* of our interests abroad, whether in Europe or the Middle East, can be best served through peaceful negotiation rather than by armed confrontation. So we also plan to withdraw our naval forces from both the Indian Ocean and the Mediterranean in the interests of peace."

"Now he's giving away the Persian Gulf!" exclaimed Nancy.

"I have agreed to meet with the Chairman of the Council of Ministers of the Soviet Union," the President said, not once raising his eyes, "as well as with the Chancellor of the Federal Republic of Germany, the day after tomorrow to discuss these and other matters."

Still more "matters"? He was obviously caving in completely. It was a walkover for the Russians and their new pals, the Germans. We were going down not with a bang but with a whimper.

After a long pause, the President added, "We shall meet in Munich."

"My God," said Sabine. "Chamberlain, 1938. They are going to make your President grovel. How awful!"

I switched off the television set. The three of us just sat there, silently. The joy was gone, the moment destroyed. The two women watched me, both obviously fearful that I would revert to the sullen condition of a few years back when things had appeared so dark.

"Frank," said Nancy, "they may have broken us for the moment, but we're not beaten. Let's remember what we still have here and be thankful."

She then stood up with a glass in her hand and in a firm voice said, "To our wonderful new life and our wonderful wine!"

She held aloft the 1985 Château Nancy Cabernet Sauvignon. Sabine and I rose and drank with her.

"And I want to drink to your country, the last home of free people," said Sabine, with tears in her eyes. And we drank again.

They waited for me.

"To the last days of America," I said.

But nobody drank to that. For all three of us knew that now the party was over.

We also knew after that that we needed each other more than ever before. So we have stayed together. Sabine now has her own ranch near ours, and she even has her citizenship papers. And do you know something? I am not so sure anymore about that last toast. Because there is a new spirit abroad in our land. We did not know what we had here until we had almost lost all of it. Now that we do know, maybe— just maybe—we shall rise again. Which would probably be the first time in history that any such thing had happened.

But why not? After all—we're Americans.

ALEXANDER VALLEY, CALIFORNIA
1992

258